ISBN 978-1-453-80469-8

Manufactured in the United States. First edition published September 2010.

This is a work of fiction. Names, characters, places and incidents either are the product of the author's imagination or are used fictitiously. Any resemblance to actual persons, living or dead, events, or locales is entirely coincidental.

# HER LATEST SUPPORTING ROLE

a novel

Cynthia Ashworth

CreateSpace—Seattle WA —2010

For everyone in advertising who has survived a pitch

# JUNE

# Chapter 1

"Where the fuck is Nick Wheeler?"

It was Monday June nineteenth and barely nine AM; Constable's shout erupted into the empty tenth floor corridor in a way that would have unnerved anyone. A moment later his frantic search for the missing Executive Producer took him to Jill Barber's desk, and he bobbed up and down before her, his cheeks flushed, eyes wild beneath the unruly mad-scientist brows.

"Where is Nick?"

"He's editing at Charlex 'til lunchtime," Jill told Constable, her voice betraying a flicker of anxiety. She slapped one palm over the mouthpiece of the phone, and with her other hand looked up a phone number on her computer. "Do you want me to call his cell?"

"Give me the number, I'll call him myself," Constable demanded, still bobbing in a slightly menacing way. He snatched the Post-It note from Jill's hand and departed, muttering furiously.

Constable was the President and Chief Creative Officer of Hambleton French Advertising's New York office. Everyone in the agency was on a first name basis with everyone else: the head of Brand Planning was known to all as Trevor, the Media Director was Suzanne, Jill's own bosses, the *Über*-producers, were Nick and Sandi. The lone exception to this code of familiarity, their President was referred to by all as Constable— just Constable, no mention of his first name (Simon) except in the industry rags like *Adweek*, and of course the *Times* advertising column where he'd received numerous mentions over the years. Like Liberace or Moby, only one name was necessary. And so it had been, the legend went, since his days as a junior copywriter at the agency's London office in the 70's. A rangy, loose-limbed Brit somewhere in his late forties, Constable had ruddy cheeks—

his face always looked as though it had been slapped long and hard—and a thatch of curly brown hair threaded with silvery strands. His slight limp was an important part of the Constable lore, the result of a near-fatal car accident during childhood, and this handicap was further emphasized by the speed with which he moved around the agency, practically galloping through its corridors, issuing three- or four-word directives at eardrum-shattering decibel levels. Often these commands were really no more than fragments of thought, the frantic and disordered output of an advertising genius, and his minions frequently puzzled over them for hours (days sometimes) afraid to ask their mercurial leader for clarification. Volatile and profane, magnetic and pansexual, Constable's ego was matched in size only by the rumored exorbitance of his salary.

It had been a little less than a month since Jill Barber joined Hambleton French Advertising. Her first real job: or at least, real job as it might be defined by certain of her high-achieving friends, for she was a failed actress-turned-almost-MFA straight out of New York University's graduate film program. Some of her oldest friends, the ones who were now working on Wall Street or at Manhattan's white-shoe law firms and who aspired to someday move back to Greenwich, Connecticut—the leafy suburban snore where they'd all grown up—might have given her a funny look when she described an average day at the New York office of America's fourth-largest ad agency. The same funny look she'd gotten when, during her previous, short-lived and ultimately abandoned career, they'd tactlessly asked if she was still "trying to act." But her degree and a couple of short films she'd made at NYU had helped her land a job at Hambleton French, and she was happy to have it. Much as it had pained her to admit it to her classmates, she didn't share their burning desire to be the next Spike (Lee or Jonze), or a programmer for the Tribeca Film Festival.

**Her Latest Supporting Role**

The more she had learned about it, the more advertising intrigued her. It seemed like a legitimate way to stay creative, and still have the time and resources to work on her own short film projects without having to be a starving artist-slash-waitress again. She'd had enough of that during her acting days. Jill desperately wanted to get going on her career, on her life; between three years of struggling to make it as an actress, and then two more in graduate school, she was already way behind most of her friends. It wouldn't be selling out, she would still be making films, Jill had reassured herself (and her skeptical classmates)—they'd just be really, really short ones. Jill had played small and forgettable parts in several commercials over the years, so she'd at least gotten a taste of the advertising business. Perhaps she'd been brainwashed by *Melrose Place* and *Bewitched* during her childhood, but Jill was genuinely excited to be there.

After nearly four weeks, though, she still wasn't entirely clear what it was she was supposed to be doing. The job had sounded like a fantastic opportunity but in fact seemed to be a glorified administrative position. She knew (from all the movies she'd watched as much as anything) that industries like advertising were all about paying your dues and being in the right place at the right time; still, she'd expected more, somehow, especially after having been put through so many interviews. A sequence of bubbly young HR girls first, and then the head of creative personnel, a fidgety brunette in an acid green mini-dress who bore an astonishing resemblance to Keith Richards in drag: that particular woman had kept crossing and uncrossing her legs like an under-cranked version of *Basic Instinct*, rapid-firing questions at Jill as if she couldn't wait to get rid of her and go "do lunch." Other agency people had looked her over with weary cynicism, as though they'd probably seen dozens like her come and go. One meeting found Jill trying desperately to impress a snarly TV commercial producer who seemed to be careening down from a cocaine high, so dark and altered was his mood by the time he'd

**5**

finished with her. And now that very man, Nick Wheeler, was her boss.

Every morning Jill took a seat in a cubicle of groovy-but-fake teak covered on one side with what resembled charcoal gray Velcro; like so many of its employees, even the agency's furniture had an air of hostile irony. She had a white iMac and her own multi-line phone—it seemed so incredibly corporate, a hundred and eighty degrees away from her former life, or lives. All day long she screened phone calls for Nick, and for Sandi Cusimano—the agency's other harried, chain-smoking Executive Producer—and booked things for them: edit suites, car service, voice-over casting sessions, rooms at Shutters Santa Monica. Plus she handled their huge and complicated expense reports (they were always traveling, traveling, traveling...LA especially): stacks of dog-eared and wallet-weary receipts which had billing job numbers scrawled on them in minute, barely legible script. Nick's writing, in particular, had unnerved Jill from the very first day— the slanted, tight little scribbles of an extremely disturbed man.

By lunch time the agency gossip network had cranked into overdrive, the reason for Constable's early-morning eruption now widely known: Tellco Toys and Games, their biggest client, had called for an agency review. The newly-hired Tellco Senior Vice-President of Marketing, unimpressed by the agency's latest round of creative work to introduce a line of pre-school toys, far from delighted with the agency's strategic thinking for the launch of Rainbow Babies—a politically-correct line of ethnic-featured baby dolls—and smarting from a two year decline in market share, had that very morning given Constable official notice of the impending review. Hambleton French had less than ten weeks to get its act together and develop a presentation that would convince Tellco not to take seventy million dollars worth of business elsewhere.

**Her Latest Supporting Role**

Nick returned from the edit house at noon. His skin was the same ashy gray color as the smoke from the twenty or so cigarettes he had no doubt consumed while supervising the editing of Tellco's new Dinosaur Valley spot. Puffed, vein-y lids obscured his dark eyes, and his brown hair was a shaggy mess. As Executive Producer and co-head of the department, Nick Wheeler oversaw all TV commercial production on the Tellco account. The agency created more spots for the toy manufacturer than for any other single client—nearly fifty in an average year—and probably half the production department's employees owed their jobs to Tellco. If the account went away, likely half of the department's jobs would, too—including both Nick's and Jill's.

He stopped at Jill's desk, and wordlessly riffled through a stack of pink message slips. A dark red gash about a half-inch long streaked across the bottom of his left cheek, and the front of his khaki shirt was peppered with more blood. Tiny spots formed a random pattern over his left pocket. Perhaps he had cut himself shaving? Jill doubted it, though; his hollow cheeks were covered with the customary two days growth of dark beard. On more than one occasion Jill had wondered how he managed to maintain his stubble so impeccably. Did he have some unusual electric razor made especially for the style-conscious, the only one guaranteed *not* to shave you closer than a blade or your money back?

"I suppose you've heard about Tellco by now," Nick said absently as he lobbed a few crumpled messages into her trashcan. Even from three feet away Jill's nose wrinkled at the smell of Marlboro Lights wafting from his hair, clothes and skin.

Jill nodded. "I guess Constable tracked you down. Sorry to hear the bad news, Nick." He merely grunted in acknowledgment. "Hey," she added. "Did you have some kind of accident this morning?"

Nick looked puzzled. Jill touched her hand against her own cheek to the approximate place where his was cut, an unconscious signal.

"Oh, yeah. The fucking just-off-the-boat, speak-no-English, turban-headed cab driver got into an accident on the way back from Charlex." Nick bristled with indignation, and for a moment stopped shuffling the slips of paper in his hand. "They had to wait for a cop, so I jumped out and hailed another cab. The first driver got really pissed when I refused to pay him and hurled something at me as I got into the other cab. Fucker got me right in the face."

He raised a hand to his cheek, then caught a glimpse of the blood stains on the shirt. His dark eyes flickered with alarm. "Jesus Christ! The bastard cut me! What the fuck did he throw?"

As Nick uttered a hoarse stream of curse words, Jill swiftly changed the subject. "So how does the Dinosaur Valley spot look?"

Still fussing over his bloodied shirt, Nick gave her a sour smile and shook his head. "Let's just say that if this is the kind of work we turn out over the next two months, we're fucked." As he walked toward his office, he shouted back to Jill. "Find Sandi for me, would you? We need to pow wow—NOW!"

Sandi Cusimano co-helmed the broadcast production department with Nick but had next to nothing to do with the Tellco account. A striking blonde of the California girl genre, tall and long-limbed, Sandi was a whippet-thin chain smoker who could match Nick Wheeler butt for butt any day of the week. Though with Jill she was unfailingly sweet and easy-going, a dream boss, Jill knew Sandi's reputation throughout the agency: that she was one tough cookie. She brought a measured, almost theatrical quality to the act of verbally beating account service guys into submission, talking them into big budget, high-risk spots with breathtaking production values, making them (and their clients) pay until it hurt. In spite of this abuse, the suits—as she called the

**Her Latest Supporting Role**

account types, with a mixture of affection and disdain—were said to love Sandi almost as much as they feared her. Marcia Brady with biker chick attitude, and the wardrobe to match: that was Sandi.

Jill didn't fear Sandi, didn't try to avoid her or kid-glove her the way she did Nick. She liked working for her, and Sandi was trying to teach Jill as much as she could about the ad business, the big budget, commercial stuff you didn't learn in film school. When Sandi had mentioned that she herself started at Hambleton French in the same lowly position Jill now occupied, it helped to reassure Jill that she hadn't made yet another poor career choice, and offered a glimmer of hope that there was indeed life after expense reports and maintaining the videotape library.

It took five minutes of roaming the halls, but Jill eventually tracked Sandi down to a music producer's tiny office. She was slumped on the couch, black spike heels resting on the coffee table, ignoring the city's indoor smoking ban. Seeing Jill's head poke into the doorway, she halted her story in mid-sentence.

"What's up?" she asked, not bothering to remove the cigarette before speaking.

"Nick needs to see you right away. He's in a terrible mood."

"Mmm," Sandi said by way of acknowledgment, and, after one final, protracted drag, swung her long legs to the floor. "There's a lot of that going around today."

Despite the agency-wide panic over the impending Tellco review, the quarterly welcome meeting for new employees was going ahead as scheduled. Sandi had insisted that Jill attend, that they could do without her for the rest of the day.

When she arrived about thirteen people were seated in rows in the big red-carpeted boardroom, and another half-dozen or so wandered in late, announcing their respective arrivals with a great noise of rattling chair legs. The boardroom was in semi-darkness. Their indoctrination to Hambleton French Advertising was presented as a PowerPoint in white type on red: it seemed to have taken its design cues from a stop sign. And after listening to an exhaustive litany of facts and figures on the international prominence of HFA (forty-two offices in nineteen countries, the flagship office in London's chi-chi Soho Square, more than six thousand employees worldwide, a prestigious client list, awards too numerous to mention, on and on and on it went), Jill's mind began to fog with boredom.

The person on her right tapped Jill's bare forearm twice with the eraser end of a pencil, pulling her back to consciousness. She turned her head and saw a casually dressed man in his early thirties; he had ultra-short blond hair and his thin face was pale, almost cadaverous in the half-light from the projector. The pencil end tapped again, this time on a pad of paper that rested on his knee. Jill strained in the dark to read the words that were written there in large, elegant capitals: CORPORATE MASTURBATION. She glanced up to see him sneak a look at her, and watched his lips part in a sardonic smile.

At last the lights went up and the woman charged with their corporate indoctrination—another bubbly blonde from HR—led a mercifully brief question and answer session before inviting them all to get to know each other at the back of the boardroom over a glass of one of their clients' supposedly fine wines. The audience, made up almost entirely of twenty-one year-old trainees from the accounting department, struggled from the chairs slowly, their senses dulled by the unexpected barrage of facts and figures, more than anyone in their right mind would ever want to know about Hambleton French.

The man to Jill's right didn't stand. Instead, he turned toward her and extended his hand. His mouth was drawn up in the same snarky smile she'd glimpsed in the darkness.

"Robin Devlin," he said, inclining his head as if she'd asked a question. "Art Director Extraordinaire. And you are..."

**Her Latest Supporting Role**

Jill shook his hand quickly. His palm was cool and dry, and she could feel all the bones in his long fingers.

"Jill Barber. I'm in Broadcast Production. How long have you been here?"

"Almost three months, and they haven't fired me yet. And you?"

"Four weeks. And ditto."

By a long table at the rear of the boardroom, the accounting trainees were guzzling glasses of Chateau Roche, a medium-sweet Long Island white. Jill watched as Robin's gaze took in the slurping trainees, then came slowly back to her.

He tilted his head toward the group. "Are you going to hang around for a glass of Chateau Raunch?"

Jill shook her head no, and crinkled her nose in disgust. If waitressing had done anything for her (besides keeping her from starving, of course) it had turned her into a terrible wine snob.

"Then you are obviously a person of both wisdom and good taste. Would you care to join me for an adult beverage or two at The Whiskey Bar?" He rolled his eyes dramatically. "After all this corporate rah-rah I could use a *real* drink."

Jill shot a look at the back of the room, where their HR hostess was bravely attempting conversation with one of the fledgling accountants, a surly-looking kid in a polyester tie so wide it could easily have doubled as a lobster bib. "Do you think we should disappear yet? It's barely five."

Robin answered with a low, reckless laugh. Jill wondered, was he mocking her or trying to be friendly?

"Live dangerously, Jill Barber," he said, jumping up from his chair. "Follow me."

Jill followed Robin to the back of the room, where he took two opaque plastic cups of white wine from the table. Passing one to Jill, he spun around to face the HR blonde, and hearing a split-second pause in the conversation, extended his hand.

"Really enjoyed the presentation," Robin announced with breezily transparent charm. Shaking her hand, he added: "Great to see you again, by the way," following it with yet another flash of his perfect, and perfectly insincere smile.

She returned his smile graciously, and nodded thanks as Robin moved behind her. Puzzled, Jill stared down into the yellow cupful of wine. A second later she felt his fingers on her elbow, and he led her toward a kitchen, which was connected to the boardroom by a narrow doorway.

"Stand here a minute," Robin whispered, positioning himself on one side of the door. "And smile."

"Do I have to drink it?" she asked hesitantly.

"Of course not—do I look like a sadist? Just try to act like you're having a good time."

*Trying to act: my specialty*, thought Jill. A moment later, she saw the blonde woman's gaze swivel around the room, at last coming to rest on Robin's tall form. He smiled and she nodded in acknowledgment, then turned her attention back to the group from accounting.

"We're out of here," Robin told Jill in a low voice, and pulled her through the open door. He dumped their wine in the sink and sent the empty plastic cups sailing into a nearby garbage can, but paused before opening another door that led to the corridor, and freedom. "Those little cups, that wine—strangely reminiscent of a trip to the doctor's office, don't you think?"

Jill sputtered with laughter, and obediently followed Robin out the door. The distant chorus of ringing telephones gave her second thoughts about leaving so soon; six was as early as she'd dared before (whether she was busy or not) reluctant to look like a slacker next to the other cube-dwellers on her floor. But her pangs of conscientiousness subsided when she remembered Sandi's words. Jill dashed to her desk to collect her purse, and then crept guiltily through the halls to join Robin at the elevator.

**Her Latest Supporting Role**

Robin led them to the bar on the ground floor of the Paramount Hotel. Though no longer particularly hot, the Whiskey Bar still had some cachet. But at this hour it was nearly empty; the poseurs, Jill knew, started drinking significantly later than mere wage slaves. A manager in a tight-fitting Euro-style shirt led them to a table near the back, and Jill slid along the cool leatherette banquette. Robin returned his Oliver Peoples sunglasses to their case with a flourish and gave a noisy sigh of relief.

"Well, wasn't *that* interesting," he announced, his tone very clearly communicating otherwise. "And now, class, we're going to have a pop quiz on what we learned. You in the front row, Jill Barber, can you tell me how many employees of Hambleton French Advertising work in the Abu Dhabi office?"

Jill smiled, playing along. She bit her lip in mock concentration. "Uh...forty-five?"

Robin tut-tutted, and gave her a stern look of disapproval. "I'm afraid that answer is incorrect. If you had been paying attention you would know that HFA does not in fact *have* an Abu Dhabi office. I'm afraid that as punishment you will have to work in accounting for a period of one week."

"Anything but that!" she pleaded, laughing.

"I'm sorry, but I'm afraid you're going to have to learn that Hambleton French shows no mercy. One glass of the house wine should be enough to convince you of that. Speaking of which, I'm ready for a gin and tonic. What about you?" He raised his hand, and a cat-suited waitress glided to a stop at their table.

The Whiskey Bar soon filled with an after work assortment of fashionable downtown types who, like Robin and Jill, apparently had to suffer the indignity of working above 23rd Street. The buzz of conversation and a gray haze of cigarette smoke wafted through the air while Robin interrogated Jill. It was just like when she'd filled out the Hambleton French job application a few weeks earlier: name, address, education, work experience. Then Robin downed the last swallow of gin, and as he fought for the attention of their now rather harassed-looking waitress, smiled at Jill. She couldn't quite decide if he was being sincere. The perfect teeth were hidden, and the look in his eyes seemed, well, kinder. Perhaps.

"So what made you want to work in advertising, Jill Barber?" he inquired. His voice had the same Serious Young Man tone he'd used with the HR lady in the boardroom, but there was still a hint of the flamboyance that he'd done little to contain since their introduction. Jill frowned, and studied Robin's tanned face. His short golden hair was so groomed, his smile so white and perfect. Jill concluded that she could be as sarcastic, as over-the-top as he was. Robin wouldn't take offence, he'd probably enjoy it.

"I don't know, Robin. The dazzling glamour of typing and distributing all those production schedules, I guess. Or perhaps the tremendous challenge of trying to keep three callers on hold simultaneously."

Jill heard her words and at once regretted them. With her voice blunted by the gin her attempt at humor had sounded not funny, but sour grape-ish.

"You hate it?" His mouth drew into a little knot of sympathy.

"Just kidding," Jill said. Then she looked at Robin and broke into a lopsided smile. The seriousness had evaporated and his face now wore a comic mask of mock-concern. So he hadn't been sincere after all. "It's actually fine. Not exactly what I expected to be doing, but fine. The problem is me, not the job. I accepted it, after all."

"Well, the job will get better. With all the experience you have from film school, you'll be a junior producer in no time."

"That's what Sandi keeps saying. She told me the story of her ascent from lowly assistant to high-powered Executive Producer, and said that could be me. So that's what keeps me going when

**Her Latest Supporting Role**

Nick sends me out to buy him cigarettes and pick up his dry cleaning."

"Have you been on a TV shoot yet?" Jill shook her head. "You should persuade Nick or Sandi to take you along to one. They can be a blast. I have one next week, as a matter of fact, a studio shoot here in the city. We're shooting another Tellco ad, for their Glow-in-the-Dark Space Alien, now that the Dinosaur Valley spot is almost finished. You should swing by."

"I would absolutely love to." Jill smiled. "Thanks. So you work on Tellco?"

"Among other accounts," he said. "I suppose you heard about the review?"

Jill nodded empathetically. "And we're still producing new ads for them?"

"Oh yeah, it's business as usual until the agency's fate is decided." Robin took a long swallow from his glass and sighed, suddenly serious. "Hooray for Hell-co."

Two drinks down and Jill was shoving a handful of wasabi peas into her mouth when she saw Robin wave to someone across the crowded bar. A tall man with hair nearly as black as her own, and dressed in a navy blazer and striped shirt moved toward them. He was probably only thirty, but his attire and sober, composed expression made him seem older.

"Hello, Robin," he said, coming to a halt at the end of their table.

He flashed a genial smile at them both, and raised one hand in greeting. Up close, the first thing Jill noticed were his slightly squinty eyes—they were an unusual shade of blue, deep-water dark—and a small raised scar that curved across his chin, centered just below the bottom lip like a second smile. Otherwise he was handsome in a bland, boy-next-door sort of way, like a G-rated Hugh Grant.

"Haven't seen much of you today," he added. "Everything okay with our little pre-historic pals?"

"Oh sure, couldn't be better," Robin assured him. "I had that new employees thing this afternoon, so I wasn't around at the end of the day. But everything's fine," he repeated, and tilted his head toward Jill. "Hey, let me introduce you two. Jill Barber, this is Graham Ferguson, the Management Supervisor on Tellco Toys. He's my favorite suit, lately anyway…my suit-du-jour. We're the Dinosaur Valley team!" Robin added with mock elation.

Graham smiled and extended a hand. "Nice to meet you Jill."

"We met at the new employees thing," Robin said. "She's in Broadcast. She works with Nick Wheeler and Sandi…Sandi…"

She finished his sentence. "Cusimano."

"Well, welcome to Hambleton French," Graham said.

"Thanks."

Robin motioned to a place in the booth next to Jill. "You want to join us? I'm going to stick around for a while, and so is Jill."

"Oh. Right," she said, steeling herself for a third cocktail, and a woozy subway ride downtown.

Graham looked down at his watch. "I shouldn't even be here—what with the account having just been put into review and all—but I had plans to meet a former client, and it wouldn't really be cool to blow him off." He squeezed onto the banquette next to Jill, and tried to make eye contact with the nearest waitress. "This guy I'm meeting is one of those people who's never on time, especially when the agency's concerned. Unfortunately, I'm compulsively punctual."

"I know what you mean," Jill said. "I was even born on the exact day I was due."

"Fortunately," said Robin, "I have a predisposition towards being fashionably late. Except where work is concerned, of course," he added, turning pointedly to Graham.

**Her Latest Supporting Role**

Graham raised his hand again, but failed to get any response. "They do have table service here, don't they?"

"Maybe it would be quicker if you went to the bar," suggested Robin.

"Either of you ready for another?"

Robin rattled the ice cubes around in his empty glass. "Gin and tonic, thanks."

As soon as Graham was out of earshot, Robin leaned across the table conspiratorially. "Now you *will* be nice to poor Graham, won't you?"

Jill frowned. "What do you mean, 'poor Graham'?"

"Girl trouble." Robin thumped his empty glass down on the table. "His fiancée dumped him—it happened right before I was hired—to marry the guy who was doing the flowers for their wedding. Can you imagine losing your beloved to the only straight florist in the tri-State area? Life can be too cruel. Anyhow, the gossip mill says that he's been in pretty rough shape since then. I mean, he's a super-nice guy, but working with him hasn't exactly been a barrel of laughs."

"You think he's depressed?"

"Or something...I just thought that a little sympathetic female company—someone young and attractive like yourself, for example—might shine a ray of sunlight on his otherwise tragic existence."

"Oh, please!" Jill gave him a chastising look. "Is that why you asked me to come here with you? To pimp me out to some guy you work with?"

"No, no, not at all. Jill!" Robin chided. "Of course not. My, aren't we sensitive today!" He glanced up to see Graham returning from the bar, drinks in hand, and lowered his voice to a whisper. "But please—be nice. I feel sorry for him, I really do."

After an hour Graham had livened up considerably, so much so that Jill couldn't see why Robin thought he was depressed and that her cheering-up services were required. Robin was keeping them entertained with his dead-on imitation of Constable—who had surfaced momentarily at the new employees' gathering—by responding to every remark with a nasal, very upper class British whine and a slightly spastic wave of his arms. Graham certainly enjoyed the show, hardly seeming to care that he'd been unceremoniously blown off by his ex-client, finally getting the call a full hour after their scheduled meeting. He laughed so loudly he even earned a couple of weird looks from the hipsters at the next table.

At a lull in the conversation, Jill reached under the table for her purse.

"Well, guys, it's been a blast," she said. "But I'm afraid I'm going to have to call it a night."

Robin frowned, and looked insulted. His voice returned to normal. "It isn't even seven-thirty," he said sternly. "You can't call it a night when it hardly qualifies as an afternoon."

"I know, Robin. But I just signed up for a summer class," Jill was suddenly nervous about having exposed herself as a not-yet-graduate of NYU—the HR blondes had quite another idea—but neither of them registered surprise. "And I want to get a jump on my reading."

"Oh Jill, you're so gosh-darned good. You can take the girl out of Greenwich…"

"Yeah, well, good or not, one more gin and tonic and I'll be lucky just to stay awake."

"All right," he relented. "You're excused."

Graham scooted over to release her from the banquette, returning her goodbye smile warmly. Robin, seeing the expression on the other man's face, gave Jill a knowing grin.

"I guess I'll see you both around the office then," Jill said, turning toward the door. "Ta ta for now."

She heard their goodbyes through a filter of rumbling conversation and clinking glasses as she pushed through the

**Her Latest Supporting Role**

crowded bar and into the fresh air. The temperature dropped a full ten degrees as she descended to the subway, and Jill smelled sweat and beer and cheap aftershave in the air. She passed through the turnstile and, with the three gin and tonics beginning to take their full effect, swayed on the platform as she awaited the downtown train.

# Chapter 2

When Jonathan Wunder strolled into the classroom on the top floor of NYU's Tisch building, casually slung an armful of books onto the lectern and announced that he'd be teaching "Novel into Film Since 1965," Jill sat up straight in her seat, genuinely surprised. In the college calendar the course—a brand new offering—had been marked *Instructor to be Announced*, but she certainly hadn't expected anyone so young. In her experience this sort of class was usually taught by phlegmatic, jaded professors in their late forties, the ones who had once been enthusiastic graduate students, but soured on academia as they settled into tenured and boozy middle age. And in film school, her younger instructors had been frenetic, edgy, dirty and black-clothed. Way too cool for school, every one of them: Tarantino wannabes.

But this instructor was an obvious exception. He was definitely young—barely thirty, Jill was sure—but extremely clean-cut, from his dark brown hair, which was stylishly, preppily cut, to his loafered bare feet. Though short, he was undeniably handsome—sort of a pint-sized Paul Rudd—and his smile was unbelievable, making Jill wonder whether great genes, or expensive orthodontia, deserved the credit. His attractiveness, however, was a little off-putting because it seemed almost calculated. Here was a man who put a great deal of effort into his image, who probably couldn't bear to pass a mirror without stealing a quick look at himself. Jill sensed this immediately, was keenly aware of that sort of thing, and all too often guilty of it herself. It was a holdover from her acting days, when, in the face of constant, audible scrutiny by casting directors (*nose too long, forehead too high, too ethnic…since when was Scottish ethnic?*) she became hypercritical of—and consequently obsessed with—her appearance.

And there was something else that struck her in those first minutes after he entered the classroom—he looked familiar. Jill felt a strange twinge of recognition as she watched Jonathan Wunder introduce himself to the class. But how did she know him, from where? It annoyed her that she couldn't place him.

Realizing that she hadn't been paying attention to his words at all (and he'd been talking for a while now) Jill made an effort to concentrate. He'd launched into an overview of the course, and most of the students around her were scribbling down the books on the curriculum: Jill copied their titles, and at the top of the page wrote his name—Jonathan Wunder with a U, that was how he'd introduced himself—underlining it with a series of squiggles. And then it all came together: the face, the name, everything. She suddenly knew why he seemed so familiar.

It wasn't that she and the instructor had met before. They definitely had not. But Jill was a chronic prowler of bookshops, not chains or the second-hand ones, but that charming endangered species of independent bookstores that stocked brand new volumes. Jill read voraciously, compulsively. The peculiar smell of a newly bound hardcover—especially the clean dry papery scent of pages as they flipped past her nose—intoxicated her as much as anything she'd ever smoked or snorted or swallowed. She had committed the floor plan of most of the independent book stores downtown to memory, knew the arrangement of their aisles and the contents of their shelves with a level of intimacy and nostalgia that most people reserved for their experiences with people, not things. And of all those stores, The Biography Bookshop was her favorite. Because it was so well-curated, and had such an inviting atmosphere, it attracted the city's hard-core book lovers, not just the literary dilettantes who cruised the best-seller tables at Barnes & Noble and Borders. Jill had even been picked up in its fiction section. Just once, by an earnest, *faux*-sensitive grad student, a PhD candidate in English Literature at Columbia who lured her out onto Bleecker Street with the promise of some lit chat and a cupcake from the Magnolia Bakery across the street, and then into his apartment by offering her a glass of cold milk to wash it down with. Jill soon learned that the doctoral student was also an aspiring pornographer—and in her admittedly amateur opinion, not even a very talented one—and he quickly abandoned their discussion of Dorothy Parker in favor of a reading from his latest composition, in an unsuccessful, though highly original, attempt to get her into bed.

It was at the Biography Bookshop—she didn't remember when, exactly—that she'd first come across the name and face of Jonathan Wunder. The photograph on the book jacket hadn't really done him justice: it was in black and white, and even from her perch in the third row she could see that he had the most extraordinary eyes, a deep, thoughtful shade of brown, long-lashed eyes that disappeared almost completely when he smiled.

As interesting as the course sounded, and as intrigued as Jill was to find herself studying under Jonathan Wunder (finally, after six years of higher education she had gotten a teacher whose book she'd actually heard of!) she hadn't planned on spending an entire summer's worth of Thursday nights in a stuffy classroom. But what had happened to Jill at the end of May, less than a month before, and delayed her graduation, had been not only unplanned, but entirely unexpected.

Gabor Czerny, an Associate Professor, taught one of the slightly provocative courses for which NYU was known, among them "Politics and Film: Espionage on Screen," and "Queer Image/ Performance". Czerny's latest academic offering, and the one Jill had enrolled in, had been called "The Art of Anti-Communism," and studied the literary and cinematic response to the Soviet Union's power over Eastern Europe, with particular

**Her Latest Supporting Role**

emphasis on work produced by expatriate artists from Hungary, Poland and the Czech Republic. Czerny himself was Hungarian by birth, though in the first class had confessed that he recalled nothing of the Russian invasion, and was only seven months old when his father, a Budapest surgeon, had spirited the family away first to London, and then, more permanently, New Jersey.

The curriculum included obscure works of both fiction and film. But the course had been her lowest priority all semester. Czerny's class was an elective, and the crushing weight of her other, compulsory classes had consumed so much of Jill's time and energy that she'd spent an embarrassingly small amount of time on Czerny's assignments, and skipped a lot of lectures too. Though when she did manage to get herself to class she'd found it extremely interesting: she recalled Czerny, sputtering and pink-faced with enthusiasm before a semi-circle of rapt students as he savored the nuances of socio-political meaning in one particularly weighty scene of film. Her major paper, however, had been decidedly lacking in inspiration, since the due date for that particular essay was two days before her final film project had to be turned in. Unimpressed, and finding her analysis "superficial," Czerny had given her paper a mark of only 65 per cent. She needed to have equaled—or bettered—that on the final exam or she could forget about graduating with the class of 2000. Crossing the school's lobby on her way to their appointment, Jill recalled with an uneasy shudder just how tough the final had been.

The door of Czerny's office was open wide. It was in an ugly, oppressively modern structure just south of Washington Square; Czerny, untenured even in his mid-forties—he'd bounced around a few East Coast colleges before landing at NYU—was unlucky enough to have been allotted one of the building's many windowless rooms. It resembled a cell more than an office, and the slightly eerie glow of a desk lamp shone weakly through its only opening. Jill's sandals made an irritating noise on the floor, *slap, slap, slap* as she walked down the hall.

He must have heard her coming. But when she reached the doorway and looked in, his back was to her; he was hunched over the desk in the far corner of his office. She raised her hand and rapped lightly on the door frame.

At once Czerny swiveled around in his chair.

"Jill...come in. What time is it?" he asked, though an elegant brushed steel clock sat in plain sight on his desk.

"Twelve-fifteen. My appointment is today, right?"

Czerny had always made Jill nervous: unsure of herself, as though he was challenging (or mocking) everything she said. It was a recurring theme. Professors nearly always made her feel like she was being tested; their mere presence put her on her guard, even the younger ones, the teaching assistants she'd had as an undergrad who had smiled nervously (creepily even) and tried a little too hard to be her pal. It could have been the lingering after-effect of the many tough House Mistresses she'd had to contend with at prep school: at the age of twenty-seven, Jill was still afraid of getting caught out of uniform or busted for sneaking into town after lights out. And Czerny's often-discussed, and in fact well-deserved reputation as someone who played fast and loose with NYU's Code of Conduct on student-teacher relations only increased her sense of unease.

"Of course your appointment is today," he said, and Jill thought she heard a faint note of condescension in his low, raspy voice, like he *had* been testing her. "I just lost track of time. I've been marking the papers from an undergrad class. You wouldn't believe how badly some of them write—not to mention the fact that only about half of them seem to have read the books on the course."

Jill swallowed a brief spasm of recognition as Czerny stood and cleared some paperbacks from the armchair next to his desk, then motioned at her to sit down. He was dressed in his

**Her Latest Supporting Role**

customary fashion—black work shirt, black pants and black boots, a downtown Johnny Cash, the combination seeming at once both sleek and sinister—and his outfit matched the dark, claustrophobic atmosphere of his little chamber perfectly. He flicked a switch and a small light came on, making the room seem somewhat less solitary.

"The Art of Anti-Communism" was not Jill's first time studying with Gabor Czerny; the previous year he'd taught one of her compulsory courses, Introduction to Film Theory. The night after the Film Theory final Czerny had held a party at his loft for the class members and various hangers-on, the so-called permanent students who had become an indistinguishable feature of the Tisch School landscape, as much a part of the school as its vintage lounge furniture. He lived in what he referred to as the "up and coming, down and out" part of downtown, on the Lower East Side near the Grand Street Settlement. His loft was on the top floor of an unrenovated ex-factory. No Tribeca-style gentrification for Czerny, no yuppie comforts in his domestic life, or at least that was the impression Jill got as she and a classmate hauled themselves up five long flights of concrete stairs to his loft.

Inside, his place was grander and more stylish than the neighborhood would suggest. And their instructor was a tolerant host: he didn't move a muscle, didn't even wince as one of the chain-smoking film students placed a sweating glass on the immaculate rosewood surface of his dining table, while the student's girlfriend trailed cigarette ash across the strip pine floor in her search for another beer. Czerny lived with a big-boned and decidedly un-pretty woman named Tess who ran a prestigious art gallery in Soho. But as soon as the party got going she disappeared to take their Great Dane for a walk, and as midnight approached Tess was still nowhere to be seen. He didn't seem to notice that she was gone, though, and Jill watched with wary amusement the way Czerny's icy blue eyes shone and

**25**

his movements grew grand, larger-than-life as he struck up an animated conversation with one of the many pretty young things from among his circle of admirers: both undergraduate and grad school women dotted the soirée. More admiring, certainly, than his faculty colleagues, who were under-represented at the party; the rumor was that Czerny barely hung on to his position, given his chronic failure to publish regularly in academic journals, or even those less-scholarly but still-prestigious forums like the *New York Times'* Sunday Magazine. But among these NYU film students Czerny's little cult of personality was clearly going strong.

For more than a week Jill had debated whether or not to attend Czerny's little get-together. She was a few years older than at least half of her classmates and, outside of the classroom, often felt conspicuous among them. But the one good friend she'd made in Film Theory, Patty (another unsuccessful actress who had decided to refocus her creative aspirations elsewhere) had dragged her along. And yet fifteen minutes after their arrival Patty got a cell phone summons to join her boyfriend at a party in Brooklyn, and, mumbling apologies, disappeared into the night. Jill ended up staying at the party, though, and made a real effort to talk with classmates she hadn't spoken to all term, suddenly concerned that they had mistaken her shyness for snobbery. With a glass of Cabernet working its charms on her inhibitions, she put on her party face and mingled.

"Everyone enjoying themselves?" Gabor Czerny asked, approaching her little group. He was circulating with a bottle of red wine, topping up every glass in sight with waiterly deftness.

"Nice party," she remarked. "You have a very cool loft." And Jill dropped her empty glass to her side, out of Czerny's reach.

He looked down at her empty glass disapprovingly.

"Had two already, and I don't want to fall asleep on the subway," she said with a little shrug of apology. "I might wake up the Bronx."

**Her Latest Supporting Role**

"Such a virtuous girl, Jill," Czerny commented to the rest of her group, his tone slightly sardonic, but he paused a second before moving on to the next little clutch of guests, and in that moment Jill felt a hand, warm and heavy, come to rest very firmly on her bottom. For a split-second she thought there was no way that this bold hand—now pressing so insistently on her backside—belonged to her professor. She turned to her left, where a greasy-looking Goth stood. He was probably one of Czerny's undergrad students—she'd certainly never seen him in any of her classes. Jill looked sharply at him, a little surprised, as if he was to blame. But that student was too busy with his beer, and just stared blankly back at her as he chugged it down. Both of his hands were in sight.

"If you'll both excuse me then, I see some more empty glasses."   Czerny's broad, heavy hand gave Jill's ass a final appreciative squeeze, and he moved on.

Jill remembered all this as she sat down on a worn armchair in Czerny's cell-like office, and he stood by the door, which he'd shut.   His back was to her again as he flipped through some folders in the top drawer of his ancient filing cabinet.

"This is the class file," he said, producing an envelope from the drawer with a flourish.   He slammed the filing cabinet shut, and it clanged with an eerie metallic boom.   Czerny sat down at his desk again, and began to thumb through pages and pages of Xeroxed manuscripts.   "I keep copies of everyone's papers for a year.   Here's yours." And he pulled it from between the others, his movement exaggerated, extravagant.   Czerny flipped to the back page, where the mark was noted, but held it up so she couldn't see. Jill found this strange, particularly because she knew what he'd given her—sixty-five percent, the lowest mark a grad student could get and still pass the course.   This little game, concealing the page from her, made the muscles in her stomach tap dance.

"How did you feel about the final, Jill?" he asked quickly.

She shifted in her chair and looked at him, not quite straight in the eye. Jill cleared her throat very softly.

"I'm not going to lie, it was hard." She flashed a nervous smile, which he missed.

Jill's twill skirt was on the short side, and she had a light sunburn. She was suddenly aware of the backs of her bare and reddened thighs sticking uncomfortably to the chair's leather seat, and tried raising one leg just a little to cross it over her knee. But as Jill brought her right leg up the seat made a strange, embarrassing noise, like from lifting a piece of masking tape, or a fart. She let the leg drop down onto the seat again, self-conscious. Czerny studied the page before him, seemingly oblivious.

"I gave you 65 per cent on this paper," he reminded her. "A passing grade—barely—but I've seen you do much better work."

Jill was beyond embarrassed by the poor job she'd done on the paper, and what she expected was an equally poor showing on the final exam. It certainly wasn't the way she'd planned to end her graduate school career. She recited the answer that seemed to work best in these circumstances: apologetic, acknowledging fault, not at all defensive, basically throwing herself on the mercy of the court. She didn't want to argue with Czerny because she got the distinct feeling that she wouldn't win.

"Well, no one's going to write an A-plus paper every time, Jill, but I'm sure you realize that the final exam is quite another matter."

"Is that why I'm here?" Jill asked. Her voice was still even, but she felt another angst-y flutter in her abdomen.

"Not necessarily." He leaned back a bit in his chair, and tossed her paper onto the desk, face down. "I ask all my graduating students to come see me after the course has ended. So I can let them have their final marks before they are submitted, but also just to talk about their experience with the

**Her Latest Supporting Role**

class. In case they have any suggestions or observations they'd like to pass on."

"Oh, okay. That makes sense." Jill breathed a little easier, and settled more comfortably in her chair. He'd said *graduating* students: that at least was reassuring. Maybe this lemon was going to turn into lemonade after all.

There was a pause, a tranquilizing silence that lasted only two or three seconds before Czerny sat up straight and fixed his stare, glassy blue and intense, on Jill.

"You failed the final," he said flatly.

At first Jill thought she hadn't heard him correctly. Her mind had wandered, she'd been trying to sneak a look at her watch to see how much of her lunch hour remained, if she was due back at the agency yet. It was her first week of work and the excitement of a new job, a real job, was still fresh; she was anxious to make a good impression on Nick and Sandi. When he gave her that strange look and then let her have it Jill was more than a little shocked.

"Sorry?" she said quickly.

"I said you failed the final. Failed. To be honest with you Jill, I was extremely disappointed when I got to your exam. Did you even read any of the books on the curriculum?"

Jill swallowed hard.

"Yes, of course, of course I did. Most of them, I mean, not all of them...but...a lot." She felt a flail of panic, an unpleasant flush coming to her face, already pink from a weekend in the sun. "But with the pressure of work from my other courses, I don't know...I guess I couldn't recall as much detail as usual."

"You couldn't recall much detail, period."

Was he enjoying this, Jill wondered as she felt the muscles in her neck begin to tense up. *Bastard.* He appeared to be. He'd always struck her as someone with a cruel streak, a bit of a nasty edge. He didn't even try to hide it; Jill recalled how Czerny had seemed to take special, sadistic delight in putting some of her fellow students (mostly men) in their place. She watched as he folded his hands across his chest, all the time watching her with his cold blue eyes.

She sat there for a moment, shamed into silence, before finally lowering her gaze. Jill examined her bare pink knees, then turned her concentration to the frayed Persian rug on the floor, staring down for what seemed like a year. Czerny remained in the chair behind his desk, and though she was looking down, Jill felt his presence in the room, heavy and oppressive. The air in the dimly lit office was stuffy and she felt its weight bearing down on her. Finally he cleared his throat, and spoke again.

"You're supposed to graduate this semester, Jill, and you know the rules as well as I do."

She looked up, scanned Czerny's face for some clue to his emotional state. He continued, and his voice was especially unsympathetic.

"You have to get a mark of sixty-five or higher to receive your degree. Those are the rules I'm afraid."

"So I won't graduate?" she asked, her voice breaking in dismay.

"I'm sorry, Jill. But you can take another course and receive your degree in January."

"In January? I'm supposed to be graduating in three weeks." Jill could hear her voice, its tone that grew thinner and higher with every word. She hated the sound of her words, hated confrontation, hated to lose control, but it was happening just the same. She stopped talking for a moment and tried to calm down.

Jill looked at Czerny's ruddy face. His mouth was closed, the corners upturned in a disagreeable half smile. More of a smirk, really, and it sent an angry rush of blood to her head. His eyes were still fixed alarmingly on her.

"I could get fired," she continued, thinking out loud. "I told them I was already a graduate on my application..." And the thought of summer school made her queasy. She was so very

**Her Latest Supporting Role**

*done* with school by now, so ready to get on with her life and her career, to catch up with her friends and, too, with her own notion of where she thought her life should be by now. Not to mention the large wad of cash she'd have to fork over to enroll in another session. She groaned inwardly, then sat forward to plead her case. "You said the marks haven't gone to the department yet. Can't I do something to bring my grade up? Another essay maybe? Extra credit?" she blurted out finally, sounding desperate, trying to appeal to Czerny's sense of decency—if indeed he had one. "*Please?*"

Czerny studied Jill's face, his features set into a smooth hard mask that revealed nothing. When he finally spoke his tone was flat and impersonal, and Jill was startled by its coldness, so much so that she actually felt herself flinch at his words.

"I think it would be unfair to let you do a make-up paper to raise your mark. I can't give you an advantage that no one else will get. The Dean would frown on that." Czerny leaned forward in silent contemplation.

Jill sank in her chair, and took a deep breath. The out-in movement of her chest, slow and deliberate, calmed her somewhat. "I can't believe this is happening to me. Total nightmare." Her body eased slightly. "I guess we're done here, huh?"

It was then that the expression on Gabor Czerny's face changed, moving from detached coldness to something much more difficult to interpret. His features took on a look so strange that even Jill, still numb from the bad news, was taken aback. She gave Czerny a puzzled look, and he smiled at her, a little ambiguously she thought. But a moment later Jill felt a sudden unpleasant twitch in her abdomen, a sickening pang of intuition. She had a vague feeling she'd seen him smile that way before.

"There is just one thing," he began, leaning forward almost imperceptibly. As the chilling blue eyes held her gaze, Jill felt the hand, bold and dismayingly familiar. Its touch suddenly, unexpectedly brought to mind the incident at his party, but this time it had a whole new meaning, signaling something much more serious. It wasn't the friendly, maybe even harmless, lechery of that evening, the genial boozy grope that was practically the party-giver's due. This was more disturbing. Jill felt his thick hand move up beneath her skirt, and into the warm hollow between her legs, coming to rest against her bare inner thigh. For a moment, she was transfixed, shocked and startled into silence. It took perhaps just a half-second for the touch itself—separated from what it actually, graphically implied—to register with her brain, and then, as if convulsed, Jill shot back in her seat and her legs came together with a faint noise, the rustle of fabric, the slap of bare flesh on flesh, the sound of brisk movement as the chair legs scraped along the floor. It all happened so fast: his hand was there, Jill reacted and then the hand wasn't there anymore. She felt a couple of the lecturer's thick fingers brush her knee as he quickly pulled away, saw the place where they'd pressed her skin, the skirt pushed halfway up, her sunburned flesh revealing a pale imprint of his hand.

Jill sensed the color spreading across her face as she stared first down at her thighs—now clamped tightly together—and then at Czerny. The meaty hand, his hand, now rested casually on the arm of his swivel chair. There was nothing casual about his expression, though. His blue eyes still looked at her with alarming certainty, and his mouth was fixed in that clever, superior smile.

"You said that you wanted a chance to bring up your grade, Jill," he reminded her coolly, and leaned back in his chair, arms folded across his thick chest once more as he gauged his advantage. "So this is your chance."

Jill's head was swimming, drowning in a wave of stunned desperation. She could feel her pulse racing, but was unsure whether fight or flight would be the more appropriate reaction.

**Her Latest Supporting Role**

And she was bewildered by how much Czerny's action had taken her by surprise. After all, his reputation was nothing if not consistent—and of course, between the ass-grab at her party and now this, well-deserved.

Finally she groped for her handbag, and when she had the strap wrapped firmly around her wrist, hoisted it into her lap.

"I don't want anything that much," Jill answered sharply. Her throat was dry, her voice scratchy and unfamiliar. Then she stood up, looking for a moment at his shiny pink face, and stared down at him with sad contempt. "I'm not that desperate to graduate."

Czerny said nothing, made no movement as Jill turned and walked out of the tiny office. She stared straight ahead as she made her way down the darkened hallway, the only noise her sandals slap-slapping again as she walked. Placing her hand on the cool knob of the stairwell door, she waited a few seconds before opening it. And then, as if in a movie, the entire episode in Czerny's office was projected before her eyes: slow motion, larger than life, until it faded to black and she found herself inside the stairwell again, overcome by a choking sigh of relief, and a shudder of disgust.

# Chapter 3

The last Saturday of June: it was nearly a month since her run-in with Czerny, and still it chafed at Jill's brain. That afternoon she and her best friend Monika were draped over long deck chairs on the roof of Monika's apartment building on West 64th Street, a boom box and a stack of CDs between them on the pebbly concrete. Every forty minutes or so they would both roll over—from stomachs to backs, then vice versa—and one of them would get her turn at playing DJ. Jewel's plaintive voice moved through the air, which was thick with humidity, blazing with sunshine.

Beneath the dark shield of her designer sunglasses Monika's eyes were closed. The music and heat had nearly lulled her into a siesta, and a thin glaze of perspiration coated her forehead and nose. Every time that Monika seemed about to drift into unconsciousness, however, Jill—who was never that good at keeping still, even on a hot day—let her feet drop to either side of the patio lounger, gripped its edges with her hands and pulled it around a few degrees to re-align her body with the sun's position. When the lounger was dragged across the concrete surface it produced an appalling noise of metal scraping across concrete, jolting Monika back to consciousness.

And Jill wouldn't shut up, either. She'd tried to distract herself with a book, was reading the first page of *The Cider House Rules* for probably the fourth time, but every few minutes she'd set it down and start talking again.

"I still can't believe it happened. Fuck," she kept announcing, or variations on that sentence. Monika was the only person she'd told about her ill-fated lunchtime encounter in Czerny's office. She'd related the entire episode to her in graphic detail, relived it in a babble of shocked outrage on the very day it had happened.

Jill watched as Monika lifted the sunglasses from her eyes, just a little, and raised her curly head.

"You know I'm not trying to be insensitive, Jill. But get over it, already. Move on." On this day her tone was even less tolerant than before. She flattened out on her lounger, and changed the subject. "Have you told your parents about summer school yet?"

"The summer school thing is definitely on a need-to-know basis." Jill sighed. "But I'm going to have to take out another loan to cover tuition. I'd rather suck it up and owe the money than tell them I failed a class. What kind of moron flunks an elective?"

"I could lend you the money, you know," Monika said, prompting Jill to wave her hand in a weary thanks-but-no gesture. "But as far as Czerny goes, you should just try and forget about the whole thing. Ease up on yourself, already."

Jill squinted at her friend. Monika's booming LonGUYland-accented voice grew even louder when she was dispensing advice—which was often. In fact, Jill was quite certain that all the other sun-seekers on the roof—and there were a lot of them, it was the first really nice Saturday in a while—could hear Monika's counsel.

"It's not healthy to think about it all the time..." Monika continued her lecture, and Jill tuned out. Her initial sympathy, the support she had offered on the night of Jill's run-in with Czerny (Monika had shared her best friend's shock and indignation, then) had quickly given way to a new attitude. The very next day, and ever since, she chastised Jill for dwelling on the incident, insisted that any time spent lamenting her dilemma was a complete waste.

*Easy for her to say,* Jill thought, and she flattened herself out again, and picked her book up from the pavement. But it was much harder to do, an act of will that Jill just couldn't seem to muster the energy for, and her best friend's lack of compassion stung bitterly.

"Right?" Monika continued. Jill sensed that the lecture was coming to an end, and her consciousness drifted back to the conversation.

Monika half sat up, and hooked a finger under the edge of her hot pink bikini bottom. She scrutinized the newly exposed pale skin, made a face and then let go so that the fabric snapped back against her hip.

"I can't see a difference." Monika's voice wilted with disappointment. She turned her gaze skyward. "I don't think it's hot enough. This may not be the best day for tanning therapy after all."

Jill reached beneath the chair and found her watch. "It's almost five," she announced; they had been lying in the sun for more than two hours. "I think we started too late in the day. Let's go in." She stood up, woozy from the heat. For a few seconds her head swum and a silver-gray haze clouded the edges of her vision. She recovered, and added shakily, "I'll pass out soon if I don't get something to eat."

"Do you want to go out or eat in?" Monika demanded as they entered her apartment and dropped their stuff—towels, boom box, assorted lotions—on the floor. They made a thorough inspection of the refrigerator—relieving it of half a carton of coffee Häagen-Dazs, some days-old Chinese food and a stale poppy-seed bagel. Even if she'd known how to cook, Monika's working life—she was about to start her third year as an Associate at a big-deal law firm (even Jill had heard of it)—didn't allow her the luxury of time to cook at home. During the week she barely had time to eat, had probably lost fifteen pounds since joining the firm: the Incredible Shrinking Lawyer.

They flopped down on the long sofa that dominated Monika's miniaturized living room. It was a cookie-cutter one bedroom in a towering new building, decorated functionally but with little thought or flair; a woman who barely had time to eat surely couldn't spend much time decorating. Still, its muted beige-on-

**Her Latest Supporting Role**

beige color scheme was tasteful enough, and a far cry from the Long Island McMansion that Monika had grown up in. Her childhood home, which Jill had first visited during their sophomore year of boarding school, was decorated in a style that Jill's mother—herself more of a Sister Parrish disciple—would have characterized as "early Mafia wife". The first time Monika had led Jill through the house's immense foyer, with its rosy marble floors, Jill's eyes widened, accustomed as they were to the restrained chintz-and-Chippendale, English Manor house-style interiors of her family's Connecticut neighborhood. And Monika, reading Jill's facial expression, had made some snarky comment, like she understood that the house was in questionable taste but just didn't give a shit. The Roth's house was huge, and crammed so full of white pile carpeting, red flocked wallpaper and shimmering gilt and crystal chandeliers that it threatened to burst open, spilling its reproduction opulence into the lush streets of Great Neck, New York.

Everything about Monika and her family was bigger, louder, and more in-your-face than Jill had ever experienced. It was true Monika could be a bit of a bitch, and her bad behavior often gave Jill pause: dressing down waitresses; rudely snubbing well-intentioned men; once (to Jill's horror) even making a salesgirl cry. But Monika also had the self-confidence, the savvy, the sheer nerve that Jill envied and lacked. And Monika's parents were equally over the top: her mother chain-smoking and profane— that Easter vacation was the first time she'd heard a middle-aged parent say *fuck*—her father with his shiny cue ball head, smooth-talking, cigar-chomping, alarmingly sexual. Was it just her imagination, or was he really checking Jill out by the pool when she was fifteen?

They'd been friends for nearly half their lives. Fate brought them together as students and house mates at a prep school in Massachusetts. When Jill's father, a career Pepsico executive, was sent to Asia to help straighten out some operational crisis, her parents had decided to ship her, their only child, off to boarding school rather than disrupt her US high school career and hurt her chances with the Ivy League. She had moaned and groaned and sulked around the house for weeks, tormenting her poor mother: her dad had already departed, leaving her mother behind to pack up the house and deposit Jill at school. But secretly Jill was happy for the change. Her freshman year at gigantic Greenwich High School had been far from wonderful: she'd had a stupid falling-out with one of her oldest friends (over a boy, of course), had mysteriously lost her will to play the piano, and had failed to make even one sports team. In the wake of so much disappointment she welcomed the chance to reinvent herself.

Her first day at prep school: her mom had already said good-bye and driven back to Greenwich, and Jill was in a daze. After a month of excited anticipation, she was wondering what exactly she'd gotten herself into. She was kneeling by her assigned bed in the four-girl room, unpacking her trunk, when a gigantically tall, curly-haired girl in skin-tight designer jeans and turquoise cowboy boots burst through the door with all the suddenness and force of a sonic boom.

"Hey there, new girls," she'd called out at the top of her lungs, although no one besides Jill seemed to have arrived on their floor yet. Monika introduced herself and then blithely explained that she'd been at Walden for a year already and would be only too happy to teach Jill all the ins and outs. From that initial and nearly wordless—on Jill's part, anyhow—exchange grew an amazing friendship. Monika craved an audience, Jill wanted someone to try out Jill 2.0 on, and in each other the two of them found exactly what they needed.

After the Häagen-Dazs and Chinese food were done and they'd had their fill of *MTV News* and *Access Hollywood* Jill and Monika jumped on the subway downtown, unsure of how to

**Her Latest Supporting Role**

spend Saturday night. Weekend evenings were a lot more predictable, sometimes annoyingly so, when you were part of a couple, but girls' night out seemed infinitely more difficult, requiring motivation and thought, endless creativity. Jill's last relationship (if you could even call it that) had finally ended in April after a few listless months. Now, with the benefit of a little perspective, Jill wondered why she'd been so bummed out by being dumped by someone as inherently mean-spirited as Jason was: or mean to her, anyhow. After all, a killer smile and a Stanford MBA only made up for so much bad behavior. And while she wasn't actively looking for someone new, the idea of sharing a long hot summer with what her best friend sardonically referred to as "that special someone" definitely had some appeal. Especially if he had good air-conditioning, since her studio apartment in the East Village was a little A/C-challenged. In Jill's position Monika probably would have hung out on the street corner, like a homeless person offering his services, with a cardboard sign resting on her lap: *WILL FUCK FOR A/C.* And it likely would have worked, too. But that was Monika—Jill was content to perspire on her own.

Monika had just been dumped, and rather nastily, two months earlier. Jill had watched the aftermath of Monika's heartbreak first with sympathy, then amazement. The morning after the breakup, her eyes brimming with Visine, Monika transformed all of her hurt and angry energy into a work frenzy that enabled her to clock eighteen hour days at her firm for twelve days straight. She kept asking for more work, and more and more. One of the partners in her department had started calling her "Killer." But now, having settled back into a more normal work schedule (normal for Monika was nine am 'til ten pm during the week, and maybe one weekend day), she seemed to be finding her summer unsettled and empty. And she suffered acute mood swings—which meant that Jill suffered too.

They ended up at Café Dante, one of the many almost identical cafés in the West Village, the touristy but fun venues that lined MacDougal and Bleecker Streets. Monika stirred five sugars into her cappuccino, while Jill tucked greedily into a large dish of tiramisu. She'd spent her three year acting career in a state of near-constant hunger, desperate to get (and stay) the kind of thin that ingénue roles required, especially on TV. It was such a relief to no longer view dessert as a career-limiting move.

"Graduation was last Friday," Jill told Monika glumly. "Or at least it would have been, if I had graduated." She fidgeted with napkins in the chrome dispenser: pushed them in hard, and jerked her hand away. They toppled like dominos onto the table between them.

"You're not missing much, believe me," Monika said, shaking her head. "I almost blew off my law school graduation to go to the beach. The place where they hold the ceremony isn't very well air-conditioned, and I heard that a couple of people passed out the year before. But my mother said she'd never speak to me again if she didn't get to see me graduate from Columbia law school." She rolled her eyes. "Like I could ever be that lucky."

"They don't have a ceremony in the fall, I asked." Jill sighed, and saw Monika wince with displeasure. The forbidden topic of conversation was back. "They just mail your diploma to you, like those cheesy schools that advertise in the back of *Rolling Stone*."

Immediately, and with no subtlety whatsoever, Monika changed the subject.

"Hey, you started your summer course this week, and you haven't even said anything about it," she said. "Did you go?"

"Uh-huh. 'Novel into Film since 1965'. Woo hoo." Jill gave Monika a grim smile and downed another large spoonful of dessert.

"Well, how was it? Any good?"

"It's okay. Hard to tell at this point. The guy who teaches it isn't a regular professor. I thought it would be some serious,

**Her Latest Supporting Role**

ultra-academic snooze-fest. But if the first class is anything to go by, it could actually be pretty interesting, and perfect for night school."

"Who's teaching it, if he's not a professor?"

"He's a writer. A novelist, actually. I think he has a PhD but said he's only ever taught once before. I guess he's doing it for the money."

"Have you heard of him? Have I heard of him?" Monika asked, perking up slightly.

"His name's Jonathan Wunder. He wrote a novel called *Groundswell* two or three years back. I remember seeing it in a bookstore a long time ago—it was nominated for a National Book Award. I bought the paperback after class but I'm only about thirty pages into it so far."

Monika licked some milk froth from her spoon, and looked at Jill with interest.

"I know a Jonathan Wunder," she said. "Short, dark hair, good looking? Kind of in love with himself?"

"How many Jonathan Wunders can there be?" Jill mused.

"He used to know my sister—they went to high school together. He's from Great Neck. And they both went to BU." Monika smiled, a little meanly. "Anya was really into him when they were up in Boston, but she made like he wouldn't even give her the time of day."

"So he's the same age as your sister?"

Monika nodded. "Mmm. Probably thirty-one. Do a web search, if he wrote a famous book I'm sure you can find out. I guess my mother has lost touch with them or you know I'd have heard about the book. Small world."

"Well, all I know is that I'm going to get an A in his course if it kills me," Jill added. "Fuck Czerny. Not literally, of course."

Monika's mouth curved downward in an irritated frown that Jill recognized from their poolside talk. She set her cup down so hard that it rattled on its saucer.

"If you feel that strongly about it then complain to the Dean. Don't just ruin your summer—not to mention my summer—by going on and on about what happened with Czerny."

Jill pressed her lips tightly together, and looked out the window. Three teenaged boys were playing ball hockey across the street. She wondered what it would be like to be that young again, free of the weight of the adult world.

"I can't. He might say that I suggested it. Make it my fault, not his."

"Well was it? No." Monika seemed impatient to finish the conversation and didn't wait for Jill to answer. "You just asked if you could do something for extra credit so you could graduate with your class. You didn't offer to fuck him."

The word made Jill cringe. It was so perfectly explicit, so obscene. She shuddered, remembering again his hammy hand creeping up between her legs, his thick fingers on her sunburned flesh.

"Look, Jill," said Monika, leaning forward across the square table. Her voice was lowered, firm but not insensitive. "I don't want you to take this the wrong way. But fish or cut bait. Either do something to get back at Czerny for that fucked-up little psychodrama in his office, or forget that it ever happened and get on with your life." She eased up a bit, and leaned back in her chair. "You'll make yourself sick over this otherwise, you know. Mentally and physically."

"Easy for you to say," Jill sulked.

"Yes, it is easy for me to say," Monika countered. "But I think you should give it some serious thought. Now what are we going to do tonight?" she demanded, changing the subject with a surge of transparent brightness.

"Movie?"

"Sure," said Monika. "What do you want to see?"

"Something stupid," Jill said quietly. "A comedy, maybe? I could use a good laugh."

**Her Latest Supporting Role**

Jill's mouth creased with sadness, and she felt the hot, angry tears welling up in her eyes.

Monika's stern look dissolved into a reluctant cringe of empathy. "He's an asshole, Jill," she said quietly. "He'll get what's coming to him soon enough, I'm sure of that. Karmic payback."

"I'm sorry, Monika," Jill said. She had narrowly avoided crying in public—which would be mortifying—but could feel her face reddening: the rims of her eyes growing pink, the two hot rosebuds of indignation blooming on her cheeks. "You know I'm not usually this bad."

"I'm sorry too," Monika said, and for only the second time in more than a month Jill saw something like real sympathy reflected in Monika's eyes. "What a fuckin' mess," she added with a sigh.

"Do I look that bad?" she asked, her voice breaking with what sounded like a cross between a laugh and a scream.

"I meant the business with Czerny. Your face looks fine." Monika lowered her voice. "You know, though, this is no place to have a teary-deary. Some Italian mamma will take pity on you, run up with glasses of water and clean handkerchiefs and you'll be so-oo embarrassed."

"I'll remember that," Jill said.

# Chapter 4

It had only been a week and a half since the bad news about Tellco. But since then the tenth floor—home to Hambleton French Advertising's creative and broadcast production departments—had undergone a palpable change in atmosphere. Normally fairly mellow, with meetings of three or four people happening in any of the red-carpeted offices, it had quickly been transformed. Staffers from almost every department—production, creative, research and planning, media and account service—swarmed from office to conference room to office again, moving fast, arguing, brainstorming, some of them scribbling notes on Post-Its or flashing rough pencil sketches at each other as they dashed through the halls.

Yet again, Nick and Sandi were behind the closed door of Sandi's office. Before they disappeared, Nick had given Jill her orders. She was to spend the afternoon in the agency's videotape library, seizing every historical reel of Tellco TV commercials she could lay her hands on. Not exactly what she'd dreamed of doing back in film school, but upon hearing the tone of Nick's voice, even more verging-on-rage than usual, she'd thrown herself at the task with a mixture of zeal and nervous energy. The account had been at Hambleton French for more than a decade, so there were scores of Tellco spots—many of the cassettes were filmed with dust as thick as dryer lint—crowding the video library's eight foot high shelves.

Jill was seated Indian-style on the floor, making a list of the cassettes that were stacked before her, three feet high, when she heard the library door sigh open.

"Remember me?" Graham Ferguson asked as he crouched down next to her. "Tellco historical reels, that's why I'm here."

He made a low noise that was half whistle, half exhale. "I guess it's all hands on deck these days."

"I think it is. I've been in here for ages."

"Well, fasten your seat belt, it's going to be a bumpy night. More like sixty bumpy nights, actually."

Jill hoisted herself to her feet, and began loading the cassettes onto a steel trolley.

"I'd bet money that everything you've seen and done so far at this agency will seem like a day at the beach by the time this is all over." Graham laughed hoarsely. He looked worn out already, tired and a little fragile, his fair skin almost gray in the library's fluorescent light. Jill wondered if he could take seven more weeks of this.

"Thanks for the pep talk, Graham," she said, and flashed him an oh brother look as she continued to load the cassettes.

"Just being honest."

"Oh, I believe you," she said. Her cart full, Jill started wheeling it to the door.

"Not only do we have to pull out all the stops to save the account. But we also have a boatload of work-in-progress. All the new commercials for the holidays—the most important three months in toy retailing—are in various stages of production right now. I just eyeballed the status report this morning. We're still in creative development on three spots—trying to come up with some ideas that the clients will buy, we already missed having them done in time for Toy Fair in February. We're in the middle of bidding out five more to directors, and we've got another three in post-production. Plus this Dinosaur Valley debacle."

Graham pinched the bridge of his nose with his thumb and forefinger. The mere prospect of the next two months seemed to exhaust him. He stood between Jill and the door, as though unwilling to let her leave, and kept talking. This happened to her a lot, and she never quite understood why: people unburdening themselves, men and women she barely knew using her as their

**45**

unpaid agony aunt. Her shyness, her instinct to hang back from a conversation with someone she didn't know well was confused for empathy almost as often as for snobbery.

"What's up with the Dinosaur Valley spot?" Jill asked, remembering Nick's words on the very day that the agency had gotten the bad news.

His eyes opened again, the whites road-mapped with red. "It sucks. Their biggest new toy launch in two years and the ads suck. But I don't think the fault lies exclusively with the agency, if you want my honest opinion. The product is a piece of junk. It's the old silk purse-sow's ear thing, and we've run up against it on this account time and time again."

Jill pushed the cart forward, but it was a little too full and cassettes started to slide off the other end. She scrambled to pick some up from the floor and stop the rest from falling too.

"Hey, let me help with that," Graham insisted, waving her away. He smiled, and let out an ironic laugh. "Never let it be said that chivalry is dead at Hambleton French."

Graham walked down the hallway beside the cart, stooping slightly as he helped Jill keep the errant cassettes on the trolley. She stopped outside Sandi's closed office door. They were still inside, though one or other had emerged briefly many times over the course of the afternoon, summoning Jill with a shout that echoed down the tenth floor corridor, loud enough to be audible (and therefore, unavoidable) even in the tape library—demanding coffee, a slew of directors' reels, Tic Tacs, Advil, menus so they could order lunch, production schedules, their messages, yellow and pink highlighter markers, Visine, reels of competitors' TV advertising, on and on and on it went.

"Thanks for your help with the cart. I'm just going to leave it here," Jill told Graham. "I don't want to disturb them. They'll open the door to ask me for something soon enough."

**Her Latest Supporting Role**

"Is Nick in there too?" She nodded silently, and touched her index finger to her lips, shushing him. "How long have they been holed up in her office?" he added, voice low.

Jill peered at the clock beside his head. "Since around eleven. Close to seven hours, I guess. They've been coming out now and then to ask for things. Cigarettes, especially."

"I bet you could cure a ham in there by now," Graham said, wrinkling his nose.

Jill gave him her see-you-'round smile. "Well, thanks again for helping me carry those cassettes over." She headed back toward her desk, and was surprised to feel him follow her down the hall. It seemed that he was slowing his natural pace a little to match hers step for step—he was a long-striding six-footer, Jill barely five-four—not wanting to overtake her.

She plopped down in her chair. Her voicemail light was on, and as she picked up the receiver to collect her messages Graham came to a halt in front of the faux-teak partition that shielded her cubicle. It stopped just level with the top of Jill's head, so he had to come right up to it if he wanted to talk to her. But did he want to talk to her? He just stood there for a moment, rocking idly from one foot to the other, examining her phone list, the skyline of buildings that shimmered through the window behind her and the series of fashion-y shampoo ads—a campaign Robin had created at his previous agency—that decorated an expanse of wall next to her computer. Jill scratched seven messages into her notebook with a dying ballpoint pen, every one of them work-related. Finally, people were beginning to know her name, learn what she could do for them: track down missing reels, tardy expense checks, junior producers gone AWOL. Jill felt her status in the department slowly rising, and it gave her hope that she'd finally found something she was good at, had gotten some momentum. She tapped hey keyboard and the screen lit up with boldface type, a wall of unread e-mails.

She finished writing down the seventh message, and sent the faltering pen soaring into her garbage can. Graham slowly lowered his eyes to meet hers, the expression on his face the picture of artful nonchalance.

"So this is where you sit, huh?" he began. "Nice view."

Jill nodded, still trying to figure out why Graham was hanging around her desk when everything and everyone else related to the Tellco account had been thrown into overdrive. She'd heard from other girls in her department about male employees (mostly account guys and creatives) who made fairly regular tours of the agency to scope out the new female "talent". At least he wasn't middle-aged or married—or both—like so many of them appeared to be.

Graham said nothing more for a second, just continued his mental inventory of the surroundings. Jill felt mildly uncomfortable with his silent, jittery presence, unsure of whether to get on with her work or make an effort to talk to him. He'd seemed so much more at ease when they first met—so much smoother, more talkative, like all the client service types she'd encountered during her short time at H-F. Now he was different: he seemed on edge, nervous, vaguely out of sorts.

"Are you on the tenth floor too?" she said at last, unable to bear the cramped silence another second.

"Me? Nope, no way. No suits allowed on ten." He let out a nervous laugh. "That's been the rule since long before I got here. Segregating the departments is sort of a Hambleton French tradition, or so they tell me. At my old agency people were seated together by account, not by department. I worked on the Foster's Lager business, and I sat with the creative teams, the media people, and the producers who worked on the account with me. Which I actually preferred."

"Now you sit with all the other client service types? The suits?"

**Her Latest Supporting Role**

"On eleven. Sad to say, yes." Graham stopped rocking back and forth, and flashed Jill a silly little grin. "A ghetto of Thomas Pink shirts and Banana Republic khakis."

"Doesn't sound too awful," she allowed.

Graham looked past Jill, and she turned her head to follow his gaze. To the agency's east, the buildings of Rockefeller Center gleamed in the afternoon sun. Then he sighed, and pinched the bridge of his nose again, shutting his bloodshot eyes tight for a couple of seconds. Even the smile-shaped scar on his chin seemed to droop a little.

"Do you realize that by the time this pitch is finished the summer will almost be over?" he said finally, opening his eyes and blinking hard at the brightness outside, like he'd just emerged from a darkened room.

"What's the date of the pitch?"

"August twenty-fourth. And Labor Day's early this year, too," he added, his voice low. "I've been on a save-the-business pitch more than once before, and I'm sure that this one's going to be a non-stop blur of late nights and weekends, just like every other time."

"Oh yeah?"

"A couple of years ago we pitched to save the Mid-lantic Express Airlines account. Hambleton French had been their agency since the airline was founded, in the early 70s." Mentioning it seemed to stir up something from deep in Graham's memory. He paused, and stared into space for a moment.

"Did we lose?" Jill asked quietly, though she already knew the answer. She'd never seen any evidence of Mid-lantic Express in the office: no framed ads in the lobby, not a single rah-rah e-mail about an upcoming campaign, not even so much as a line on her time sheet.

Graham sighed. His good-natured smile was replaced by something else: a slack line, thin and without humor.

"Of course we lost. The incumbent nearly always does. And they laid off about forty people the next week. It's just the way these things go. If there's something about you they really can't stand, can you change it in two months? And even if you can, will you be able to convince the client that the change is real and lasting, not a superficial act of desperation? Bottom line, to most clients it's the old old-dog-new-trick thing."

He looked so down. Jill, who'd been mildly annoyed since he'd accosted her in the videotape library, finally warmed up to Graham. She put on her comedy voice, chirpy and nasal.

"Well, thanks for stopping by, Mister Cheerful," she said. "I guess I'll plan to stay late tonight and get my résumé in order."

Graham's smile came back immediately—tempered with a big dose of sheepishness—and he let out a guffaw. Jill felt relieved. Maybe now that he'd snapped out of it he would buzz off and let her get some work done.

"Sorry, sorry, sorry," he said with a pleading groan. "Feel free to tell me to shut up. The creatives do all the time. Just ask Nick and Sandi. Or your pal Robin."

"No biggie," Jill said, swiveling her chair a few degrees toward her computer, trying to signal that she wanted to get back to work. Graham just wasn't getting the hint, though.

"You know, Jill, this is probably the last weeknight I'll have free for a long, long time. For ten weeks—sorry, now it's more like nine, but who's counting, haha." He looked at her nervously. "Anyhow, I'm desperate to make the most of it. And besides, it's so beautiful outside." Graham's voice trailed off for a few seconds. He seemed dazzled by the sight of the cityscape.

He cleared his throat and began again. "Tonight I was going to take a walk up to the park. Watch the sun set, maybe have a few drinks at the Boathouse—do some of the things I planned to do this summer...now, while I can. My batteries sure could use some recharging," he added. Then he stood up very straight and

**Her Latest Supporting Role**

looked Jill right in the eye. "Can I persuade you to come with me?"

"Me?" Jill said, caught completely off guard. "You want me to come with you?"

"Sure. I've depressed you enough for one day, haven't I?" He smiled appealingly at her: the smooth, confident client-handler once more. "Now you can let me cheer you up."

"That's really nice of you," Jill began. The invitation had taken her by surprise, particularly since he'd spent the last quarter of an hour filling her head with doom and gloom. The Tellco review could well be the beginning of the end of her unspeakably short career at Hambleton French, and now he was asking her out? The only thing that made sense of it at all was his silly appearance at her desk, the rocking back and forth and looking around her little corner of the tenth floor with all the subtlety of a B-movie actor. Probably checking to see if she had a picture of some boyfriend on her desk: just the kind of feeble detective work that Jill herself would attempt.

"That's really very nice of you, Graham," she continued. "But I'm afraid I can't, not tonight."

"Oh," he said quietly, his mouth closed tight around the word. The look of naked disappointment on his handsome face almost made him look like a teenager. "Other plans?" It was a question rather than a statement, and the tone in which it was delivered just begged for an answer, some elaboration. On almost any other day he likely could have wormed the information out of her, but this afternoon—her nerves sharpened by that unwelcome glimpse of the specter of unemployment—she wasn't really in the mood to talk.

"Uh huh. Sorry." Jill smiled at him, and she tried to make it a warm smile—teeth, gums, the works—afraid he'd spend the rest of their office interactions thinking of her as some chilly bitch who'd blown him off without giving it a second thought. She remembered him from the bar, with Robin, and he seemed nice enough, really. She felt a little sorry for him, too. Robin said he'd just been dumped, and Jill certainly knew what that felt like. Strange: there was something about his eyes, their deep blue streaked here and there with red, the skin around the corners pale and netted almost invisibly. They made him appear tired, for which the Tellco account could almost certainly be blamed. But there was something else, too, more than just simple fatigue. Graham looked world-weary, beaten-down, almost like he'd had it with life. "But have a great time," she added cheerily.

He nodded, and with a smile that struck Jill as lifeless but sincere, said goodbye and began the retreat to his office.

At that very moment Robin Devlin—Art Director Extraordinaire, as he was so fond of calling himself—came sailing down the corridor, head turned, eyes bright, shouting directions at some unseen person who trailed in his wake. It looked as though he was going to run headlong into Graham, but then he deftly moved his narrow body away, averting collision at the last possible second. When he recognized Graham, and then Jill, Robin came to an abrupt halt. He said something sharp and unintelligible to the junior art director he'd been shouting at and the poor girl scurried off, her iBook clutched to her chest.

"You two!" Robin said pointedly, and looked from Graham's face to Jill's and back again. He came around to the side of Jill's desk so that he stood right between them, then beamed suggestively at each one in turn. Though nothing of substance had passed between her and Graham—a date had been proposed and then graciously declined, end of story—Robin's expressive stare made Jill's cheeks turn pink.

Robin was wearing an ensemble that was preppy yet outrageous: Topsiders so decayed that the front of one shoe had lifted away from the sole almost entirely, revealing three long and extraordinarily hairy white toes; and khaki safari shorts cinched around his thin waist by a braided tan belt, the cotton fabric fashionably distressed but immaculately ironed. On top was the

**Her Latest Supporting Role**

*pièce de résistance*, the item that brought the whole ensemble together, and gave it meaning and life. Emblazoned in hot pink letters across the front of Robin's navy T-shirt was the proclamation: *I Cross-dress My Barbies*.

Graham's attention drifted from Robin's smirking face to the front of his T-shirt. His bloodshot eyes opened wide, one of those expressions she'd seen all the time in movies, but that in real life are much more rare.

"Jesus Christ! Where did you get that shirt?"

"A friend gave it to me when he heard I was working on a toy account. Some vintage Barbie dolls, too," he added archly, "if you ever want to borrow them."

"Just do me a favor, Robin." Graham's voice betrayed mild annoyance. "Don't wear it around the office, okay? I mean, what if the Tellco clients were visiting the agency?"

"Why should they mind? They don't make Barbies."

"Yeah. I know, I know. But it's a family-run company, and the folks there are all church-going, solid-citizen, pillar-of-the-community types from Ohio. Somehow I don't think they'd take too kindly to the idea of gender-bending toys, even as a joke." Graham's tone softened, became pleading. "Please, Robin. The account's ready to walk out the door."

"All right, all right," he said, fanning his skinny arms as though trying to shoo the topic away entirely. "'Nuff said. Consider this T-shirt officially retired from my workday wardrobe." Robin winked at Jill, "At least until the pitch is over."

"Thanks," Graham said quietly.

Robin sneaked another quick look at his T-shirt and gave Jill a conspiratorial smile.

"Look, kids," he said. "I've got to dash—I don't know where that wench Petra has run off to—" Petra Marks was his creative partner, an H-F lifer with a shelf full of copywriting awards, "but we've got some non-Tellco work to finish for a meeting in the morning. Should be done in a couple of hours, though, if the two of you," and he put such unmistakable emphasis on the word two that Jill felt her cheeks sizzle all over again: *who died and made you Miss Lonely hearts?* she wanted to shout, "would care to join me at Julian's for a cocktail. You could go run along now," he added transparently, "and I'll meet you there when Mad Madam Marks is done with me."

Graham looked at Jill. Robin looked at Graham, then followed his gaze to Jill, and an awkward asymmetrical silence hung in the air between them.

Jill broke it first. "I'm sorry, but I've gotta go, right now," she said, and backed her story up by grabbing her phone to call Nick and Sandi, telling them she had to leave, that there was someplace she had to be, though in fact class didn't start until seven-ten. "Sorry, Robin," she added as she hung up.

"Right. Well, it was nice chatting with you again Jill," Graham said, perhaps a little sadly. "Robin," he added with a polite nod, and turned away from the desk. "I'll see you 'round."

"Round like a doughnut," echoed Robin. A second later Graham was gone.

Robin took a giant step, so that he ended up standing squarely in front of Jill's desk. He folded his arms across his chest and looked her straight in the eye.

"What?" Jill asked. She averted her eyes and bent to fish her purse out of a desk drawer.

"I bet he asked you out, and you slam-dunked his poor fragile recently-jilted ego, didn't you, naughty girl?"

Jill felt herself shrink a little, and frowned. "Was it that obvious?"

"No, not really. But he did kind of ask me about you. The old social background check, you know how it is." Robin raised his eyebrows for physical punctuation. "I told him you were a smart girl—you laugh at my jokes, after all—an entertaining lunch partner, and totally unattached. I told him, in other words, to go for it.'"

**Her Latest Supporting Role**

Jill groaned. "I wish you'd told me, Robin, so I could have declined his invitation a little more gracefully."

Robin put both hands on his hips, and gave Jill a look full of reproach.

"Why did you say no in the first place? I think you two are the perfect couple, a pair of cute, intelligent, high-strung WASPs. You even look kind of alike. And you both have this weird character trait too—no offense. You have this crazy mega-reserve. It must be a WASP thing –" he mused, wagging one long finger at her, "because I sure don't have it. But once you get past it you're this nice, fun, warm person. And with Graham, same exact thing. You two are made for each other," he said with finality.

"He's not my type," Jill countered, although it was a lie. Graham was just the type that appealed to her, physically and otherwise. He was intelligent, accomplished, and blessed with great (if a little too conservative) style; she and Monika were always commenting, certainly more than the subject warranted, on how New York was filled with straight men whose good looks were completely, tragically overshadowed by their awful taste. And Graham seemed nice enough:  not one of those slimy, untrustworthy modern-day Larry Tates, the so-called "empty suits" that Robin complained endlessly about. She wasn't sure why she didn't want to come clean with Robin—tell him how wary she was of an office romance, that the thought of breaking up with (or worse, being dumped by) someone and then having to see them day-in, day-out was almost her worst nightmare.

"Too bad, 'cause he's totally my type," Robin gushed. "Problem is, he's on *your* team."

"I hear you," Jill said. "The thing is, Robin, I'm more of an 'opposites attract' kind of gal."

"Oh really?" Robin said. "Well, if I meet any ugly, mean, dimwitted jerks I'll let you know, shall I?"

The conversation was going downhill fast, this much Jill recognized, and the only thing to do was make a quick exit. She slung her gigantic bag across her body, bike messenger-style, and rotated in her chair. As she stood to leave Robin was still anchored before her desk wearing that tsk-tsk expression.

"Bye, Robin," she said with a quick wave. Then she firmly fixed her eyes on the passage to the elevator. "I've got to run—night school beckons—but call me tomorrow. Maybe we can have lunch."

"I might know more about the boy-girl thing than you give me credit for," he began, his tone almost sulky. But then his voice brightened, and he was instantly his amusing old self again. "Though of course, not from personal experience. But lunch tomorrow is time enough for your lecture."

They walked together toward the elevator, though Robin peeled away from Jill at the last possible moment, and turned down another corridor, narrow and windowless, bustling with Tellco-related activity.

"Now where's that silly bitch Petra?" he demanded of no one in particular, and disappeared into a shadowy alcove of offices, while Jill slid her MetroCard from her purse, preparing for the subway ride downtown.

The class discussion was cut off promptly at nine-thirty. Jill shoved the books and papers into her bag, and practically sprinted to the building's front entrance. Monika had offered to meet her after class, and she absolutely hated to be kept waiting. But at nine forty-five Jill was still alone on the sidewalk of West Fourth Street, her cell phone silent, with the distinct feeling that Monika's work had once again gotten the better of her and she'd been dragged into an office or conference room, unable to escape. Jill tried Monika's desk, then her cell, letting her know that at nine-fifty Jill would be bailing on their plans. Then she

**Her Latest Supporting Role**

walked back up the building's steps, dropped her bag and sat down, exhausted from her long day of work and school.

A minute later Jill heard footsteps coming from behind. When the sound stopped suddenly, she turned her head and looked up. Jonathan Wunder stood beside her, silhouetted by the light from the building's entrance, his face obscured.

"Hey, you're in my class, aren't you?" he asked, tilting his head toward her.

Jill peered up at him, but his expression was hidden by darkness. "Yes...I am," she answered wearily.

"Got a name?"

Jill climbed to her feet. With her low-heeled sandals on they were exactly the same height, and she looked squarely into his brown eyes.

"Oh, sorry. I'm Jill Barber. Hi," she added, feeling slightly foolish.

"Good to meet you, Jill," he said. "Are you in the English program? Picking up a quickie summer credit to lighten your course load next year?"

She shook her head. "Neither, actually. I was supposed to graduate last week with my MFA, but I —" For a moment the words eluded her, and she faltered. "I wound up short on credits. I have a full-time job, so I only had night classes to choose from, and yours was the best fit," she said with a self-conscious laugh, suddenly realizing how idiotic this rationale sounded.

"I'm flattered that you found yourself so drawn to my course," he said archly.

"Sorry," Jill said. "It does seem like it'll be interesting," she added, angling for forgiveness.

"Don't worry about it." Jonathan Wunder laughed. "So what do you do in this job of yours?" he asked.

"I work for an advertising agency in midtown. It's called Hambleton French."

"Oh sure, I know them," he said, and nodded solemnly. "They created some really famous campaigns. Are you a copywriter, then?"

"A writer? Oh no, God no," Jill said with a twitchy laugh. "I'm low man, at least...low girl on the totem pole in the production department. A mere cog in the wheel. More like an assistant mere cog, actually. I work for the two people who oversee all of the agency's commercial production. Nothing too glamorous, I'm afraid," she added with a shrug.

"Well, can I ask what you think of the class so far? This is my first time teaching this course, and for that matter, at NYU," Jonathan Wunder's handsome brow creased amusingly, and his voice took on a tone of mock seriousness. "You can be brutally honest with me, Jill. I can take it."

"It's very, um..." She plumbed her brain for a suitable adjective, trying to impress him, a writer. "Very thought-provoking. I really enjoyed tonight's class."

"Oh yeah?" he said, not quite concealing a smile.

"Sure. The whole literary structure to cinematic structure thing," she added, hoping that maybe she could get some participation marks this way, since she'd been all but silent throughout the last two sessions

"If you were so intrigued you should have said something. What held you back?"

Jill shrugged and said nothing. She felt a mild flush of embarrassment and was thankful for the cover of darkness.

He smiled at her, that much she could see, and the skin around the corners of his dark brown eyes creased appealingly. "Well, I hope you'll say something next week, Jill, when we discuss *Slaughterhouse Five*. You were in the first class, weren't you?" Jill nodded yes. "So you know that class participation counts for a large part of your grade?"

"I remember. So I guess this little exchange doesn't count?" she added hopefully.

**Her Latest Supporting Role**

"Nice try. See you next week." And with that, Jonathan Wunder slung his backpack over one shoulder and turned to leave.

"I'll get into the discussion next week. Promise," she called down the steps to him.

Jonathan Wunder reached the sidewalk at the very moment that Monika did. Jill saw her look first at Jonathan's face, then up at Jill.

"Hey," Monika said to him. "I know you."

Jonathan Wunder stopped on the sidewalk, and turned back to face her. "Excuse me?" he said, looking a little bewildered, like maybe she was a crazed fan or even just a garden-variety NYC nutcase—though how many of those were so impeccably suited-up for business?

"I know you. You went to school with my sister."

Jill waved to Monika and descended the stairs to join them.

"Great Neck North High School," Monika continued. "Anya Roth? You guys went to college together too, I think." She extended her hand, precise and formal, like she was meeting a client for the very first time, not someone from her hometown. "Monika Roth."

"Shit, of course!" Jonathan shook her hand and stepped back to take another look at Monika. Illuminated by streetlights, Jonathan Wunder's features registered familiarity. "How's your sister doing? We kind of lost touch."

"She's good. Lives in Paris now. Married a guy who works for Lazard Frères."

"Really." Jonathan Wunder pondered for a moment. "Well, tell her I said hello the next time you talk to her. Small world," he added with a shrug.

"I just came here to meet Jill. We're about to jump in a cab," Monika said. She raised one blue-suited arm and as if on cue a yellow taxi cruised to a stop on the street next to her. "We're heading east. Can we drop you anywhere?"

"I'm actually walking uptown. But thanks for the offer."

"Well, I'll see you next week," Jill said quietly, moving toward the cab and opening the door.

"Right you are, Jill." He smiled, then shook his head slightly, as though stirred by a passing thought. "By the way, you two, I'm having a party tomorrow night. If you're going to be in town, consider yourself invited. I can't promise any other refugees from Great Neck," he added for Monika's sake, "but you never know, right?"

Jonathan pulled a pad and pen from his bag and passed it to Jill. "Write down your e-mails, I'll send you both an invite when I get home."

"Thanks a lot, Jonathan." Monika tapped her forehead with one finger. "I'm probably going to the Hamptons this weekend. You'll be in town, though, won't you, Jill?"

"Probably," she admitted, and made a little face. "I may have to work."

"Then please come if you're free. And bring whoever you'd like, of course."

Jill and Monika said goodnight to Jonathan Wunder, then slid into the taxi and headed for NoLita. Monika caught Jill's eyes closing and gave her a quick poke in the ribs.

"Hey, wake up!" Monika demanded. "Aren't we going out for coffee?"

Jill sat up straight, and nodded wearily.

"How long were you two talking before I showed up?" she continued, raising her voice over the screech of traffic and the buzz of talk and music as they passed the outdoor cafes along Lafayette.

"Not long," Jill said. "Five minutes or so."

"So did you tell him how you stayed up all night to read his book?"

**Her Latest Supporting Role**

"Not yet." Jill turned her head and stared out the window at the traffic. "I need to ponder it a little more before I mention it to him. I haven't quite figured out what I think of it yet."

"Are you going to ask him if it's autobiographical?"

A loaded question, Jill realized. She'd been awake half the night finishing *Groundswell*, and spent most of her free moments that day reflecting on its disturbing action, turning the story's elements over again and again in her mind. The gushing tributes that decorated the back cover of the paperback edition revealed relatively little about the book's subject matter. *Groundswell* was the grim tale of a suburban family that was dysfunctional in the extreme. Reading late into the night—*Groundswell* was a thin volume of barely two hundred pages—Jill felt herself at the same time gripped and repulsed, the way people must feel while slowing the car down to catch a glimpse of a traffic accident. Nothing in Jonathan Wunder's breezy, charming classroom manner, nothing that she'd heard about him from Monika—that he was an average Long Island Jewish Prince, from an average Great Neck family—made her think the story was autobiographical. But at the same time, she was curious about where he'd found his inspiration. She read enough to know that most first novels were really thinly veiled version of their authors' own coming-of-age stories. What had led him to write such an unrelentingly grim tale? The story contained strong measures of both hatred and revenge, most of it directed toward the father, and that unsettled Jill. Head inclined against the cab window, her brain cells churned through the novel's darker passages. Again she saw the family's conflict acted out in her mind—this time with a New York traffic soundtrack throbbing in the background—until she nodded into sleep.

# Chapter 5

It was the last day of June, a Friday night and for most New Yorkers, the start of a long holiday weekend. Jill had lucked out and didn't have to spend any part of the long weekend in the office working on the Tellco pitch—Broadcast Production's heavy-lifting would supposedly happen much closer to the big day—though Robin and many other creatives had not been as fortunate.

Jill arrived on the doorstep of Jonathan Wunder's apartment at nine-fifty, and stood there in anticipation for at least a full minute before raising her hand to the bell. Though almost obsessively punctual when it mattered, Jill made a point of never being on time for this sort of gathering. She hated nothing more than being among the first to arrive, standing awkwardly in a corner of an empty room, scanning the faces of arriving guests as though she had nothing interesting or social in her life except a silly little party. Even if it was true: being desperate was one thing, looking it was quite another. But through the closed door she could hear the reassuring buzz of conversation and a stereo's pounding bass.

Her clothes, at least, gave her some confidence. She was wearing a favorite outfit from her acting days, the one she wore to auditions when her agent told her they were looking for an "Ingénue With Edge" type. The Ingénue With Edge look was comprised of a black scoop-neck T-shirt of thin cotton jersey, low (but not too low) faded Seven jeans, and a ribbon choker with a pink enamel daisy at its center. She tottered slightly on wedge-heel sandals, a bit higher than she was used to; Ingénue With Edge hadn't come out much of late. From within she heard a slight stirring and then the lock clicked. Jonathan Wunder pulled the door open and smiled a host's smile, boozy and genial.

"Jill Barber. Hi. Welcome, I'm glad you could make it," he said, and stood to one side of the doorway, ushering her in with a sweep of his arm. "No Monika tonight?"

She returned his greeting with a slight nervousness—being at his party brought back a momentary flash of that evening at Czerny's. But Jonathan's amiable, handsome smile soothed her. He was really more of a peer, after all: only a few years older than her, and not even a real faculty member.

Her left hand was clutching the neck of a bottle of wine. "Thanks. For you—happy drinking," she said, offering it to Jonathan, who quickly relieved it of its wrapping and peered down at the label.

"Umm, French. Thank you. Good stuff, this," he added appreciatively. She had learned a thing or two about wine during her waitressing days: so, she thought with a little inward grimace, not a total waste of three years.

Her host placed a hand on Jill's bent elbow. "Let's get you a drink, all right, and then I'll introduce you to a few people?"

Jonathan Wunder's home was low ceilinged but surprisingly airy, the entire lower ground floor of a brownstone a half-dozen blocks north of Gramercy Park. The main room, where about fifteen guests in their late twenties or early thirties stood in groups of three or four—and, she noted with little spasm of dismay, not a familiar face among them—was large and long, with a large carved wood mantel and very few pieces of furniture. Though somewhat sparse, the furniture was tasteful and looked fairly expensive: mostly gray and black, and arranged precisely around the edges of a zebra-patterned wool rug. On three sides of the room the walls were painted pale gray, and decorated here and there with framed prints. The front wall, which was painted a cold, flat white, was dominated by two very tall windows; they were criss-crossed on the outside by a grid of skinny iron bars. The Venetian blinds were partly opened, but the evening sky was invisible, concealed behind brownstones and high-rise apartment buildings.

His kitchen had a tidy, minimalist appearance, and an air of disuse about it. Laid out across the unmarked white counter was an impressive array of liquor. Spirits of every imaginable variety and color winked at her: Grappa? Buffalo grass vodka? Hardly the type of party she was used to—an ice-filled bathtub brimming with beer and wine bottles was more her speed—and Jill suddenly felt a little out of her league.

"Hey, did you knock over a liquor store this afternoon?" she inquired jokingly, and motioned toward the rows of bottles.

"Oh, no. Not quite," Jonathan answered with a laugh and a quick lift of his dark eyebrows. He opened the fridge and squatted before it, slotting her bottle of wine in among what appeared to be at least a dozen others. Then he stood again, right next to her, and rubbed his palms together with enthusiasm. "So what are you drinking?"

"Well..." She paused, and bent over the counter a little, scrutinizing the labels. She settled her hand on a half-filled bottle of Absolut Citron and picked it up. Just for a moment she felt like Alice clutching the DRINK ME bottle and felt lightheaded, quite suddenly. "I wouldn't say no to some of this," Jill said and to her horror, giggled lamely. *Cool at all costs*, she silently admonished herself, Ingénue *With Edge*. She added, with much more composure, "with tonic and ice, please."

Jonathan complimented her on her daisy choker (cute...was he mocking it?) and they returned to the living room. She scanned the little clusters of guests again, searching for a familiar face—someone else from the class, maybe—but still recognized no one. So many women! She remembered the dedication page of *Groundswell*; it read To K. With idle curiosity she wondered if "K." was his girlfriend—and if so, which one was she?

Before he could begin to introduce her around the bell sounded again and Jonathan excused himself. Jill was beginning to

**Her Latest Supporting Role**

regret that she hadn't pressured Monika more, guilt-tripped her into blowing off the Hamptons and coming along. After all, she was the one who had pushed Jill into attending, curious about Jonathan Wunder and his post-Great Neck life, wanting some gossip to report back to her older sister. Jill took a large sip of her drink, not yet feeling psyched or intoxicated enough to walk over to a group of strangers and bulldoze her way into their conversation. This was one of the reasons (and there were so many) that she'd failed as an actress. She couldn't just turn it on in any situation; she was a studier, a preparer, a rehearser, and there was so little rehearsal time for the auditions she was sent on, and in life even less.

She moved to the nearest wall to examine the framed artwork on display. The first thing she noticed was a dust jacket from Jonathan's novel. It was mounted flat and framed by glass and brushed steel. She'd read his book only ten days before, in paperback, and the design for the hardcover dust jacket was very different. The book's front cover featured a rather impressionistic drawing of a body of dark water which lapped at the foundations of a row of houses, a suburban skyline. The back of the book jacket appeared in the frame's left side, a curious reversal: the handsome, rather serious face of the young and then-unknown author appearing to gaze over at his book's front cover. In the black-and-white photo Jonathan's expression was unsmiling, joyless and a little distant, as though he was working the brooding, tortured artist angle.

She glanced toward the front door where he was admitting another guest. From where she stood Jill could see only the guest's arms; it was yet another woman. She looked at them all, standing around the living room, only a couple of men among them, here and there, overwhelmingly outnumbered. This new woman's arms were short, and red-sleeved. They wrapped around Jonathan's back, and then moved downwards in what appeared to be an extremely personal greeting, as the top of her white-blonde head bobbed against his shoulder. Jill looked back at the framed book jacket, took a long swig of her vodka tonic, and turned, ready to face the party at last.

She swiveled around, and out of the corner of her eye saw the host leading his newest arrival toward her—on their way to the kitchen, she assumed—when the albino tint of the short hair and that dwarfish stature became instantly, alarmingly familiar. Jonathan led Justine DeVries through the room, and Jill felt an unexpected surge of annoyance: Justine, the straw-haired pygmy who had caused her no end of angst during their three long years together at prep school. Jill recalled their final year, when they had shared prefect duties, with a special shudder of distaste— their mutual aggravation society. An entitled brat who'd spent her entire life in Manhattan, Justine had mocked Jill's suburban upbringing mercilessly; Jill in turn retaliated with barbs about Justine's impossibly, comically short stature. Now Justine entered the room, hanging on Jonathan Wunder's bent arm (though decidedly below-average in stature himself, Jonathan towered over Justine) her smile displaying an expanse of baby-pink gums, and a decidedly horsy overbite that seemed to have become even more pronounced since their last encounter.

Fuck. Jill breathed in sharply as they headed right for her. She'd run into Justine so many times during the years since they'd left boarding school—to Jill's extended chagrin, they had wound up as college classmates at Vassar, both majoring in English—but it was those terms at Walden Academy that brought on a strange nausea of remembrance. From their first encounter at age fifteen, Jill had taken an intense, profound dislike to Justine DeVries, a sentiment which Justine had more than adequately returned. Jill had spent three years locked in a struggle of unending one-upmanship with her, while Monika—who didn't like Justine any more than Jill did—watched their rivalry from the periphery, too cool for school even then.

**Her Latest Supporting Role**

Now Jill watched Justine take mincing baby steps from the door. Walking alongside Jonathan, she talked nonstop as she scanned the trios and quartets of guests. Inevitably Justine's stare locked onto Jill, and her pale, round face changed in expression for just an instant, shifting from mindless enjoyment to unpleasant surprise. Justine stopped chattering at Jonathan and halted in front of Jill, looking her over from head to toe.

"Jill Barber!" she exclaimed with just a trace of sourness, adding a patronizing smile that was a millisecond flash of too-big pink gums and red lipstick.

Jonathan smiled blithely and looked first at Jill, blank faced, backed up against the living-room wall with her fingernails tapping a nervous rhythm against the side of her glass. Then he shifted his gaze to Justine. The strangest look —very enigmatic, nearly a smile—spread across Justine's face.

"Hi Justine." Jill finally found her voice. "I haven't run into you in quite a while."

"So you two know each other then," Jonathan said brightly. Turning to Jill, he added, "and you were worried that you wouldn't know a soul."

She looked to him, then at Justine's withering scarlet smile, and laughed weakly. "Oh, we go way back."

Jonathan disappeared to fetch Justine a drink, managing to free the arm she had gripped so tightly since her arrival. Jill and her old classmate were left standing in an empty corner of Jonathan's living room, compelled to make small talk until he returned. It was like being back at Walden.

"So what are you up to these days, Jill?" Justine began, likely trying to conceal her true, nastier intentions behind a veneer of mere nosiness. "Still in grad school, or trying to be an actress again?"

She took a second to look Justine over before countering (under her breath, inaudible) *cow*. Jill smiled pointedly, and took a long swallow of vodka.

"I was just curious, you know?" Justine continued, working her powdery-pale face into a wide, gummy smile again, and pushing a lock of whitish hair away from her eyes. "I mean, I haven't seen you in a while. At least not since that bank commercial you were in stopped running." Her pale brow furrowed thoughtfully "And that doesn't really count, does it?"

"Mmm." Jill looked down into her drink, momentarily mortified to be reminded of her role in a banal TV spot for a New York bank. She'd played a teller, smiling inanely for all of the four seconds she'd appeared on screen. Jill swirled the little nubs of melting ice round and round. Maybe if she didn't respond, didn't put up a fight, then Justine would just leave her alone, like an animal that loses interest when its prey pretends to be dead.

"Any other great roles on the horizon?" Justine wasn't letting her off the hook tonight—she smelled blood. She had a real smile across her pale moon face now. In it Jill read volumes of superiority and satisfaction.

Jill moved away from the wall slightly and inflated her lungs with a calming breath. She reminded herself that no matter what words passed between them, she would always have an absolute physical advantage, and that very fact had been eating away at Justine since the tenth grade. Though by no means a giant—Jill seemed a little stunted herself next to Monika's decidedly Amazonian proportions—she was by now at least five inches taller than Justine, and blessed with longer legs, bigger breasts and an actual waist. Justine resembled nothing so much as a bleached-out beanbag, small and shapeless, blobby, devoid of color save for the ever-present bloody gash of lipstick. So why did she always make Jill so nervous, sabotage her with insecurity? Justine DeVries would always be tottering through life on high heels, Jill thought with a silent little *ha!* of satisfaction.

"Actually, I am still in grad school," Jill finally answered. She was amazed how easily the admission came out of her mouth.

**Her Latest Supporting Role**

After more than a month of borderline despair over the incident with Czerny she was finally moving on. "I'm taking an evening class, from Jonathan in fact," she added, tilting her head in the direction of their host and hoping her matter-of-fact tone of voice would convey Justine that it was all a complete non-issue.

"Oh. So he's your teacher, then?"

"That's right. I'm his star pupil," Jill added, letting the vodka do the talking. She looked plaintively toward the kitchen, but their host was nowhere in sight.

Unable to get a real rise out of Jill, Justine nonetheless kept talking, almost exclusively about herself: her job (working at the literary agency that represented Jonathan, very prestigious, very glamorous, though Jill suspected the position was as borderline-secretarial as her own); her new apartment (she'd just closed on a one bedroom co-op in a doorman building—with the help of her rich daddy, Jill was certain); and her amazing new boyfriend (yet another investment banker, of course). Jill stood there silently with her mind going blank from boredom, wishing that Justine would collect her drink and move on. Or leave, remember another engagement and clear out altogether. That would be too wonderful for words: oh, that she could be so lucky.

Justine closed her mouth for a moment. Gooey scarlet lips pursed tightly, she scrutinized Jill once again.

"So," she began. There was a protracted pause, heavy with meaning. "Are you actually working, then?"

"I've got a job at Hambleton French. Actually," Jill answered coolly. "It's a big multi-national ad agency in midtown. Perhaps you've heard of it. I've been there since May."

"Doing what?" Justine's lip curled a little as she spoke, like she'd caught a whiff of an offensive smell.

Jill turned her head. Through the propped-open kitchen door she could see Jonathan's back as he stood before the refrigerator, its freezer compartment wide open. He seemed to be having serious problems with his ice cube trays, and there were shards of broken ice and tiny pools of water all over the floor. He was clearly a little drunk, and that wasn't helping matters any. She wished he would sort it out and hurry up with Justine's drink, give her something, anything other than questions to keep her big mouth occupied.

"I work with the Agency's two Executive Producers. They're in charge of the broadcast production department, which makes all the TV and radio commercials."

"Oh. Like a secretary?"

*Bitch*, Jill breathed again, her lips barely moving. She shook her head slowly. "No, not like a secretary. I handle the production schedules, book editing and recording time, round up directors' reels, stock music, things like that. Last week I went on a TV shoot for the new Caramba! instant coffee spot." *Yeah, to deliver a cassette that Nick forgot to take to the studio*, she added mentally.

"Really. How interesting," Justine said, though her tone implied exactly the opposite.

Jill rolled her eyes and gulped down the last of her drink. At that precise moment Jonathan Wunder emerged from the kitchen and handed a glass to Justine, who received it with almost aggressive thanks. Jill smiled at Jonathan, a warm, wide, familiar smile that succeeded in shifting his attention almost completely away from Justine.

"Did you sort out your little problem with the ice?" Jill inquired.

He laughed, slightly embarrassed, and looked down at the front of his fashionably worn blue Oxford shirt, which was mottled with dark wet circles.

"I did have a hard time with the ice. Sorry there's none in your drink Justine," he said, with a cursory nod, then looked at Jill again. "So how do you two know each other?"

Jill tilted her head a little. She was doing everything in her power to keep Jonathan Wunder focused on her. That would

**Her Latest Supporting Role**

piss Justine off. "We went to boarding school together—Walden Academy in Massachusetts. We were in the same house."

Jonathan's brown-eyed gaze, dark and friendly, remained on Jill as she spoke. With a faint thrill of revenge she saw that he was all but ignoring Justine. It was in his body language; although he stood between them, his shoulder angled in Jill's direction, partly blocking Justine's short blonde head as he spoke.

"Really," he said to Jill.

"Really," Justine repeated loudly, in a pissed-off tone of voice. Jill grinned: Ingénue With Edge one, Blonde Troll zero. She raised her glass in a sort of mock toast, then swilled down nearly half her drink in two short gulps.

"You'll excuse me, won't you both," Justine said with a stiff smile. "I think I see someone I know." Then she turned on her high wedge heels, and wobbled off to the other side of the room.

Jill followed Justine's departure with perverse interest, and watched her approach a squat, completely bald man who was dressed entirely in white. She let out a long sigh of relief.

"Check out Justine and Mister Clean," she said. Almost as soon as the words had left her mouth, Jill regretted them. Jonathan Wunder mixed a lethal vodka tonic—or at least that would be her excuse. "Oops. Sorry—is he a friend of yours?"

Jonathan looked across the room and shrugged.

"I forget his name. He came with a friend."

"Oh." Jill relaxed a bit, then gave him a perplexed frown. "So do you know Justine DeVries very well?"

"Not really. She works for my agent. She only started a few months ago, but she seemed pretty nice. We met on her first day, when I stopped in at the office. Then I called a couple of times to talk to Annabel, and Justine would always say hi, ask what I was up to. So I invited her to the party."

Ah-ha. Jill gloated inwardly: despite her boasting, Justine was merely his agent's secretary. "That was nice of you. You know, I saw you with her when she arrived—and I got the impression you'd known each other for years."

Jonathan smiled crookedly. He ran one hand quickly through his dark hair. It was an affectation she'd seen in class, when he was trying hard to think of something to say.

"Uh-huh," he said, then exploded into an embarrassed laugh. "I guess she's a really affectionate person, right?"

"Justine? Affectionate, no. Scary, maybe," Jill said with finality.

Jonathan smiled and his eyes wandered to her empty glass.

"Can I get you another? Hey, why don't you come with me?" Jonathan added agreeably as he took the glass from her. "Maybe you can sort out the problem with the ice cube trays."

"And portion control," she said, following him to the kitchen a little unsteadily.

It was way past midnight, and about twenty people were standing or sitting around Jonathan's living room in shadowy semi-darkness. No lights overhead: just the pale glow from a frosted-glass wall sconce near the front door and from a floor lamp in the corner, its shade upturned, beaming a column of white to the ceiling. She'd been talking to Kurt, a sculptor, for quite some time, listening with feigned interest as he explained—in exhaustive, unwelcome detail—how he had obtained virtually all the materials for his upcoming show from an auto graveyard in Jersey. The show's theme, as he described it (in a bombastic monologue with lots of dramatic arm-waving) was basically the decline of meaning in late 20th-century America. He claimed that its most obvious manifestation was people's obsession with machinery and gadgetry, particularly their cars. For the show he was using only parts from cars built since 1995. Of course, he said (inhaling deeply from a noxious European cigarette) no car that young had died of natural causes. He'd even been fortunate enough to have stumbled upon two new-ish cars, their upholstery

**Her Latest Supporting Role**

covered with dried blood. In a confidential tone, Kurt explained that he was a sucker for realism.

Then he snuffed out his cigarette in one of the empty martini glasses, and offered to share half a gram of cocaine with Jill. She thanked him very politely, but explained that she was an old fashioned girl and as such would prefer to drink herself into a coma. With a grunt Kurt disappeared into the bedroom, and she was left alone once again. She began to search the living room for her purse, preparing to head home.

Stooping in a corner of the room—where the hell was her handbag?—Jill felt a light tap on her shoulder, and turned her head.

"Hi. I'm playing the attentive host." Jonathan Wunder stood behind her, a little unsteady on his feet. A smile was on his face, his brown eyes sparkling. "So what did you think of Kurt? An interesting case, isn't he?"

Jill nodded. "The very first thing he said to me was 'last year I did a series of sculptures using only electric typewriter parts'. Nothing as mundane as 'Hello, my name is...' for him."

"I saw that show last summer. Very intense guy, Kurt," Jonathan added, the smile suddenly fading from his lips.

"He's in your bedroom now, destroying the lining of his nose." Jill laughed and raised her glass in silent tribute. "He offered to share, but I seem to be doing pretty well on the vodka"

"On that note, can I offer you another?"

Hell no, Jill thought, I can't even find my stupid purse. She already felt like she was losing her edge. And she liked her edge...Ingénue With Edge. What was it that Robin had called it? Her reserve, whatever. But she said nothing when Jonathan took the glass from her hand, just frowned a little at him.

"I'll only freshen it up a bit," he insisted playfully, holding the glass at arm's length, away from her. "Just a touch more vodka and some ice. I promise. You can even watch."

Jill lowered her voice. In a bold moment of drunken flirtatiousness—forgetting for a moment how they knew each other—she gave him a slightly woozy smile. "You're treating me far too well, Jonathan. I'm not used to it, you know."

Her host smiled enigmatically, and placed a warm hand on Jill's elbow, guiding her away from the window. "Then you obviously haven't been hanging around the right men."

They wove through the cramped living room. A few more people had just arrived: Jonathan stopped moving for a moment and placed his hand lightly on Jill's waist, bringing her to a gentle halt beside him. He introduced them to her first as a group— they were in a band that had enjoyed some success on the independent music scene, its name only fleetingly familiar—and then each in turn. Their names evaporated from Jill's mind almost immediately in a filmy haze of vodka and music and conversation. Then Jonathan Wunder led her into the kitchen and poured a small measure of vodka into Jill's glass. He swiftly downed a shot of tequila, without salt or lime.

The white kitchen was the one well-lit room in the apartment, and cooler than the crowded, sticky living room. Fresh drink in hand, Jill moved to return to the party, but Jonathan motioned for her to stay.

"Have a seat. Please." He waved his arm toward the tiny table, and she sat. Then Jonathan pulled out the chair next to hers and lowered himself into it. He rested his forearms on the table, and stared at her wordlessly, intensely for a moment, his brown eyes unreadable. Jill felt her mouth twitch into a nervous smile.

The hand flicked through the hair again. "I'm glad you stuck around. I've been feeling guilty," he explained. "Abandoning you in the middle of the party, when you didn't know anyone. You seem a little...a little shy, I guess."

Jill lowered her eyes for a moment, embarrassed. Though shy was better than stuck up, that other frequent charge.

**Her Latest Supporting Role**

"Well, don't feel guilty. Besides, I knew Justine," she added with a hoarse laugh.

"Oh yes," he said. "Your pal Justine. What was up there?"

"She hates my guts. She thinks Monika Roth and I tried to kill her when we were seventeen."

"You certainly don't fit my image of a teenage murderess," Jonathan said, lifting his shoulders questioningly.

"It's a long story. Long and stupid."

"Ahhh, my favorite kind," he said. "Go on."

Jill drained her glass in one long swallow. She wiped a thin mustache of wetness away with the back of her hand, and settled in her chair again.

"Well," she began. "Monika and Justine and I all lived in Tait House."

"Girls' dorm, yes?" he interjected.

"Correct," Jill said. "Anyway, the food at school was pretty appalling, but there was a little kitchen, where some of us Tait House girls used to make brownies and cookies and things. In our junior year Monika and I did it all the time. We'd skip dinner and just eat brownies all night. "

"Nice," Jonathan added.

"And since we weren't allowed to keep food in our rooms— probably the only rule we always followed, because who wants mice? —we used to leave it in the house fridge. Well, Monika and I noticed that our brownies were mysteriously disappearing. At first it was barely noticeable, maybe half a brownie cut away in a corner of the pan. But as time went on, the thief got bolder and bolder. By Christmas, we were losing half a pan of brownies a week to this mystery snacker. We couldn't guard the fridge all the time, but the whole thing was really pissing us off. It became our little obsession.

"Anyway, that's when Monika got this great idea. A way we could catch the culprit, not exactly red-handed, but the proof would be there for everyone to witness."

Jonathan hunched forward in his seat. He was obviously trying to anticipate the story's ending—was that the writer in him?—but his expression betrayed only confusion and intoxication. "And the plan was..." he coaxed.

Jill smiled, a parody of sweetness.

"Ex-lax brownies. We made a whole pan of brownies that were chock full of laxative. We used up a whole box, and we laughed so hard while we were making them, our house mistress kept popping in to see if we were getting high."

"Let me guess. Justine was the culprit?"

Jill nodded. She felt an evil, victorious smile spreading across her mouth as she remembered the night in question. "We baited the trap that night, cutting the brownies into squares and throwing a few in the trash, in case their edibility—is that a word?—was called into question. And our plan worked like a charm. The next morning six more brownies were gone. That's like a quadruple adult dose of Ex-lax.

"Justine didn't show up for breakfast that morning, and she was the only Tait House girl missing. So Monika and I ran back to the house where we found her locked in the third-floor bathroom, moaning so loud you'd think she was dying." Jill was laughing, choking on the words. "What a racket! It sounded like someone was torturing a cow. She was still locked in there when everyone came back from breakfast. Monika and I got a whole bunch of people leaning up against the door so they could get an earful of Justine in all her glorious misery. We were merciless. And the part that burned Justine up the most was that Monika and I got off Scot free. She couldn't turn us in to the house mistress 'cause she was the one who had broken house rules in the first place by stealing our food."

"Poor Justine." Jonathan didn't sound that sympathetic, was still laughing, hard, as he spoke. He reached up and wiped one merry tear from the corner of his eye.


**Her Latest Supporting Role**

"So now you know why she hates me," said Jill. "Well, one of the reasons. And I'm not exactly her biggest fan either."

Jonathan's laughter was finally dying down. He looked at Jill and said, "I'm glad you came, you know? I thought you might not want to."

She answered him with a nervous smile. "Why wouldn't I?"

"Oh, I don't know," he said, and looked reflective. "Because I knew Monika, I supposed, and she couldn't make it. And you probably see me as a teacher, not a peer, which is still kind of a weird role for me to find myself in."

"I've been to teachers' parties before," Jill answered, remembering Czerny's loft. She swallowed. "No biggie."

Jonathan pushed his chair away from the table slightly and surveyed the kitchen, which was empty except for them, and a complete mess. Kurt the sculptor appeared in the doorway for a moment. Jill turned her head in time to catch him staring at Jonathan. Kurt's eyes narrowed to slits: a long, chilling look that was impossible to interpret. Jonathan didn't even notice until at last Kurt lowered his gaze almost to the floor, and muttered something about meeting friends at a club in Chinatown. Jonathan waved his arm, said a few not especially friendly parting words, and then turned back to Jill.

"Not exactly your scene here, is it?" he said, shaking his head. "To tell you the truth, I'm not even sure it's mine."

Jill nervously moved a hand up to finger the daisy hanging from her neck. "I'm pretty adaptable."

"You must be pretty tolerant too, to have kept Kurt occupied for so long."

"I just listened while he kept talking about himself. After about ten minutes I started to get the feeling that talking about sculpture was as important to him as actually doing it, you know?"

Jonathan was silent for a moment, his eyes unfocused. With his arms loose, shoulders forward slightly and that glassy stare, it seemed like he'd fallen into a shallow trance. She probably lost his attention for no more than five seconds, but it felt like ages. Finally he blinked, and with a deep, noisy breath, sank back against the chair. His dark eyes met her own, and fixed them with fierce concentration.

"Well, I talk a lot about writing. About other people's writing, like in class. Plus endless dissection of what other people put down on paper, in my book reviews. And my own writing too. I don't think that talking about your art, or your work or whatever you choose to call it precludes being into the creative act itself."

Jill felt a twitch, a pang of remorse as she watched the angry words leave his mouth. "Whoa...I'm sorry if I offended you, Jonathan. I wasn't trying to make any blanket statement about the creative process. It's just that after talking to Kurt..." Her voice trailed off.

He dismissed her words with a flutter of his hand. "No, no. My bad. You're entitled to your opinion. But personally, I think if you're really an artist then you have to talk about your work—it's an iterative process. I don't know any artist who works in a vacuum. Maybe some do, but they must have a whole lot more talent—or self-confidence anyway—than most of the ones I know."

Calmer, silent at last, he searched her face for some kind of response. Jill cleared her throat nervously, a little afraid of making another conversational misstep.

"You are probably right," she allowed. "But with Kurt it wasn't truly a discussion. More of a diatribe. I don't see anything iterative in that." The glass of vodka in Jill's hand was by now almost warm. She raised it to her lips and observed Jonathan over the rim. "And by the way, if you really believe what you so very eloquently told me just now, why have you never talked about your own work in class?"

"I'm not part of the curriculum," he shot back. "It's Novel *Into Film*, remember?"

## Her Latest Supporting Role

"Well," she countered, suddenly feeling energized by their discussion. "Don't you think that our thirty young, fertile minds might be useful to your creative process?"

Jonathan's face looked again as it had when he'd slipped away from their conversation only minutes earlier: distracted, disinterested, far away. His mouth became the same slack line, betraying no genuine, readable emotion. The only difference was that his brown eyes had become smaller: but it was impossible to tell whether it was from weariness or the endless shots of tequila, or from something else entirely.

"Jonathan?"

He reached for a liter of Coke that sat on the table. When he took a long swallow, his face contorted into a grimace of distaste.

"Listen," he said. A moment later he set the bottle down so hard that foam surged over the top and trickled slowly down, creating a frothy puddle on the table. But then he shook his head, and let out a sorry laugh. "No, forget it. I'm sure you've heard enough about the so-called 'creative process' for one night."

Jill cocked her head slightly. The boys from the band were getting rowdy now, and they argued noisily on the other side of the open kitchen door. Jonathan turned briefly toward the noise, and an uncomfortable lapse in their conversation followed. Jill felt the silence weighing down on her, causing something in her head and neck to throb. She thought that it was definitely time for her to leave, and sneaked a quick look at her watch: almost one. Stay or go? Although tired, she was mildly curious about the rest of the party, wondered who else would turn up, and what else Jonathan Wunder's drunken moodiness would reveal.

Jonathan picked up his cigarette—it had been burning in the discarded lid of a spaghetti sauce jar—and flicked its enormous ash deftly into an abandoned bottle of beer. "I've got to give up this disgusting habit," he muttered to himself, and took a long, thoughtful drag, the end glowing bright red, then fading again.

"I've read your book, you know," she said, raising her voice against the background din. As soon as the words were out, she was briefly, violently embarrassed by the tone of her admission. The vodka was talking again: it had come out sounding like a parody of enthusiasm, rampant teacher's pet iness. "I really admire your writing," she added, this time much more subdued.

"You read my book. No joke?" He sounded surprised. Smoke curled from his lips as he spoke. "When did you read it?"

"A couple of weeks ago. I bought it after the first class."

"Oh? And what was your critical opinion? I mean, as a student at the esteemed Tisch School for the Arts, of course." Was he mocking her? Jonathan Wunder considered Jill's face, her hesitant frown, and added, "Don't worry, I won't hold it against you. I'm just curious, that's all. And I'm sorry if I lost my cool at you before."

"Well," she began slowly. "As I said, I admire your writing. A lot..."

"Come on Jill. I want to hear your opinion. I'm a big boy," he added with a breezy laugh. "I can take it."

"Fine." She sat back in her chair and answered as she might in class, her delivery cautious and slightly impersonal. "I thought it was a great read, but for me there were two problems. The first was the way it ended—I don't think the ending fit the rest of it." Jonathan nodded his head as she spoke, probably more to demonstrate how carefully he was listening than in agreement.

"And why do you think I ended the book like that?" he asked. His speech was slow and measured, slightly slurred but still thoughtful; it was impossible to tell whether she'd pissed him off or not.

"I'm not sure."

"Want to guess?"

## Her Latest Supporting Role

Jill shifted in her chair. It suddenly felt like she was back in the role of student again—being cold-called by a professor—and it unnerved her. "Not really."

"A lot of the critics loved the book's ending. Not all of them, but some. *The Washington Post*, for example. Not to name-drop or anything"

Jill waved her hand, as though trying to erase the entire conversation. "Well, I'm just a lowly grad student. I knew I shouldn't have said anything." Her tone clearly said, *I told you so.*

Jonathan reached across the table and ground out his cigarette. Then he laughed, his dark eyes flashing with amusement.

"Look, I'm not upset. I meant it when I said I wanted your opinion. You seem like a bright person, and I wanted to hear what you had to say."

Jill gave him a confused look.

"I really don't mind," he assured her. "You're not the first person who's told me that the ending didn't work for them. My sister completely loathed that part."

"Well, it's not that it didn't work at all," Jill allowed, trying to revise her previous criticism, without letting her reversal be detected: one of her favorite ploys. "But it was hard to swallow, given the way the protagonist behaved for most of the story. It threw me, I guess. It was a shock."

Jonathan's head bobbed gently in agreement, his smile ironic. He seemed to be enjoying her discomfort, and listened intently as she tried to eat at least some of her words.

"Okay, that's one," he said. "You told me that there were two problems with the book. So what else?"

"Well..." Jill hesitated. "Something else kind of disturbed me, right from the beginning."

"Oh yeah?" He looked right at her, intrigued. "Well, let me have it."

"Why did you set the story in the Midwest, when you were so obviously describing the New York suburbs? You took great pains to create this Midwestern suburbia. But the geography, and the mindset of its people made it so patently obvious, to me anyway, that it's set right here."

"That bothered you?" he asked, one eyebrow creeping gracefully upward.

"Except for prep school I've lived in the area my entire life."

"Me too," said Jonathan.

"So I know it's New York," Jill said with authority. "It seemed a little disingenuous, a bit...well, phony to say it was the Midwest."

Jonathan Wunder looked thoughtful for a moment. "Well, you're not the first person who's busted me on that, either," he said. "Far from it."

"Okay, well, you've heard enough of my drunken literary criticism for one night, I think," Jill said, and sat up very straight, as if trying to will her body back into sobriety. "So are you working on a second novel now?"

There was a long, long pause. "Well. I started it last year," he began. She detected a heaviness in his voice, something she hadn't heard there before. Jill glanced at the glasses and bottles that littered the kitchen counter, and wondered how much he'd consumed in the course of the evening. A lot. He was probably pretty drunk, and yet his words had a calculated rhythm, like he was afraid of saying the wrong thing, revealing too much. Jonathan lit another cigarette from the pack lying on the table, inhaled deeply and then opened his brown eyes wide.

"Like I said, I started the new book last year. End of January, to be accurate. But unfortunately my muse took a powder shortly thereafter."

Jill tipped her head sideways, not quite understanding.

"Sorry? I don't get it...was your muse a real person?"

**Her Latest Supporting Role**

"No, no, not at all. Forgive me—I was being overly dramatic. I just mean I can't write fiction any more." Jonathan took a long, pensive drag from his cigarette, leaving Jill a moment of silence to digest his last statement.

She considered his words. "Do you mean you can't write, or you don't write?"

"Can't. I try but it's garbage. The words seem so stiff and unnatural. I can't get a fix on the story line either, it's going everywhere and nowhere, all at the same time, spinning out of control," he said, waving his hand about almost angrily. "And not in any good way—not like experimental fiction. It's just pretentious, unreadable trash." He avoided looking Jill in the eye as he spoke. "So I tossed it out. I've got barely twenty pages, and since then it's all been crap."

Jill was suddenly all too aware of her surroundings: the dull electric monotone of the refrigerator, the stale cigarette smoke. In the other room a throbbing musical beat, the party's pulse: she wished she could be in there now, away from the growing tension of this conversation, but no graceful escape was in sight.

"Maybe you're being too hard on yourself," she suggested haltingly. "Why not take a month off—don't try to write, just take it easy and let your imagination run wild. See what you come up with after that."

"That would be an okay suggestion," he answered bitterly. "Except that my imagination has practically ceased to exist. When I was writing *Groundswell*, I had the most incredible, vivid, almost surreal dreams. You're a film student, you must have seen *Un Chien Andalou*, right?" She nodded. "That was my imagination—like a Salvador Dali-Luis Bunuel film festival was playing in my head. I kept a notebook next to my bed, and boy, did I ever have something to write about in the morning. Some of the more, uh, disturbing images in my novel came out of that notebook. I'd wake up at dawn and then spend half the morning trying to wrap some language around all the things I'd dreamt.

Now I can hardly get to sleep at night, and when I do it's like watching TV when the cable's not working—endless gray static. Nothing."

"Nothing at all?"

"Nada." Jonathan Wunder ran his left hand through his hair again, and sighed.

"I'm sorry to hear that," Jill said gently. "You're very talented."

She'd complimented people's talent so many times in recent years. It was the way all the actor-slash-somethings propped each other up, supported friends in the face of so many rejections and so little praise: Jane's a very talented performer, Scott's an incredibly talented comedian. They'd all been each other's personal booster squads, introducing talented but unbookable friends that way to those who'd never met them—and certainly never heard of them—at parties and bars and auditions. But this time she really meant it. Jonathan Wunder was one of the most genuinely talented people she'd ever known, and it upset her to hear him confess to this creative drought.

He took another puff from his cigarette, wincing.

"So." He exhaled a long gray ribbon of smoke and placed one warm hand over hers, a maybe friendly, definitely inebriated gesture. His voice rose with indignation. "So in December I started whoring myself, teaching creative writing to semi-literates at City College, and now I'm teaching this silly summer course at NYU."

When their eyes met he revised his tone slightly. "The NYU gig isn't too bad. But you know the famous saying of George Bernard Shaw's: 'He who can, does. He who cannot, teaches.'"

"'And he who cannot teach, teaches gym class'," Jill added in what she hoped was an amusing tone. She was relieved to see a genuine smile spread across Jonathan's face, the first in a while.

"Thank you," he said softly.


**Her Latest Supporting Role**

"You're welcome. It was someone from one of my previous classes, by the way, who said that. I can't take credit." She looked around. The kitchen was empty, except for them, and the party was winding down. Through the kitchen door Jill noted that most people were slung across chairs, or half-slumped on the rug. A foursome stumbled together toward the front door, managing a quick backward salute of thanks as they departed. Her watch said twenty to two, not so late, but at this hour the thought of striking up a conversation with another Kurt-like character did not appeal at all. She stretched her legs out beneath the table, and yawned silently.

"I'm about to turn into a pumpkin," she said, pulling herself to her feet. "I have to take off."

Jonathan's face fell. "You're not leaving yet, are you?" he protested, his voice fuzzy and low. Then he got up from the table and, stretching his arms and legs out wide, blocked the door. He smiled drunkenly and was more declarative this time: "You're not leaving yet."

Nothing in his expression made her afraid of him, made her want to pry him free of the doorway and run from his apartment the way she'd fled from Czerny. Jonathan Wunder was a handsome, intelligent man—her teacher, yes, but a bona-fide author too, which was much more impressive. And now that she'd seen him outside of the classroom, where he could be a little looser and show more his true self, she had to admit that he was actually kind of sexy. And though he was rapidly disappearing into a gray fog of inebriation, he seemed to be one of those fairly harmless drunks who simply become more fun, more interesting when lubricated by alcohol. Just how drunk was he? He'd seemed fairly lucid when they discussed his book, considerably less so now. She'd watched him down shots of tequila and straight vodka in the space of maybe an hour. He didn't look like a hard-core drinker. Jill remembered Monika's assertion: Jews don't drink, she often said—though Monika herself was the exception that she claimed proved the rule. Jonathan wasn't a very big guy, either; it had to be having some effect on him. Like the vodka was having on her.

"I'd stay longer," she white-lied, "but I promised to meet a friend for an early breakfast tomorrow, and I need to get some sleep."

He let his arms flop down to his side and stepped out of the doorway.

"Okay. Well, I'd really like to hear more of your thoughts on Groundswell," he said, leading her into the living room. "Maybe we could talk some more next week?"

"You'll see me in class, remember?" she said, a note of surprise in her voice. Had he already forgotten who she was? "Thursday night? I'll be in the third row, as usual."

"Oh, right. Right," Jonathan repeated, sounding confused.

Jill stooped to collect her purse from beneath the coffee table, and she bumped into him as she stood up straight again. She felt his warm breath behind her, and her nose wrinkled at its smoky alcohol scent. Jill turned to face him.

"So maybe after class, then?"

"Sure. If you want. Whatever." Jill took a step toward the front door. "I'd better make a move."

Jonathan was still staring right at her, and she lowered her eyes. It was the same at the movies, where Jill stared at the screen for as long as she could, becoming absorbed in the story, letting herself be reeled in. But when something became too frightening, or embarrassing—earnestly incompetent acting, perhaps, or one of those situations that were just too painfully familiar, inevitable heartbreak or fractured hope—she had to look away. Monika was always berating her for being too sensitive. Jill didn't think sensitivity was such a bad trait, but what she perceived in her own behavior wasn't anything as noble as sensitivity. She saw it as gutlessness: fear plain and simple.

**Her Latest Supporting Role**

"Thanks for everything, Jonathan," she said, hurrying for the door. "I had a great time, and it was really so nice of you to invite me. Good night."

Jill took one last look around the living room. No one was standing any more, and someone had replaced the electric lights with candles: insta-mood. She only recognized a handful of the remaining partiers. A few seemed to have arrived without bothering to seek out their host, if they knew him at all. Maybe they were guests-once-removed, acquaintances of friends of someone Jonathan knew. Justine was still there, seated in a far corner of the room, her chunky shoes and too-short legs dangling from the deep armchair like a big rag doll's. The white straw hair had fallen over one eye, but she'd done nothing to brush it away, so apparently engrossed was she in conversation. Jill paused to check out her partner, and let out a tiny hiccup of shock. Seated on the floor next to Justine, his ruddy face and slick black hair only partly obscured, was Gabor Czerny.

Jill hurried to the front door. She'd thought she was over what had happened in his office, was sure of it until just a moment before, and her sudden weakness upset her. She turned to face Jonathan, and was ashamed to feel her mouth twitching nervously. Jill found her voice and told him good night a second time.

"You feeling okay?" he inquired, as she reached to unlock the door. She blinked in the harsh light; a halogen bulb filled the tiny foyer with white. "You look pale."

Jill pointed to the lamp in wordless explanation. "I'll see you in class. Thanks again." She was halfway through the door when she stopped. "Was that Gabor Czerny in the living room?" she asked, trying to disguise her distress as vague curiosity.

"Oh, he showed up?" Jonathan turned to scan the dark living room. "I better go say hello. Do you know him?"

"I'm a film student, remember?" she said, trying to sound offhand. Her heartbeat was percussive in her ears.

"Oh yeah. I ran into him down at the *Observer* last week. I'm doing the odd book review for them, and he's been a contributor for eons. I'm actually amazed that he put in an appearance. I guess that now that we're colleagues of sorts it's different. He never seemed to think that much of me in class." Jonathan tilted his head in Czerny's direction. "He was one of my instructors at BU," he explained.

Jill was silent.

Looking over his shoulder once more, Jonathan smiled. "He seems to be quite taken with your old pal Justine."

"Well, he's welcome to her. I think they make a lovely couple," Jill said quietly, barely able to conceal her distaste for them both. She pulled open the front door, and bolted through it. "Thanks again," Jill sang out, without turning back. "I'll see you in class."

**Her Latest Supporting Role**

# AUGUST

# Chapter 6

It was now just three weeks until the big pitch, and things weren't going at all well in H-F's bid to save the Tellco business. Now everyone in the agency referred to them (not even under their breath, anymore) as "Hellco," and the conflicts that were constantly erupting among members of the team couldn't bode well for the agency's chances. That particular Friday, tempers had flared all day long; Jill had never seen Nick Wheeler in truly good spirits, but after that morning's gigantic Tellco status meeting his mood had become even darker. Constable had verbally pummeled him in front of a roomful of shrinking onlookers, each one no doubt mortified to witness this very public humiliation. With the conference room door ajar, some of Constable's more rabid abuse had floated toward Jill's desk. Out of sympathy and embarrassment, unable to listen to their President's tirade any longer—Nick was an unpredictable boss, even frightening sometimes, but no one deserved what Constable was dishing out behind that half-closed door—Jill finally fled to the ladies' room. But amazingly, upon her return the barrage of cruel insults was still going on, seemingly uninterrupted. She'd never heard one man call another a cunt before, did it even make sense? And she dashed into the comforting silence and isolation of the videotape library, remaining there until the meeting adjourned and its attendees began drifting in and out in search of various old Tellco commercials. By the end of the day, the half-circles below Nick's eyes were so dark that they resembled bruises, a sore and angry shade of blue-black.

At eight-fifteen, as Jill finally got ready to leave the office, Sandi reminded her (adding at least three *I'm sorrys*) that they needed her back at noon the next day: Saturday. Weekend work had become the norm, and there was in fact surprisingly little bitching about it; though it was rarely voiced, everyone on the team seemed painfully aware that losing to another agency meant losing their jobs. That weekend, Nick and Sandi, together with the agency's video editor and a pair of young art directors (recent graduates of the Miami Ad School who were renowned on the tenth floor for their great ideas and terrible attitude) would be producing three rip-o-matics, combining footage swiped from commercial directors' reels into sample ads that would help sell Tellco on the agency's own ideas.

Jill would pass her Saturday, the day she usually spent with Monika, holed up in the video library. A couple of weeks earlier she would have quietly resented the way her job was encroaching on her social life. But Monika had been working her butt off too, though with a different purpose. The following Wednesday she would be taking off on vacation, a much-needed two week trip to see her sister in Paris, and until she departed the partners would continue to squeeze as many billable hours out of her as they could. Of course Jill was genuinely sad that Monika was leaving: August, normally a sunny, lazy, enjoyable month, was starting to look like a write-off, between her course work—she was still determined to get that A, Czerny be damned!—and all the overtime she was logging on the Tellco pitch. But Jill realized that if Monika were around, she'd just be irritated by how little time Jill had to spend (or gossip with) her.

It wasn't just the weekends that had disappeared: with the black cloud of the Tellco pitch looming on the horizon free evenings had been just as rare. But over the past month Jill had managed to spend a few of them with Jonathan Wunder. He'd cornered her at the end of class, the very first Thursday after his party. Until that happened Jill had convinced herself that he'd forgotten their conversation, that it would have faded away by the time he awoke the next morning, its memory replaced by a throbbing hangover, the result of the six or eight drinks she'd watched him consume during their extended conversation. She

**Her Latest Supporting Role**

herself woke up the next morning with a bad case of cocktail flu, and a sinking feeling that the vodka that made her head hurt so had also caused her to say and do some things that she normally might not have.

At his urging she'd joined Jonathan Wunder for an after-class coffee at a place near the university, a dive restaurant run by three generations of unsmiling Greeks, inexplicably popular during the school year and always jammed with students. But in July the place was quiet. They talked for more than two hours that night. The coffee long gone, they had ignored sour looks from their waitress, who was clearly attempting to move them along: first about movies and books, then on to more serious and personal issues. It was small talk really, getting-to-know-you stuff. His tone was engaging and spirited, light years away from their heavy discussion at the party. Jill's instructor subjected her to a friendly interrogation, and she was amazed to see him showing what she thought was real interest in her responses. He seemed genuinely surprised when Jill told him she was an only child—a "lonely only," he called it. In turn he revealed a few personal facts of his own, though between Googling him after the first class and a long download from Monika she didn't really learn that much new.

"This is my deal." That was how he put it, and it charmed her. He was the youngest of four children, the baby of a boisterous Jewish family from Great Neck. His father was a second-generation garmento, his mother was big in the JCC. Of course his family drove him crazy—whose didn't? he'd asked with a comical shrug of resignation—with his father always offering him unsolicited career advice, his doctor brother trying to fix him up with beautiful young interns from Mount Sinai. Nonetheless, Jonathan seemed especially close to his family, admitted that he couldn't imagine what it would have been like to grow up, as Jill had, without brothers and sisters, and with your parents living on the other side of the globe.

They didn't talk about his writing at all that night, and though Jill was dying to raise the subject again, she yielded to his endless string of questions mostly with good-natured smiles, though once or twice she felt an odd shiver of embarrassment when the inquiries got too personal. It was nearly midnight when he dropped her off—taking the taxi far out of his way so that she could get home first. But not before Jill had promised to accompany him to an Ingmar Bergman double bill the following Sunday.

His attentions were both flattering and vaguely disturbing. On the one hand Jill—the prowler of bookstores, the not-so-secret admirer of literature and the literate—could hardly imagine anything more exciting than spending her free evenings with a real live novelist, a published (and acclaimed!) writer. She even briefly considered bringing along her copy of Groundswell to one of their get-togethers, for him to sign. And yet Jill felt uncomfortable being out in public with her instructor: she was able to rationalize her way through it, but barely. Monika's sister was the extra-curricular link that had brought them together, she explained to herself, working her mind through the slightly convoluted circumstances of their acquaintance over and over again. It was because of her friendship with Monika and Anya that she'd been invited to his party, and because of the party they had become chummy. So it was all above-board. After all, no one could seriously consider these rendezvous to be dates, Jill assured herself. They were just friendly little encounters; each time she paid her own way, and to her immense relief there seemed to be no expectation of anything more. And yet something about it still felt weird, and a little inappropriate: was there any better proof than the fact that she had shared barely anything about these get-togethers with Monika?

Jill had finally put the whole ugly scene with Gabor Czerny behind her, and was secretly proud of the progress she'd made. She rarely thought about it any more, and when she did it was

**Her Latest Supporting Role**

with an almost eerie sense of detachment, like the entire incident had actually happened to someone else. Still, as their evenings together drew to a close and Jonathan seemed keen to see Jill again, to meet outside of class, it gave her a strange sensation, the exact same one she's had at the end of his party. As she rode the elevator down from her office, and exited into the swelter and bustle of a summer Friday evening, Jill wondered what Jonathan Wunder had planned for her that night.

She met him at a hip little bar across from Tompkins Square Park called Niagara. It was as dingy and narrow as a bowling alley, its only ornamentation a few crackling neon signs from the 1950s that advertised Pabst Blue Ribbon and Schaeffer beer. At eight thirty it was packed, the crowd made up not of the suited and skirted masses that frequented the bars near Jill's office, but of men in jeans and motorcycle boots—they might have been artists, musicians or construction workers—and needle-thin women with a decidedly downtown sense of style, all dyed-black or platinum-blonde hair and short skirts, their bony arms shackled with rows of heavy bracelets. Jill felt a stab of self-consciousness as she elbowed her way through this crowd, her long brown hair secured with a tortoiseshell clip at the base of her neck, the flowered skirt stirring around her bare knees when she moved. She felt as conspicuous as a bride stumbling into a funeral.

She spied Jonathan near the back. He was dressed in jeans and a worn black T-shirt, nursing a Heineken as he watched TV on a small screen above the bar. He nodded and waved when their eyes met.

"Good evening, Miss Barber," he said with a smile that was a parody of waiter-ly obsequiousness. When she heard his voice it stirred up a fleeting memory of his party, and Jill decided that he must be on his third beer, at least. "And how are we doing this evening?"

"Sorry I'm late." They were supposed to meet at eight, and he hadn't answered his cell when she'd called to push it back. "We have had a day from hell," she said. "Although at least we were given time off for good behavior." She glanced at her watch and made a face. "Seriously though, total nightmare. The more I hear from people, the more I think we're going to lose Tellco. And according to the rumor mill two other agency accounts are on Dotcom Death Watch", she added glumly. The months since the NASDAQ's crash had not been kind to the advertising business, and the steady stream of new accounts that had come to Hambleton French at the tail end of the 90's had first halted, and then begun to reverse itself. "There's a serious possibility that I'll be looking for a new job after Labor Day."

His features creased with concern. "I'm really sorry to hear that."

Jill waved one hand in dismissal. "Don't be," she said with a resigned smile. "In the words of the great philosopher, 'Que sera, sera. Whatever will be, will be.'"

Jonathan lowered the bottle from his lips and sputtered with foamy laughter. "That's the first time I've ever heard anyone refer to Doris Day as a 'great philosopher.'"

"Well," countered Jill, "I bet she gets quoted—by the population at large, anyhow—a whole lot more than, say, Sartre or Bertrand Russell." Then like an eager child she searched his face for a flicker of appreciation, any sign that she'd impressed him with her little riff straight out of Philosophy 101. But his expression was impossible to fathom.

It was good to be away from the office at last—that day especially, eleven hours had seemed more like a eleven hundred—but now she felt dispirited and drained, had lost the sense of elation that she usually felt as Friday's workday drew to an end. Jill turned around and surveyed the crowded room. Overhead, two ceiling fans whirred at top speed, but the air

**Her Latest Supporting Role**

inside the bar was heavy, and she felt her T-shirt clinging damply to her back.

"Let me get you a drink," Jonathan said, fighting for the bartender's attention. "What would you like?"

Jill was dying for some wine, a glass of Chardonnay to chill her overheated body and soothe her frayed nerves. Niagara, however, was more of a beer joint than a proper bar—just the type of establishment that would carry the dreaded Chateau Raunch on its wine list, and precious little else. She swiveled her head round to see the bartender eyeing her expectantly. Behind him dozens of liquor bottles reflected the flickering neon of an ailing sign, and twinkled like Las Vegas.

"Vodka tonic," she called out with a shrug.

The day's pressures had taken a bigger toll on Jill than she'd imagined, for she realized—with mild chagrin quickly giving way to resignation—that she'd emptied her glass in only fifteen minutes. The vodka worked on her like some magic elixir. She felt the knotted muscles in her back begin to slacken, her thumping heartbeat ease into a comfortable, slow-dance rhythm. Jill's good spirits, her usually Friday night attitude, slowly crept back, and she ordered another drink, vowing to make the next one last longer. Jonathan had downed the rest of his Heineken almost as rapidly, and Jill noticed how his fingers worked the bottle as they talked, meticulously peeling off the label and then sticking it back on the bottle's face—upside down—never pausing, not once, to inspect his handiwork.

Departing the bar, Jonathan and Jill strolled through the East Village. The temperature had finally fallen below eighty degrees, and she felt a light breeze at her back as they crossed Tompkins Square Park. They zig-zagged along the sidewalk on Avenue B, which was mobbed with tourists and Friday night revelers, and crossed the street a couple of times in search of a restaurant. The bistro they finally selected—Casimir—was noisy and aggressively air-conditioned. Jill closed her eyes and let it cool the vodka flush that had spread across her cheeks.

A table in the back, a bottle of wine with the first glasses poured into those cheap juice glasses that French bistros at this price-point and zip code seemed to favor: by that time, Jill was feeling much better, more relaxed, and she peered over the top of her menu, watching Jonathan Wunder as he studied his own intently. She stared at his thick brows, admired the way that they arched above his brown eyes so gracefully. A fine cobweb of lines appeared below the corners of his eyes when he smiled or concentrated, became lost in thought. He'd done both several times in Jill's presence, at his party and then at their subsequent meetings, of which this, she remembered, was the fourth. Those lines were the only physical sign that he was well over thirty—during one of their conversations it had come out that he was in fact two years older than Monika's academically precocious sister, and nearly seven years older than Jill—otherwise he could have passed for a fellow graduate student, twenty-five, maybe twenty-six tops. She realized then with perfect clarity something that had been in the back of her mind all along, since that very first class. He was a startlingly attractive man—not just sexy, but handsome, and precisely her physical type, save of the slight misfortune of his height. He was attractive in a way that Jill could feel in the tips of her curling toes, and a faint tingling sensation in her abdomen. And the whole tortured artist thing only made him more appealing.

As the waiter relieved them of their menus Jonathan Wunder raised his glass spiritedly. His brown eyes darted from his glass to the perspiring bottle before finally coming to rest, locking Jill's gaze with his own.

"A toast to the summer," he said. "I realize that it's more than half over now, but better late than never, yes?" Jonathan laughed, and it surprised Jill to detect what she could swear was a hint of nervousness in his voice. "Well, anyhow, if I hadn't run

**Her Latest Supporting Role**

into you and Monika on the college steps that night after class you would have been just another semi-anonymous student, just a name on an essay and a raised hand in search of class participation marks."

Jonathan Wunder released her from his gaze, and his head dipped down for a moment. He appeared to be staring at the table, like there was something there that he needed and couldn't quite find. When he looked up again, he grinned at her.

"I feel very lucky to have had my class, my first class at NYU, selected for your last academic hurrah. Teaching that course has been a pretty good experience, so far. I'll remember it forever, I'm sure. And I'll remember you, too."

Jonathan Wunder concluded his little impromptu toast by tapping his glass against Jill's, and a bell-like sound echoed around them. When their two glasses parted Jill found herself momentarily speechless. The unexpected toast to their acquaintance swirled up into the air and fogged the space between them. By the time the power of speech came back to her—enough, at least, that she could respond to the toast with a whisper of thanks, a choked *here, here*—her head had already grown helium-light, and her hand trembled so badly that the glass bumped against her jutting lower lip. Jill was alarmed to feel her heart plummet through her chest, as doomed as an elevator with a severed cable.

She passed through dinner in a haze. This wasn't the party; she couldn't blame it on the vodka. Something else had happened between them. A strange chemical reaction had suddenly transformed one substance—their student-teacher acquaintance —into something entirely new and different: human alchemy. At some moment during the meal, between bites of pumpkin tortellini so rich and delicious that she was convinced that she'd never again dine on anything quite so heavenly, Jill had an epiphany. By the time her wine glass was empty and the waiter appeared to refill it, she realized it with a sickening pang of self-knowledge. She had it bad for Jonathan Wunder—and that wasn't good.

This was more than just a crush, definitely more. She could feel the difference as clearly as the difference between a headache and a head wound. She'd sailed through crushes on dozens of men, taking pleasure in each without putting too much emphasis on any one in particular, eyes always wide open and looking ahead to the next with as much excitement as for the last. She knew that she could save herself if she put some distance between the reality of this evening and the feelings that it stirred in her—keep it light, bring it back to crush-land, trot out a bit of that infamous reserve Robin Devlin was always razzing her about—and yet she resisted, without really knowing why.

Jonathan stabbed at his steak frites with a fork and chattered amiably about a new art gallery in Williamsburg that he'd visited that afternoon. But although Jill saw his mouth curve around the words, she just barely understood what Jonathan was telling her. She was trying to collect her thoughts: they'd scattered, were moving about in her head as wildly as mercury liberated from a thermometer. A question darted to the front of her consciousness: should she let him know how she felt? Give him some sort of signal? Then just as swiftly, an answer: God no, no way, that was a recipe for disaster. In the first place, he was her instructor, and the whole teacher-student thing, in addition to being an embarrassing cliché, was kind of sleazy. Even though Jonathan Wunder was relatively close in age to Jill (unlike Czerny), unattached (ditto) and (on the surface at least) there seemed to be some willingness on both sides.

What if she did say something? After all, he was the one who kept suggesting they meet up, get together, four times in two weeks now. Nothing physical, not even a good-night kiss, had passed between them. She drew up a mental list of his possible responses, from revulsion to shock to a flattered thanks-but-no, and, at the far end of the spectrum, reciprocation. Then she

**Her Latest Supporting Role**

ordered and reordered them from most to least likely. Like a deck of cards she shuffled his responses time and again, but reciprocation never made it to the top. Jill felt herself growing irrational from longing and then, only a moment later, thwarted by reason: a heart-stopping fear that he would somehow find her lacking, and reject her.

A strange sound snapped her attention back to the table.

"Paging Jill Barber," Jonathan Wunder said, echoing into his fist, a pretend microphone. Jill felt the color rush back to her cheeks, and she mumbled some lame excuse about a crazy day at work.

"It's okay." He smiled, defusing her embarrassment. "I just noticed that you haven't touched your dessert yet."

Had she ordered dessert? Looking down, Jill saw that a ramekin of *crème brulée* had magically appeared before her on the table. She picked up a spoon and dipped it in, as tentative as a toe in a swimming pool. Fat blobs of custard slid down her throat like oysters.

There was an awkward silence between them, and Jill groped through her mind for a topic of conversation. But the only thought that came to her was the class, and she wanted to steer way clear of that.

"So Jonathan, tell me," she said. Jill heard her own voice clearly over the buzz of restaurant noise, and became instantly self-conscious. How much had she drunk? Maybe she had miscalculated, forgotten something. "Summer school is almost over. What are you going to do when it finishes? Are you teaching any more classes?"

He answered her with a strange smile, one that telegraphed anxiety rather than happiness.

"Yeah, I can't believe we only have three more weeks," he said, his tone slightly sour. "Three more weeks of scintillating over-analysis." She nodded as he spoke, hearing bitterness in every one of his words. "And after that it's time for me to throw in the towel on the full-time writing thing and go back to school myself."

Jill tipped her head to one side. "Sorry?"

"I thought I told you this last week. Maybe not. I dropped out of the PhD program in American Studies at B.U. when *Groundswell* was accepted for publication. I'd passed my orals, and taught some undergraduate sections, but hadn't finished my dissertation. My heart just wasn't in it." He paused and pursed his lips. "I was only working on my doctorate because an academic career seemed like the most palatable option open to me, kind of the path of least resistance; I had no desire to be a doctor like my brother, or a lawyer. And the thought of going to business school turned my stomach: really, I wanted to write. But my parents were very intent on us all getting graduate degrees, all becoming professionals, since neither of them went to college. And then while I was working on my dissertation I sold a couple of short stories—one to *Esquire*—and it felt like I had finally found my calling and proven myself."

"So you left school and to become a writer, full-time?"

"Yeah, sort of." He chewed thoughtfully on a forkful of carrot cake. "I moved to the city, it was only going to be a break from my studies, and I was supposedly going to be doing some research for my dissertation. My parents thought the writing thing didn't seem very stable. But then *Groundswell* was published and after that came the National Book Award nomination, and the option for the movies, and it felt a bit more legitimate to them. I had an out. And I just couldn't go back to Boston."

All this surprised Jill. She'd supposed that he had always been a writer, imagined years of toil on his first book: that writing, like acting, was one of those careers you slogged away at for years, with a talented (or lucky) few actually making it, and scores more throwing in the towel and settling for Plan B. She had not yet told Jonathan much about her brief and unfortunate foray into acting. She envied him his easy success, his certainty about having found

**Her Latest Supporting Role**

his true calling. Jill had never felt that way about acting: it was an adventure more than a calling. At Vassar it had helped her overcome her shyness around others during her freshman year: to step into character was to become someone smarter, savvier, and more fun to be around. After moving to New York, in the company of a few other actress-slash-waitress types from her class, it provided a soft landing into the real world.

"There was something so liberating about being far away from my old self, from my old life in Boston." Jonathan Wunder's impassioned voice fell silent for a few seconds. He looked so terribly sad. "The book was well-reviewed, it sold okay, and the award nomination definitely helped me coast along for a while. But the royalty checks have slowed to a trickle now, and it's been optioned twice for the movies but nothing more has happened there—and this last time the option wasn't renewed. Book number two just isn't happening: I got a decent advance but I won't see another dime until I actually deliver the manuscript. Which is why I have to teach and do book reviews and all that other stuff too. Not that I mind...it just makes me think about that old 'those who can, do...those who can't, teach.'".

"Don't kick yourself, I'm sure you have another book in you," Jill assured him. "A bunch more." She could feel her face shining with helpless admiration, and while it embarrassed her she was also powerless to stop it. "You should be happy that you succeeded on your own terms, rather than caving in to your family's wishes."

"That's right," he said. "Succeeded. Past tense. Like I told you at the party, I haven't been able to finish even a short story since *Groundswell*. At first I thought I just needed a little holiday from writing fiction. Working on the book with my editor was pretty intense. I was so exhausted I practically fell into a coma every night—I remember that's when I stopped dreaming. But I thought it was from exhaustion, so I took a couple of months off."

"There's nothing wrong with that," Jill said quietly. She could see the frustration building up inside Jonathan Wunder. Jill sensed an unfamiliar combination of passion and sympathy stirring in her chest. As much as she admired him, she was beginning to feel both privileged and vaguely embarrassed that he'd chosen to unburden himself to her yet again, and she shifted uncomfortably in her seat just as she had at his kitchen table a few weeks earlier.

"Here's the problem," he said, in a strained voice that had dropped to little more than a whisper. "When the holiday was over, I couldn't write anything I was satisfied with. I wrote half-a-dozen first chapters at least, and threw them all away in disgust. Then I started doing the odd book review, so I could still at least be acknowledged as a novelist, as a fiction writer. I was going through the motions—I still am, for that matter—without actually being capable of writing anything. But the money from *Groundswell* has almost dried up—just like my talent," he added in a rueful aside. "I can't support myself with book reviews and spotty teaching jobs."

"And you're still not dreaming?" Jill asked.

"Nothing I can remember, nothing that inspires me the way I was inspired while I was writing *Groundswell*. Just call me 'One Hit Wunder', like my brother does," he added with a bitter laugh. "So I'll finish my dissertation, start applying for tenure track jobs. In eighteen months' time I'll probably end up teaching American Studies in Bumfuck, Indiana or some other cultural backwater. Goodbye, New York—God help me."

Then he fell silent. The waiter passed their table, and Jonathan motioned dispiritedly for the check. When it came, he insisted on paying for dinner, and though Jill felt guilty letting him—he'd made it so painfully clear that his money was running out—it also gave her hope, let her think for a second that she was more to him than just a sympathetic ear, let her believe that everything Jonathan had said when he had raised the glass of wine to her was absolutely, irrevocably true.

**Her Latest Supporting Role**

By the time they left the restaurant it was almost midnight. Beneath Jill's feet the sidewalk felt treacherous. She moved slowly, and Jonathan, who was only an inch or so taller, matched her stride with ease. He seemed more at peace with himself than he had during dessert, as if the cloud of anger had flashed and then passed by him quickly. And although she kept expecting, kept hoping to feel his arm curve around her shoulder or waist, it didn't happen. Above them the August sky was an inky blue. She paused to admire it and spied a constellation—stars were such a rare sight in the New York sky—but when she pointed it out to him, the beauty of its connect the dots puzzle, Jonathan seemed strangely unmoved, and Jill felt her hopes deflate a little.

Neither of them had mentioned a destination when the walk began, but eventually their footsteps led them to Jill's street. They were silent when they rounded the corner.

She unzipped her purse and groped inside it for her keys. Jill lived in a studio apartment on the second floor of a brownstone on East Ninth Street, in a once-lovely single family home that had been carved up into tiny apartments long before she was born. Jonathan followed her to the front of her place, but went no farther. Jill was already halfway up the steps by the time she realized that he wasn't right behind her. Her mind was still fogged with wine, her body weighed down by all the rich food she'd consumed. But as awkward as it felt, she slipped back down the steps so that they ended up face to face on the concrete path.

"Hey," she said quietly, hoping for a response: a word, a touch, anything. He remained silent and still before her, and Jill strained her eyes to read his face. Milky light from the streetlamps covered his handsome features with shadows. Jonathan didn't appear to be smiling, or unhappy, or anything else that Jill could easily interpret.

She watched him blink—two, three times—and then spoke again.

"Can I invite you in?" she ventured. As soon as the words were past her lips, Jill cringed. Such a weak offer, it revealed so little about the way she actually felt, though her feelings pinched like a too-tight dress.

Jonathan inclined his head to one side, and a shaft of light lit his brown eyes. Jill suddenly felt something fall through her body in a rapid, endless descent, a stone dropped into a well.

"I'd love to," he said edgily, and flicked his fingers through his hair. "But I can't. I have a review due on Monday morning, and I'm only halfway through the book, if that." She watched his lips part into a smile that was pleasant but noncommittal. "Maybe some other time," he added.

Behind her back, Jill gripped her key ring. Her hand trembled so badly that the touching keys made a small noise.

"Not even some coffee? One cup of the stuff I make and you'll be able to read all night." Jill winced at the edge of desperation in her voice, and was grateful for the cover of darkness. Coffee was really only part of what she was offering Jonathan, but she wasn't sure whether or not he realized this. In the same situation Monika would have just grabbed him by the hand—or by the belt, if she was good and drunk—and dragged him up the stairs. But that wasn't Jill's style.

Jonathan looked down and shook his head.

"I really can't," he said quietly. "I'm sorry."

"Okay." Deflated, Jill felt her shoulders slump.

"But I'll see you in class on Thursday night, right? And let's do something next weekend. How's Sunday for you?" His tone brightened considerably, and he didn't wait for her to nod. "We can go see the Egyptian exhibit at the Met, and then my parents are having a barbeque. I'd love it if you could come along—and save me from my family!" he added with a laugh. "Not to scare you off or anything. They're perfectly harmless but a little, well..." He struggled for an appropriate analogy. "Ask Monika, she'll give you the dirt."

**Her Latest Supporting Role**

.

Jill swallowed her frustration, and smiled at him. "This is the first time anyone's ever given me homework for a date," she said, feeling reckless or drunk enough to use the word that had been on her mind, in the form of a question, for hours. "I think you might be taking this student-teacher thing a little too much to heart, Jonathan," she added in a serious tone.

"So we're on then?"

She nodded silently.

"I enjoyed dinner, Jill," he said, and took a half-step into the space between them.

Jonathan Wunder moved his head toward Jill's. This was the moment that she'd thought about all during dinner. She had imagined that his lips would be soft and cool, with the slippery naked wetness of sushi, his tongue warm, his breath perfumed with wine. But instead of lips and the inside of his mouth she felt an unexpected sting, the stubbly cheeks grazing her own once, twice as he kissed the anonymous night air.

Jonathan stepped away from her quickly. "I'll see you in class," he said, then turned and hastily retreated down the path to the sidewalk, not even waiting to see that she got inside the front door safely.

Jill mounted the steps again. Slower this time, her limbs dull and heavy with disappointment. She slipped her key into the lock and the door opened, the click of the latch echoing through the stillness and dead air of the foyer. When she reached her apartment door she heard a muffled whirring noise and realized that she'd left the window air conditioner running since she had departed for work that morning. Not the first time this had happened, and she sighed, thinking of her enormous electricity bills, and that her place would by now be as clammy as a meat locker.

She slipped into the apartment without bothering to switch the light on. Chilly air rushed out to greet her, and gooseflesh rose on her bare arms and legs. Jill switched off the humming air conditioner, and opened the other window as wide as it would go. The warm August night spilled in as Jill undressed slowly, in darkness and silent frustration, and crawled between the sheets of her bed.

**Her Latest Supporting Role**

# Chapter 7

At one o'clock the following Thursday Jill stuck her head inside the open door of Petra Marks's office. Petra—a tiny, corkscrew-curled blonde, Robin's creative partner since he joined the agency—was sitting at her desk, nibbling at the corner of a half-wrapped bar of chocolate with great concentration. A hardcover *Roget's Thesaurus*—old, thick as a family bible—lay open next to her notepad.

Petra's sunny office was a time capsule of souvenirs from nearly a decade as a copywriter at Hambleton French. Since she'd joined the agency the prefix "copy" had been banished from the H-F lexicon. They were just writers now, a title which was supposed to be more dignified and serious, more erudite. Most of the writers Jill had come across during her brief tenure at H-F were none of these things (Petra included) but they were endlessly amusing, and Jill was on friendly terms with—sometimes even worshipful of—half a dozen of them. She loved eating lunch with them in the cafeteria, trading paperbacks and glossy Eurostyle magazines with them, lending a hand with the incredibly elaborate practical jokes that they were constantly perpetrating on each other. Out of all of them Petra was her favorite by far. She was like the cool older sister that Jill had never had.

On one side of Petra's desk, rising from the floor in a fairly obscene fashion, was a three foot high inflatable hot dog stuffed in a flesh tone bun, a keepsake from her award-winning TV commercial for French Frank's frankfurters. A multi-hued acrylic plush parrot, poised for attack, stood on her bookcase next to *LIFE Goes To The Movies* and a biography of Edie Sedgwick. The parrot had been presented to Petra for MC-ing the talent show at the company golf tournament the previous summer, and people around the agency still spoke reverently of her hilarious, risqué commentary, which had completely eclipsed every other performer. And on the wall behind her desk, flanked by huge French posters for *Gentlemen Prefer Blondes* and *Rebel Without a Cause*, was perhaps Petra's most prized possession, the gold One Show pencil she'd won for writing the "Please Squeeze Lee's" radio commercial, heralding the introduction of Lee's Soy Sauce in a squeezable plastic bottle.

Petra raised a hand, and waved Jill into the office. The other hand still held the chocolate bar to her mouth, as she gnawed away at the corner, a ferocious look of distaste on her doll-like features.

"Fuck!" she exclaimed, and let the bar drop onto her open thesaurus, where it landed with a faint thud, scattering little blobs of chocolate across the pages. "Where's that slacker Robin? He's supposed to be in here doing his fair share of the work, not off playing with toys in the Tellco War Room. I'm going to have gained twenty pounds before I come up with even one decent line for this stupid Big Bite campaign."

"How many have you eaten?" Jill asked as Petra grabbed her mug and gargled noisily with a mouthful of tea.

"Yuck. Look in there." She kicked the waste basket next to her desk. Jill stepped forward and peered down obediently. Three or four crumpled yellow and red Big Bite wrappers, together with a few half-eaten and discarded stumps of chocolate bar, lay forlornly in the bottom of the basket.

"And that's just this morning. I asked the Account Executive for a product sample, and the silly bitch gave me an entire box," Petra added in disgust, taking another large swig of tea.

"Well, what have you come up with so far?" Trying to be helpful, Jill walked around to Petra's side of the desk. The Powerbook on her desktop wasn't even switched on. A ruled legal pad was covered with scratched out lines of copy, leaving a messy trail of turquoise Sharpie ink before she had wisely switched to pencil. Jill scanned the page. Halfway down, there was one line that hadn't been crossed out. It read:

**Her Latest Supporting Role**

*Big Bite. The most chocolate-y chocolate bar, bar none.*

Jill looked up from the page, said the line aloud. It wasn't embarrassingly, painfully bad, like some of the lines that her writer friends tested on her, but it didn't exactly set the room on fire either.

"I think that's all right," she ventured.

"Sucks," Petra said flatly. "The creative brief says that we have to 'communicate that Big Bite contains more chocolate than any of its competitors in the non-moulded bar segment.'"

"Hmm." Jill pursed her lips. "I suppose you have done that."

Petra tore the sheet from the pad, wadded it up in her hand and sent it sailing over the side of her desk to join the crowd of Big Bite wrappers. Then she reached for a stapled document on top of the bookcase, and set it before her.

"The creative brief," she announced, eyeing it suspiciously. Petra turned ninety degrees in her swivel chair and looked up at Jill. "It also says that we're supposed to give the Big Bite bar contemporary cachet and glamour, 'to make it the Absolut of the chocolate candy category.' That sounds like it came straight out of the idiot client's mouth, right?"

"That's a big ask," Jill allowed. "I certainly love Big Bites—but glamorous?" She paced beside the desk, and then looked again at Petra's movie posters. Jill spun around on her heel and clapped her hands, a very Petra-esque move. "I know—what about this? Kind of a Hollywood glamour thing." She gave a quick snuffle of laughter. "Is that a Big Bite in your pocket, or are you just pleased to see me?" Petra crossed her abundantly braceleted arms, and gave Jill a sour smile.

"Like that's really going to get by the network standards people," she said.

Jill shrugged. "Hey, lighten up. I just came to see if you wanted to get lunch. Sandi told me to take a break. Apparently it's going to be another late night—what a shocker." She eyed the wastebasket. "But I guess that under the circumstances you'd rather not."

Petra pushed her chair back and leapt to her feet.

"*Au contraire, ma chère.* And fuck the circumstances, as I always say," she added emphatically. With one hand Petra gave the inflatable hot dog a friendly stroke, sending it into a provocative sway beside her desk. "I could use a change of scenery."

By the time the waiter emerged with dessert the restaurant's patio was almost empty. Petra stirred a packet of raw sugar crystals into her coffee, and peered at Jill through the dark cats-eye lenses of her sunglasses.

"What's on your mind, doll?"

"Huh?" Jill said through her first mouthful of banana cake, then swallowed. "What do you mean?"

"You seem a little off today," Petra said. "You were okay at the office, but you've hardly said a word since we got here. Not like you. Nick and Sandi riding you too hard?"

"What? Nick and Sandi? Oh no, not really. Although they're both going crazy with the Tellco pitch."

"Aren't we all." Petra laughed, then tipped her curly blonde head back and blew cigarette smoke into the air. "It must be a boy trouble, then," she said finally, and Jill's eyes widened in amazement. "By the time you're thirty-five you'll develop, like, a sixth sense about these things." She waved one hand for emphasis, and the bracelets jangled together. "Trust me."

Jill laid her fork down. Her eyes, unshielded from the sun, met Petra's, and she spoke slowly, desperate for guidance but a little embarrassed at the thought of sharing her predicament with a co-worker. "Did I tell you about the party I went to about a month ago at my lecturer's apartment?"

"Rings a bell. It is someone you met there?"

**Her Latest Supporting Role**

"The host, actually."

"Oh, right Wonder-Boy." Petra nodded her head sagely, and took another long drag from her cigarette. "Or is it the Boy Wonder? The novelist, right?"

"Jonathan Wunder," Jill corrected. "With a U. He's teaching the summer course I'm taking. It's the last credit I need for my degree." Jill gave Petra a cautious look. "And by the way, HR thinks I already have my MFA, so keep that last bit to yourself if you don't mind."

Petra smiled. "I didn't even finish college. Trust me, it's no biggie at H-F."

Then Jill lowered her voice. She'd decided that not only could Petra be trusted—she might even know what to do. "Anyway, about Jonathan Wunder. He's kind of been pursuing me...I think. Kind of but not really, and that's what's bugging me. We hit it off at the party—he told me all this fairly private stuff about some problems he's been having with his writing—and I've gone out with him, like, five times since then."

"But who's counting, right?" Petra said with a knowing grin.

Jill paused, and felt her cheeks redden. "He's got this incredible magnetism, which is a totally cheesy word but I can't think of anything more appropriate." She frowned and stabbed another square of cake with her fork. "I mean, he's good-looking, but it's more than that. When we're together we have the most amazing, stimulating conversations—about everything: books, movies, the meaning of life."

"Oh yeah?" Petra's pink-glossed lips pursed with interest. "Sounds intense."

"I've never met anyone quite like him, really. At the party he kind of scared me. I think he'd had a lot to drink—for that matter, so had I—and the conversation was getting pretty heavy. About his writer's block, I mean. He was very wound-up: you know, sort of the tortured artist thing, which is so hot, by the way. But since then I've really had the most amazing time with him. I know it sounds clichéd –"

"Circle-bar clichés," Petra shot back: one of her standard responses. On her office door was a warning sign, the silhouette of a briefcase-toting businessman inside a red ring, a red slash going diagonally across it: circle-bar client service people.

"Well, I'll say it anyway." Jill clamped her bare arms tightly across her chest. "I don't think I've ever felt this strongly about a guy before, and it's sort of freaking me out."

Petra motioned to the waitress for more coffee. "And you're worried about dating your teacher? Is that the problem?"

"Am I dating him?" Jill sighed. "I don't know. Every time I see him—I mean, outside of class—he's so anxious to make plans for the next time we'll get together. It's like he's afraid that if we don't set up something else right then and there, I'll get away from him. And a couple of times he's said things that make me think he's actually into me."

"For example?" Petra leaned back in her seat and studied Jill intently.

"Well, at the party he was being so solicitous toward me, almost to the point of ignoring his other guests. I made some nervous drunken remark, like 'Oh, Jonathan, I'm not used to being treated so well by men, ha ha ha,' and he gave me this weird, totally riveting look and said 'Then you obviously haven't been hanging around with the right men.' What the fuck was that supposed to mean? And more of the same, every time we go out."

"Like?"

"Like we went to dinner on Friday, and he made this big to-do, a toast to our relationship, and it absolutely floored me. I mean, I could hardly speak after that." Jill sighed noisily, and slumped back in her chair. "I've really got it bad for him—and it's flipping me out. I need to figure out how to stop myself."

## Her Latest Supporting Role

"Stop yourself? Why would you want to?" Petra asked with a wry smile. "It sounds like a little slice of heaven to me."

"But it's *not* heaven, Petra." Jill heard her voice, the blatant anxiety. Petra wasn't exactly coming through with the kind of big-sisterly advice she'd hoped for. "In all this time he's barely laid a hand on me. For instance, we had this wonderful, perfect night out on Friday. He walked me home, we stood in the moonlight, and when he said goodbye he gave me one of those Euro air-kisses—you know, both cheeks, making that fake kissing noise? God, I hate those. They're so..."

"Non-WASP?" she said archly. Petra's bright lips curved into a smile.

"*Touché*," said Jill. "But this thing is really giving me a complex. I mean, he keeps asking to see me again, and he seems so into it, but at the end of the evening—nothing."

"And while the class discussion rages on around you, you're spending all that precious time imagining what he looks like naked." Petra smiled sympathetically.

"Sort of." Jill lowered her gaze for a moment. It upset her to be so transparent.

"Been there, done that," said Petra.

"I want to let him know how I feel." Jill confessed. Her voice was little more than a whisper. "But I'm not sure how to handle it. I couldn't bear it if he blew me off, and then I had to see him in class again. It would just be too awful."

A thoughtful expression crossed Petra's face, and she was silent for a moment. Then she set her coffee cup down, and smiled crookedly at Jill.

"Unzipping his trousers with your teeth is pretty unambiguous, as heartfelt declarations of feeling go."

The tension was suddenly gone. Jill gave a big snort of laughter and one hand flew across her mouth.

"Or—he's a teacher, so he's got to have an office somewhere, right? Just walk in one day and like, lie down on his desk. That ought to get the message across."

Jill stopped laughing, and took a deep breath. "If it were just another crush I could deal with it, you know? But with him it's like I can't bear the thought of something not happening between us, and yet I haven't got the guts to make it happen, either. I guess I'm just going to have to wait it out." She inhaled again, noisily. "I don't know why I'm bugging you with this, Petra. I suppose it's because you don't know him. You can be objective—about the situation, I mean. And you have a lot of experience to draw on."

Petra's brow furrowed above the feline sunglasses. "Thanks."

"Don't get insulted," Jill countered. "You know what I mean."

"Yeah, I do know. I remember—barely—how it was when I was twenty-seven. Of course, when I was your age I was living with a fifty-year old artist, so it's kind of not the same thing. By the way—apropos of nothing—can I tell you that I had great tits when I was twenty-seven? Fred, that's the guy I lived with then, he called them champagne glass tits 'cause when I bent over they looked as if they would fit perfectly into a couple of champagne glasses," she added.

At the only other occupied table, a middle-aged man in a rumpled linen jacket tipped his shaved head slightly in their direction. Petra didn't miss it, though. She raised her voice to him, and with both hands gestured lewdly at her chest. "Yeah, check 'em out, why don't you?" she urged, as the man hunched further into his table, his face florid with embarrassment.

"Anyway," she continued, with a smile of exaggerated sweetness. "I think maybe the reason that Boy Wonder hasn't put the moves on you already is that he's afraid you'll take it as some kind of teacher-student power play."

## Her Latest Supporting Role

Her mind went back to that day in Czerny's office. Had it really been more than two months since she'd fled in disgust? She felt a cold spine-twitch of remembrance.

"But I've never said anything like 'No' to Jonathan, never turned him down, not even once. Last Friday I was trying to encourage him, I mean how could he have missed it?" She smiled hopefully at Petra. "Do you really think that's it, the student-teacher thing?"

"I'll bet he thinks he's pushed his luck already with those ponce-y little air-kisses you hate so much. He probably won't go an inch further than that until your class is over." She grinned wickedly. "And then he'll waste no time in jumping your bones. That's my prediction."

Jill let out a long, almost noiseless sigh, and shifted against her chair.

"I'm really glad you said that, Petra." Jill's brow wrinkled. "I mean, I was beginning to think there was something wrong with me."

Petra shook her head. "I seriously doubt that. You're a pretty girl, and obviously smart enough to hold his interest. Why else would he keep asking you out? I absolutely think it's the student-teacher thing that's holding him back. He's probably afraid of being tossed out for sexual harassment."

"Well then, I guess I should just wait it out." Jill pushed her long hair away from her face and smiled nervously. "There are only two more classes to go. I guess I can stand a few more air kisses if I have to."

Petra laughed. "Who says you have to?"

Jill frowned, not quite understanding.

"Why wait? If it's bothering you that much, just go for it. Close the deal. You see the guy every week, right? I mean, don't throw yourself at him in class or anything. That's a bit tacky, really. But one night get him drunk —or get yourself drunk, if that's what it's gonna take—and tell him what's on your mind. Or better yet, just jump him and get the damn thing over with!" She paused, and added thoughtfully, "A little alcohol can work wonders in situations like yours. I'm sure once he knows that you're willing—more than willing—he'll take the hint. He's a man, after all."

"Well..." Jill began to demur, but Petra cut her off with authority.

"Just give him a chance," she insisted.

Petra looked up as the waiter swept over to them with the check, and placed her hand over it with authority.

"This one's on me. It can be our celebration lunch. To launch your new campaign d'amour," she added. Petra was still smiling, though her voice had a funny edge to it, as she whistled and said, "Fuck, to be twenty-seven again!"

Jill escaped from the office a little after seven, though the agency seemed even busier than after she'd returned from lunch. The Tellco pitch was now just two weeks away, and the agency rumor mill was abuzz with tales of infighting among team members, and an inability to reach any sort of agreement on the agency's strategy recommendation. Constable was heading one of the warring factions, supported by the agency's research director and a couple of mid-level creative teams who'd worked on the business for years. In the opposing camp were most of the Tellco client service-types and Bateman and Brinder, the two Executive Creative Directors who oversaw Tellco.

At the elevator bank she ran into Graham Ferguson, who was just back from a meeting in Ohio with the Tellco clients. One look at his face and she was afraid even to ask how things were going, let alone press him for details of the alleged hostilities on the account. His dark blue eyes seemed to be sinking into his skull, mired in fatigue. He perked up a little when he saw her though, politely inquiring how she was, and this little exchange brought Robin's words of advice painfully to mind. Jill lived in fear

**Her Latest Supporting Role**

that Graham was going to ask her out, that she would have to slam-dunk his poor lovelorn ego yet again. She fled into the elevator, and threw off a quick wave as the doors closed between them.

Yes, he was charming and really very cute, but she just couldn't risk getting involved at the office: especially now. Jill was loath to hurt Graham, she really was—he was so sweet, it would be like kicking a puppy!—but it was Jonathan Wunder that consumed her interest. Talking it over with Petra at lunch had only made the problem more acute: she'd been a mess all afternoon, had made mistake after mistake, causing Nick (himself beginning to crack under Constable's relentless abuse) to shriek at her, enraged, until his face turned as red as the agency's famously red carpeting and her eyes welled briefly with tears.

It was Thursday night, and for Jill the distance between Hambleton French and the NYU campus measured not in miles or even city blocks, but in terms of the book stores that lay between her subway stop and the school. She'd lately been haunting her favorite booksellers even more than usual, desperately seeking a topic for her second and final paper for Novel Into Film Since 1965. Jill had turned in the first essay just a couple of weeks earlier, a terse and incredibly well-researched little analysis of *Marathon Man*. Never before had three thousand words seemed so long! Jill had labored over every sentence and paragraph, refining her use of language, distilling her argument. Her intellectual rigor was fueled in equal parts by an overwhelming desire to impress Jonathan Wunder with her mind, and a chilling fear that the academic nose-dive she'd taken in Czerny's course was not an anomaly, but a warning.

She ventured inside the last book store along her route, an indie on the west side of University Place, having stumbled, quite by chance, upon her essay topic. The store's wide front window featured a display of literary fiction and among these books she saw the perfect essay subject: *The English Patient*. How she'd loved that book, had read through the night to discover what happened to the doomed Count Almásy—so sexy, so romantic. If she couldn't ignite a flame of desire in Jonathan Wunder's body, she could at least try to arouse his intellect, seduce his mind with an amazing essay about a provocative, non-linear book and the equally challenging film adaptation. She'd briefly considered Petra's idea—getting him drunk and laying her cards on the table—before discarding it as far too risky. She hated confrontation of any kind; and besides (though it had remained unmentioned) Petra's scenario contained the very real possibility of Jonathan rejecting Jill, and she just couldn't bear the thought. Not until class had ended anyhow, and though the end of class was a mere week away, it felt like years, unbearable years. She'd spent the entire afternoon playing and replaying dozens of possible romantic scenarios in her head, and just thinking about the ones in which Jonathan Wunder turned her down sent liquid misery pumping through her heart. Something much more subtle would have to do.

**Her Latest Supporting Role**

# Chapter 8

The following Thursday night Jill stood outside the door of the lecture room, waiting for Jonathan and feeling as silly and shameless as a groupie. A student that she was on friendly terms with gave her the oddest look when she saw Jill loitering by the door, and didn't seem terribly convinced when Jill stammered out her lame excuse: that she needed to wait for their instructor because she couldn't read the comments on the essay he'd just handed back.

Jonathan appeared a scant minute after the last students had disappeared down the hall. Their voices still bounced and echoed off the ceiling as he stepped through the door, and the sound made Jill uneasy, like they were being eavesdropped on. In his crinkled linen shirt and aged Levi's, with books and unclaimed papers tucked under his arm, he could himself easily have passed for a grad student.

"Hey, Jill," he said when he saw her hovering, a note of surprise in his voice. He obviously hadn't expected to see her after class. They had already made plans to go to the Metropolitan Museum on Sunday afternoon, and then he was taking her to a barbeque at his parents' house: their first time paired in public. She'd realized it only that afternoon: their evenings together always followed these carefully constructed plans. They never got together spontaneously, or called each other up out of the blue just to say hello as she was accustomed to with other men. And they rarely e-mailed. It was as if there was a Standard Operating Procedure for their relationship, a way that he thought things should be done, and Jill had blithely followed these unwritten rules without ever giving them much thought. And she hadn't even dragged Monika along on any of her get-togethers with Jonathan, as she had been in the habit of doing with other men, to provide a second opinion. It was mostly because she was so afraid of getting told off by Monika: for Jill's best friend, there was no gray area when it came to ethics, or to relationships with men. Jill still cringed when she recalled how disappointed Monika had been to find out that Jill had thrown herself at her instructor—for Jill had finally come clean about it the previous Sunday. Especially since (and Monika reminded Jill of this at least twice during the conversation) she'd had to listen to her moan and groan about Czerny for weeks. The irony of her current situation hadn't escaped Jill.

"Hi Jonathan." She gave him a rapid-fire smile.

"Hey." He surveyed the empty hallway, and then brought his gaze back to Jill. "I guess you're waiting for me, huh?"

"I thought you might want to walk over to the East Village for a drink. It's a beautiful evening, and we could sit outside..." Jill faltered, and heard the drumbeat of her heart pounding in her ears. "Or somewhere else, if you like," she added.

Jonathan shifted his weight from one foot to the other. He was silent for what seemed like an eternity, and Jill could feel two little rosebuds of dampness blooming, one under each arm of her turquoise T-shirt. She was about to open her mouth and save face, tell him well, maybe some other time.

"I'm sorry, Jill." She'd waited a second too late. "I'd love to, but I really can't do it tonight." He smiled at her, and for a split-second Jill thought she detected something patronizing about his attitude toward her: the smile a little less than sincere, the tone a bit too smooth for her liking. Since the night of his party she'd been conscious of the difference in their ages, but she'd never before felt like this: like he was talking to a small child, like he was humoring her. But perhaps she was just overly sensitive, because he'd said no.

"That's too bad. I hope you're doing something fun," she added, seeing if he'd take the bait.

"Oh, you know. Nothing too fabulous," he said, and shifted the books and papers from one arm to the other. Again, a

**Her Latest Supporting Role**

current of doubt jolted her. Was he being evasive, or was Jill just paranoid? There was a moment of heavy silence between them: Jill's heart was beating hard, and she could feel the wet stains beneath her arms growing larger and darker. To hide them she kept her palms flat against her sides, while she stood the middle of the hallway feeling perplexed and foolish.

Jonathan flicked his wrist and glanced not-too-subtly at his watch. He looked, if not exactly mad at her, then certainly impatient to get away.

"I'm sorry, Jill, but I've got to run. I'm really late," he explained. When his eyes met Jill's and he saw her discomfort— it must have been so painfully obvious—Jonathan's tone became kinder. "But we're still on for Sunday, right? The Met, then the barbeque, all that good old summertime stuff, yes? I'll call you Sunday morning," he promised, hurrying down the deserted hallway. "Bye," he added, his words still echoing between them long after he had disappeared around the corner.

Jill had forgotten to turn her cell phone back on after class, and missed Monika's call. If it weren't already so late she would have called back as soon as she heard the message, but her best friend had left for France the day before and, with the time difference, was probably still asleep. Despite Monika's dim view of the whole Jonathan situation, there was no one else Jill could share her predicament with, and ask for advice. Sure, Petra hadn't judged when they'd talked the previous week (kind of the opposite, in fact) but Jill's other friends would be shocked enough if she told them that she was in this nebulous date-like relationship with one of her male instructors. How would they react, how bad would they make her feel if Jill were to admit that she might even be falling for him, and had even invited him home with her? During Jill's first year of college her residence adviser, a beautiful third year Classics major, had gotten pregnant by, and subsequently moved in with her faculty adviser, a forty-ish professor only recently separated from his wife. Even at Vassar—hardly a hotbed of social conservatism or piety—the incident had been whispered about in scandalized tones the entire year. There was no way she was going to fall into the rumor mill like that: not if she could help it.

Jill slumped onto the sofa, and fumbled between the flowered seat cushions for the TV remote, buried deep and encrusted with cookie crumbs and stray pillow feathers. The local news was almost finished, and she surfed aimlessly from station to station until she found an old black-and-white movie that looked familiar. Then she settled back and let her mind become as fuzzy and grainy as the images that flickered across the screen.

Her ringing cell phone snapped her back to consciousness. Jill rubbed her eyes and peered at the glowing numbers displayed on the front of her VCR: one-twenty a.m. The movie was over, and now an infomercial was playing. Identical twin dwarves who promised to share the secrets to getting rich in real estate, apparently a subject of intense interest to insomniacs and night owls. Jill struggled to her feet, slamming her shin against the coffee table and sending precariously-stacked magazines scattering along the slippery hardwood floor. She lunged across the kitchen counter for her phone, grabbing it on the fourth ring, beating her voice-mail by a split-second.

"*Bonjour, Mademoiselle.*" Monika's voice was obscenely cheerful, wholly inappropriate for both the time of night and Jill's mood. "Did I wake you?"

"What do you think?" Jill answered wearily. Her shin throbbed, and she glanced at the magazine-littered floor with annoyance.

"Well, I tried calling you earlier, but you weren't home from work yet."

"Thursday is school night, Monika. You know that," Jill said, yawning directly into the receiver. "So where are you, anyway?"

**Her Latest Supporting Role**

"Paris. We arrived today around eleven, just in time for Mom to go out and empty every shop on the Avenue Montaigne. Anya says hi, by the way. You should see the apartment that she just moved into. It's amazing, totally sick, with a courtyard and everything. Though of course my mother hated it, it's a little too boho for her taste. So we're staying at the Ritz."

"How long are you going to be at the Ritz?" Jill asked sleepily.

"Twelve days here, a quick detour to London and then home." Monika said this as nonchalantly as if she was describing a trip to the corner for a carton of milk. Jill had been dying to speak to Monika, all afternoon and evening she'd longed for a phone call, for words of reassurance and advice from her closest friend (even if it was accompanied by an I told you so or two). But now that she had what she'd wanted Jill felt not grateful, but abandoned and irritated.

"Enough about all that. How are you? How's everything going with Jonathan Wunder?" Monika asked pointedly. "You still in quasi-love?"

There was an edge to Monika's voice that Jill didn't like. She had used the very same tone when they'd met for breakfast on the weekend, when Jill had recounted—in graphic, disappointed detail—the story of her Friday night with Jonathan. When Monika was in a relationship she wished the world well, but when she wasn't she displayed an extremely low tolerance for other people's love lives.

"I don't know," Jill answered ruefully. Their intercontinental connection left something to be desired. Her words echoed back at her through the phone, a disturbing audio effect. "But I can't get him out of my mind. I was so wound up about it this afternoon that I fucked up this big schedule I was working on and my boss screamed at me in front of half the department."

"Poor Jill," said Monika, and for a moment she almost sounded empathetic. Almost.

"Anyway, I was hoping to get together with Jonathan after class tonight—kind of a spontaneous thing, you know, to talk it over—but he blew me off without a moment's hesitation."

"Hmm." There was a long silence, and all that Jill could hear was a burr of static across the line. "Hmm," Monika repeated, a little ominously. "Do you have any idea why?"

The kitchen where she stood was dark and shadowy. Jill bent low over the counter, and studied the way that light from the living room silhouetted her head and shoulders against it. Her image perfectly mirrored the way she was feeling: like an outline of herself, a shadow, not quite solid.

"I don't know. But he seemed to be in a hurry to get somewhere." A spur of anxiety caught her voice as she added: "A big hurry. Do you think that maybe he's seeing someone else?"

"Jill?" Monika's voice was low and serious. "If I tell you something do you promise not to get upset?"

"I know you're going to tell me anyhow, so why not just spit it out?"

"Well..." Monika began, and then faltered for a couple of seconds. Her best friend was uncharacteristically at a loss for words, which alarmed Jill. She stood up straight, preparing herself. "I was talking to Anya," she began: Monika's sister, Jonathan's high school class-mate. Uh-oh, Jill thought, something from Jonathan Wunder's past is coming back to haunt him. Yet at the same time she was relieved. Some dirt from high school, how bad could it be? He'd been suspended—expelled—gotten someone pregnant. Big fat hairy deal. Or an unspeakable nerd, president of the math club, a calculator-holder swinging from his belt. She didn't care, it wouldn't upset her. He was smart and funny and handsome and talented now; an imperfect past humanized him, made him more real and therefore even more desirable to Jill. And at the same time she felt a stab of compassion. Jill herself lived in fear of having a few pieces of her

**Her Latest Supporting Role**

own personal history made public. The story she'd told at his party was by far the least damaging to the image that she so carefully maintained.

"I told Anya that you and Jonathan Wunder were sort of seeing each other. I didn't mention that he was teaching your summer school class. I know you don't want to be too public about that," she added emphatically.

Jill kept her thanks silent, not wanting to slow the story down. She was dying to know what Anya had to say.

"She seemed really surprised. Anya said something like, 'That's good, I guess. I always thought he was a bit suspect, you know.'"

Jill frowned and leaned against the doorframe. "What's that supposed to mean?" she said.

"Well, I pressed her on it. She kept saying 'It's nothing, I'm sorry I said anything' and all that. But after I bugged her enough –" Monika paused, "Anya told me that in college she suspected Jonathan Wunder was gay." And then Monika was silent, and there was just the faint hiss and crackle of the telephone line.

"That's what you called to tell me?" Jill said with a noisy puff of laughter. She was sure that Monika's anti-romance attitude had gotten completely out of hand. "That's why you thought I'd be upset? How could you tell me that with what I can only assume is a straight face? There is absolutely no way that Jonathan is gay."

"Look, I'm not saying he is," Monika insisted. "I'm just telling you what my sister said. She told me that at B.U. he hung around with this group of guys that her friends referred to as The Vienna Boys Choir: kind of swishy but undeclared. Most of them dated but supposedly never slept with any of the girls they went out with, or at least that was the rumor."

"Well, she's wrong," Jill said. Incensed that Monika had even raised this issue, she plumbed her memory for substantiation. "There have been plenty of women in his life, Monika. Jonathan told me he was even almost engaged once—I think she must be the 'K' that he dedicated his book to—but he broke up with her when he went off to graduate school."

"That might be true," Monika said guardedly. "But Anya told me that she ran into him in the city right after his book was published. And even after all those years, she still had the same weird sense about him."

"Look, you told me yourself that Anya had the big-time hots for him in school but he wouldn't have anything to do with her," Jill reminded her friend acidly. "Whatever your sister may think, not wanting to date her doesn't make Jonathan queer."

"Maybe not," she countered. "But you said you practically threw yourself at him on Friday night, and that he turned you down flat."

Jill tried hard to recall the scene in front of her building: the pavement shaky beneath her feet and the vodka and-wine transfusion coursing through her veins. A trick of memory: in her mind, the events of that night were rendered impressionistically, more a series of effects of light and color than distinct images. She had a strong sense of the evening, of what passed between her and Jonathan, without being able to remember the exact details of their exchange. Except for the Euro air kisses, the sandpapery sensation of his cheeks against hers. That faint irritation, the redness where his whiskers had scratched against her own smooth skin stayed with her until the next morning and was—like her throbbing head and arid mouth—undeniable proof that their evening together was more than just a fantasy.

"Well," Jill reasoned, "saying that I threw myself at him might have been a bit of an exaggeration. When we got back to my place I asked him inside—you know, for coffee—but he made his excuses and took off. All that talk at dinner and then not even a real kiss good night," she said bitterly. "It's my fault, though." Jill remembered Petra's words at lunch. "I should have made my

**Her Latest Supporting Role**

interest a little more, well, obvious. I think he's probably hung up on the student-teacher thing. That's what's holding him back."

"I'm not saying that he's definitely gay or anything," Monika cautioned. She was using her lawyer-giving-advice voice, serious and stern. "I'm only telling you what Anya said. Just be careful, and keep your eyes open, okay? I don't have to remind you about Phillip –"

Jill cut her off. "No you don't," she said quietly. "I'll talk to you in a couple of days. Bye."

Phillip was Jill's first New York City boyfriend, a fellow wannabe she met while tending bar to support her acting habit. They became lovers the night they met, and thereafter settled into cautious, then comfortable coupledom. After they had been dating for three months she found an anonymous note of warning in her mailbox. She had no idea who sent it; its purple prose-y intimations had almost surely been cribbed from some trashy bodice-ripper. The note informed Jill that Phillip was three-timing her. He was, it transpired, the urban equivalent of the sailor with a girl in every port, for Phillip very nearly had a girl in every part of the city: a sexy painter in Williamsburg, a sweet Barnard College junior, and Jill in the Village, blissfully naive and then utterly heartbroken. Stealth dating was common enough in New York—especially among her friends who were meeting people online, juggling two or three dates a night sometimes. Still it amazed Jill that she could have been seeing someone for months, thinking that she knew, if not his every thought and movement, at least the set of possibilities that defined their relationship. It was especially humiliating to discover—and by third-party intervention, no less—how very wrong she'd been about Phillip.

And though she had no concrete reason to believe it was true, it occurred to Jill that Jonathan Wunder might be playing Phillip's game. She wholeheartedly believed that he was straight—was certain as she could be, having no real evidence— but how much did she actually know about him? His friends?

She'd met a few at his party, but that group had all the markings of a "crowd," people drawn together by shared circumstances, the self-conscious quest for all things hip and cool. She had never heard him speak of a real, enduring friendship like the one she and Monika had. But if there were other women whose existence was a mystery to Jill, then why was Jonathan Wunder wasting his time with her? Why did he insist that she come along to the barbeque, why did he want Jill to "save" him from his family? She was hardly a parent's dream date, not his parents', anyhow: so much younger than Jonathan, and conspicuously un-Jewish. And perhaps most damning of all, she was one of his students, and therefore a walking, talking testament to their son's bad judgment.

Agitated and unable to sleep, Jill lay in her bed and stared at the ceiling. Although the precise details of her dinner with Jonathan had become fuzzy, the way she felt that night had stayed with her, that peculiar stirring in her abdomen, the dull dragging ache of desire. Monika's phone call hadn't upset her—not exactly—but it made Jill think about her current situation in an entirely new way. She knew that something was not quite right between herself and Jonathan, but whether it was real or imagined, she couldn't be completely sure.

**Her Latest Supporting Role**

# Chapter 9

The weekend felt empty, and a little lonely, with Monika out of town. Sure, Jill had been at the office for most of the day: the entire team had. With less than a week until the big presentation it was all hands on deck. But under no circumstances did Jill want to spend Saturday night alone at home, stewing about Jonathan Wunder, obsessing over the next day's barbeque—what to wear, what to say—and making herself crazy over Monika's middle-of-the-night phone call. Instead, she went to the movies with Petra and Robin. Over lunch in the Tellco War Room they'd had a long debate about what to see: Jill was lobbying hard for *Chuck and Buck*, while Robin was pushing for the new Margaret Cho documentary, which had just opened that weekend to stellar reviews. Petra was to cast the deciding vote—and when Robin declared that Margaret Cho was (like Petra) an avowed fag hag, it was all over for Chuck and Buck.

Jill wandered back and forth in front of the Angelika, waiting, unable to keep still despite the oppressive heat and humidity. The summer weather clung wetly to her skin, and the forecast called for more of the same, and the possibility of thunderstorms arriving late the following afternoon: bad news for the Wunders' Sunday gathering.

Petra arrived next. She strolled over from Sixth Avenue, bopping happily to the sounds from her Walkman, oblivious to the human traffic that bounded past her on the busy sidewalk. She was dressed in a fairly subdued, at least for Petra, outfit: a sleeveless baby doll dress printed with pink cabbage roses as big as Frisbees, and black flip flops. Her eyes were shielded as always by the cat's-eye sunglasses, though at eight-fifteen there was little sun to bother her pale eyes and paler skin. Petra waved when she spied Jill, causing a Slinky of thin silver bangles to slide down her arm. Jill's nose wrinkled slightly at the smell of Petra's favorite perfume, Poison. She wore nothing else despite unrelenting abuse from Robin, who referred to her eighties throwback scent as *Poisson*.

"Hi sunshine," trilled Petra. She yanked the headphones off and retired the Walkman to her leather knapsack. "Where's young Robin?"

"He hasn't shown yet."

"Why am I not surprised? I always give him a fake time—tell him to meet me fifteen minutes before we really need to be somewhere. Then, if I'm lucky, he'll actually be only five or ten minutes late." She laughed. "That man is his own time zone."

"Robin Standard Time." Jill nodded. "Now I know."

By the time Jill returned from the box office with their tickets, Robin had made his entrance. He stood next to Petra on the sidewalk wearing a familiar T-shirt.

"Hi Robin," Jill said. She pointed to his chest. "We haven't seen 'I Cross-dress my Barbies' since Graham Ferguson banished it."

"Ah yes. It's been relegated to weekend wear only, I'm afraid—at least until the fate of Tellco has been decided. To be truthful, Jill," he added, "I don't see what the big deal is, but I'll do anything to keep your boy Graham happy."

Jill looked abashed. "He's not my boy, Robin."

"Not yet, anyhow," Robin said. "That's right, I forgot. Rumor has it that you've given your heart to another. So how is everything with the Boy Wonder?"

Jill shot Petra a dismayed look, one that said *you told him?* She wondered just how much Robin had heard, and realized that—despite her efforts to keep things quiet—the circle of people who knew about her extra-curricular acquaintance with Jonathan Wunder was expanding, and before they were even officially a couple. Monika and Anya knew, Petra and now Robin as well. And then she'd bumped into a couple of her old acting-class friends when she was exiting a restaurant with Jonathan, and

**Her Latest Supporting Role**

knee-jerk politeness compelled her to make the introduction. In her mind she saw the number of people who knew about the relationship increasing exponentially, spiraling out of control. It was just like that old shampoo commercial: she told two friends, and she told two friends, and so on, and so on...

Jill was suddenly angry with Robin, and answered him in a tone so uncharacteristically curt that it precluded further discussion. "Jonathan Wunder," she said, "is just fine, thanks."

She'd never been to the movies with Robin before, but Petra was a veteran. The theater was blissfully air conditioned, and they sat Jill down in what Petra called the sandwich spot, with Robin in the customary aisle seat, his long legs nearly sabotaging several popcorn-toting moviegoers, while Petra took her place on Jill's other side. That way Jill could take full advantage of what they both called "The Robin Devlin Movie Experience." It began with the opening credits, when he launched into a monologue he called "Name That Face." His years in the University of Delaware's ad program had clearly not been wasted, for as the names of the writers and producers flashed onto the screen Robin dramatically announced the name of each and every typeface that the film-makers had used. "Comic Sans," he hissed as the first title appeared, loud enough to earn a couple of irate Shut ups from nearby patrons, those humorless movie addicts who were known to frequent the Angelika.

As the last title (*Bembo Italic and Comic Sans Light—Would you shut the fuck up?*) dissolved from the screen, Jill felt something cold and metallic bumping against her arm. She looked down at an open flask glinting in the theatre's near-darkness, then saw Robin's mouth curve into a mischievous grin. Jill raised the flask to her mouth and swallowed straight pepper vodka, letting loose a silent gasp before wiping a greasy half moon of lipstick from its neck and passing it on to Petra.

As the closing credits rolled they hurried up the theatre's aisle. One more round of "Name That Face" and Jill was sure the angry fat man seated two rows ahead would turn on them; a guy that size could snap Robin's skinny frame as easily as a Popsicle stick. She felt herself weaving slightly from the combination of too much vodka and no dinner.

Petra stopped when they reached the corner of Sixth, and surveyed the assortment of neon-fronted bars and restaurants that stretched out along the avenue in either direction. Her gaze at last came to rest on a bar a couple of blocks north. It was housed in a former bank, the neo-classical facade still stonily imposing.

"Anyone care to make a withdrawl?" she said, stretching one rattling arm toward the bank-bar.

"No more booze!" Jill pleaded. She could still taste the metal of the flask, and feel the vodka after burn in her throat. "I'm still recovering. Can we go for a coffee instead?"

Robin joined in. "I've got an even better idea. Why don't we head over to my place, and I'll fire up my cappuccino maker? If you don't mind –" Petra shrugged her assent. "It's very close by and Jill, I think you'd get a kick out of seeing it. Plus I'm starving, and I happen to have in my apartment every delivery menu for any restaurant ever located in the West Village since 1994."

They headed west, and a ten minute walk took them to Robin's building, a low-rise 1920's-vintage structure in the shadow of the White Horse Tavern. He pushed open the door of his apartment and stepped back with a flourish. "After you, *mesdames*," Robin said, waving Jill and Petra into the darkened foyer. He flung the door shut and switched on the lights.

"Taa-daa!" Robin swept one arm out dramatically, and they followed him into the living room. Jill took it all in and let out a low whistle of amazement. Though neither large nor especially luxurious, it was nonetheless the most impressively-decorated, wildly original living room she'd ever been inside. For just a second Jill sensed what it might be like to read *Elle Décor* on acid. The walls were a bold but pretty shade of yellow, with moldings

**Her Latest Supporting Role**

and wainscoting painted a glossy, blinding white. All of the furnishings were of the traditional sort—things that would be found at a Connecticut yard sale, or inherited from a maiden aunt—but they had been recovered, restyled and accessorized by Robin in a completely unexpected way. A Queen Anne sofa dominated one wall, its lime-green velvet upholstery obviously brand new, and tucked into the corners were two square-ish throw pillows needle-pointed with the face of Botticelli's Venus— the Andy Warhol version. Above the sofa was an ancient-looking wall hanging, though it was not, as one might expect, suspended from an elegant pole: instead, a hockey stick was threaded through a row of loops on top of the tapestry. The stick's red- and blue-striped blade pointed downward; it appeared to be nailed right into the wall. And pairs of antlers, big and sharp and yellowing with age, were everywhere. They sprouted from door frames and wall sconces and there was even a pair suspended from the ceiling, artfully draped with a cloud of gold-colored netting.

"This is amazing," Jill marveled. "What exactly would you call this design style, Robin?"

His suntanned brow creased in thought. "Good question. It's sort of a hybrid of French Provincial Camp and Upstate Hunting Lodge *Moderne*."

"Did you decorate the entire apartment yourself?" Jill watched Petra make herself right at home. She sat down on the sofa, and slung her bare feet onto the coffee table, which was really just a thick oval of glass resting on two pieces of gracefully-peeling tree trunk.

"Well, I used to date an artist," Robin said. Jill's expression registered her surprise. This was the first time she'd ever heard Robin mention his love life; it seemed that he was usually too busy plotting everyone else's to bother with his own. He gestured to a mantel stenciled with tiny gold stars; above it hung a huge, gaudy abstract painting. "He broke my heart," Robin added, uncharacteristically bitter, "but I got the apartment as compensation."

"You got the better deal by far, babe," Petra reassured him from the couch. "This place is utterly fab." She peered around the room with a perplexed expression on her face. "But you've done something new to it, haven't you?"

Robin nodded, his good spirits restored by a dose of home fashion flattery. "Check over the table," he hinted.

Jill turned around. Robin's famed dinner parties—she'd heard all about them from Petra, was dying to be invited to one—were held around a well-worn pine refectory table. A black iron chandelier was suspended above it, tiny round pink candles perched on its spidery limbs. Around the matte black chain that joined the chandelier to the ceiling were a couple of Barbie dolls, hands linked, one of them natty in a tiny tuxedo of powder blue velvet, the other naked save for a pair of flowered boxer swim trunks that obscured her shapely plastic rear.

"Holy fucking God," exclaimed Petra. "Too much. I totally love it."

"I had a couple of dolls just like those when I was five years old," Jill mused. "But it never occurred to me to dress them in Ken's clothes."

Robin crossed his arms over the T-shirt's slogan with an air of satisfaction. "Call it truth in advertising," he said with a grin.

By midnight, Jill was wired. She kept shifting on the scratchy canvas cushions of Robin's huge armchair, unable to get truly comfortable. Robin, playing the consummate host, was constantly in motion: changing discs in the CD player, offering refills of cappuccino, practically force-feeding Jill and Petra from a half-frozen pan of brownies. Petra had produced two joints from the depths of her knapsack and passed them around in rapid succession, but even those hadn't succeeded in mellowing Jill out.

**Her Latest Supporting Role**

The joints and some vintage Ella Fitzgerald had lulled Petra into a quiet daze. From the sofa she observed Jill in lazy silence, watched her fidget. When their eyes met Petra gave her a curious, sleepy look.

"Hey, doll," she said, and eased herself into a half-sitting position. "I'm not trying to pry, but is something bothering you?"

Robin looked up from the floor, where he sat flipping through a stack of CDs. "Yeah, you've been wound up all evening. And don't you dare try to blame the cappuccino," he added scoldingly. "It was decaf."

Jill coiled her hair around one hand as Petra and Robin watched her expectantly.

"Can I ask you something, Robin?" Jill said finally.

"Fire away."

"I figure you're as much an expert as anyone. So how can I tell if a guy I have the hots for is queer?" she asked, sinking back into the cushions with a sigh of frustration.

Robin gave Jill a fishy kind of look—lips pursed, eyes open wide—not angry exactly, but perhaps a little taken aback. "Truthfully," he said, "I prefer the term 'Noted Aesthete.'"

Petra shook away her sleepiness and sat straight up. "Jesus, what brought this on?" she asked. "I assume you're talking about the Boy Wunder."

"Who else?" Jill answered with an uneasy shrug.

"Jill told me about her last date with this Jonathan Wunder guy," Petra said, clueing Robin in. "She's pretty into him, but at the end of the night when he walked her home, she...you asked him in for coffee, right?" Petra looked to Jill, who nodded unhappily. "Which is girl code for 'I want to see you naked and sweaty.'"

"Not just *girl* code," Robin corrected her.

"OK, whatever. Anyway, Boy Wunder said thanks but no, and Jill hasn't quite been her cheerful old self ever since, am I right?" She continued without waiting for an answer. "I thought he was probably playing it safe until she was no longer his student. I mean, who wants to get turfed out of a job on some sexual harassment claim? You don't think that one disappointing evening is any reason to suspect that he's playing on the all-boys team, do you Jill?"

Robin rolled his eyes at Petra. "All-boys team?" he repeated skeptically. "Trust a copywriter to call a spade a 'flat-bladed, long-handled tool used for digging.'"

"Sorry, Robin." Petra looked sheepish. "Like you said, synonyms are my life. So Jill, what's the deal? Is there something about Mister Wunder-ful that you're not telling us?"

"Well, it's just that I got this weird phone call from Monika, my best friend. She's kind of the reason that I got to know him in the first place."

Petra looked confused. "I thought he was your teacher."

"Oh yeah. Yeah, he is. But when I was hanging out in front of the building after class waiting for Monika, I ran into Jonathan and we started talking. Then Monika showed up, and he went to high school with her sister, and that's when he invited us both to her party. Only Monika couldn't go so I went alone," Jill said.

"I know there's a point to all this," Robin interrupted. "Right?"

"Sorry," said Jill. "Long story short: Monika is visiting her sister in Paris, and told her sister that I was dating Jonathan Wunder. And her sister says, 'oh how weird, I always thought he was gay,' or words to that effect. Monika called and told me this Thursday night. End of story."

"So you believe your friend's sister who knew him, what— ten, fifteen years ago?" Petra asked.

"At first I laughed and said no way. I mean it seemed so ridiculous, there's nothing about him that's—you know." Aware that Robin was watching her intently, Jill faltered. "But then I started thinking about everything that he's said and done since the night of his party. His trendy friends, the way he dresses, some

**Her Latest Supporting Role**

of the offhand comments he's made that could be, well, taken another way, shall we say. And then there's last Friday night. Explain that?" she challenged.

"So now you think maybe your friend's sister was right after all," Petra said. She looked thoughtful for a moment. "Ouch."

Robin offered an enigmatic look, and said nothing. Jill turned toward him.

"Don't just sit there!" she insisted. "I need your expert opinions, both of you. A guy asks me out five, six times. He tells me the story of his life, he tells me I'm smart and cute and that he's so happy he's met me. He wants to introduce me to his family, even. But then, when it's time to say good night," Jill paused and tipped her head back so she was staring straight at Robin's bright white ceiling. The angry expression gave way to one of confusion and worry. "When it's time to say good night he does just that, says good night and practically sprints away. What would you think if you were me?"

He tilted his head to one side, and folded his skinny arms across his chest, a familiar Robin gesture, an attempt at seriousness. There was an awkward lull in the conversation. The only sound Jill heard was Ella's Fitzgerald's soaring voice as she sang of love gone wrong.

"I don't know," he said finally. "The things that you've told me about him don't necessarily make him gay. He might just be emotionally fucked-up—you know, jerking you around for kicks. Or there's the teacher thing, too –" he nodded deferentially to Petra. "Maybe he's afraid of looking like he took advantage of you."

"If I beg him to come home with me I'm hardly being taken advantage of, am I?"

"Depends on who you talk to," Petra chimed in. "Maybe he's been watching a little too much CNN. An hour or two with Greta Van Susteren and next thing you know, Boy Wunder's worried about defending his good name and reputation in court."

"Yeah, right," Jill said, irritated.

Petra sank back into the lime green upholstery. No one spoke for two or three minutes; they all just listened to the music vibrating through Robin's gorgeous, outrageous living room.

Finally Jill hoisted herself from the chair and wandered barefoot to the window. It was after one o'clock. A hundred thoughts crowded her brain, competing for her attention like impatient, spoiled children. One of them was pushing a little harder than the rest.

"Robin?" she asked, still staring out the window. "What are you doing tomorrow afternoon?"

Jill stared at Robin's reflection in the window, watched him stretch his long legs out across the floor, ease his upper body back so that he ended up semi-reclined on the rug, propped on bent arms. His head fell back lazily.

"The usual Sunday stuff," he said. "You know, head into the office and finish some more Tellco comps."

Jill did a little half-pirouette. She ended up facing Robin, and waited for him to look up.

"Can I borrow you for an hour or so?" she asked, her tone deliberately mysterious. "I need your expertise."

Petra peered at Robin from the depths of the sofa. "Why do I have a feeling that it's not your considerable skills as an art director that she's after?"

"Petra's right," Jill said. "Jonathan and I are going to the Metropolitan Museum tomorrow afternoon. I got special dispensation from Sandi, and I'm only going to have to be in the office until about two. I was wondering if maybe you could 'run into' us there. Just look him over for a minute or two and give me your honest opinion. I mean, you can usually tell, right?"

Robin sighed and raised himself to a sitting position. "Well if you must know, yes, I usually can. But I'm warning you right now, my gay-dar is not 100 percent accurate."


**Her Latest Supporting Role**

"I don't care. I'm getting really close to having a nervous breakdown over this." She looked down pleadingly at Robin. "I'll be in your debt forever. Please say you'll do it."

Jill saw a look of hesitation cross Robin's face and felt her heart begin to slip.

"For God's sake, Robin," Petra practically shouted at him. "Stop torturing the poor girl and say you'll help her out."

Robin looked Jill straight in the eye. "You shouldn't ask a question if you aren't prepared to hear the answer," he cautioned her.

"I've got to know, Robin," Jill said. "And you're the only one I trust to tell me."

"Then just let me know where and when," he sighed, and flopped back down on the carpet with an air of resignation. "I'll be there with bells on."

# Chapter 10

Wandering through the modern art wing, Jill tried to keep her fidgeting to a minimum as she marveled at a group of gigantic Clyfford Still canvases. Together they reminded her of nothing so much as a series of Rorschach tests, or the "before" segment of the product demo in a detergent ad she was helping out on. Jonathan paused next to her in the chilly gallery, arms crossed over his chest. "I could swear I painted something just like that in third grade," he said with a grin.

Jill turned toward him, and coaxed her facial muscles into a smile. "You're in an amusing mood today," she said, without actually letting her gaze meet his, afraid that he'd see the uncertainty in her eyes.

Shifting her weight uneasily from one foot to another, Jill stalled for time while he strolled on to the next cluster of paintings. Once his back was to her, she turned and scanned the gallery for Robin. She checked her watch again, irritation momentarily clouding her features. It was twenty minutes past the appointed hour; too late, she remembered the concept of Robin Standard Time. Soon they would have to head to Penn Station, catch a train to Great Neck for his family barbeque. Her much-anticipated first meeting with the Wunder clan: Jill rubbed her bare arms briskly and felt gooseflesh beneath her fingertips.

She caught up with Jonathan beyond the next corner of the gallery, staring as an enormous Jackson Pollock. In her mental state Jill couldn't look at the paint-spattered canvas for long without feeling a dull throb of pain behind her eyes, the sensation of her pupils contracting. It was then that Jill felt a bony jab at her right shoulder. She turned to see Robin beside her, staring straight at the Pollock canvas. His lips were parted in a wry smile, one that seemed to ask, *Okay, now what?* Jill wasted no time in taking his cue.

"Robin Devlin," she exclaimed, perhaps a little too brightly, and turned in his direction. "Long time no see. What are you doing here?"

Robin surveyed the gallery, apparently looking for Jonathan Wunder, before meeting Jill's gaze. He inclined his head toward the Pollock. "Oh, I'm a real culture vulture," he announced. "I'm always looking for new inspiration. You know, museums, galleries—movie theatres," Robin added with a sly wink in her direction. "What's your excuse?"

Jill furtively checked out Jonathan's reaction. He had half-turned his body away from them, as if unsure whether to join their conversation.

"I just love the Met," she explained with a wave of her arm. "Always have, especially the Temple of Dendur. When I was a kid I made my mother bring me here at least once a year."

Jill beckoned to Jonathan Wunder. He stepped toward them, hands digging deep in his pockets, his body language still tentative.

"Jonathan, I want to introduce you to someone," she said cheerily. "Jonathan Wunder, this is Robin Devlin, Art Director Extraordinaire. Robin was almost the very first person I met at the agency. He and Petra, who's his partner—she writes the copy—they kind of adopted me right after I started."

"We're so proud of our little girl!" Robin interjected, but his outburst hardly caused a ripple across Jonathan's placid expression.

"He's working on the Tellco Toys pitch too," she added, trying to prop up the flagging conversation, then watched with intense interest as Robin gave Jonathan a strange smile that was at once supercilious and slightly amused.

"Robin," she continued, "this is my —" For a moment Jill faltered, unsure of how to introduce Jonathan. My friend? That was way too impersonal. My teacher, my instructor? No way, that raised a red flag. Jill pressed her damp palms together. "This is Jonathan Wunder," she said finally, with a self-conscious smile, "the novelist."

Robin extended a hand, and for a moment it dangled in the air between them like an awkward question. After waiting a beat, Jonathan fished his right hand from the pocket of his shorts, and gave Robin's a perfunctory shake.

"Pleased to meet you, Robin," Jonathan said, polite but unenthusiastic.

"Oh, the same." Robin smiled at Jill, then turned his attention back to Jonathan Wunder. "Jill's told me so much about you," he said with a knowing smirk. Jill thought his tone was a little too breathless, his movements too stagy. This performance: the walking, talking stereotype bit was over-the-top even for someone as open about his preferences as Robin. Could it be part of his plan? Jill suppressed a critical glance, and folded her hands demurely as she watched Robin go to work on Jonathan.

"Really?"

"Really. How much she admires that book you wrote, for starters," Robin continued. "She even tried to get me to buy it. But I must confess to being more of a non-fiction man."

"That's too bad," Jonathan said, his quiet laugh teetering on the edge of sourness. "I could definitely use the sales."

"So celebrated novel *numero deux*'s not about to set the literati on fire then?" Robin asked, one hand positioned inquiringly on his hip, his brow creeping upward with interest.

At that, the conversation died before Jill's eyes. She saw Jonathan begin to form a sentence and then, on second thought, wince and let it slip back down his throat like a bitter pill. She watched those brown eyes—the ones that sent her pulse into a cha-cha and made her grow all hot at the wrists and behind the knees—as they flickered with something like despair. She glanced edgily at Robin. A no-man's land of silence lay between the three of them. They all just kept eyeing each other cagily until finally Jill

**Her Latest Supporting Role**

could stand it no longer. She thrust herself right into the space between the two men and linked arms with them both in a show of desperate enthusiasm.

"As we might say at The Tisch School," she trilled at Robin, pulling them both away from the display. Robin moved beside her with ease, played right along, but she felt a certain shock or resistance on Jonathan's side before at last he yielded, and grudgingly matched his pace to Jill's. "Jonathan is experimenting with some new narrative forms at the moment. But enough about all that. I'm dying of thirst—I walked here all the way from the office in that hot sun. Before I expire would you guys please take me to the cafeteria for a cold drink?"

Setting down his empty plastic cup, Jonathan Wunder excused himself and headed down the hallway in search of better cell reception. The conversation had gone on and on and they were running late; he wanted to tell his family they were on their way. When he was well out of earshot, Jill leaned across the table and whispered to Robin.

"So?" she hissed, her voice betraying the anxiety that had plagued her all day. The tension between them in the upstairs gallery had been palpable, and made her almost unbearably nervous. Fortunately, it had evaporated the moment they'd reached the café. After a bumpy start, they seemed to get along quite well. Wisely, Robin had steered clear of all but the most innocuous lines of questioning thereafter: movies, contemporary art, and even that safest and most boring topic of all, the weather.

Now Jill realized that the moment of truth was staring her in the face. She couldn't look away, it was much too late for that. Her gaze met Robin's across the tiny café table, and Jill gnawed at her lower lip as she awaited the verdict.

"So?" she said again, her voice barely audible over the dozens of art-happy tourists clamoring around them.

"Well, my dear," Robin said, running his fingers through his stiff blond hair. "I don't think he's gay. But I personally wouldn't be sorry if he was, if you get my drift."

Jill gave Robin a cross-eyed look. "What's that supposed to mean?" she squeaked. "You think he's hot too?"

Robin smiled placidly. "Let's just say that I wouldn't say no to him."

"Well, thanks for the stamp of approval, Robin—I guess. But the question that's been eating me up is what if Jonathan says no to me?"

Robin considered this for a moment. "Class is over, right?"

Jill bobbed her head from side to side as though unwilling to commit to the idea. "One more to go, actually. This Thursday night, when my last paper is due," she explained.

"Okay. So you have to drop off a paper, write an exam, blah, blah, blah. But what I mean is you don't actually have to see him any more, correct?" Jill shrugged a reluctant yes. The thought of no longer being sure that she'd see Jonathan regularly was an unhappy one. "So you should look at it this way: what have you got to lose? If he says yes– and P.S., he's a guy, so he probably will—you get what you wanted. And if he says no then you never have to see him again."

Jill bowed her head slightly. "The thought of him turning me down—it's just too awful. Every time I go to say something to him, try to let him know what's on my mind, I just clam up. I can't do it, you know? I want to, but I...I can't."

"Listen, sweet pea," Robin said, using his best Dear Abby tone. He leaned toward her, a position so intimate that their foreheads almost touched. "Don't take this the wrong way. But it's time to put the ice princess in the microwave."

Jill jerked away from him and looked extremely taken aback. "Thanks for the outpouring of friendly concern."

"I'm not saying it to be mean, Jill," he insisted. "I'm trying to help you. I know how you are, how you hate scenes—don't deny

**Her Latest Supporting Role**

it. But if you don't do something soon it may be too late. *Carpe diem* and all that bullshit. If you wind up dropping the ball," Jill gave Robin a funny look, "or whatever sports analogy you prefer, you truly never have to see him again. I mean, you and Jonathan have one or two mutual acquaintances tops, right? And one of them lives in France, if I remember correctly. So your pride may be a tad wounded, your poor heart may get roughed up a little, but it won't wreck your life, right? It won't be a public failure—I promise you, those are the worst kind, all those pitying looks." Robin paused, his face contorted by a memory. "It won't be a public humiliation, just a private heartbreak."

Out of the corner of her eye, Jill saw Jonathan heading toward them. She made a small slicing gesture across her throat. Robin dutifully closed his mouth, and pulled himself to his feet. Jill watched as he extended his hand again. This time Jonathan took it much more readily.

"Very nice to meet you, Jonathan," said Robin. "I know you two are dashing off to your barbeque, and I want to pop upstairs and look at a couple more exhibits before the museum closes." He leaned down to kiss Jill on both cheeks—singing a barely audible Good Luck into one ear—before disappearing up the stairs.

Jill looked at Jonathan, again searched his face for meaning. "Are we late?" she asked apologetically.

"No, not really." Jonathan seemed less than enthusiastic about their next destination. "But my father worries."

They were on their way out of the museum, descending the long stairs to Fifth Avenue when Jill heard her name being called out from behind them. The voice was loud, insistent, and familiar.

"Jill! Jill Barber! Jill!"

That last time Jonathan heard it too, and as they neared the bottom step they turned in unison. Jill shielded her eyes against the sun and breathed a silent oh no as she watched Justine DeVries totter down the concrete steps towards them. She was dressed as ever in the too-high heels that always made her walk seem stilted, wind-up doll-like, and a sundress made from some stretchy taupe material that was weirdly reminiscent of a tensor bandage.

"Jill Barber," she chided. "I must have called your name a half-dozen times." Justine's beady gaze took in Jonathan Wunder and Jill as they stood side by side on the pavement, and her red-lipsticked mouth dropped open. "Are you two together?" she asked with thinly veiled shock.

"We just came from the modern wing. Did you see the exhibit?" Jill asked, trying to deflect the question, and suppressing her bitch reflex for Jonathan Wunder's benefit.

"No, no, no," Justine said, swinging her head back and forth, the exasperation visible on her face. "I mean, are you two together? Like going out. An item."

Jonathan glanced at Jill, his face a mirror image of her own nervousness, and there was a moment of uncomfortable silence while Justine stood before them: looking impatient, looking pissed-off. Jill watched Justine fold her short arms across her chest, caught a glimpse of one high-heeled foot tapping on the stair, and in that half second it dawned on her. Justine DeVries fancied Jonathan Wunder, liked him every bit as much as Jill did. Jill had sensed it briefly at his party but only now in the bright light of day (and complete sobriety) was it all clear to her. And Justine was shocked and dismayed to see the writer she secretly pined for spending a beautiful Sunday afternoon with her old frenemy.

He looked a little stunned, as though he had forgotten who Justine was. But Jill's reaction was entirely different, and it surprised even her. Buoyed by Robin's good news, and her hope that an invitation to the Wunder family barbeque was a positive development, a turning point in her relationship with Jonathan, Jill's chagrin at running into Justine rapidly turned into something else: a glimmer of opportunity, the thrilling possibility of revenge.

**Her Latest Supporting Role**

The words tumbled from Jill's mouth almost before she had time to think.

Jill looked away from Jonathan, because she knew that if she still saw discomfort on his handsome face the words would die in her throat. Instead, she fixed Justine with a stare every bit as intense as the one Justine had trained on her, and boldly, recklessly gave her answer.

"Together? You might say that," Jill said.

And then she grabbed Jonathan's unready hand and pulled him in the direction of the subway, bidding Justine a hasty goodbye.

They weren't the last ones to leave the barbeque. But by the time Jonathan and Jill had said their goodbyes to all of the Wunder siblings and cousins it was nearly ten o'clock. His brother Adam, the doctor, stood in the middle of the perfect green lawn and waved them off. Next to him was Adam's new wife, Randi, a raven-haired beauty who seemed a little tired: perhaps, Jill thought wickedly, from an entire day spent lugging around her engagement ring, weighed down by its snow globe-sized diamond.

As they climbed into the black sedan—his parents had kindly offered them car service back into the city, wouldn't hear of them taking the train so late at night—Jill noticed a handful of stars fighting to be seen despite the abundant ground light. They winked knowingly at Jill. She was looking for some sign, anything that could offer her a transfusion of courage. She'd tried to find her nerve earlier that evening by downing a series of cold beers: five or six in rapid succession, always making sure that the garage, the location of the all-important beer-fridge, was Wunder-free before tidily slipping her green bottle into the case of empties and sneaking away with another cold Heineken.

A moment of truth was staring her in the face again: two in one day, surely some kind of personal best. Jill touched one hand to her chest and felt that same elevator-with-a-severed-cable sensation she'd suffered before in Jonathan's presence. As the car made its way along silent streets, Jill slid her window down, tipped her head back against the headrest and let the night breeze cool her cheeks.

All evening long she'd answered the Wunders' questions, been paraded by Jonathan before family and friends. Jonathan had guided her around the yard with a light touch—so thrilling to Jill, as he'd barely laid a hand on her since his party—sometimes brushing her elbow, sometimes her waist. Yet he always introduced her in some friendly but non-committal way. "I'd like to introduce my friend Jill Barber," or simply, "This is Jill." It was a family barbeque, for God's sake, she told herself as a spasm of irritation passed through her body. Not something you'd just bring a random date to, or a friend, at least not in Jill's circle. Even Petra had agreed: this was an event, something of potential significance to their relationship. Now if only Jonathan would acknowledge what others seemed to be taking for granted.

She'd grinned at curious aunts and cousins, all of whom seemed extremely happy to meet her; made pleasant conversation with one and all on a range of subjects from the interesting to the banal. She got a tour of the house, which was sprawling, huge, its living and dining room furnishings immaculate and oppressively modern, like she'd stepped into a Roche-Bobois showroom rather than someone's home. She'd scanned the endless family photographs—they were plastered across the den walls, peeked out of bookcases, grew like moss in the most unexpected places, on small dark tabletops and bathroom shelves—seeking a clue, the Rosetta Stone that would unlock the mystery of Jonathan's life and, even more elusive, his feelings for her. Now the party was over, and still his intentions were obscure.

With a small jolt Jill realized that they were headed south from the 14th Street exit, towards her apartment. She shuddered, thinking of that Friday night, his cheeks grazing her

**Her Latest Supporting Role**

own, her confusion at being left standing in front of the building as Jonathan practically sprinted away. Well, sprinted was an exaggeration, but the image of his body retreating from her own didn't exactly help her wobbly self-esteem. If he took her home now she would instantly lose her nerve—she was sure of it. Her mind raced until it came upon a suitable excuse.

"I'm wired," she began, and suddenly sat upright to make her story more credible. In fact, she was feeling weird rather than wired, what with everything she'd consumed at the party, an underdone hamburger floating on a sea of beer in her stomach. "I don't know what I ate and drank back there, but I feel like I'll be up half the night."

"Really?" Jonathan looked at her quickly.

"I know what I need!" Jill practically shouted across the car at him. "That book!"

"What book?" They were only ten blocks from her building, Jill noted. She had to work fast.

"Two weeks ago you promised to lend me that book by the American Studies guy at Yale. The one that's out of print," she reminded him.

"Why do you have to read it now? Tonight?" he asked.

Three minutes from home. Jill saw her opportunity slipping away. In desperation her voice grew childish, petulant.

"My final paper," she lied. "I have to finish it tomorrow. The Tellco pitch is on Thursday, and I just know that work will be crazy this week—I'll probably have to stay late every night too— which means I won't be able to get any schoolwork done."

Jonathan muttered something Jill couldn't quite hear.

"Please, Jonathan. I want to do well in this course, and I know I can—without any special treatment from you," she added, though neither of them had mentioned that possibility anyhow. Ever. Her mark on the first essay had been good but not spectacular, though that was before—in Jill's eyes, anyhow—their relationship had truly blossomed. "Can't we swing by your apartment and get the book? I can take a cab home from there," she added in a final burst of desperation.

Jonathan said nothing for a moment, but then Jill felt a surge of hope as he leaned forward to redirect the driver.

He led her into the apartment, which was warm and dark, the blinds closed tightly. Jonathan flicked on a couple of lights as he passed through the foyer, then the living room. Jill paused before the familiar framed book jacket while he continued on to the bedroom where she supposed his bookshelves were located. She studied the cover of *Groundswell* again, the two opposing images—author's handsome, detached expression and the impressionistic skyline facing him—looking for a clue, anything that would explain his behavior.

When she heard footsteps, Jill darted to the couch and took a seat. Jonathan appeared with the book in one hand, raised above his head like a trophy.

"Taa daa!" he said. Jill breathed silent relief to see that he was almost smiling, his mood vastly improved since they'd left the barbeque. He'd been silent and uncommunicative during the drive back, and it had worried her. "I knew it was in there... somewhere. You know, I had this book when I was at B.U. And I seem to remember that I got a shitty grade on the paper I used it for," he added, moving toward the couch but holding the book just out of reach. "You sure you want it?" he teased.

"Yes, I want it." Jill rocked up from her seat to snatch the book out of his hand, then landed back on the couch. Jonathan stood before her expectantly, but Jill refused to stand, had no intention of going home yet. After a couple of seconds he gave up, and took a seat: not beside Jill as she'd hoped, but in a chair that was positioned at a ninety-degree angle to the sofa.

A single track light shone overhead, bathing the gray-toned living room in shadows. Jill studied Jonathan Wunder's profile, the stray wisps of hair that licked his face; she felt a stab of

**Her Latest Supporting Role**

tenderness in her throat as he sighed, sank back in his chair, and let the lids flutter down over his eyes.

"Did you have a good time tonight?" she ventured, still scrutinizing the contours of his face. "You seemed a little tense, you know? Especially on the way back. Not quite yourself."

The head tipped back and Jonathan's eyes rolled open to stare at the ceiling. His nostrils quivered with a big intake of air.

"Family bullshit." He addressed his comments to the shadowed surface overhead. "Every time I walk into that house I am reminded of all my shortcomings."

"Like what?"

"My stalled career, my stalled life. Thanks for putting up with them, though. I think they liked you a lot."

"Can I ask you something, Jonathan?" Jill sat up on the sofa and planted both feet solidly on the floor, seeking strength, and grounding. Without waiting for a response, she forged ahead. "Why did you ask me to go with you?"

He closed his eyes again and slid further down in the chair. "They like to know what's going on in my life, how I spend my time, who I spend it with." His mouth twitched almost invisibly. "I see them so rarely, considering that they only live twenty miles away."

Her voice caught with disappointment. "Oh. I see," she lied. Jill felt the all-too-familiar frustration slip over her again. "I thought maybe it was something else," she added, fishing.

Sterile silence surrounded them. Jill fixed her eyes on Jonathan. Slumped back, disappearing into the armchair, it was difficult to discern even if he was awake, let alone what was on his mind. With a pang Jill remembered her last visit to his apartment: the night of his party, the turning point in their relationship. She now recalled their conversation as vividly as if it had happened ten minutes ago, the angry outpourings about his writing career, his wretched account of fruitless work and dreamless sleep.

"Jonathan?" His name caught in her throat, making Jill's voice a choked whisper.

"Mmm." His lips barely parted to answer her.

"Can I ask you one more thing?"

Again: "Mmm."

Jill took a deep breath, and plunged in. "Has your muse come back? I mean, have you written anything—anything you were happy with—since the night of your party?" Hands clasped together, Jill's nails carved little half moon-shaped welts into the tops of her knuckles. "Have you been able to dream again?"

Without raising his head Jonathan slid one eye open and gave Jill a fishy stare, one that drew all the air out of her.

"Why do you ask?" he said. "Were my parents quizzing you on my output today?"

"No, no, not at all. I'm the one who wants to know."

"Well," said Jonathan, his voice growing louder, fueled by irritation. "The answer is a resounding no. Book reviews, articles, sure, but 'celebrated novel *numero deux*'—as your friend Robin so charmingly put it—remains wholly unwritten."

"I'm so sorry, Jonathan. I didn't mean to upset you." Jill stopped talking and was alarmed to hear what she took to be the sound of her own heart thumping insistently in her ears. "I want to help you, so much more than you probably realize."

Jonathan's eyes slumped shut once more, as though attempting a speedy retreat from their conversation. He sounded skeptical, and angry. "How can you help me, Jill? How can anyone?"

Noiselessly Jill got up from the couch and rooted herself before him on the black and white rug. She gazed down at Jonathan, watched the long sooty fringe of his eyelashes tremble so heart-wrenchingly with the listless in-out rhythm of his breathing. She crouched down before him so that their faces were level and no more than a couple of feet apart, though Jonathan's head still lolled restlessly backward. Robin's earlier

**Her Latest Supporting Role**

exhortation—time to put the ice princess in the microwave—echoed inside her head, and spurred her on.

"I want to be your muse," Jill announced, her words quiet but insistent. She watched Jonathan Wunder's head tilt forward, the dark eyes fly open. She was chagrined to see surprise there, as well as in the slight but unmissable drop of his jaw. She forged ahead anyhow, adding, "My rates are very reasonable," with a silly little smile, an attempt to diffuse his shock. Then her tone grew deadly serious again. "I dream about you, Jonathan, and not just when I'm asleep, either. At my desk, on the subway, in that restaurant you took me to. I can hardly concentrate in class, except I'm trying so hard to impress you with my mind that it forces me to speak up."

"What?"

Still crouching, Jill laid one hand, then the other, on Jonathan Wunder's knees, more than anything just to steady herself. She'd noticed at the barbeque the way his khaki shorts rode up whenever he sat. Now from her vantage point she studied the twin shapes of his exposed thighs: near his knees they were brown and weathered-looking, the dark hairs curling like iron springs across his tanned skin. But just a little farther up the leg became suddenly pale, with skin far more fragile in appearance, the hair straight and soft-looking. Sensing no reaction from him one way or the other, Jill moved her hands slowly upward, bringing them to a rest when the tips of her fingers reached that delicate skin just past his tan line. With amazement Jill noted that her hands were no longer shaking, and the skin across her knuckles no longer pale.

"Jill," Jonathan found his voice, and—wide-awake now—hunched slightly forward in the chair. Whether intended or not, this movement brought their faces even closer together. A gap of less than a foot separated them now, and with a sting of delight Jill felt the warm air that touched her as he spoke. She greedily sucked in the smell of his breath, as ripe and beery as her own.

And her eyes locked onto Jonathan's, which were clouded with shock.

"Jill," he repeated. "This is my fault. I think I may have—" And then he stopped in mid-sentence. Jonathan Wunder, the tragic prisoner of writer's block, had choked yet again. Even now—with Jill sharing her true feelings for him—he was unable to complete a simple sentence. Jill felt her vital organs churning with a mixture of pity and desire. She picked the conversation up where he'd fallen away.

"Don't worry." Jill shook her head gently. "Don't think you led me on. I was, I am a willing participant, believe me. I'm sure the student-teacher thing is bothering you, but I swear to God, I'm not going to run to the Dean and blow the whistle or anything like that. I want to help you…to inspire you. Make your dreams come back, Jonathan." She smiled encouragingly. "I believe great things about you. Things I bet you don't even think are true."

Jill eased her head forward and closed the shadowy gap between them. When her lips met Jonathan's she was thrilled by their feel, the pulpy softness. She pressed her head forward insistently and at last felt Jonathan's mouth yield. Her tongue collided with his and the sensation made something drop through Jill's body. Wordlessly she climbed into his lap and touched Jonathan's face, which had gone slack with desire or bewilderment or abandon. It was impossible to tell, and it scarcely mattered now.

It was tight and sticky with the two of them clamped together in the armchair. She beseeched him in silence, using only her body. With her tongue Jill drew a line down the side of his neck, and thrilled to feel a single awkward kiss whispered against her clavicle. Her skirt hiked up and her bare thighs moved, curving themselves around Jonathan, enclosing him until finally she felt an erection stirring in his lap.


**Her Latest Supporting Role**

Jill wriggled out of her clothes and abandoned them on the floor—and she pulled Jonathan from the confining armchair to the soft wide depths of his gray couch. She slipped naked across the shadowy room, moved stealthily toward the bathroom, a woman on a mission. She found the condoms right where he'd said they would be, hidden at the back of the neat medicine cabinet. Jill was grateful for the semi-darkness as she returned to the living room, where Jonathan Wunder was sprawled on the couch, half-naked and glistening with perspiration.

When she approached, he raised himself up on one elbow: it almost looked like he was going to stand, and she moved quickly to him, afraid he was going to call the whole thing off. As she had so many times before, Jill found the expression on Jonathan Wunder's face difficult to interpret, and she felt a stab of frustration. It wasn't a look she was used to in this type of situation: wasn't gratified or self-impressed, wasn't giddy with desire or taut with anticipation. More than anything, the oblique arrangement of Jonathan's features suggested simple confusion.

"Hi," Jill said quietly, suddenly at a loss for words. She paused before him and trembled, despite the warmth and humidity of the room.

He stared straight into her eyes with a questioning look, and Jill lowered herself, kneeling before the couch, right in front of Jonathan. With a tentative movement, she reached for the hand that wasn't propping him up. She avoided his face, his eyes for just a moment while she pulled herself together.

"This is what you want," he said. It sounded more like a statement than a question.

In a rush of anticipation, Jill answered him—not even considering Jonathan's words, or why he'd said them. "Yes, this is what I want," she echoed. Her voice was low, like a prayer.

Jonathan Wunder's living room was almost dark, the air around them tepid. They made love in near-silence, disturbed only by the sound of their own movements and the creak of the sofa, its springs complaining quietly before yielding beneath them. Jill tried hard to abandon herself to the moment, to shut out everything but the present reality of skin meeting skin and commingled breath and the movement of so many muscles she'd nearly forgotten she had. But dozens of thoughts crowded her brain. The moment she'd been thinking about for weeks, aching for: it had finally arrived, and yet something seemed to be, well, not quite right. Astride him, she arched backward slightly and studied his face. His eyes were closed, and his black eyelashes moved almost imperceptibly, as though shutting Jill out from whatever was taking place behind them. Jonathan's face was virtually expressionless except for a slight downturn at one corner of his mouth, and a twitch that suggested intense concentration. But Jill could read nothing in his features that implied desire or excitement or any of the things that, less than half an hour ago, she'd been so desperately sure she felt for him. In fact, Jonathan's expression was—more than anything that came to Jill's mind—suggestive of a man working on a math problem or perhaps doing his taxes: that air of concentration and worry, the features set in a grim mask of resignation. Her body entwined with Jonathan Wunder's, both of them close to climax, and Jill was suddenly overcome by this image of a man laboring over his income tax: patient, resigned, duty-bound. The picture that pushed its way into her mind was alarmingly clear, and the accompanying litany of instructions throbbed in her brain like an ad jingle from hell: total income from all sources, less adjustments to income equals adjusted gross income, less deductions...

This unnerving image crashed into the reality of her situation—she was purposefully, passionately making love to Jonathan Wunder while his eyes remained closed in indifferent silence—and brought Jill to an unwanted but inescapable epiphany. Jonathan wasn't doing what he was doing because it was something he wanted, because he felt something for her or

**Her Latest Supporting Role**

even because he believed she could somehow help him. He was only there because it was what Jill wanted. With a pang of despair Jill realized that with everything that had passed between them—the anguished exchange at his party (and the several that followed) capped off by dragging her to what seemed, at least to him, like an excruciating family get-together in the 'burbs—after putting her through all of that Jonathan Wunder probably felt like he owed her. She didn't feel like a muse, like his creative salvation—far from it. Jill felt like an idiot.

Whatever it was that Jonathan wanted or needed, whatever it was that could turn his situation around—if indeed anything could—Jill knew now with stunned, painful clarity that it wasn't her. She loosened her arms from around his neck and shoulders and the breath left her body all at once, like a sob. Then she felt a hot angry flush of blood rise to her cheeks, and suddenly the thing she'd wanted so badly and waited so long for had turned into an interminable nightmare. She could hardly wait for it to be over, for Jonathan finally to finish with her and fall asleep or disappear into the bathroom or whatever. Then she could pick up her clothing from his living room floor, and retreat home in shamed silence.

# Chapter 11

The day before the Tellco pitch passed for Jill as if in a dream. Parts were fast and frantic, flew by in a blur of noise and activity, while others were so prolonged, so excruciating that it felt to her—and must have to everyone else caught up in it—that the pre-pitch nightmare would never end. For weeks it had seemed as if the entire agency was fighting to save the Tellco business; but as hard as they labored, there was always the sour whiff of desperation on everyone's breath, and a cloud of disaster hanging in the air.

The final presentation was scheduled for Thursday morning, and—just as Jill had feared—the days that week were insanely long. On Tuesday morning a handful of people had staggered into work shortly before seven to find two junior creative teams still holed up in one of the smaller conference rooms, OD'd on caffeine, winding up an all-night brainstorming session. Even the most driven H-F-ers on the team, the ones who constantly bragged about their crazy hours and seemed to live for the adrenaline rush, looked completely fried by mid-week.

Legions of Hambleton French creatives had been drafted into helping save the Tellco account. All day long they raced through the agency's corridors, rushing from the color printers to the War Room with a never-ending stream of creative work to support dozens of advertising and collateral and promotional ideas—point-of-sale materials for retail promotions in toy and department stores, television storyboards, ideas for theme-park tie-ins—only to have the overwhelming majority of this work killed by Constable, work which he might have already approved only days or even hours before. As the big day approached Jill became even more pessimistic about the agency's chances of keeping the account. Again and again she watched creative teams rush into the War Room, full of enthusiasm and a sense of purpose, only to be told—with the brutal, ego-flattening honesty which was Constable's trademark—that they, and their ideas, were not any good. The teams would reappear what seemed like only seconds later, and trudge past Jill's desk with their eyes lowered and shoulders slumped, either trailing their rejected work behind them or balling it up and slamming it into the trash.

At this point there wasn't much that Jill could do for Nick and Sandi, other than bring them a steady supply of double espressos from the ground floor Starbucks. By Wednesday morning the two *Über*-producers had been up for more than forty-eight hours straight, editing a slew of rip-o-matics: TV commercial concepts "ripped" from other advertisers' work. The bulk of these never made it past Constable, despite the fact that he'd green-lit the scripts earlier that same week. And they were endlessly re-cutting a montage of the agency's most successful Tellco commercials, the so-called feel-good reel that would accompany Constable's opening remarks in the meeting.

Late Tuesday things took an unexpected turn for Jill when her services were appropriated by Sally Leyton, the Executive Account Director on Tellco. Her assistant, apparently a notorious hypochondriac, had bailed out earlier in the day and Sally, desperate for competent support, had been put in touch with Jill, who was nearly always willing to work late in exchange for time-and-a-half and car service home to the East Village.

Sally Leyton was holed up in her disordered, toy-filled corner office on the eleventh floor, furiously writing and re-working the strategy portion of the presentation, endlessly finessing the wording and rationale of a recommendation that would set up the barrage of new creative work to be presented. Her pale blonde hair was obviously dirty, and she had pulled it away from her face with a fraying velvet hair band; bits of mascara had drifted onto the shadowy skin just beneath her eyes. Every hour or so she would present Jill with a new sheaf of yellow paper, where she had outlined the strategy discussion of the moment in a scrawl of sky blue: her lucky fountain pen left oddly-shaped splotches of ink here and there on every page, cheerfully colored little Rorschach blots. Some of the ink was still wet when she handed these stacks to Jill, and there were streaks of blue like fat veins climbing the surface of Sally's fingers, wrists, and her long white throat.

Late Tuesday night—Jill had sleepwalked out of the agency some time after one—and all day Wednesday she typed for Sally, turned the ink-splotched yellow pages into neat and orderly stacks of PowerPoint slides. Jill would work furiously for forty minutes at one stretch, an hour sometimes, completely focused, uninterrupted. All that existed was the scrawl on the page and the blinking monochrome of her computer screen: no world outside her dim, chilly cubicle on the tenth floor, no personal life, and—as much as she could prevent them from popping up—no thoughts of Jonathan Wunder and what had happened on Sunday night. The few times that Jill did think about him, about what had gone on between them, it wasn't with the dull dragging ache of desire she'd felt for so long; instead, a gnawing sense of regret ate away at Jill's psyche, the emptiness she'd felt as they made love slowly being replaced by despair.

When the typing was done she'd slip upstairs and deliver the work to an embarrassingly grateful Sally, who would either be slumped over her desk clutching a coffee cup as if for dear life, or in a meeting with some of the Tellco team, the air charged with nervous and sometimes hostile energy. Jill had seen Graham there a couple of times, hunched forward in one of Sally's leather director's chairs, his shirtsleeves rolled up almost to the elbow and the Windsor knot in his tie askew. An unusual sight: Graham was usually so perfectly attired, he could have been the poster child for good grooming. While talking with Sally—his tone of voice sometimes agreeable, but often not—Graham always found a half-second to favor Jill with a quick wink or a surreptitious smile. But she was too self-conscious to return his

**Her Latest Supporting Role**

greeting, always trying to blend into the background, all too aware of her very minor role in the drama unfolding around them. She would go back to her desk and listen to the radio, sipping Diet Coke and waiting patiently for Sally to reappear, fresh from an audience with Constable, the crisp white pages stained bloody with red ink: deletions, corrections, whole new pages to be added, all in Constable's frenzied and virtually indecipherable hand.

Seven o'clock came and went: the night before the pitch, and Constable was still making changes to every facet of the presentation—revisions to storyboards, endless re-wording of the research results and strategy statements—which meant that Sally's portion was nowhere near finished. At eight-ten Jill delivered the latest round of typing, then returned to her desk, where she slipped off her sandals and stretched her arms and legs out with a long low sigh of fatigue. When she pressed a button on the clock-radio her small corner—murky gray, bathed in shadows cast by the almost-vanished summer sun—filled with music, a moody instrumental with a pulsing and insistent drumbeat that perfectly matched the throbbing atmosphere of Hambleton French Advertising. She felt her eyes flutter closed, until all she saw was the foggy gray-pinkness inside her eyelids.

A loud noise, a throat being cleared—obviously, purposefully—and her eyes snapped open. The display on her clock radio glowed in the near-darkness, and told her it was eight-thirty-four. She swiveled her head and was surprised to see Graham Ferguson in front of her desk. He held something out to her, wrapped in a sheet of waxed paper that was beginning to unfold at the ends.

"Here," he said, and placed it gently on her desk. "You missed the food in the conference room. I thought maybe you were stuck with Sally but she's nowhere to be found." As Graham pointed to the paper parcel and smiled a little nervously,

Jill felt a rush of *deja vu.* "I hope you're not a vegetarian. It's chicken salad on whole wheat."

"Thanks, Graham," Jill said. She was suddenly hungry, and pulled the sandwich toward her, gingerly unfolding the waxed paper to peek inside. "That was really nice of you."

Graham waved, slicing the air noiselessly with his arm, as though her gratitude embarrassed him. His expression was restless, uncommonly tense. His appearance, usually crisp and immaculate, had undergone a remarkable change too, his blue-and-white striped shirt rumpled and partially unbuttoned, the tie now abandoned. Seeing Graham so disheveled and forlorn made Jill feel another small rumbling of doom.

"Can I ask how things are going?" she asked warily. "Or is it still too soon to tell?"

"I really don't know." He rubbed his eyes with the palms of his hands and blinked, hard. "I've lost all perspective. We might save the business—might—but right now I wouldn't bet money on it. I just came from the boardroom. They started their first run-through of the presentation about fifteen minutes ago, although Constable keeps changing everything. They haven't even got half the boards ready to go because they've only just decided what's going to be shown. So they sort of skipped over the introduction and launched straight into the creative. It was pathetic." He glanced down the silent corridor and lowered his voice, which nearly shook with anger. "I got so disgusted with the whole thing I had to leave. Constable was up there talking, just like he will be tomorrow, and Bateman and Brinder —" Graham named the two co-Executive Creative Directors on Tellco: Stu Bateman, a wheezing, middle-aged alcoholic, a man almost as big around the middle as he was tall; and his partner Sam Brinder, handsome, ironic, cooler-than-thou, a transplant from the L.A. office. "They were scurrying around behind him like morons with the storyboards. The three of them looked like

**Her Latest Supporting Role**

Larry, Moe and Curly, goofing around in the boardroom. I had to get out of there," he added with a pained whisper.

Jill winced in sympathy. "I suppose I should spend tomorrow getting my resume together?"

"Well, if anyone asks, you didn't hear it from me, okay?"

She gave a quick nod that was meant to encourage Graham. Unfortunately, it seemed to have no effect on his grim mood.

"Was Sally up there for the run-through?" Jill asked.

"Sure. Why?"

"I'm still waiting for the latest version of her pages. And the studio told me that on pain of death they need to get my PowerPoint files by midnight."

"Why so early?" he said. "I thought they only needed a couple of hours to make the boards."

"Well, they worked the schedule all out with Sally's assistant long before I arrived on the scene. I'm surprised Sally didn't fill you in on it. She's got these little round yellow and navy blue stickers—the colors of the Tellco Toys logo—and she wants to put a sticker over every bullet point on every board in the entire presentation."

Graham rolled his eyes so far back in their sockets that Jill stopped talking, almost worried they would stick that way.

"Yellow, blue, yellow, blue," she continued in an edgy sing-song. "It's going to take hours. Plus, if one of the boards comes back and we find something wrong with it, we need enough time for a do-over before the pitch starts at nine. She's got the whole thing worked out, it's on a little critical path diagram that Grace typed up before she bailed yesterday. The problem is, I need to re-type her stuff, and then she has to get Constable to personally OK all the pages—the research, the media plans, everything—before we send them to the studio. Plus, I called Constable's secretary before I fell asleep, and Anne said his pages aren't ready yet, either."

"And you're taking care of all this with the boards?"

Jill nodded. "And the leave-behinds. Anne was supposed to, but her daughter is sick, and she doesn't want to leave her with a sitter overnight. She's just staying 'til Constable's stuff is done. Apparently he doesn't like to have anyone but her do his typing."

He let out a harsh laugh. "She's probably the only one who can read his writing."

"It is pretty indecipherable," Jill said. "Maybe he was a doctor in a previous life. They say doctors have the worst handwriting of anyone."

Graham shook his head slowly, and his mouth dipped into a frown. "I couldn't tell you exactly what Constable did in his previous lives, but I seriously doubt that he was in any kind of caring profession."

Just then Sally Leyton appeared next to Graham. He nodded deferentially.

"Hey Sal, what's all this I hear about dressing up all the bullet points with blue and yellow stickers?" His tone was bitter, very nearly mocking, which surprised Jill. After all, Sally was his boss. "Some trick you picked up during your Gamma Phi days?"

Graham's irony went right over Sally's head. Her answer was so earnest that it almost pained Jill to hear it. "Oh, no, it's something we tried during the Heartland Cereals pitch last year. Fly the company flag, show some spirit, all of that."

He frowned at Sally, and shot Jill a strange and unnerving look. "We lost the Heartland pitch."

"That's hardly the point, Graham," Sally answered defensively. "And besides, Constable was all for it."

"Oh, well then. Far be it from me to second-guess our fearless leader."

"My sentiments exactly," she said, and turned away from him. Sally handed Jill a stack of white paper, slashed and scribbled on with a red felt-tip pen, so much ink that on a couple of pages it had soaked right through. "These are the final, final corrections to my part of the presentation. I'm sorry it took so long," she

**Her Latest Supporting Role**

said wearily and, putting one hand behind her neck, arched backwards for a quick stretch. "When you've finished correcting these pages please bring them up to the boardroom for me to proof. And check with Anne around eleven, would you? Constable's pages should be ready by then, if we're lucky."

Sally spun on her heel, and hurried for the stairs to the eleventh floor. She was almost to the stairwell, her back to them, when she called out, tight-throated and angry: "Graham, you might want to join us upstairs in the boardroom. If you think you can bear it."

A flash of irritation crossed Graham's face. "Duty calls," he said in a low, choked voice, and stalked off after Sally.

Witnessing these scenes—it was by no means been the first time she'd seen this kind of tension between Graham and Sally—made Jill incredibly uncomfortable. Their attitudes toward the pitch were so radically different. Sally was the cheerleader, the eternal optimist, continually trying to boost flagging morale among members of the Tellco team. A few days earlier Graham had told Jill—only half in jest—that he lived in fear of Sally interrupting one of the many pitch brainstorming meetings to suggest a group prayer for their success. His attitude was darker, much more guarded: Graham was working just as doggedly as the rest of the team trying to save the business, but his tone and body language made Jill believe he had suspected disaster early on, and that his sense of foreboding was growing with each passing day. He definitely wasn't an Eagle Scout, the steadfast company man he'd seemed on the night they met. Graham Ferguson actually had a little edge—maybe a dark side, even—which actually made Jill like him much more.

Left alone in her dark corner, Jill reflected on the situation. It wasn't quite as shocking as she'd first thought, the way that Graham had bolted from the run-through, overcome with disgust, and how he'd so blatantly mocked Sally's plan to decorate the presentation boards. He had a huge stake in the outcome, and that gave him every right to be horrified by the way that the pitch was finally coming together. The battle to keep the Tellco account was being waged at the agency's highest levels and while Graham, the Management Supervisor on the Boys' Toys part of the business (and basically middle management) certainly had some role on the pitch, his most critical responsibility was to keep the account running smoothly, brilliantly, until H-F's fate had been decided. He had been killing himself to make sure that Tellco clients received the very best service possible; after all, H-F was still Tellco's agency, at least until August 25th, and they were in the middle of producing more than a dozen commercials for the Christmas toy season, buying tens of millions of dollars worth of TV time and placing countless magazine ads too.

Everyone was praying that the Tellco clients would walk into the boardroom for Thursday morning's meeting with their blue-suited chests nearly bursting with goodwill toward the agency, and (together with his counterpart on of the Girls' Toys side of the business) it was Graham's responsibility to make it happen. It was supposed to be Sally's job too, he'd pointed out to Jill, at least until she'd withdrawn almost entirely from the day-to-day running of the account to focus on the pitch. Constable, Sally and everyone else wanted to ensure that the Tellco marketing group would be able to reflect on the agency's dazzling strategic thinking (they hoped it was dazzling), and the brilliant creative work (if it wasn't brilliant, they were toast) with a tremendous sense of well-being, confident that H-F had not just the ability to wow them with a two hour presentation, but the well-oiled machinery needed to create and produce advertising that would build their sales year in, year out.

At ten on Wednesday night Jill slipped into the boardroom to hand the corrections to Sally. The run-through had been abandoned, and eight or nine people were slumped around the long table, smoking or picking at a tray of oozing sandwiches and broken cookies. Heavy hitters, every one of them: gazing

**Her Latest Supporting Role**

surreptitiously around the room, Jill realized that Graham was the most junior person there. The air was nauseatingly heavy with smoke and the agency was risking a big fine if they were caught. Worse, how would they ever get the room clean, the air breathable by the time the Tellco clients arrived in just eleven hours? Nick and Sandi weren't there—probably dozing in their offices, overcome after back-to-back all-nighters—but the fruits of their labor were. The familiar videocassettes—all those days and nights, and only five had passed muster with Constable— were lined up neatly on a table at the front of the room. On the big video monitor in one corner, a Rainbow Baby doll's dark face was eerily freeze-framed, much larger than life, its guileless baby smile so skewed and distorted that it seemed to mock the very proceedings being held in its honor.

Shortly after eleven Jill headed over to see Constable's secretary, Anne. The rest of the pitch—strategy, research and media plans—had been approved by Constable, retyped one last time, and then proofread by three different people. Jill had sent those pages to the studio, where most would be blown up to thirty-by-forty inch size and mounted on stiff foamcore board. Constable's pages—which would accompany the presentation's opening remarks—were the only ones still not done.

As she approached his office Jill heard two voices, a man's and a woman's, and a rapid volley of unintelligible words. She moved closer, strained her ears; it was Sally and Constable, locked in a heated argument, though it wasn't clear what about. Jill eased her head around the corner and saw Anne sitting at her desk, Sphinx-like, guarding the path to Constable's office and studiously ignoring the noisy duet of curse words and pleading that drifted from inside.

Jill silently mouthed a question—*are his pages ready?*—but before Anne even had time to nod or shake her head Constable burst through the open door, trailing Sally, red-faced and frantic, in his wake. His limp was almost comical, exaggerated by the speed and gracelessness with which he galumphed toward Anne's desk. He dropped a sheaf of papers in front of his secretary as Sally looked on, aghast.

"Fix these and my bit's finished," Constable barked at Anne, and made an awkward half-turn. His seething gaze met Jill's. "What the bloody hell are you doing here?" he demanded.

Surprised, Jill opened her mouth to speak, but Sally jumped in before she could get the words out.

"Jill's helping me," Sally explained, her bloodshot eyes flashing with anger, her voice unusually forceful. "She's supposed to be getting all the presentation boards made, which she can't do until you get Anne to finish your section. Correctly," she added, exasperated.

Anne turned first to Constable, then Sally, with a look that would freeze the East River.

"Look," Anne said, in an impatient tone that she alone could use with Constable. His temper was legendary; if anyone else tried that tone they'd be taken out of the agency on a stretcher. But it was rumored that Anne had the goods on Constable, was privy to some information so scandalous, so monumentally damaging that his career would be ruined if ever it got out. "I can type this stuff horizontal, or I can leave it vertical. I really don't give a good goddamn to tell you the truth. But my kid is sick, and I've gotta get home by midnight. So make up your mind."

"Leave them vertical," Constable said dismissively, and staggered back into his office.

"Constable, no," Sally pleaded, and the look she shot at Jill suggested that if Sally lost this argument the world would almost certainly end. She chased after him. "The whole presentation has been laid out horizontally. Your boards will stick out like a sore thumb—they'll look stupid—" She held a photocopy of the rest of the presentation out to Constable, unavoidably close to his face, then slapped it dramatically to draw his attention to neat rows of typing laid out across the white paper. Even from ten

**Her Latest Supporting Role**

paces away Jill could see that Sally's hands were shaking, her knuckles white with fury.

Constable took a clumsy half-step backward as though she'd slapped him. There was a brief, agonizing pause, and for a fraction of a second Jill almost thought he was going to give in. Anne would re-do all his pages in the same horizontal format that had been used for the rest of the presentation and in fifteen minutes Jill and the studio manager would be starting their blue and yellow stickering in earnest.

Then Constable's normally ruddy cheeks grew livid. He moved without warning, took one menacing step toward Sally until their faces were no more than a foot apart.

"You look here," he began quietly. But he was quiet for only a moment. His next declaration exploded from his lungs in an ego-fueled fire of rage. Jill saw Sally jerk quickly away from him, her reflexes taking over as though she'd touched an open flame. "*I'm* the big fucking kahuna around here," he screamed, his British-accented voice so loud, so horribly shrill that she was sure he could be heard throughout the agency's eleven floors. And there were still plenty of people around to hear Constable's tirade: lonely souls lurking the halls, small groups lounging in conference rooms as they took a collective breather from getting the agency ship-shape for the big meeting. "*I'm* the fucking man who makes it happen. I am the *goddamned President* of this bloody agency. How dare you sashay in here and *presume* to tell me how to make my bloody presentation tomorrow? How *dare* you? Who put *you* in charge?"

Their confrontation was a terrible thing to see, and yet it riveted Jill's attention. Words seemed to have failed Sally, and she stood there with her mouth hanging open, her weary eyes round with shock.

Finally it was Anne—impatient, no-nonsense Anne from Bay Ridge, Brooklyn, God bless her, Jill breathed to herself—who blew away the mushroom cloud of tension that had gathered

overhead. With a shrug and a put-upon little sigh she hoisted her
fleshy body up, steadying herself with both palms on the desk the
way an arthritic twice her age might do, and planted herself
squarely in the doorway of Constable's office.

"So I guess it's vertical," Anne said, to no one in particular.
Her voice was flat, even bored. Swiveling her head toward Jill she
added, "Give me five minutes, kiddo."

By three-thirty Thursday morning the boards were finished at
last. The Tellco team was down to a skeleton crew: those who
had anything to do with the pitch, whose presence was required
bright and early the next morning—whether presenter or peon—
were being put up at the Crowne Plaza two blocks away. Every
contingency had been planned for; God forbid the agency's bid to
keep Tellco from walking out the door should be sabotaged by a
problem on Metro North, or an accident on the FDR Drive.
Constable, as ever, was the lone exception. He had eschewed
accommodations that had been deemed good enough for the rest
of the team, and decamped to the relatively palatial splendor of
the Waldorf Astoria on the other side of town.

A few agonizing hours of tossing and turning in the
hermetically-sealed comfort of his hotel room had convinced
Graham that he'd be better off without any sleep at all; or at least
that was what he told Jill as they sat cross-legged on the War
Room floor, adorning the faces of forty-six foamcore boards with
navy blue and yellow beauty marks. Facing the big morning on a
surge of adrenaline would be immeasurably better than grabbing a
couple of hours of fitful shut-eye and then being caffeinated into
consciousness, only to spend the rest of the morning praying that
the coffee buzz would outlast the agency's long-winded appeal to
save the business. He didn't have to stand up and present,
anyhow. He was just supposed to sit there in the boardroom
with a gang of suits and creatives and media people and planners,
on display for all the Tellco clients to see and admire, a living,

**Her Latest Supporting Role**

breathing example of the tremendous human capital that Hambleton French had invested in their business.

"So you really think, in your heart of hearts, that we're going to lose?" Jill asked him, sliding another finished board onto the growing pile. She paused for a moment to watch Graham apply the little round stickers, so serious and painstaking that he might have been performing open heart surgery. First he lifted the sticker from its backing with the tip of an X-Acto blade, then lowered it perfectly onto the bullet point, smoothing it down oh-so-carefully with the blade's dull edge.

He looked up from his handiwork, and moved his mouth to speak. His gaze locked with Jill's for half a second and the words seemed to evaporate from his lips. She dissolved into a nervous little fit of coughing and bowed her head while Graham recovered himself.

"I really don't know anymore," he answered finally, with a dismayed laugh. "I know when the review was first announced I told you I was convinced that we'd lose the account. But I wasn't serious, then. I mean, it was one guy in the marketing department—their new Senior Vice-President—who instigated the review. Almost everyone else at Tellco felt pretty good about Hambleton French, the CEO included. We've been their agency for a lot of years, after all. We know their business, we have a relationship with their key trade partners and their sales force; it would be like breaking up a marriage! Plus, there was a healthy dose of the old Devil-you-know psychology working in our favor, and we leveraged it to the hilt with the clients."

"So do you still feel that way?"

Graham flattened his palms on the carpet and rocked from side to side while he considered his answer. "I wish I knew. I mean, Constable's a brilliant guy—I still get goose bumps watching the spots he wrote for the British Gas Board in the eighties—but I don't think he's much of a leader. He wasn't able to rally the troops early enough, especially the creatives. You probably heard that there was all this in-fighting about the strategy—" Jill nodded. "Well, Constable reversed his decision on that less than two weeks ago—against almost everyone else's recommendation—and all the campaigns that had been developed up to that point were scrapped. I'm sure you saw how much of Nick and Sandi's stuff was just thrown out. It was the same in every department. And the work that Constable and his henchmen presented during the run-through tonight didn't exactly blow anyone away.

"So, net-net, yes. I guess I think we're going to lose," Graham said finally, with an unhappy sigh. "I honestly do."

"Wow," Jill said soberly.

"Wow, indeed." He sat up straight and raised both hands to massage his temples. "What a year this is turning out to be."

They went back to sticking colored dots on the presentation boards, finishing the task in silence. Finally, all forty-six were complete. Jill gave a goofy little cheer as she heaved the very last one onto the stack between them, and Graham checked his watch.

"Four thirty," he said. "Only four and a half hours until show time. Are you going home?"

Jill shook her head. "There's no point. Sally's coming in at six o'clock to personally inspect all forty-six boards. There has to be someone available in case there's a typo—and you're looking at her."

"Good old Sally," Graham said, and rolled his eyes once more. "What a piece of work she is."

"I really can't say anything bad about her." Jill shrugged. "She's been nice to me, despite all the pressure she's under. Nick hates her though. He always refers to her as Sally the Stewardess—to her face, even. I once heard him tell Sandi that the only words that should come out of Sally's mouth in a professional capacity are 'Chicken or Beef?' Ouch." A quick, guilty laugh escaped from her mouth. "I feel kind of sorry for her,

**Her Latest Supporting Role**

too. She and Constable had a real screaming match at eleven o'clock. Over these stupid boards," she added, tapping the stack that lay between them on the floor. "I only caught the tail end of it, but he was really nasty to her."

Graham gave her a funny look. "Well, there's more there than meets the eye."

"Like what?"

With a guarded smile, he continued. "Well, I shouldn't be telling you this, but a lot of people know already, like pretty much the entire agency, actually. Sally Leyton and Constable had this really hot, super-secret affair a couple of years ago. I guess they carried on for six months or so without anyone getting wind of it—Sally was still married at the time—and then someone saw them leaving the Hilton together at lunchtime and the word spread. Stu Bateman came up with this really nasty nickname for her, 'Lay Down Sally.' Whenever she missed a Tellco meeting, he'd ask 'Where's Sally Lay-Down?' but he'd make it sound just close enough to her real name that the joke went over the clients' heads."

"That's wild," Jill said. "I'd heard rumors about Constable and his conquests. No names, though. I never would have guessed that Sally was one of them. I heard he was into men too—that's what Robin told me, but he's just loves to stir up trouble, so who knows? Sally seems so...I don't know, so Susie Sorority, really. I just can't picture her getting down with someone like Constable."

"You and me both."

"Is that the information that Anne uses to keep him in line?"

He shook his head. "You heard that, but not the Constable and Sally thing? Weird."

"I'm a little more plugged in to the Creative rumor mill," Jill explained. "The Petra and Robin factor."

"Well, the Sally thing is small potatoes...and ancient history. I think Anne has something much more sordid on Constable. I don't know, young boys maybe," he mused. "Or heroin. There's been lots of speculation, but no one really knows for sure. Except Anne I suppose, and she's not telling. It's the ultimate in job security."

"This place!" Jill said with an exasperated laugh.

Giddy from sleeplessness, she stole a sideways glance at Graham, then unfolded her crossed legs and let them flop down on the red carpet. She tapped Graham's knee with the tip of her sandal.

"Are you going back to the hotel?" she asked.

"No way, not for a while. If I go to sleep now I'll be a zombie in the morning." He shook his head, stifling a yawn that seemed to be forming in his throat. "Sally wants everyone here by seven, so I'll head back at six to shower and change. Why?"

"'Cause I'm really hungry, but no place is going to deliver at five a.m. You want to jump in a cab and go have breakfast at the Empire Diner? I can drop you at the hotel on the way back."

There was a moment of silence as Graham placed one bent finger on his chin—whether planned or not, this gesture covered the pale scar almost completely—and frowned.

Jill said, "What's wrong?"

"I'm just a little surprised, that's all." He gave her a perplexed look. "In a good way."

"What's that supposed to mean?"

"Well, it's seemed like you've been trying to avoid me for a couple of months now—ever since the day Tellco gave us our notice, as a matter of fact."

"Oh yeah?" Jill's brow edged guiltily upward.

"I thought maybe I'd said or done something to offend you, but for the life of me I didn't know what. Whenever I smiled at you, you would get the oddest expression on your face, almost like you were mortified to see me. It's a strange feeling, to run into someone in the halls all the time and have this voice inside you say, 'That person does not like me.'" Graham glanced down at the floor nervously, and his voice softened. "Because most

**Her Latest Supporting Role**

people do like, me...at least I think they do. And because I like you."

Jill coughed into her fist. "You didn't do anything to offend me, Graham. Far from it. It's just ..." she searched for the right words. "I don't know, it's been a weird couple of months for me. I've been under a lot of pressure—personally I mean, not just at work—and I'm sure it's affected the way I behaved toward everyone here, including you. I'm sorry. It was nothing personal."

She gave Graham a sad smile, suddenly feeling very guilty about the fact that she had avoided him, ever since that first night he'd asked her out. She couldn't even fall back on Jonathan Wunder as an excuse. The Graham Avoidance Plan had started way before she fell for Jonathan, with her vague and untested theory that it would be best to avoid an office romance. And the way Robin had repeatedly and blatantly tried to get them together had made it worse, really gotten her back up, forcing her stupid assertions that she could take care of her own love life, thank you very much. She had in fact done a horrible job taking care of her love life; falling so hard and unrequitedly for her lecturer showed much worse judgment than having an office fling.

And why was it that Robin's none-too-subtle attempts to bring them together had only made her more wary of Graham? She was starting to think she'd been mistaken about him, one-hundred-and-eighty-degrees wrong: as she'd been with almost everything else in her love life, at least since she'd moved to the city. Jill was only too aware of just how bad her track record with men was. Sunday night's little interlude with Jonathan Wunder had brought that even more sharply into focus, and the memory of it still pained her. Why was it that she nearly always wanted the men she couldn't, shouldn't have—and only them?

Graham looked straight at her, and pressed his hands together as though at a loss for words. Jill stared back. His eyes were so much darker, a more intense blue than her own: the color of a Van Gogh sky.

For a few seconds neither of them said anything. Graham's expression was sober, his mouth flat and still. Then she saw a slight twitch, no more than a tiny flicker that creased the pale skin around Graham's eyes as he began to chuckle. It started as a tiny puff of laughing breath, and then grew stronger and more uncontrolled, until the War Room seemed an echo chamber, with Graham's laughter reverberating off its four walls.

Jill waved her right arm helplessly, struggled to get his attention back.

"What are you laughing at?" she demanded, and, when she got no response, repeated herself, louder this time.

At last Graham's laughter subsided. He dabbed at his eyes with a plaid handkerchief that he'd unfurled from his back pocket, and smiled a little crazily at her.

"I'm sorry," he said, and let out one final, choked laugh. "It's not you Jill. I'm laughing at myself. Because I've spent the last two months thinking you hate my guts, and apparently for no good reason. Oh boy." He exhaled noisily, dabbed at his eyes again, then folded the handkerchief neatly and stuck it back into his pocket. "I think this business is getting to me. It really is. This summer I'm suffering from paranoid delusions. What's next? They're going to have to fit my office with rubber walls soon."

Jill said nothing as Graham checked his watch, then leapt to his feet. He extended a hand, which she took, and helped pull her to a standing position.

"We only have an hour and change until Sally wants you back. And the Empire Diner awaits!" he said, sweeping one arm out to let Jill lead the way.

The War Room's open door cast an eerie, solitary shaft of light on the tenth floor's darkened corridor. Jill and Graham walked swiftly through it and headed toward the elevator a couple of paces apart, as quiet as thieves.

**Her Latest Supporting Role**

# Chapter 12

At six-thirty the Tellco War Room was silent except for the soft sound of forty-six foamcore boards falling one at a time onto the red-carpeted floor. Sally Leyton—her pale brow furrowed, eyes bleary—carefully inspected every single one before they were to be taken upstairs and stacked on easels in the boardroom. That was just one of so many items that filled a five page checklist of final preparations for the big meeting. The Tellco pitch had been planned, worried over and second-guessed for weeks; now it was just two and a half hours until show time.

Alternately, Jill stood behind Sally, awaiting orders to redo any or perhaps all of the forty-six charts, and stepped into the hallway to look out for new arrivals. Sally flipped through the stack, and Jill saw the boards topple, their blue and yellow beauty marks winking brazenly at her. At least that was how it seemed, her mind screwed up from lack of sleep, her body caffeinated into twitchy alertness by four cups of the Empire Diner's high octane coffee.

Jill hovered, flicking the tips of her fingers against the doorway in a dull, mindless rhythm. She stared at Sally's back; the scarlet suit jacket was already off, draped over an empty chair, and two half moons of nervous perspiration were spreading out from her armpits, staining her cream silk blouse.

"Can I do anything for you, Sally?" Jill asked, fidgeting with the handle of the War Room door. "Do you want me to take any of the boards upstairs?"

Sally waved her hand for silence. Barely a minute later she let the forty-sixth board fall to the floor, and swiveled in her chair to face Jill. Sally's cheeks, normally round and rosy, sagged alarmingly—had they been like that last night, Jill wondered—and the thick crescents beneath her eyes appeared to have been drawn with purple eye shadow. Jill's pounding, over-caffeinated heart went out to her; the long hours and her battles with Constable had obviously taken their toll. In the harsh light of the War Room, she looked unnaturally pale, and a great deal older that her thirty-something years.

"You and the studio guys did a great job with the boards—they're perfect," Sally said. She stood up and joined Jill in the doorway, gave her a little arm-pat of gratitude. "And the yellow and blue dots look great, don't you think?"

Jill nodded noncommittally. "Do you have anything else for me to do?" Her heart was still pounding so fast. She wasn't in pain, though—far from it. Jill felt light-headed, hyper, rubbery enough to bounce off the War Room walls like a squash ball.

Sally picked up the checklist. Five pages of things that had to be accomplished before the clients arrived at nine o'clock, typed by Sally's assistant right before she took to her bed. Copies of the list could be found all over the agency, various tasks highlighted or circled with neon-hued markers by the people responsible for completing them. Fishing a pen from her skirt pocket, Sally crossed out one more line on the list, and Jill realized with a grateful sigh that at last things were coming together.

"Would you be an angel and take these boards upstairs?" Sally asked. "Just lay them against the wall at the front. We should wait for the other presenters to make sure they're in the right order before we stick them on the easels."

"Sure. No problem," said Jill.

"Great. I'm going to my office to put on my makeup. We don't want to scare Tellco away from Hambleton French, do we?" she asked with a grim laugh.

Jill acknowledged her with a twitchy smile.

"Everyone staying at the Crowne Plaza is supposed to be here by seven, and the caterers are coming to set up at eight. If you'd be a doll and look after them, make sure breakfast gets laid out nicely at the back of the room that would be super." Sally

**Her Latest Supporting Role**

scooped her jacket up, and disappeared out the door. "Tell everyone where I am, okay?" she shouted from somewhere down the hall.

It took four trips for Jill to ferry all the boards up to the boardroom. This is why I went to graduate school? she thought. The endless, wearying activity of the past three days, however, had wound up being a blessing, had prevented Jill from torturing herself over her troubled encounter with Jonathan Wunder. Still, what a relief to think that it would all be over soon, the agency's fate sealed one way or the other. Though lurking at the back of Jill's mind was the very real possibility that she might soon be unemployed; the rumor mill had speculated that if Tellco left the agency's production department would likely be halved. Freelancers would always be available to pick up the slack, and they weren't considered "headcount" by the bean-counters—making it an attractive cost-cutting measure.

The low bong sound of the elevator, announcing its arrival at the eleventh floor, echoed in the deserted hallway. Morning light poured through the east-facing windows. A diligent late-night cleaning crew and a couple of guys from Audio-Visual had miraculously transformed the dump-cum-boardroom she'd visited only a few hours before—littered with rotting food, air ripe with the smell of stale coffee and cigarette smoke—into a sparkling, high-tech conference room of the future, the horseshoe formation of oak veneer tables gleaming, the two dozen chairs aligned with military precision. The television monitors at the front had been wiped free of dust, and on their screens was the Hambleton French logo, reproduced in a hundred tiny squares as a video test pattern, its stylized white initials afloat in a scarlet sea, the letter F emerging from one limb of the H like Eve from Adam's rib.

"Hey there, Caffeine Queen!" Graham's smiling face appeared around the edge of the door, newly shaven, his black hair damp and glistening. "You surviving your all-nighter?"

Jill waved one trembling hand in greeting, and eased the last load of boards down against the wall. "Is it seven o'clock already?" she said. "How time flies when you're having –"

"The shakes?" Graham teased as he stepped inside. His lightweight navy suit was immaculate. With it he wore a crisp white shirt, its French cuffs twinkling with gold, and a polka dot tie, penny-sized discs of white on a background of Hambleton French red. Jill's gaze traveled downward. She could have put her lipstick on in the reflection from his just-shined shoes.

"Sorry—" he continued. "I interrupted you. Actually, I thought maybe you were going to say fun. After all, breakfast was fun." It sounded as much like a question as a statement. "Though you can't say I didn't warn you about that fourth cup of coffee," he added, full of humorous reproach.

"I feel fine, Graham," Jill insisted, though her hands probably would have registered a seven on the Richter scale. "Besides, Sally said that as soon as the presentation begins I can go home. Take the day off. The caffeine will have worn off by then, and I'll be ready for some serious pillow time."

"Well, don't sleep through the party. There's a post-pitch bash planned for one o'clock. We're taking over McNeal's for the entire afternoon, on H-F's dime. The old work-hard-play-hard thing's kind of a tradition here, so it should get pretty wild."

"Oh yeah, Sally mentioned it to me. I'll be there."

Jill could hear the low murmur of conversation outside the door. A couple of people streaked past, no doubt making sure that a few more items got crossed off Sally's all-important list. She and Graham emerged from the boardroom to find a small battalion of people gathered in the north-east corner, near Sally's office. The arriving elevator sounded again, and four more people appeared. They hurried to join in the Tellco rally.

The time that Sally had invested in putting on her makeup was time well spent. Gone were the circles that had seemed indelibly etched below her eyes, and she had powdered and

**Her Latest Supporting Role**

plumped and rouged her cheeks so competently that she now appeared the retouched picture of health. Chanel No. 5 wafted from her, and she had slipped back into her scarlet jacket, the ensemble now both blindingly cheerful and appropriately businesslike.

Sally's copy of the checklist was attached to a clipboard. Nick was right: her pose was reminiscent of an extremely competent stewardess. She drew a circle around various tasks as she doled them out. The bustling little crew that surrounded her was made up of all types of H-F-ers: there were secretaries; two Account Executives who worked on Tellco; Graham's counterpart—the Management Supe on Girls' Toys; Nick (sans Sandi, who was still probably sleeping off their string of all-nighters); and several A/V guys. Also hovering in the hallway were a few of the presenters: the Media Director, Suzanne, *très chic* in a little black suit despite the fact that temperatures had topped eighty all week; and Bateman and Brinder, the Tellco Co-Executive Creative Directors, surly and loafing in a corner, sucking coffee from matching Starbucks cups.

Jill glanced at her watch: seven-fifteen, less than two hours to go. The caterers weren't coming until eight—she had more than enough time to tackle another item on Sally's list, maybe even two. She saw Sally whisper something to one of the A/V guys and he hurried away, walkie-talkie raised officiously to his lips.

As more people joined or left the crowd, Sally flipped a new page to the top of her clipboard. Yet another list: she looked at it and then scanned the group, crossed something out with her pen and then repeated this whole series of actions again and again. Jill saw Sally's eyes meet Graham's, then slash another item off the list. Immediately she understood: Sally was taking attendance, just like a teacher, though at least she'd spared everyone the indignity of having their names called out and answering "Here."

Her head nodded as she silently ran down the list one last time, and then her brow furrowed with concern.

"Where's Constable?" she demanded of nobody in particular.

A low murmur went through the gathering. No one had seen him since the final run-through the night before.

"Did anyone see him at the hotel this morning?" Sally demanded, her pep squad voice now straining upward with alarm.

"How the fuck could we?" Stu Bateman replied sourly, and in doing so sprayed tiny droplets of coffee all over someone's secretary. "He stayed at the Waldorf, didn't he, while the rest of us were billeted at the fucking Crowne Plaza."

"That's right," Sally muttered softly, her tone distracted. She disappeared into her office, and the conversation died down. Everyone strained to listen as Sally addressed Anne, Constable's secretary, on the speakerphone.

"Call his cell, try the hotel if he's not picking up, and then call me right back. On my cell," Sally demanded before hanging up

Gently, Graham touched Jill's elbow. When she turned he shot her a concerned look. Jill tipped her head in the direction of the clock. "He's only a little late," she mouthed, still hopeful.

At exactly seven-thirty, Sally's cell phone bleated loudly. She snatched it from her jacket pocket and flipped it open before the first ring had finished.

"Not there? Well he's certainly not here! Where the hell could he be?" Sally's words echoed through the hallway, which had constrained itself into silence once more: her voice, usually cheerful and efficient-sounding, telegraphed panic. "Jesus God, the clients will be here in an hour. Call me if you hear from him," she said, and then there was a loud crack as she slammed her cell down on the desk.

Sally stalked out of her office and halted in front of the group, still clutching her clipboard to her chest as if for dear life.

"Graham, you've got to go over to the Waldorf right now and see if you can find Constable. They tried ringing his room and there was no answer, but he could have been in the shower or something. The front desk told Anne that he hasn't checked out yet."

"Did they go into his room?" Graham asked.

"They wouldn't do it, but maybe you can persuade the manager. Slip him some money if you have to. Nick?" she called out.

The hallway was flooded with morning sun. To say that all this light was unflattering to Nick Wheeler would be a triumph of understatement. Jill's boss stood slightly away from the rest of the group, looking pissed-off and rumpled and positively cadaverous—his skin with a dingy pallor, hair dirty and matted-looking, his squinting eyes rimmed with red as he nursed a Styrofoam cup of coffee.

"Uh-huh," he grunted, barely audible.

"Could you please go to the hotel with Graham? You can split up when you get there, to save time. Check the lobby, the restaurant, the barbershop. You know what Constable's like, he refuses to wear a watch, so he might not even know just how late it is."

"Christ, Sally, can't you send someone else?"

"The presenters have to get ready," she pleaded, "and I need everyone else to help with the last-minute preparations. We still have to set up all the toys in the reception area and decorate the elevators."

Nick rolled his eyes in disgust, then tapped one finger to his forehead in a mock salute that was decidedly mean-spirited.

"Go team," he said sarcastically, and disappeared down the hallway, trailing a few steps behind Graham.

Jill checked her watch: eight-fifteen. She was developing a nasty case of carpet burn on her bare knees as she knelt in the eleventh-floor reception area, helping Graham's secretary and two Account Executives who worked for Graham put the

**185**

finishing touches on a massive display of Tellco products. It had completely taken over a ten-by-ten foot space at the end of the elevator bank, this wildly-colored exhibition of every single toy, every last game in Tellco's fall lineup.

Some items had been salvaged from the shelves of creative teams who'd worked on Tellco commercials, or been taken from Sally's office, which had—in her three years of running the account—turned into a virtual toy museum. Molded plastic action figures defended the frontier of her desk, while a multi-ethnic brood of Rainbow Babies spilled from her sofa like so many abused and abandoned children. As for the rest of the items in the Tellco line—games that weren't advertised, or, as often happened, the agency sample had been appropriated for someone's kid—they were all on display too. A vast array of toys and games had been purchased by a trio of Account Executives dispatched to Toys'R Us on a thousand dollar shopping mission. As Jill pulled herself to her feet—brushing the itchy red fibers from her bare knees—she let out a long low whistle of amazement. The four of them had artfully ordered nearly a hundred playthings on and around a long conference table, the quantity and arrangement of these items so imposing, so majestic: they had turned the reception area into a towering shrine to Tellco Toys and Games.

As she admired their handiwork, Jill's still-buzzing mind tripped back to the scene outside Sally's office. She wondered whether Constable had arrived, and if not, whether his mysterious no-show had yet given Sally an aneurism. The Tellco client entourage would be arriving in less than half an hour, and according to Graham they were absolute fanatics about punctuality. It would be the kiss of death for Hambleton French's chances if they had to stall for time while their missing President was located.

**Her Latest Supporting Role**

The elevator sounded. *Bong:* another new arrival in Toyland. Robin Devlin strode silently, reverently toward the Tellco shrine, and slapped one hand over his mouth in amazement.

"Well, well, well, what have we here?" he marveled. "I feel like I've died and gone to K-Mart."

Jill replied with a jittery smile, and a sweep of her arm.

"Care to say a prayer for H-F's salvation at the altar of toys and games?"

Robin grimaced. "Ever since this debacle began I've been praying—that I'll hang onto my job."

"I know what you mean," Jill said cautiously. She returned to the table, and shifted the Glow In The Dark Space Alien a couple of inches to the right. One of the Account Executives murmured his approval.

"So it's all ready for the big event?" Robin asked. "I came in early just to peek at everything before show time." He glanced at his watch, then regarded Jill with concern. "You look a little tired, sweet pea. What time did you get here?"

"Get here? Ha! I never left."

Robin looked impressed. "You were here all night? How come?"

"Sally needed someone to hang out and do some things for her, so I volunteered—I Heart Overtime! A bunch of people pulled all-nighters to get the place ready for this morning. Graham was here most of the night, for one."

Robin gave her an accusing look. "You and Graham...together all night in an empty office. How convenient..."

"Would you cut it out, Robin? How many times do I have to tell you that nothing's going on with him? We went out for breakfast this morning and I told him that I was..." she faltered, searching for an appropriate word. "Sort of...unavailable right now."

"Ah, yes. Mister Wunder-ful," he said, his tone ironic. "You know, Jill, you should give this whole thing some thought."

"What's that supposed to mean?"

"Just that someone like Graham doesn't come along every day. Someone real," he added cryptically.

"Well, if it makes you feel any better, I told Graham that I'd have dinner with him tomorrow night—just as friends—to celebrate the end of the pitch. Just friends," she repeated, reading Robin's mind.

He shrugged and took a step back to get a better look at the Tellco shrine. Jill and the others deferred to his skill as an art director, and he fussed with the arrangement of the Rainbow Babies for a few minutes, attempting to give them a more heroic role in the display.

"Hey," Jill said when Robin moved away from the table, finally satisfied. "I forgot to tell you about the little drama this morning. Constable went AWOL. When he didn't show up Sally sent Graham and Nick over to the Waldorf. I went to help the caterers at eight and there was no word yet. For all I know he might still be missing."

"You know he's terribly unpunctual."

"Sure, sure," Jill said. "But this isn't just any old meeting. I thought poor Sally was going to lose it. She and Constable had this big fight late last night, and now this happens." Jill sighed. "Around midnight she was definitely a woman on the verge of a nervous breakdown."

Graham's Account Exec, Lee, had disappeared while Robin was finessing their arrangement of toys. Now she was back, admiring his work.

"I just saw Sally outside the boardroom," Lee said. "They found Constable. He was at the hotel."

"Thank God!" Jill breathed a happy sigh. "What happened to him?"

"Well, I asked." A puzzled look crossed Lee's face. "But no one really knows. Or at least they're not saying. Stu Bateman was bugging Sally for details, but all she would tell him was that

**Her Latest Supporting Role**

Graham and Nick had found Constable, and that they'd be back with him by eight-forty."

"He was supposed to be here at seven," Jill explained to Robin. "That's weird."

The elevator sounded again—that low bong noise that vibrated all around them—and then, like an actor dutifully responding to his cue, Constable appeared from between its parting metal doors, trailing Graham and Nick in his wake.

With just a casual glance, anyone would have said that it was the same old Constable who stepped out of the elevator. Maybe he even looked better than usual: the wooly mad scientist brows seemed somehow to have been tamed, and he was dressed for business (a rare sight, Constable in a smart Prince of Wales check suit—and a tie! albeit one with a large wet stain on one side). But Jill stared. She couldn't help it: after observing his fight with Sally, and then hearing about his early-morning disappearance she'd developed this strange curiosity about Constable, a mixture of fear and fascination. And as he blasted past her and the others on his way to the boardroom, she noticed that something was not quite right. For one thing, Constable's always-flushed cheeks were absolutely colorless. In the bright light of the eleventh floor reception area he looked alarmingly corpse-like. And his limp had become so pronounced that it was way past comical, like someone's cruel and vulgar imitation of a spastic. When he disappeared down the hallway, Constable appeared to be cradling his left wrist as though it was injured.

Jill's eyes met Graham's as he strode by, keeping a few safe paces between himself and their wildly lurching President. Nick skulked after them both, his mood obviously no better than when he'd departed. Jill tipped her head questioningly, and Graham shot her a look that seemed to say *don't ask*, then headed straight for the boardroom.

At nine-oh-five the news spread around the agency. The Tellco clients had arrived, the pitch had begun. Everyone who worked on the eleventh floor went about their tasks with the silent and exaggerated movements of a mime troupe, anxious not to disturb the proceedings behind the big double doors.

Robin stood next to her desk and watched Jill take her purse from the bottom drawer.

"I feel like I could sleep for a year," she told him. After three and a half hours the caffeine buzz had finally worn off and she was crashing hard. "I don't think bed has ever looked so good."

Robin nodded kindly. "Go home, go to sleep. You've earned it," he said. "But I do hope we see you this afternoon at McNeal's. It should be quite the party. Petra's going too—and of course your new pal Graham Ferguson..."

Jill gave him yet another dirty look.

"And Jill, since you're so tight with Graham maybe you could find out exactly what happened to our fearless leader to make him so late this morning. Enquiring minds want to know!" he crowed. "Of course there are all sorts of nasty rumors flying around the agency, but I want the real dirt."

"Rumors like what?" Her voice rose with interest as she remembered Constable's dramatic entrance.

"Well," Robin said, and as he leaned over her desk he lowered his voice. "You know how his wrist was all bandaged up?" That detail had escaped her notice, but it explained why he was cradling his left hand as he flew past. "Someone heard—I don't know how, maybe they got it from Nick who has a mega-mouth. Anyway, they heard that Graham and Nick had to bribe the hotel staff to let them into Constable's room. And what did they find there but our esteemed President and Chief Creative Officer: buck naked, handcuffed to the bed posts, and—this is my favorite part—gagged with his very expensive Hermès tie so that he couldn't call out for help."

"Oh my God!" Jill said. "That can't be true, can it?"

**Her Latest Supporting Role**

"Well..." Robin said quietly. "Stranger things have been known to occur. I mean, there are so many angles to consider. You know that a while back he broke off his secret-affair-that-the-entire-agency-knew-about with Sally. Maybe she flipped out and wanted revenge."

"And she would screw up the pitch to do it? Risk her job?" Jill shook her head. "I seriously doubt that."

"Ah yes, but you said that she sent Graham and Nick to the hotel, right? Rather than make the trip herself."

Jill considered this for a moment, but it was just too implausible. Sally wasn't crazy, just a little frayed at the edges from too much work, and the pressure of trying to save the business.

"I can't believe you could think that's what happened, Robin," she said dismissively. "You'll have to do better than that."

"All right then." He demurred with a wicked smile. "The Sally thing was just a thought. But the bit about Constable being tied up and gagged is bona-fide agency scuttlebutt. I did not make that up. What probably happened is that he paid someone to tie him up last night, and then they nicked his wallet and left him there. Constable has some, well, unusual preferences. Or so I've heard," he added enigmatically.

Jill looked thoughtful as she stood up from her desk. Intrigued. "Maybe it was someone from another agency, trying to seduce and then sabotage Constable so that HFA would blow the pitch," she suggested "Some ad agency Mata Hari."

"Or Mata Harry," Robin countered with a sly grin.

# Chapter 13

Jill opened her eyes very slowly. The bedroom was dark and chilly. Her sheer curtains billowed softly above the whirring air conditioner, and a filigree of maple leaves moved outside the window. For a moment she felt confused, disoriented. She'd gone to sleep in daylight and awakened in darkness—a strange reversal, something she hadn't done in years. Jill leaned across the bed and looked for her alarm clock. The glow in the dark face informed her that it was well past ten p.m. She'd slept the clock around and then some; apparently the week leading up to the Tellco pitch had taken a greater toll than she'd realized. The bedding was strangely unmussed, too—none of the usual twisted sheets or pillows tossed onto the floor. It looked as if she'd fallen into a dead sleep, undisturbed and motionless.

She eased herself up into a sitting position, her head feeling dense as a sandbag. Her eyes, too, felt strange, the lids leaden and vaguely crusty. She got out of bed and opened the front door of her apartment, only to encounter a wave of heat and humidity that hit her like a smack. But putting on her ratty old bathrobe made Jill feel much better, and she shuffled back to bed, leaving the door open in an attempt to warm up her chilly studio.

Only when she was beneath the covers again did things start to crystallize in Jill's mind. Past ten o'clock: without a doubt she had missed the post-pitch bash at McNeal's. There was no point even stopping by; the hardiest of partiers, a group that almost certainly included Petra and Robin, would have moved on to another, cooler bar by now, while the casualties would have been loaded into cabs and sent home to sleep it off. Jill rolled over and sighed. She was sorry she'd missed the festivities, but with any luck the pitch had been a stunning success and she'd last at the agency long enough to take part in a future bash.

Then, as the brain fog slowly lifted, Jill became conscious of the fact that the McNeal's party wasn't all she'd missed. It was Thursday night, the night of Novel Into Film Since 1965, the class at which they were supposed to hand in their final essays. With a start Jill realized that her magnum opus on The English Patient was still in the manila envelope, rolled into a fat tube and sticking insistently out of her handbag. Class had ended more than an hour before and so—according to the rules, anyway—her paper was officially overdue. And while she didn't doubt for a second that Jonathan Wunder would cut her some slack, grant her an extension without even needing to hear whatever excuse (real or imagined) she could drum up, she was loath to ask. From now on Jill wanted to keep the whole situation with Jonathan as above-board as possible. Or even better, never see him again; humiliation still clouded her senses, and though she was trying hard to let it go, that was easier said than done. When she considered the events of Sunday night—and she had done so again and again over the past four days—Jill was convinced that she'd made a very big mistake. The only way to purge herself of the memory forever was to act like nothing had happened between them.

By the time she dressed and walked over to NYU the building's doors were locked tight. Her plan—now thwarted—had been to slip her essay under the door of his temporary office, with a note explaining why she'd missed class, a very short and business-like apology. But it was too late for that. Jill fingered the crinkly tube of paper absently while she considered her options.

Washington Square faced the building's steps, and it was silent, empty, dappled with leafy shadows. A few hunched students filed noiselessly out of the business school library: eleven o'clock, closing time. Jill frowned, wondering what she should do. She could return first thing in the morning, when the college reopened, and slip it under the door then. But as she passed the tube of paper from one hand to the other Jill realized just how much she wanted to get rid of it. Turn in the essay, pass the course, complete her degree and move on. It was what Monika would do, would insist upon.

Jonathan Wunder's apartment lay twenty blocks or so northeast of the campus. It was late, but she'd just woken up, and wouldn't be able to get back to sleep for a while anyhow. If she could slip the essay into his mail slot he'd receive it in the morning, and that barely qualified as overdue. She'd done it before. Just last October her Film Criticism professor had given the class a midnight deadline, and at twelve-oh-five she'd run into a half-dozen breathless classmates, jamming papers into the hands of his laughing doorman.

She hovered on the sidewalk outside the brownstone where Jonathan Wunder lived. A low wrought iron gate separated the pavement from the path to his doorway; the door to his apartment sat beneath high steps leading up to the parlor floor. Jill eased the gate open; it made a low sigh, barely audible as she slipped through and made her way to his door. Then she could access his mail slot, shove her paper through and be rid of the paper, of him, of summer school: done with this annoying and humiliating chapter of her life.

She pulled the envelope from her purse and made one last attempt to smooth out its wrinkly curve before crouching down to slip the essay through the narrow brass flap at the bottom of his door.

"Damn," Jill breathed aloud after a full twenty seconds spent trying to cram the too-thick envelope into the mail slot. She slipped the essay out of the envelope and tried again. The paper was too wide to fit unless Jill folded it in half, and once she'd done that it was too thick to slip through the mailbox's narrow opening. This mail slot was clearly more fashionable than functional, for her paper was no larger than an average issue of *The New Yorker*.

**Her Latest Supporting Role**

She pulled a green felt-tip pen from her purse and, in the dim light from the street scratched a note on the envelope. The explanation was simple and truthful, its tone studiously non committal: Sorry this is a bit late. Pulled an all-nighter at work and missed class. Thanks, Jill Barber. Then, crouching again in front of the apartment, Jill flattened the envelope out as well as she could, and propped it against the door.

She moved to stand up but something hard and wobbly was under her right foot and she staggered back, trying to regain her balance. But to no avail: with a shocked little *oof!* she lost her footing entirely, and landed flat on her ass.

She'd just placed her palms at her sides, ready to push herself back onto her feet and make a mad dash back to the sidewalk when without warning the apartment door swung open. Jonathan stood in the doorway, silhouetted by bright light. His features were barely visible until he took a step forward and stood directly in front of Jill. Then she watched his dark eyes narrow with surprise.

"Jill? What are you doing here?"

Mortified, she scrambled gracelessly to her feet, and rubbed her palms clean on the seat of her flowered shorts.

"I, uh..." She faltered, started over. "I missed class, and by the time I got to the college to hand in my essay the doors were locked." Jill paused to study the uncertain frown on Jonathan's lips, then added: "I hadn't asked you for an extension, and I didn't want to get marked down for being late."

"Oh," he said quietly. He hadn't seen the message she'd scrawled across the envelope: it lay at his feet. "Oh."

Behind him, she could see a sliver of his all-too-familiar living room. The memory of her last visit came flooding back—just four days had passed but in the wake of the nervous exhaustion brought on by the pitch it seemed like weeks, even months ago. Five minutes earlier she'd been sure that it would be so easy to slip her essay into the mailbox without incident or detection, and then disappear into the night with everything behind her, the entire awful sequence of events that had defined and destroyed her summer: the encounter with Czerny that had landed her back in summer school; her serendipitous acquaintance with Jonathan Wunder; and the way her feelings for him had so unexpectedly surged and then had ebbed just as quickly, marred by Jill's own self-doubt, and her doubts about him. She felt a hard, tight knot growing in her stomach as the encounter flashed through her mind. The way she had climbed into his lap—and his reaction, that look of bewilderment, speechless surprise. Now she looked at his dark eyes, the puzzled frown at the corners of his mouth. It appeared that she had a knack for surprising him.

She heard someone pad across the living room floor, and a voice—unusually quiet, but still inescapably familiar—called out. And then Robin Devlin appeared in the foyer behind him. The look on his face confirmed the exact moment he realized that the mystery visitor was Jill. He blinked once, hard, and for the very first time since they'd met it seemed that Robin was at a loss for words.

"Robin?" Jill stared straight at him. He stood motionless a few paces behind Jonathan. The first thing she noticed was that his feet were bare, but otherwise he looked very much the same as he always did, the eternal refugee from the pages of *Details* Magazine in his neat khaki shorts and blindingly purple shirt.

And then her gaze moved from Robin back to Jonathan, and she gave him the exact same toe-to-head appraisal. With her senses made more acute by the surprise—no, shock—of finding them together in Jonathan's apartment Jill saw for the first time just how many outward similarities there were between them. Jonathan too was fashionably, immaculately dressed. Then there was the apartment straight out of an interior design magazine, and of course the air of someone who spent a little too much time worrying about the enhancement and preservation of his own good looks.

**Her Latest Supporting Role**

All of it came together in Jill's mind with such sudden force that she literally felt a burst inside her head, worse than feeling her ears pop, much more unpleasant and unexpected. Context was everything: at last she saw with excruciating clarity what had pitched people into doubt—first Anya and Monika, herself only much later—and had finally destroyed her feelings for him. Vienna Boys Choir indeed: Anya had been right all along.

She snatched her purse up and took a step backwards. Then she turned and bolted through the gate to the sidewalk. About halfway down the block Jill slowed a little, and finally at the corner of Third Avenue she paused. Her heart was pounding and her breath came in labored, choking gasps. Clutching one hand to her waist—she'd developed a stitch in her side—she swallowed the warm night air in painful gulps.

When Jill looked in the direction of Jonathan's building she was alarmed to see Robin running along the sidewalk, his advance now and then obscured by shadows from the brownstones lining the block. Even from a distance she could tell that he'd taken a moment to put his shoes on. It was pointless trying to get away from him; Robin was taller, much quicker on his feet and Jill was already completely winded. She wiped a film of perspiration from her nose and forehead, then crossed her arms in front her chest.

"I really don't feel like talking to you right now, Robin," she announced as he came to a halt beside her. The harshness of her voice surprised even Jill, and she watched Robin flinch so very slightly when she said his name. "Sorry I interrupted." Her hands dropped to her sides and she walked away, turning right on Third and scanning the traffic for a cab.

"Hang on, Jill." His tone was so serious—so, well, un-Robin. She heard his footsteps behind her and then felt him lay one hand on her bare elbow. Her reflexes took over and she shrank from his touch.

"I have to get home." She directed her comment at no one in particular as one arm flailed through the air, though no available taxis were in sight.

"You can spare five minutes." Robin actually sounded pissed off. Before Jill even knew what was happening he had seized her hand out of the air, and linked her arm with his in a vise-like grip. Then he practically dragged her for twenty or thirty paces along the sidewalk and into a dreary, nearly-empty diner.

At the back of the restaurant he stopped and, releasing her arm, commanded her to take a seat at the corner table. Jill answered him with a look of cold fury before sliding onto the vinyl banquette.

"You said five minutes, Robin." She removed her watch and laid it on the table between them. "Go."

"Jill." He looked right into her eyes for at least five seconds, something he'd never done before. His hyperactive gaze was always on the move, as though afraid he'd miss out on something. What she read in his eyes and thin face, that mixture of pity and remorse, curdled her stomach. She dropped her own gaze to the table, and as she studied its glittery Formica surface with inordinate interest Jill felt the burning in her cheeks and forehead. Never before had she felt like such a likely candidate for spontaneous combustion—so entirely, unstoppably flammable. If he laid a hand on her again she was sure that she'd burst into flames, and—like those people that seemed to interest the *National Enquirer* so much—end up as a smoldering pile of ashes and tooth fillings and earrings on the banquette of the Ideal Coffee Shop.

It was Jill who broke the unnerving silence.

"I thought you were my friend," she said finally, trying—and failing—to keep her voice smooth and controlled. A golf ball-sized clot of anger was forming in her throat, making speech all but impossible, and tears inevitable. Her gaze met Robin's once

**Her Latest Supporting Role**

more, and she felt a hot trickle slide down beside her nose, then bump over the ridge of her open mouth.

Robin jutted out his lower lip and let a long, exasperated stream of breath blow over his face. He shook his head as if he too couldn't believe the way things had turned out.

"I am your friend, Jill."

"Then how do you explain—" her voice caught again. She took a deep breath to recover. "Explain tonight. And what was that little farce at the museum on Sunday afternoon, Mister 'I don't think he's gay, but I wouldn't be upset if he were'?"

Robin waved one hand in silent protest. "You're jumping to conclusions, Jill."

"Oh. Okay," she countered abruptly. Her arms snapped closed across her chest once again. "So why don't you tell me what really went on, then?"

"All right." Robin gave her a doleful smile that sent her eyeballs swimming. Hot with shame but unable to stop the flow of tears, Jill dabbed at her face with a napkin as he began to speak.

"First of all, I am your friend. And what I told you about Jonathan on Sunday, well, I meant it. I really didn't know he was gay. The whole 'gay-dar' thing—" Robin stopped and sighed as he watched Jill attend to her leaking eyes. "I mean, I may make it sound like a fucking party trick but there really are two standard responses I get when I meet a gay man—whether he's completely out, a total closet case, or anywhere in between. Usually they look back at me with, shall we say, intense interest, recognizing a fellow-traveler and all that. Or else they completely avoid my gaze and try to get away as quickly as they can. The second response is more typical closet-case behavior: like they're afraid I'll blow the whistle. But your boy Jonathan did neither. He didn't seem to be avoiding me; he just didn't seem to care much for me, one way or the other. When I met him on Sunday I kind of got the sense that he was dismissing me as some silly fag friend of yours. Studied indifference, you know what I mean. It threw me off the scent."

Jill wadded up a couple of soggy napkins and stuffed them into the pocket of her shorts. While she did this a panda-eyed waitress arrived with drinks that Robin had ordered. Jill mumbled her thanks and, awash in self-pity, emptied a half-dozen sugars into her coffee.

"So he fooled you on Sunday," she said, sounding unconvinced. Then she lowered her head to take a noisy sip. "What about tonight?"

"Tonight." Robin paused, and wrung out his teabag thoughtfully. "You missed the party at McNeal's."

"I went to bed at ten a.m. and didn't wake up until a couple of hours ago. Don't change the subject."

"I'm not. It's just that things there broke up around nine, and by then I had quite a nice buzz on and was looking for a party. Anyhow, I grabbed this nice young fag from the media department and dragged him off to the Boy Bar to see what was going on. I was there for an hour or two—my little pal went home at ten but I stuck around—when who should walk through the door but your friend the Boy Wonder. It's dark as hell in there, but I knew right away it was him."

"He walked into a gay bar. On purpose." Jill set her coffee cup down so hard that it rattled on the saucer. "Was he alone?"

"Oh yes, all alone. But when he hit the bar and got a good look at yours truly I thought those big brown eyes were going to pop out of their sockets. He was busted wide open, and he knew it. And since he knew I was your friend and would rat him out—like, right away—he thought he might as well come clean about the whole situation."

Jill's mouth fell open. "So did he?"

Robin nodded solemnly. "We went to his place around eleven, just to talk. He only lives a couple of blocks from the bar.

**Her Latest Supporting Role**

And that is what we were doing when you showed up. He seemed to have a lot on his mind."

"Like?"

"Like—the plot sickens. I don't know how much I should tell you, Jill. I mean, it's pretty personal stuff, and I promised him I'd keep it *entre nous*. But your friend Jonathan is one messed-up individual. I think he's been playing some major head games with you: and with himself. I'm still not sure he intended to lead you on as much as he seems to have. But just let me say that I don't think his appearance at the Boy Bar was a first-time thing. Like I don't think he was just curious, if you know what I mean."

Jill scrupulously avoided Robin's glance for at least a full minute while she absorbed his words. Steam rose from her cup, clouding her vision, beading like dew on her mascara-clotted lashes.

Robin broke the silence. "Are you okay, Jill?" he asked softly.

"Jesus," she said, her voice low and toneless. "I fucked him, Robin."

He gasped. "You didn't!"

Jill raised her head and blinked very slowly. "I did. On Sunday night. I attacked him after his little family barbeque. We went there after the museum, after you gave me the 'all-clear' sign, Mister 'It's time to put the Ice Princess in the microwave'." Her words stung with reproach. "Mister 'Go for it.'"

"Oh my God, Jill." Robin's mouth was so often twisted into an ironic or reproachful grin, but now it just hung open. For a moment he didn't say anything. In fact, he barely seemed to be breathing. When at last he recovered Robin added in a small, pained voice, "I really, truly did not know."

Angry tears sprung to Jill's eyes again, and she reached for a fresh wad of napkins from the greasy dispenser.

"The ironic thing," she told him with a sharp laugh that almost broke into a sob, "is that I did know. I mean, I didn't, but I did. Something about him wasn't quite right from the very beginning.

When we first met and I went to that party at his apartment he seemed so keen on me. And I was worried that he was some sleazy teacher putting the moves on me—believe it or not, it's happened before. The whole scene kind of gave me the creeps." The image of Gabor Czerny and his dim little office momentarily chafed at her consciousness. "Anyhow, that's not important. I didn't exactly blow Jonathan off but I certainly kept him at arm's length, for a while, anyhow. That's probably what he was looking for all along. Someone he could go out with, a girl he could conveniently parade in front of his friends and family without having a real relationship. Too bad I fell for him after all, and spoiled his plans," she added with a bitter laugh.

Robin looked across the table at her. "I feel awful about all this, Jill." He bit his lower lip. "I really did want to help you, you know, and now I feel like I pushed you off a cliff instead."

"It's not your fault, Robin." She exhaled deeply, felt herself begin to calm down. "I shouldn't have made it sound like it was. Not your fault, probably not Jonathan's either. It was just—oh, I don't know—circumstances. I guess. But I feel so horribly weird about the whole thing now. Like a complete idiot. The signs were there all along, and I refused to get a clue."

He appeared a little happier after Jill said this. A bit of the old Robin was visible again. He raised one eyebrow archly, and fixed Jill with a curious look.

"So my dear, what happens next? He knows you know—you ran away and I went after you, so he must."

Jill frowned and took a deep breath as she considered the situation.

"I don't know, Robin," she said. "I must admit that I don't have a lot of experience in this sort of thing. Your guess is as good as mine."

"I think he'll try and talk to you. The expression on your face when you saw me in his apartment, they way you looked us both

**Her Latest Supporting Role**

over—you were one unhappy camper. I think he'll try to salve his guilty feelings. Maybe not right away, but at some point."

Jill gave a little shudder, and blew her nose yet again. "Later rather than sooner, I hope. If ever. You know, I really don't want to see him for a while. I don't need to be reminded of my mistake just so he can make himself feel better. And—no offense, Robin—but you need to forget about it too. Not a word about this to anyone, please. Not even Petra."

"I know you don't believe it, Jill, but I really can be the soul of discretion," he insisted. "And I am truly, truly sorry about this whole mess. I feel awful about it." Robin sighed as he fished a handful of singles from his pocket and dropped them on top of the check. "Not that it's supposed to make you feel better or anything, but he fooled me too, and that doesn't happen often."

By the time she got back to her apartment it was almost one. She'd ignored her cell phone for hours and saw she'd missed a call at twelve-forty. Who would call so late tonight except Jonathan? Robin maybe, checking up on her, making sure she hadn't had a change of heart on the way home and thrown herself in front of the M15 bus. Jill stood paralyzed in the blackness of her apartment and stared hard at the phone, afraid to listen to the message and afraid not to.

Then she couldn't bear it any longer. She heard a whirr of static, the crackle of a bad connection before Monika's disembodied voice filled her ears, unconscionably cheerful and larger than life.

"Where are you?" she called out. "It's almost seven in Paris, so why aren't you answering?" Monika tsk-tsked noisily. "If you're still partying up a storm then have fun, but if you get this tonight give me a call." A rapid sequence of fifteen digits followed.

Jill switched on the light and then replayed the message, scratching the numbers onto the back of a bill with a dying Sharpie.

"It's me. Jill." Her voice quivered so very slightly.

"Hey! I called you not fifteen minutes ago."

"I'm fine. You don't sound so good, though. Your voice sounds kind of weird. Are you sick or something?"

"Oh, no. Not exactly. I'm just not feeling too great tonight. I, um—" Jill faltered, unsure of how to explain the night's events. After a pause she continued. "I've had, well, kind of a bad shock, I guess."

Monika's voice grew low and serious. "What's up?"

"Oh, remember what you told me about Jonathan Wunder?" Jill began in her normal voice, but hearing Monika's tone of concern set her off. Her throat began to constrict and the words became muffled, barely audible before they even reached her tongue.

"Oh fuck! Fuck fuck fuck! Oh, poor Jill. I'm so, so sorry." Monika shouted when the story was finally over.

Jill was crying now, not even trying to hold it back. Her voice shook and fat warm tears ran down her face. "I fell for a man who had absolutely no interest in me—except maybe as a way to keep his family off his back. And I let him reel me in, just like that. I feel so –" a sob choked the last of her words.

"Poor, poor Jill," Monika's voice was in turns booth soothing and admonishing. "I've been worrying about you ever since I left. Sometimes you are innocent to a fault."

**Her Latest Supporting Role**

# Chapter 14

Jill felt truly awful. The sinking feeling that had plagued her all day long was slowly giving way to an entirely different state.

She looked down to the half-eaten cherry cheesecake, now a sticky disgusting mess on her kitchen counter. There were fragments of cracker crust everywhere—on the floor, the counter, some had traveled even farther and scattered across the stainless steel sink. *You could at least have used a plate*, she thought woefully, and pushed the uneaten cheesecake out of her sight and back into the box, which she then forced into an already-overflowing bag of trash beneath the sink. Her stomach felt huge and bloated. She had a sudden anguished urge to stick her finger down her throat, only that method didn't work anymore: not since tenth grade, when it had worked a little too well. Jill imagined herself in the familiar about-to-be-sick position, bent double over the toilet. If she tried that now her throat would just ache as though someone had tried to strangle her.

Her cell rang. Probably Monika again: she'd been checking in almost hourly since the morning.

"Yes? Hello?" Jill heard the familiar crackle of dead air.

"It's me." Monika's voice echoed across the line. "Were you asleep? You sound terrible."

"I feel terrible," Jill said. "In the ten minutes since I got home from work I managed to scarf down half a cheesecake."

"Hmm. What kind?"

Jill reached across the kitchen for a dishtowel, and pushed some of the scattered crumbs toward the sink.

"Sara Lee Deluxe Cherry Cheesecake. Preferred three to one by bulimics everywhere," she added sourly. Jill turned on the tap and watched the crumbs swirl before disappearing down the drain with a loud sucking noise.

"If you just ate half a cheesecake then I guess you aren't feeling much better after all."

"I was only going to eat one tiny piece," Jill explained, "just to cheer myself up." With that she felt a lump of self-pity growing at the back of her throat, and words failed her.

A shower, she reasoned, might make her feel better, and Jill was letting the hot water pound against her body when she thought she heard her phone ring. Faint, almost drowned out by the *sst sst* noise and muffled by the steam. Although she didn't especially feel like talking to anyone—except maybe Monika—to Jill the sound of a ringing phone was irresistible. She groped for a towel and ran to pick up.

"Hello?"

"Jill?" A male voice: familiar but not immediately recognizable. Not Jonathan Wunder, calling to tell her that the whole thing was just a practical joke gone wrong, an awful misunderstanding.

"Yes?" Jill looked down and saw a puddle developing around her feet. She clenched the cell between her shoulder and head, and attempted to rearrange the towel into a slightly more effective position. Still the pool of water grew until, exasperated, she finally let the towel drop onto the floor and stomped until it was soggy.

"Jill, it's Graham." Graham Ferguson? "How are you? Have you recovered from the pitch, Caffeine Queen? You missed a good time at McNeal's yesterday," he added cheerfully.

"Huh? Oh, yeah. I was still catching up on my sleep from the night before, and I slept right through the party," she confessed. "Pathetic, right?"

"Not at all, not at all. Hey, I missed you at the office. I was at a TV shoot most of the day. Did you get my e-mails, or the message I left you?"

Her mind was still fogged up from the shower. She hadn't gotten any messages from Graham. Or had she? Jill had found it

**Her Latest Supporting Role**

impossible to concentrate all day, had barely even bothered to turn on her computer. At one point she'd answered the phone only to become inexplicably mute as soon as the receiver reached her mouth.

"Oh, I just got in and jumped into the shower," she ad-libbed. "Haven't checked my messages in a while."

"You haven't forgotten about tonight, have you?" he chided amiably.

"Tonight..." Jill repeated, stalling.

"Peking Duck in Chinatown," Graham said. "Our little I-survived-Hellco celebration dinner."

Friday night! She'd been in a trance all day, suffering through the aftershock of her confrontations with Jonathan and Robin. Jill had completely forgotten she'd agreed to have dinner with Graham, a promise made at the Empire Diner in a giddy-from-sleeplessness state. Then she clutched her bare abdomen and remembered the cheesecake. She still felt dizzy and ill: too much sugar always gave her this weird buzz which started well but ended very badly. And sick with guilt, too, because she'd turned Graham down time and again. Their middle of the night conversation in the War Room suggested that he'd developed quite a complex about it.

"Of course I haven't forgotten. Sorry. There's still a lot of water in my ears." What a lame excuse. Still, Graham seemed to have bought it. His voice had all of its usual liveliness, and—in a triumph of guilt over good sense—she agreed to meet him downtown in a couple of hours.

Jill swept the crumbs from the kitchen floor and mopped up the water. It looked normal again; all the telltale signs were gone. This was the way she liked things: smooth, bare, unmarked surfaces, even if behind its orderly facade the shelves were disorganized, the garbage overflowing, the refrigerator filled to bursting with rotting fruit. Jill took out a glass and poured herself a large, cold drink of water. Her stomach was already beginning to feel better, emptier. Maybe.

She debated what to wear for a little while. The weather had been hot and humid, typical of August in New York. But the sun would be going down soon and when the air cooled its dampness would feel less heavy on her clothes and skin, this day would stop weighing her down.

They were meeting for dinner at Shanghainese, which wasn't your usual Chinatown restaurant: no comfortingly tacky jumble of institutional white dishes and those colorful paper placemats decorated with pictures and descriptions of all sorts of strange alcoholic concoctions, Rob Roys and Angel's Kisses and Mai-Tais. It referred to its trendy cuisine as *Nouvelle Chinoise*, and boasted a taciturn Asian Manager-cum-Maitre D' who, according to *New York* Magazine dressed exclusively in Miyake and spoke with an unmistakable New York accent. The chef, whose name was Soong—just Soong, he seemed to aspire to the one-name fame enjoyed by Constable—was forever popping up in the city's most style-conscious magazines and newspapers, where a photograph of his puckish, tea-colored face shared space with rapturous descriptions of his way with bok choy and dried black fungus.

Jill pulled her sleeveless black dress from its hanger. Straight and knee-length, with a deep U-shaped back that made it impossible to wear a bra, it was the most chic thing she owned, probably the only thing in her wardrobe that was worthy of dinner at Shanghainese. Jill wanted to look nice but not too attractive, so maybe the low back was overkill. She needed to keep her distance from Graham—and maybe from all men—for a while.

By the time she'd rallied—dried her hair, painted a hot-pink smile on her lips—it was too late to make the trek downtown by subway. As the cab inched down Second she sat by the window and looked out at people strolling along the sidewalk in the fading light, or sipping drinks and laughing, enjoying life on the patios of a

**Her Latest Supporting Role**

dozen cafés and restaurants. Dressing up usually improved Jill's spirits; this time though it was having the opposite effect. She grasped the hem of her dress, which was riding up, a little higher with each tiny movement of her bare legs, and yanked it down as far as it would go. Then she rested her forehead against the cab's window, feeling deflated.

She walked into the arctic chill of Shanghainese at eight thirty on the dot, and caught sight of Graham, already seated about halfway back. An excellent table, she thought. He must have given the Miyake-d Maitre D'—who was headed her way in a cloud of Hugo Boss for Men—a pretty good tip. The restaurant was full, packed wall-to-wall with the usual young style junkies and curious trendies, and Jill felt a quick wave of relief, glad she'd dressed the part.

Graham rose from his seat as she approached. He was wearing a pale linen jacket with a blue shirt, the kind of Euro-cool look she would never in a million years have imagined him in, and his dark hair was slicked back. He looked happy, and eager, and absolutely gorgeous.

"Hello, Graham." Jill took a deep breath, and smiled.

"Hello there yourself. You look great," he told her as they sat down. "What a beautiful dress."

"Thanks. You look nice too," Jill said. She added a little more quietly: "And P.S. I don't think they'll even seat anyone who doesn't."

"You're probably right," he said, with a knowing lift of his dark eyebrows. "Check out this crowd. It looks like half of them stepped straight out of an Armani ad. But to be fair, I've heard that the food here is amazing." Graham smiled warmly. "I hope you're hungry."

The waiter took their drink orders and glided away in the direction of the bar. A square glass vase sat on the table between them, filled with speckled orange lilies. Jill touched one of the cool petals idly with her fingers as Graham continued to comment knowledgeably on the restaurant's menu.

"So," he said as the waiter set their drinks before them. "A toast."

Jill blanched, remembering another toast only weeks before. When she reached for the Cosmo her hand trembled with a sudden palsy.

Graham watched her with concern. "Whoa!" he said. "You okay? I was going to toast the fact that we both survived the Tellco pitch, but maybe you haven't totally recovered yet. Did you get enough sleep last night?" Jill had hidden her dark circles with makeup, but there was nothing she could do about the network of red lines that stretched across her eyes.

"I'm fine," she assured him. She wrapped her fingers tightly around the stem before touching her glass to his. "And speaking of the Tellco pitch, I haven't seen you since you and Nick and Constable dashed past on your way to the boardroom." Her voice rose with modest curiosity. "So what was going on there? There are all kinds of wild rumors floating around the agency. I must have heard five or six versions by now, but I wanted to get the straight dope from you."

"Just what did you hear, exactly?" Graham feigned disinterest, but Jill could tell he was dying to know. "I was out of the office all day, so I've been totally out of the loop. It's not exactly the kind of thing you email about."

"Well," Jill began cautiously. "They are all variations on the same theme, really. Which is that you found Constable tied to a bed in his room at the Waldorf."

"Oh yeah?" Graham said, more out of encouragement than agreement.

"But there are a lot of different versions of the story. Like some say he was found facing up, others say face down. Someone claims that you found him, well..." she paused before blurting it out, "smeared with shit. I also heard—I forget who

**Her Latest Supporting Role**

told me this—that Constable had been gagged with his own Hermès necktie. So Graham –" Jill gazed at him questioningly over the rim of her glass. "What's fact and what's fiction?"

"Sorry, Jill." Graham rested his hands on the tablecloth and smiled enigmatically. Long fingers interlaced, they looked like the hands of an artist, graceful and surprisingly expressive. It was the first time Jill had noticed.

"Oh, come on. Don't be like that."

"It's not that I don't want to tell you, Jill. Believe me, it would make a great story. But I really can't say anything. It would be, shall we say, a very poor career choice on my part."

"God, Graham. Did Constable threaten to fire you if you said anything?"

"No, no, no," he insisted, throwing up his hands in a kind of 'I surrender' motion. "But he's the one person in our office who can make you or break you. So I don't really want to wind up on his shit list."

"Okay, got it," Jill relented. She took a long, stomach-settling swallow from her glass. As she surveyed Shanghainese's smartly dressed patrons she could feel Graham's eyes on her, studying the curve of her jaw and the slope of her bare neck. She shivered slightly—in New York the more pricey the restaurant, the more over-air-conditioned it was—and deftly changed the subject.

"So Graham, you can tell me this much without risking your job," Jill said in a confidential tone. "Are we going to keep Tellco? You were there in the room. Did the pitch bomb? Today Nick told me that he thinks Tellco is as good as gone."

There was a short pause and then, unexpectedly, Graham laughed.

"Ah, Nick." He gave her a sly smile. "Jill, do you know the painter Ad Reinhardt?"

She shook her head.

"How about Mark Rothko?"

Puzzled, Jill said yes.

"Well, I've been working at Hambleton French long enough to know that talking to Nick Wheeler is like looking at a certain group of Mark Rothko paintings. At first you look at them and they're almost all black, hardly any color to speak of, just vast expanses of darkness. But then you look at it more closely and you realize that there are shades of black, shades and textures."

"Uh huh..." Jill murmured, not quite getting his drift.

"The point being this: Nick is hands down the most negative guy at the agency, and you have to know that to be able to discern the difference between things that are truly terrible and things that Nick just says are terrible."

"The shades of black?"

"Exactly. I think that Nick was feeding you his typical response, all doom and gloom, when things really aren't as bad as all that. He wasn't in the room, you know. Constable, for all the trouble we had getting him there on time, was truly brilliant during the presentation. Sam Brinder had them mesmerized and Stu Bateman even managed to convey relative sobriety."

"So it went well?" Jill asked with a mixture of surprise and relief.

Graham smiled and downed the last of his martini, almost gasping with satisfaction. "Extremely well," he assured her. "I mean, we won't know for sure until after the Labor Day weekend. But I'm cautiously optimistic."

"That's really great. I was beginning to dread looking for another job. You know that if we lose Tellco probably half my department will get pink-slipped. I think that's what's been bothering Nick."

"Well, he's been on his way out for a long time anyhow. Confidentially, the word around the agency is that Constable's wanted to get rid of Nick and put Sandi in charge for a while, but the circumstances have never been quite right."

"So if we lose Tellco, I guess Constable will get rid of Nick, huh?"

**Her Latest Supporting Role**

"You'd think so, wouldn't you?" he said cryptically.

Jill deferred to Graham when the waiter came to take their order. She felt her stomach wobble when he mentioned the Peking Duck—Shanghainese's signature dish—and fought a small wave of nausea as he made his selection from the wine list. Graham was so intent on the ordering process he seemed not to notice her discomfort, the perspiration on her forehead despite the blasting A/C. And that was just fine with Jill.

"So..." she ventured as the waiter receded from view.

"So?" echoed Graham with a silly smile.

"So Graham, what's your story? You know something about me—at least, the Robin Devlin version of my life—" When she said this Graham looked abashed, his cover blown. "But I don't know much at all about you. Where are you from?"

"Just the facts, right?" he said playfully.

"That's a good place to start."

"Well," he began, settling back in his chair a little. "I spent a lot of my childhood overseas: mostly in Africa and the Caribbean: Senegal, Grenada, Haiti. We split our time between developing countries and the DC suburbs—Bethesda, Maryland, to be specific. I was a diplo-brat," he explained. "My father's been with the State Department his whole career. When I was twelve my parents sent me back to the States to go to prep school. After that I went to Princeton, and then got my first job in advertising, at RMB&P."

"Foster's Lager, right?" recalled Jill.

"Good memory!" Graham sounded impressed. "I stayed there for two years, and then I was lucky to get a job at Hambleton French, where I've been for, oh, almost five years now. I started out on the Breeder's Choice Pet Food business...a real dog of an assignment."

"Ha ha ha," Jill said, her tone appropriate for such a bad joke.

Graham grinned guiltily and continued. "It was sort of a pay-your-dues thing. After that I worked on Bank of New York for a couple of years. Eighteen months ago I got promoted and moved onto Tellco, which is where I hope to stay, at least unless I can get an international transfer. That's what I really want to do, go to one of HFA's European offices. But until the fate of Tellco Toys is decided I guess my future is one big question mark."

"Even if Tellco stays put, I'm really not sure how long I'll last," Jill admitted. "Aside from the whole glorified secretary thing, which is starting to get on my nerves, I just don't know that I'm ruthless enough to get ahead in advertising. Don't get me wrong, I still think it's a very cool business; I just don't think my skin's thick enough, if you know what I mean."

"Nonsense," Graham said sternly. "People aren't really ruthless. It's just that this business attracts a lot of very different—and very strong—personalities. From buttoned-up business types a thousand times stuffier than me to computer geeks and wannabe Warhols. And everyone's trying to assert themselves all at once, make themselves heard."

"That's for sure."

"You just have to find something you like to do, that gives you a buzz and makes you happy to go to work in the morning, and find someone good to work for. The rest comes naturally." He smiled encouragingly at her. "I've heard great things about you, and not just from Robin either. Sandi thinks you're a total rock star, and though he'd probably never admit it, I'm sure that Nick values you too. If things pan out with Tellco you might want to talk to them about an Assistant Producer position. Throw your name into the hat for the next opening." He smiled appealingly at her. "If you want to, that is."

"That's funny. Petra Marks gave me the exact same advice, just last week."

Graham shifted a little in his seat, and moved ever so slightly toward her. "So you're pretty good friends with Petra, huh?" he asked.

**Her Latest Supporting Role**

"Sure. She and Robin are kind of a matched set, aren't they? She's a doll."

"Absolutely, I like her a lot. Very talented writer." He lowered his voice. "A bit too much of this, though," he added, pressing a finger to one nostril and sniffing slightly.

"Really?" Jill asked, genuinely surprised. "Well, she's never offered me any."

"She was one of the ones involved when there was a drug bust in the creative department about three years ago. Huge scandal!"

"A drug bust?" Jill's open mouth widened.

"Hard to believe, right? Or maybe it isn't. A narc came into the agency posing as the new guy in the mail room. A junior art director was selling the stuff, and he actually went to jail. A couple of other people got fired, but Petra got off with just a warning. She was very lucky—or had friends in high places."

"I guess."

Their waiter, all stiff hair gel and elegant efficiency, poured red wine into their glasses. Graham raised his swiftly and Jill followed suit.

"Well congratulations, Jill. We made it," he said, and looked pointedly at her over the wine glasses.

Jill thanked him quietly, embarrassed by Graham's lavish attention. She lowered her gaze down into the glass as she drank.

Jill forced one last sliver of duck into her mouth, and chewed with little enthusiasm. It all tasted the same to her by the end of the meal—the duck, the rice, sauce and pancakes—and she had sloshed it down her throat with liberal swallows of red wine, just trying to get through dinner without letting Graham know that anything was wrong. On top of her growing physical discomfort, she was consumed by guilt. Graham was charming company, he was really making an effort, but everything that had happened in the past week had sapped all of her positive energy—physical and

**215**

mental; at this point she was just going through the motions. With a shudder of dismay Jill wondered if she could ever fall for a truly nice guy, one who wasn't completely self-absorbed, or burdened with a thousand hang-ups, or a downright fraud: someone like Graham. She kept thinking about Jonathan Wunder, she couldn't help it. Jill saw herself standing on his doorstep the night before; the image was so clear, and so relentless, like a video loop from hell that played back again and again.

Graham set down his chopsticks and looked across to Jill.

She put on a faint smile for his benefit. "Wow. That was a great dinner. I'm absolutely stuffed. I was a total piglet."

"You didn't eat that much," Graham countered, unfailingly polite, though in fact he was right. For the first ten minutes she'd more or less just flung the food around on her plate, finally managing to slide a few mouthfuls down her throat. That was the great thing about chopsticks: through sheer lack of coordination, she rarely got much to eat.

"You don't want anything else? I hear they have this amazing green tea *crème brulée*."

"Oh God no, thanks. I couldn't possibly eat one more thing," Jill said, though in her mind she added: *just a large Alka-Seltzer, please.*

He reached for the bottle to offer Jill a refill but she declined. They'd both had quite a bit to drink but it hadn't affected Graham, just made him more pleasant, if that was even possible. Jill on the other hand felt strange, not drunk but light headed, almost separated from her body. It was quarter to eleven, not so late, but still she wanted to go home and crawl into her own bed, just forget about everything and fall asleep.

Graham motioned for the bill, and paid quickly. Jill looked at the total unobtrusively, a curious glance. It was an awful lot—going to these places of the moment was never cheap—and idly wondered how much money Graham made. Her forehead

**Her Latest Supporting Role**

knotted with concern. Had he spent this much taking out any other cute young ad girls, or was he really, seriously interested in her?

They stepped out of the restaurant and into the warm night air. Jill scanned the traffic for a cab, but she couldn't see one that was free.

"Let me drop you home. I bet we can find a cab over on Lafayette," he said, and placed a gentle hand on her bare arm, guiding her in the right direction.

"But I'm out of your way. You live on the Upper West, right? Why don't I just get another cab, and save you the trouble?"

"It's no trouble at all, Jill. Please," he insisted, and with one cool hand against her bare elbow Graham led her away from the bright neon glow of Shanghainese.

They didn't say much as the cab drove uptown along busy streets. Friday night revelers packed the sidewalk cafés in Jill's neighborhood.

"Turn right. The brownstone with the black steps," she said as they approached her building. The cab pulled up to the curb and Jill and Graham sat there for a few seconds in awkward silence.

"I'm really happy you could make it tonight—" Graham began, but before he could say more Jill cut him off.

"Thank you so much for dinner, Graham." She stared straight ahead at a line of parked cars. "That restaurant was fantastic. And I apologize if I haven't been the best company. It just hasn't been a terrific day."

"Don't apologize, please," he insisted, a little too urgently for her comfort. "You were great. Really...great."

The silence felt oppressive. Jill swiveled her head a few degrees in Graham's direction. He was looking toward her—though not at her, exactly—with an expression on his pale face that made her feel at once both very alluring, and very odd. It was a nice confidence-booster to have a guy like Graham stare at her this way, especially so soon after her most recent romantic disaster. It made Jill feel special. It also made her very, very nervous.

"Do you want to come in for coffee or something?" Jill stammered. She regretted the offer the moment the words were out of her mouth. Her stomach was still churning, and as indebted as she felt to Graham for his hospitality and good-natured company that evening, it probably wasn't such a hot idea to encourage him. She knew better than anyone the perils of leading someone on. "You probably want to get straight home, though," she added hopefully.

Graham's hand shot out of his breast pocket, clutching his wallet.

"Sure, I'll pop in for a coffee, if it's no trouble." He quickly shoved a ten dollar bill at the driver; it was as though he was worried that if he took too long Jill might change her mind.

"Of course it's no trouble. I was going to have one myself," she lied.

Graham stood examining the spines of all the paperbacks in Jill's bookcase with exaggerated interest while she struggled with the coffee maker. Ground coffee scattered across the clean countertop as she tried to spoon it into the paper filter cone—how much did she have to drink? She stared down at her hands, which were trembling slightly, and at last managed to get the whole operation going.

"Shall I put on some music?" he asked when he saw her stereo, which was wedged into the bottom shelf. She murmured her assent and in what seemed like only seconds Bryan Ferry's mournful crooning filled the room.

Jill gave a little sigh of satisfaction when she heard the faint gurgle of hot water, saw the vapor rising like breath against the inside of the pot. "Won't be long," she called out to Graham, who was now hunched on her flowered couch, hands on his

**Her Latest Supporting Role**

knees. He turned his head toward Jill and gave her a funny half-smile.

The cups and spoons rattled noisily on their saucers as Jill carried the coffee into the living room. She set them down on the table—without spilling a drop, to her surprise and relief—and took a seat next to Graham. She had so little furniture in her dollhouse of an apartment there was actually no other option.

"Thanks," he said, lifting the steaming cup to his lips.

"Not at all." Jill raised a hand to her temple. She felt very odd for a moment, again like she was standing outside herself. Then she moved her hand to rest on the arm of the sofa: only it didn't really feel like her hand. Finally she picked up her cup with both hands and was relieved to feel it, smooth and almost painfully hot to the touch. Then it wasn't just her hands that were warmed; the heat seemed to spread to her face and she felt a strange and unpleasant flush.

Graham set his cup down on the table and drew a little closer to Jill. He gently brought his dark blue eyes up to meet hers.

"I really had fun tonight," he said. His tone was all earnest sincerity, but the faint tracings of a smile flickered across his face. "I've wanted to..." He seemed at a loss for words. This was a rare occurrence among polished client-service types like Graham, and it unnerved her.

One hand muffled a nervous cough and then he started over. "I've wanted to get to know you for quite a while now, but things never seemed quite right, you know?" His eyes sent out a brief appeal and Jill nodded. "You're...you're very –"

With the coffee still warm on his lips and Bryan Ferry's throbbing vocals urging him on Graham leaned over, and to Jill's shock planted a long and surprisingly soulful kiss on her unready mouth.

His eyes were closed while he kissed her but Graham must have felt the tension in Jill's response, for as he drew his head back he surveyed her features with a mixture of wonder and concern.

"Hey, are you okay?" he asked, his voice soft and low and not entirely sure of itself. "Did I do something wrong?"

Jill shook her head. "It's not what you did."

"Then what is it? What's the matter? The look on your face is...I don't know, tragic. Like you lost your best friend." He breathed deeply, noisily. "Can I help?"

"Graham, you are such a nice guy, you know?"

His face creased with dismay. "Uh-oh," he said. "Why do I think this is going to be something I don't want to hear?"

"It's not you, Graham, it's me. I've—how can I put this?" Jill stared down at the floor for a second, carefully choosing her words. "I've had, uh, kind of a romantic setback recently. Very recently." Jill let out a pained little fragment of a laugh. "I've been doing a lot of soul-searching, and I've come to a few not-very-flattering conclusions about myself."

"Oh?" he said slowly, looking perplexed and a little pained. "Like?"

"Like when it comes to romance I think I'm basically a Groucho Marxist."

For a moment he didn't say anything but the look on his face was utter confusion, like she'd opened her mouth and babbled something in Thai or Finnish or Portuguese.

"A Groucho Marxist," he echoed.

"Yeah." Jill grinned nervously, trying to turn the whole crazy thing into a joke because she feared she was hurting him. "You know that famous quote of his that goes, 'I wouldn't want to belong to any club that would have me as a member'? That's me. Where my relationships with men are concerned I want what I can't have, and ruin what I can. I'm not proud of it and I want to change, but—well, no buts about it, really, that's just the way it is right now. I'm sorry to lay all this heavy stuff on you, Graham. But I don't want to take advantage of your...your good nature, so

**Her Latest Supporting Role**

I might as well be honest with you." She saw the slightly crumpled look on his face and added, "I guess a little self-knowledge is a dangerous thing too, huh?"

"You know Jill, Robin and I were together on a shoot today. I mentioned to him that we were having dinner tonight."

Jill felt a small chest-thump of panic when she heard Robin's name. "Oh yeah?"

"Yeah. He told me that you've had kind of a rough summer—"

She bristled, and folded her arms tightly across her chest. "Robin Devlin should mind his own business, if he really wants to help me through my so-called 'rough summer'."

"No, Jill, listen. He was genuinely concerned about you. You know," Graham drew close to her, and Jill had a sinking feeling that he was going to kiss her again. But he didn't: instead his voice grew quiet, soothing. "I've had kind of a romantic setback myself. Not too long before we first met—remember, you were with Robin in that bar? I was engaged to a woman that I thought was the love of my life. And without any warning whatsoever she left me, took off with some guy she'd only just met, and not even a month before the wedding."

"I'm so sorry, Graham," Jill breathed.

"Thanks. Thanks a lot." He paused. "Anyhow, in the days and weeks that followed I tortured myself over it. Why hadn't I noticed that she was unhappy? How could she leave me for someone she hardly knew? What had I done wrong? I was really beating myself up over it, losing all kinds of sleep and screwing up badly at work, too."

"So what happened?"

"Well..." Graham took a deep breath. "A friend of mine gave me the name of this great therapist, an older man who had helped him through some rough spots. I started seeing this guy every week, and pretty soon—I know this sounds like something out of a cheesy TV movie—" he cautioned, "I had a breakthrough.

I realized that obsessing about the past was pretty much keeping me from any kind of present or future happiness. I was expending all of my energy on something that I couldn't change, instead of using it to have a positive effect on the rest of my life."

"And once you realized that you were fine?"

"More or less. I mean, it wasn't quite so simple or quick as I've made it sound. But I stopped seeing the doctor a couple of weeks ago, anyhow."

Jill loosened her arms from across her chest. "That's funny. My best friend has been telling me the same thing for weeks. Not specifically about my rough summer, but more about life in general: that I've been dwelling on stupid things that don't matter instead of getting my act together. Mind you, her standards are almost unattainably high."

Graham laid one hand on top of Jill's encouragingly. "A friend from my old agency—someone who actually reminds me a lot of Robin—has a saying that kind of sums it up perfectly," he said. "'Regrets are for dinner parties,' this guy told me. 'Move on'."

"Regrets are for dinner parties," Jill echoed. She laughed quietly, and then the laugh turned into a hiccup which turned again into something even less pleasant. When Graham looked at her, she read the concern on his face.

"Jill, are you all right?"

She rose unsteadily from the couch, and could feel something inside her moving in the very same direction.

"Will you excuse me, please?" Jill said in a halting voice, and made her way quickly toward the bathroom. She banged against one wall with her hip, and turned sharply into the doorway. There was barely enough time for her to drop to her knees on the cold tiled floor and bend over the bowl. The water was a dark pool that reflected her head in silhouette against a shaft of light from the hallway. And then it happened: a great bitter stream of vomit rushed from her churning stomach, and she choked it up, the taste sour in her aching throat and mouth as

**Her Latest Supporting Role**

she pressed her bare arms down on the toilet seat and convulsed again and again.

Jill leaned back for a moment in the darkened bathroom, arms still resting on the seat. Her face and chest were covered in sweat. Weakly turning her head Jill heard rapid footsteps, and Graham appeared in the doorway.

"My God. Jill, are you okay?" He went down on one knee, and was almost beside her on the floor.

She pulled back from the toilet a little, and woozily pulled the handle. Her building was old, and faulty pipes sang out as the bowl's contents swirled away.

"Could you just leave me alone for a second?" she pleaded, her voice shaky. "Just for a second." Graham rose and backed out of the bathroom. Then, with legs that felt like twin Slinkys Jill stood, reached over to switch on the light, and shut the bathroom door.

She filled the glass with water and rinsed out her mouth. But still she didn't feel right, didn't feel like it was over, and a few seconds later she was hit by another wave of violent sickness, and dropped to her knees once more.

When Jill was through she flushed the toilet again, twice, and sat back on the bathroom floor, legs bent, head resting on her knees, her bare back flat against the cool tiled surface of the wall. Her face was still damp, and she felt exhausted, completely drained, like her stomach had just run a marathon and dragged the rest of her body along out of spite. Her throat ached, and there was a horrible sour taste in her mouth. She could smell it too, almost enough to make her sick a third time.

After perhaps five minutes down on the floor, Jill hauled herself up to her feet. She put one shaking arm on the towel bar—it felt like she'd just been kicked, her stomach ached so much—spat into the sink, filled her mouth and spat again, and finally, brushed her teeth with unusual violence.

When she emerged Graham was waiting just outside the door, an extremely worried look marring his handsome features.

"Jill –" he began, but she cut him right off.

"I am so embarrassed, Graham." Jill's voice was flat and hollow, barely audible even to her. "And I'm so sorry, but I think it might be better if you go home now." She cast her eyes downward as she moved, very slowly, toward the living room, flattening one hand against the wall here and there to steady herself. "I've really screwed up your evening, haven't I?"

Graham followed her down the hall, then stood and watched nervously as Jill slumped down on the sofa.

"Of course not." He shook his head a little too insistently. "I had a great time, really. You know that I did. But listen," Graham said, and crouched down, so his eyes were level with hers. "I'm worried about you. Are you going to be all right? Can I get you anything? Maybe I should stick around for a while, in case you're feeling worse. Or need to go to the Emergency Room."

Jill shook her head slowly, eyes half-closed. "No, I'll be okay. And I am so, so sorry," she repeated weakly. "I think I'm coming down with something. Maybe I should just go to bed."

"I'll go if you want me to," Graham said, and Jill nodded, her eyelids already slumping. "But before I leave, do you want a glass of water, or some aspirin?" He bolted to the kitchen. Jill let her eyes shut for a moment, and felt a gray fuzziness swelling inside her head. She heard the sound of water running, and it grew fainter and more echoing until it was like an ocean's roar inside a seashell.

"Jill?" She made an effort to open her eyes and saw Graham standing over her with a glass of water. "You still don't look too well. Why don't I help you to your bed?"

"How romantic," Jill said with self-pitying irony as Graham took her hand and helped her to her feet. She considered the bizarre turn that the evening had taken, and laughed silently at her own bitter humor. But it didn't seem that Graham had heard

**Her Latest Supporting Role**

her, his concentration was so intense as he helped keep Jill from swaying on her bare feet. At what point since arriving home had she lost her sandals? Jill hadn't a clue. With Graham's arm solid around her back she eased herself down onto a corner of her bed.

"Right," Graham flicked off the lamp. His voice was low and soothing in the semi-darkness, his outline traced into her consciousness by light flowing in from the kitchen. "If you're really sure you're going to be OK I guess I'll take off."

"I'm so sorry, Graham," she repeated. "You can't imagine how awful I feel."

"Shhh," he said quietly, and bent over her like he was soothing a small child. "Lie down. Just get some sleep. You'll feel much better in the morning."

"Sorry," Jill murmured again, sinking backward on her bed.

Graham leaned down and kissed her gently on the forehead. With one hand, he smoothed the damp, ruffled hair "Good night, Jill," Graham whispered, and backed out of the apartment, pulling the door closed behind him.

# Chapter 15

The insistent pounding on Jill's front door synced almost perfectly with the throbbing inside her head. Someone was playing a bongo drum there, its surface stretched across the vast, aching grayness between her ears. When her eyes finally worked their way open the first thing she saw was her clock: nine-thirty. She rolled over with a groan, and sat up on the bed. The black dress which had appeared so immaculate and chic only twelve hours before was now a sorry, wrinkled mess. The once-fine linen bunched uncomfortably under her arms, its hem had climbed nearly to Jill's waist, and the small satin bow beneath its scoop neck was now crumpled and wretched-looking.

She fell back on the bed and lay there for a while, hoping that if she ignored the sound whoever it was might give up and go away. One, two minutes passed: no such luck. There was a buzzer for each apartment, but the building's front door had apparently been left open by another of the other tenants, allowing access to her door one flight up from the street: thus the pounding.

After five minutes, Jill gave up on ignoring the noise—it was making her headache worse, much worse—and hauled herself off the bed. Freeing her body from the wrinkly black dress, she slipped her ratty bathrobe on and struggled to the door.

She pulled it open and squinted past the chain, from shock as much as from the hallway's bright light. Jonathan Wunder stood before her, cradling his right hand with the left as though it was injured.

"Oh," she said after a moment's pause. Her voice was painfully dry and scratchy, as though she hadn't spoken for weeks.

She'd thought that if anyone would arrive on her doorstep that Saturday morning it would be Graham: concerned for her well-being, checking up on her. Jill's memories of the previous night were vague, especially the part after she disappeared into the bathroom. The pounding headache interfered with her memory, though her breath—sour with a pungent mixture of vomit and Crest—was an inescapable reminder that things had not gone particularly well. But instead she found herself face to face with Jonathan Wunder, who looked artfully disheveled in a worn white golf shirt and ancient Levi's with holes in both knees.

When he saw the look that she gave him, Jonathan's brown eyes took on a wounded expression. Jill felt a sudden stab as she remembered how the appealing crinkle at their corners had once made her helpless with desire. Before she knew.

"I need to talk to you." His words brought Jill painfully back to the present.

"Oh?  Well, I don't need to talk to you," she rasped, still unable to locate her real voice. She tried to pull the door closed but Jonathan placed one hand firmly on the knob and gripped it as though he meant business.

"Jill, come on," he pleaded.  "I want to talk to you about the other night.  Please take the chain off and let me in."

"No offense, Jonathan, but I don't really feel like listening.  As you may have noticed—" How could he not?  Her breath was strong enough to wilt flowers, and when she blinked Jill could feel globs of makeup that had lodged in the inner corners of her eyes. "I'm not feeling too hot today.  And if you'd just let go of the fucking door," she added, briefly losing her cool, "I'd like to get back to bed."

Jonathan Wunder stared at her, hard.

"I can't go.  Not until I explain."

"Look, Jonathan. I don't want to hear it, okay? I just want to get on with my life and forget that we ever knew each other. I'm not mad at you, I'm not bitter—" Despite Graham's little pep-talk the night before this wasn't entirely true, but what Jill really wanted was to get Jonathan off her doorstep, and go back to bed.

"I just don't want to see you anymore. All right? From this day on pretend we never met."

"I need to tell you something, okay?" When this got no response from her, he added angrily: "You know, your friend Robin came to see me last night."

The previous night had left Jill pale and shaky, but she grew paler still when Jonathan mentioned Robin's name. He'd certainly been busy since their little heart-to-heart at the coffee shop. First blabbing to Graham—and now, she found out, he'd talked to Jonathan too. She felt a wave of panic as she considered who else might have been brought into the loop. Did Petra know the whole sad tale now, too? Would she soon be calling to offer her condolences? Who else had he told?

"Robin came to see you," she echoed.

"Yeah, and really tore a strip off me, too. Said I'd probably scarred you for life, said he wouldn't be surprised if you joined a convent after what had happened."

"Oh really?" Jill fought to conceal a tiny smile.

"That's why I came over. I mean, I needed to speak to you anyhow, but..." His voice trailed off for an uneasy moment. "Believe me, Jill, I feel awful. I...I know I misled you, but not intentionally. I mean, I guess some of what I did was intentional, sort of, but I never dreamed you'd actually get hurt."

He made one last appeal with his eyes. From the way they glistened Jill was suddenly afraid that Jonathan Wunder was going to break down and cry right there on her doorstep. That was something she knew she couldn't take, especially in the exceedingly fragile condition—both physical and emotional—that she was in. With a sigh of surrender she took a step backward, slipped the chain off and admitted him into her apartment.

When they reached the sofa Jonathan hovered nervously, waiting for Jill to take a seat. She flopped down at one end, curling her feet tightly beneath her. Jonathan eased himself onto the other end and hunched forward. He looked at her uneasily,

**Her Latest Supporting Role**

and when he began to speak his tone was pained, like a suspect on Law and Order who'd finally been badgered into confessing.

"The summer after I graduated from B.U.—" He lowered his eyes to the floor, and Jill heard the labored in-out of a deep breath, "I told my father that I was gay."

Though Jill already knew it was true, it pained her enormously to hear him say the words. More surprising was the fact that she also felt the strange thrill of a voyeur. As curious as she'd been all summer long, Jill now had a sickening suspicion that Jonathan Wunder was about to reveal more about himself than she ought to know. She kept absolutely still as he spoke.

"I'd been pretty sure about if for years, but I'd gone through all the usual motions. I had a girlfriend in high school and a couple of others during college. I guess back then I believed that maybe it was just a passing thing, a phase, and if I found the right girl—well, that would be the end of it. But instead, that summer..." Finally, he peered up, and his eyes narrowed, deadly serious. "I met Mister Right.

"I'd always been close to my father. Much closer than to my mother, who's kind of, well, distant. I mean, you met her at the barbecue, you saw what she's like. Very materialistic and kind of judgmental: a total 'keeping up with the Joneses' type. We never really had much to say to each other. I was actually afraid to break it to her—tell her that one member of her perfect family wasn't quite what she thought. But my father—he'd always been there for me. We were close. I had thought a couple of times that he might have even suspected the truth about my... feelings. Maybe. In any case, I was sure he'd understand, and he'd be there for me."

After a long and uneasy pause, Jonathan found his voice again. "I couldn't have been more wrong about my father." A sigh escaped through the tight O of his mouth. "My father, the one person I thought would be so sympathetic, he didn't take it well. At all. He kind of flipped out, started crying uncontrollably, said he couldn't bear the thought that I wouldn't have children, said I'd be facing a lifetime of discrimination, and where had he gone wrong that I had wound up like this. It broke my heart to see him like that, Jill, it really did. I guess in retrospect I should have been more prepared for the way he reacted—I mean, he's a *shmatta* guy from the Bronx, a middle-aged Jew who manufactures raincoats for God's sake, not some liberal New Age Dad.

"Anyway, when I finally got him calmed down a bit, then he started in with the whole denial thing. Said it was probably just a phase I was going through, even though I pleaded with him to accept that this was who I was and swore I'd known this about myself for years. Still, he begged me not to 'give in to it', as he put it. Said I probably just hadn't had a good relationship with a woman and that once I met 'the one' everything would change."

At that Jonathan folded his arms across his chest and fell back against the sofa, a stricken look on his face.

"And that was how long ago?" Jill asked quietly, still trying to process everything he'd just thrown at her.

"Ten years."

His confession made her strangely bold. "And since then, what?"

"Well, I felt so goddamned guilty about what I'd put my father through that I tried to do what he wanted, tried to find the right woman…any woman, really. And I moved back from Boston for a while, lived on the Upper East Side and dated a girl I knew from high school, Debbie Birnbach. I'm sure Anya remembers her. Probably hated her, too, she was a snooty Long Island JAP, but she fit the bill and my parents—especially my mother—loved her. They thought the sun shone out of Debbie's backside. After about two years, though, they started dropping hints about what a wonderful wife Debbie would make and how they were dying for grandchildren. I'm actually surprised it took them that long.

**Her Latest Supporting Role**

That's when I knew that I had to get away, and I started applying to graduate programs."

"And when you left," Jill said. "That's when you wrote *Groundswell?*"

Jonathan nodded vigorously. "I can't tell you how happy I was in to be back in Boston after the whole Debbie charade in New York. I was close enough to home that I could see my family regularly, but far enough away that I could be myself. I didn't really hang with many people from my New York past, and it was so...so, well, liberating. In my first semester I met this guy named Kurt. He was doing an Masters in studio art. Sculpture. Really talented but a bit bizarre. Anyhow, I fell for him in a big way. Groundswell was sort of inspired by stories he told me about his own family: he had a pretty fucked-up childhood. I used to dream about the things he told me, only in the dreams I was him and it was my family, my story."

Jill's forehead wrinkled when she heard the familiar name. "Kurt? From your party? The guy who makes sculpture out of mangled machinery?" Then an image shot to the front of her consciousness, the dedication page of his novel: To K., for everything...

"That's right, you met him." Jonathan took a deep breath, and stared at the floor again. "It ended a long time ago, him and me I mean. My father got prostate cancer right around the time I finished the book, and I spent a lot more time with my family, ended up moving back to New York and dropping out before I finished my dissertation. Found a publisher, you know the rest. I broke up with Kurt when I left Boston; all that time with my father while he was sick made me realize how conflicted I was and I just couldn't put Kurt through my fucked-up little psychodrama. I went back to my parents' world, back to living the way my father wanted me to live. Back to dating women." Jonathan Wunder looked up at Jill, and his brown eyes shone with frustration. "That's when I stopped dreaming, and when my second book ground to a halt, almost before I started it."

An uneasy silence filled the apartment. Jonathan continued to stare at Jill with a look that broke her heart all over again: it begged for understanding, for her forgiveness. But she couldn't bear it, not yet anyhow, and she looked right past him out the window.

"Not to change the subject," Jill said finally, still not quite focusing on him, "but can I ask you one thing?" He nodded solemnly. "Why me?"

"What do you mean?"

"I mean, why did you choose me?" She knew she should be more compassionate but her voice had an unmissable edge of bitterness. "You needed someone to parade in front of your parents at the family barbeque, right? Didn't you have some understanding woman friend who would have gone with you, instead of perpetrating this huge mindfuck on an unsuspecting student?" Jill felt her throat constricting; her words were choking her. "I mean, I felt something for you, you know? I really did. And you were just using me."

"It's not like that, Jill," he said defensively. "Not at all. When I met you that night on the steps of the school I thought you were this smart, cool girl, and you obviously had some opinions of your own, something to say. But you kept hanging back in class, you hadn't uttered a word and that kind of intrigued me. I wanted to draw you out, you know? When I discovered that we had Anya Roth in common I thought I would invite you to my party and find out what your story was. It was all perfectly innocent. I mean, I talked to you, I liked you, and I wanted to be your friend, Jill: just a good friend. I'm sorry if you think I led you on. I guess in a way I knew that something strange was going on because I could sense that you were, well, developing some feelings for me. But I really thought that if I kept you at arm's length you wouldn't get hurt."

**Her Latest Supporting Role**

Jill's throat tightened even more. "But how do you explain last Sunday night?" she said. She closed her eyes and again saw the dispassionate look that on Jonathan Wunder's face as she had tightened her body around him. The image had burned itself into her brain as an inescapable reminder of the awful mistake she'd made. A fierce loathing shudder went through her body. "You could have pushed me away, you know, could have kicked me out of your apartment." She added hurtfully: "God forbid, you might even have told me the truth."

"I didn't want to hurt you Jill. I always tried to avoid going home with you, or having you come home with me. I thought you'd get the picture. I guess I was just kidding myself. But when you came to my apartment that night after the barbeque, and you...you reached out for me, it wasn't until then that I realized just how out-of-hand things had gotten. It was an impossible situation, Jill. When I looked into your eyes I could see how much it meant to you, and my body just kind of gave in."

"A mercy fuck," Jill said, humiliated. She could feel her eyes begin to swim in their sockets. "That's great, Jonathan. Thanks a lot."

He shook his head sadly. "It wasn't like that at all."

Jill pulled herself to her feet, and drew her bathrobe even more tightly around her body. She tipped her head in the direction of the door. "I think we're done here."

Jonathan rose, but remained in front of the couch a moment longer. "I'm truly sorry if I hurt you, Jill. After I saw your face on Thursday night, the way you looked when you saw Robin in my living room, I knew that I'd done something really, really wrong. He's the one who insisted that I come here today, that I come clean with you once and for all. Of course I don't blame you if you hate me, but I still care about you and want to be your friend. Whether or not you want to is completely your decision. I won't push. But if you feel like calling, you know how to get in touch."

He took a step in her direction and for a split-second it looked as though he was going to reach out and give Jill a hug; but after he read the look on her face he changed his mind and kept moving.

When he got to the door Jonathan Wunder turned and looked at her sadly. "Can I tell you one more thing?"

"If you have to."

"Your paper on *The English Patient* was outstanding. Well thought out, beautifully written—the best essay in the whole class, a real A-plus effort. You'll get an A in the course, Jill, and you've certainly earned it."

Jill didn't reply; she couldn't. The pounding that had started between her ears had spread to the rest of her body until she was one giant throbbing pain that stretched from head to toe. She waited until she heard the apartment door close, and then hugged the robe tightly around her, and flopped back onto her bed.

**Her Latest Supporting Role**

# Chapter 16

It was the Wednesday morning after the pitch, and Jill was more than an hour late for work. She'd been at the dentist's having a broken filling replaced, and—thanks to a generous shot of Novocain—the left side of her mouth felt like a flesh-tone sandbag. As she walked down the tenth floor corridor to her desk Jill noticed an unusual silence and lack of activity. She passed an open door and was surprised to glimpse a pair of solemn-faced producers engaged in hushed conversation.

Sandi appeared beside Jill's desk while she was collecting her voicemail messages.

"Hey, I was looking for you."

Jill tapped a finger against the swollen side of her mouth in reply.

"Oh yeah, I forgot you had to go to the dentist." Sandi gave an empathetic cringe. "Anyhow, I thought you'd want to know right away. We lost Tellco."

Jill gasped. "You're kidding. I thought we weren't supposed to find out until after Labor Day. Don't they still have a couple more pitches to see?"

Sandi nodded. Her pretty face looked tight and drawn; her skin had an unusual yellowish cast and this was only the second time in nearly four months that Jill had seen her glamour-puss boss without lipstick. "The president of Tellco phoned Constable last night. Thanked the Agency for all the hard work, but said they'd already seen better. Quite a 'fuck you very much', apparently. At nine-thirty Constable called an agency meeting in the cafeteria and broke the bad news to us. We're supposed to be transitioning off the business during September and October—start handing stuff over to their new Agency as soon as the winner is announced—and all our work-in-progress, meaning all the stupid fucking spots that are currently in production or post, they're supposed to be finished by October 31st."

"Jesus. Did Constable say anything about layoffs?"

"Not in so many words. But between us—and I really shouldn't be telling you this, Jill—it's going to be a bloodbath. Probably forty people, maybe even more. It was our biggest and most labor-intensive account by far."

Jill whistled. The Agency only had six hundred employees to begin with. "Any idea when it's going to happen?"

Sandi shook her head. "Dunno. But soon, probably. The account will be out the door in 60 days. The powers that be will have to start cutting their headcount by then or they'll get their asses kicked by London."

Jill shook her head slowly. "I never really thought of myself as 'headcount' before."

Sandi 's naked lips curved into a tragic smile. "Welcome to the glamorous world of advertising."


After making a few quick revisions to her résumé and printing twenty copies—Jill had no idea how quickly things would happen but wanted to be ready in case she wound up on the hit list—she wandered down the hall in search of Robin. She hadn't seen or spoken with him since their midnight exchange at the coffee shop; amazingly, almost a week had passed since then. Though she had tried to stay mad at him for opening his big mouth to both Graham and Jonathan, over the past couple of days Jill had come to realize that she was actually grateful for his intervention. Now she knew why Jonathan Wunder had acted the way he had; now (for better or worse) Graham Ferguson knew where he stood with her.

Robin wasn't in his office, but the half-eaten bagel on his desk told her he was definitely in the agency. Jill found him sprawled on the couch in Petra's office, where the two of them were conducting a post-mortem on the Tellco pitch.

**Her Latest Supporting Role**

"Hey," Jill said.

Robin looked genuinely surprised to see her. He swung his legs onto the floor to make room on the couch, and she sat down beside him, shooting a conciliatory smile in his direction. "I was at the dentist's this morning, and I just heard the news from Sandi. So what did Constable say at the meeting?"

"Nothing too illuminating, I'm afraid," Petra said. Jill watched as she dumped three Sweet'n Lows into her coffee and stirred it with the business end of an X-Acto knife. "Nothing we haven't heard before." Her voice took on a Constable-like tone of sneering self-importance: "'I think everyone who worked on the pitch is to be commended', '...we did some of our best work ever, work we can really be proud of', '...everyone really pulled together in true Hambleton French fashion', blah, blah, blah...'"

Robin nodded agreement and his narrow shoulders rose in a cynical shrug.

"I guess they're going to let a lot of people go, huh?" Jill said quietly.

"Well, I know that I plan on spending this afternoon working on my book," Robin said.

"Ditto," Petra added and, nodding toward the open door, lowered her voice. "I actually got a call from a headhunter yesterday about a great job at Saatchi. I told her I wasn't interested, but after this morning's newsflash I've reconsidered." She smiled wickedly at them both. "Haven't you always dreamed of saying, 'you can't fire me—I quit'?" She turned her attention to Jill. "And what about you, doll?"

"I just put the finishing touches on my résumé," Jill admitted, and slumped down into the spongy depths of Petra's sofa. "But in my heart of hearts I think getting fired would be sort of a mixed blessing, you know?" They both gave Jill a look of genuine surprise. "I mean, the people have been great," she said, sweeping one arm around the room to let Robin and Petra know she meant them in particular, "but the work hasn't been especially, well... fulfilling. I know I need to pay my dues but I'd also like to find something that's a little more...something... before my brain begins to atrophy."

"Know what you mean, Beauty Queen," said Petra, and a brisk nod of her head set the halo of curls in motion. "Believe it or not, I myself started out as a so-called Creative Assistant-slash-Dogsbody-and-Coffee-Bitch. And to the exalted big cheese himself—Simon Constable."

"You were Constable's assistant?" Jill's face registered astonishment.

"God's honest truth." Petra planted her Doc Martens on the red carpet and moved to shut her office door. "Robin and my old partner know the story. A couple of other people too, now that I think about it. He's sworn to secrecy," she said, pointing in Robin's direction. "And if you promise not to blab I'll tell you too." She smiled mischievously. "How I got my big break in advertising."

Jill raised one hand as though being sworn in

Petra's eyes glittered as she settled back in her chair. "Well, I took this Creative Assistant's job when I was twenty-five," she began. "I'd been trying to get a job at every agency in town but even though everyone told me they liked my book, no one would actually hire me as a writer. I'd dropped out of college and kind of frittered away a few years of my life—waitressing, trying to launch a stand-up act, nothing that looked too promising on a résumé. But luckily I'd taken a high school typing class, and that was what ultimately got me hired at Hambleton French.

"They put me to work for this creative group that happened to include our esteemed President among its members. At the time he was a Creative Director who had just arrived from the London office, incredibly talented but lazy as shit and everybody knew it. Quite a partier, too, in those days. I was always covering for him because a lot of times he wouldn't get to the office until eleven or noon and even then the smell of booze was

**Her Latest Supporting Role**

still seeping from every pore of his body. In exchange for me running interference with the account people and his boss, Constable agreed to help me with my book. You know, go over the spec ads I'd written and help me tighten them up, make them more professional.

"Anyhow, about eight months after I started the bastard stole one of my ideas. Once I started at HFA most of the ads I did were for our own clients, because I could more easily get my hands on visuals and logos and stuff. It was a print ad for Caramba! coffee, which was an account that Constable worked on at the time. He hid it from me, I didn't even know it was being produced until an art director brought me a proof he'd seen down in the production department. This guy—who by the way hated Constable because Constable was the Executive Creative Director's fair-haired boy and was always getting away with murder—he knew the ad was my idea. He'd helped me work on it six months before the real assignment ever came up.

"So I marched right into Constable's office and went ballistic. Screamed bloody murder and threatened to blow the whistle. To shut me up—I had the support of another C.D., after all, it wasn't just my word against Constable's—he got me hired as a junior writer, in someone else's group thank God. And the rest," Petra added, her light eyes twinkling, "as they say, is history."

"Incredible," Jill said. "What I want to know is this: is there anyone in the agency—other than me—who doesn't have something on Constable?"

Robin made a strange, knowing face which suggested to Jill that he too knew something that was not quite public information.

"Probably not. From what I hear about the morning of the Tellco pitch, the list is getting longer all the time," Petra said. Out of the corner of her eye Jill saw an odd look cross Robin's face. "But I wouldn't lose any sleep over it, Jill. Like you said, this may not be your dream job. But you'll figure out what you want to do, and then you'll do it. As I said before, I wish I were twenty-seven again."

When Jill got back to her desk she found Graham in her chair, scribbling on a hot pink Post-It. Fierce morning sun was streaming though the window, doing odd things to his hunched form: creating golden epaulets atop his crisp khaki suit, adding a backlit shimmer to his shiny black hair. When she cleared her throat he looked up and gave Jill a warm but questioning smile.

"Oh, there you are," he exclaimed with what sounded like relief. "You know, I was out of town for the last two days at a Tellco meeting. I wanted to see how you were feeling. You were so sick on Friday night, and then when I called you over the weekend either you weren't in—or you weren't answering," he added, sounding the faintest bit put out.

"I'm better, thanks," Jill answered, flashing an uncertain grin. She'd lived the past few days in a state of total mortification. She'd never, ever treated a date as badly as she had treated Graham on Friday night. Jill was shocked that he was even talking to her, let alone concerned. "Much, much better."

"Good. Great." Graham sat there smiling inanely, as though he didn't know what else to say.

"I was so sorry to hear about Tellco." Jill gave him a look that was sympathetic and serious. "I know how hard you worked trying to save the account."

"We all did." Gracious Graham. "You, Nick and Sandi, the whole agency really pulled out all the stops. But I'll admit I was surprised," he allowed. "Especially with the way they dismissed us so soon, before they'd even seen all the other agencies' presentations. It seemed a little...I don't know, rude I guess. Kind of a 'Fuck You'. But what's done is done, you know? I'm not going to beat myself up about woulda-coulda-shoulda."

"Regrets are for dinner parties, right?"

Graham sputtered with laughter. "Exactly."

**Her Latest Supporting Role**

"So what's the note say?"

Graham ripped the pink square from her pad and held it up. "Yankees tickets: tomorrow night, seven-thirty. If you come I promise not to feed you anything that will make you sick." He gave her a slightly uncomfortable look. "And I promise to, um...leave you alone."

Jill gave her head a wary shake. "Oh, Graham—it's really kind of you to ask, but I can't." Her mind flashed back to Friday night (or at least what she could remember of it): to throwing up her half of a two hundred dollar dinner; and to reacting so badly when he'd kissed her. But it was guilt that was eating at her, not regret. She didn't want to lead him on, to encourage him when there was no hope—and right now things felt nothing if not hopeless. She'd been on the receiving end of that with Jonathan, and she couldn't do it to Graham, especially since he had only just recovered from his own romantic disaster. And she hadn't completely bounced back herself, still plagued by that raw, torn feeling, the sensation that her entire body was covered with exposed nerves. She needed a break from dating.

He smiled and eased himself up from the desk. Was she imagining it, or did his shoulders sag a little now from her rejection?

"I'm sorry you feel that way Jill, but I'm not going to push. If you change your mind, you know where to find me."

Jill watched Graham stroll down the corridor. He paused and took one quick look back in her direction before disappearing into the stairwell, heading back to the safety of the client-service colony on eleven. Then she took a deep breath and settled herself at her desk. Jill eyed her silent phone nervously, wondering if the Tellco loss left her anything to do at Hambleton French.

# SEPTEMBER

# Chapter 17

After Labor Day things started to happen even more quickly than Jill had anticipated.

Extra-long holiday weekends were an H-F summer tradition: one for Memorial Day to kick off summer, a second for July 4th, and another over Labor Day to mark the season's end. Jill's extra day off had helped them beat the westbound crawl of traffic to the Hamptons, and avoid the frustration of the usual Friday night exodus. On Friday morning Monika, just back from vacation and wide awake from jet lag, had started calling Jill every ten minutes from seven on asking, was she ready to leave? They made it to Southampton in time to have a barbeque lunch on the Roth's deck, and passed the rest of the weekend sunning themselves by the pool and trading stories from the last two weeks, filling each other in on the few things they hadn't covered in calls and e-mails.

Though Jill certainly hadn't made a big deal of it, she was desperately, almost embarrassingly happy that Monika was home. She knew that she needed to be more independent, to stand on her own both socially and emotionally—especially now that they both had their feet firmly planted in the so-called "real world". And yet she couldn't help wondering if things might have turned out differently had Monika not been too busy to see her that much over the summer, and then gone on vacation. Monika's reaction after Jill had told her the truth about Jonathan Wunder—the way she'd poor-baby'd her, called her innocent to a fault—was that much more painful because Jill knew that it was true. Jill spent the Labor Day weekend reconsidering the events of the last three months, examining them from every angle. But she decided that it would be best to say nothing more about it to Monika: at least for the time being.

On Tuesday she got to work early, well before eight-thirty. After four days of sloth Jill was overcome by a sudden wave of industry: this despite the fact that since the Tellco loss had been announced the previous week she had much less than usual to do. As the minutes ticked past and people wandered in—nine o'clock, then nine-thirty, members of the creative department were not the agency's earliest risers, especially after a four-day weekend—Jill set about reorganizing the files in her computer, placing each on the server in a newly-created directory that was named for the appropriate producer. A little after ten-thirty and there were only a half-dozen files to go when she got a call from Victoria Walker, the head of creative personnel. As Jill hung up she noticed that her hand was shaking. She tried to swallow but her mouth was suddenly dry. Victoria wanted to see Jill in her office, right away.

Victoria sat up on twelve, and though Jill usually took the stairs two at a time she suddenly found it difficult to summon the energy. Exiting the stairwell she nearly plowed right into someone she vaguely recognized, a junior person from the media department: young, only a couple of years out of college. Her gaze met Jill's for only a half-second before she stalked away. A brief glimpse of her eyes—red-rimmed and teary—sent a spasm of panic through Jill.

The door to Victoria's office was open and she beckoned Jill inside. Today's outfit—skin-tight black leggings and a long cotton sweater with a leopard-spot pattern knit into it—made her look more than ever like a cross-dressed Keith Richards. When Jill sat down Victoria got up and closed the door. She took her seat again and the black Aeron chair made a small high noise like a sigh.

"So how are you?" she began, and Jill thought she actually saw a flicker of concern in Victoria's eyes. She remembered their first meeting, when Jill was trying so very hard to get hired: how different, how brittle and even hostile Victoria had seemed then.

**Her Latest Supporting Role**

Had she really changed so much, or was it just Jill's memory playing tricks on her?

She replied, "I'm all right, I guess. Kind of wondering why you wanted to see me though."

Victoria shifted, pressing her bony legs together tightly. Her wide mouth twitched.

"Jill, I don't want to play any games here. I'm afraid this is not going to be a good meeting. You know that losing the Tellco business was a big blow to the agency. A lot of people worked on that account, and while I truly wish that we could find a place for everyone on other pieces of business, at the end of the day it just isn't possible." Jill heard Victoria draw breath, and then she said, "I'm afraid we have to let you go. I'm very sorry about this," she added, looking straight into Jill's eyes, "and I want you to know that it had nothing at all to do with your performance. Sandi and Nick were extremely pleased with your work, but losing the Tellco business has left your entire department in an extremely, well, awkward spot."

Jill stared at her, but didn't utter a sound. After a moment of uneasy silence Victoria continued. "Today will be your last day at the agency. You'll get two weeks severance, plus pay for whatever vacation time you've accrued." She tipped her dark head sideways and added, "If you'll just pop next door and see Merry, my assistant, she'll go over all the details with you. You'll need to clear out your things and turn in your employee ID by five o'clock. Jill, again, I'm really very sorry about this. Best of luck to you."

Jill didn't get all teary like the girl she'd nearly run into. Still, as she wandered down the stairs and headed for Robin's office a strange numbness overtook her. She wrapped her arms in front of her chest, only they didn't really feel like her arms. She pinched the skin at her waist but felt no pain.

Robin's office was empty, but she could hear his voice drifting down the red-carpeted hallway. She followed the sound to its source and took a couple of tentative steps into Petra's office. They both caught the full impact of the expression on Jill's face and then sprang into action; Robin grabbed one of her folded arms and pulled her inside while Petra leapt up from her desk and shut the door. Jill eased herself away from Robin and took a seat on the couch, one leg tucked beneath her skirt.

Petra was the first to break the silence. "I'm afraid to ask why you look the way you look. But I think I know the answer."

Jill took a noisy, deep breath. "I just got canned. Haven't even been back to my desk yet—I came straight here."

"Oh, that's terrible, that's really terrible." Petra, normally so mellow and in control, actually sounded distraught. She bolted out of her chair and stood by the window for a moment, staring out at a construction site to the west. She addressed Robin and Jill without turning to face them, her voice quivering. "You know, I've been through probably half a dozen of these mass layoffs, and it never gets any easier. Ever. Sometimes I wonder if I wouldn't be happier as a goddamned civil servant or something."

Robin winked at Jill in a transparent attempt to lift her spirits. "A civil service copywriter? Now that's a scary thought," he admonished Petra. "Shame on you for even suggesting it, silly bitch."

Jill tipped her head backward until it touched the wall. Addressing her remark to the ceiling she said, "I guess a lot of people are getting fired today, huh?"

"You don't know the half of it," Robin told her quietly. "Constable axed Brinder and Bateman first thing this morning. I guess they're taking the fall for the Tellco loss. Or at least that's the official story. Whether it was their fault or not is quite another matter." He glanced nervously towards the door, making sure that it was closed before adding: "But Constable's not exactly going to fire himself now, is he?"

Petra turned away from the window, and wandered back to her desk, her shoulders slumped. Even her springy halo of curls

**Her Latest Supporting Role**

seemed to have lost some of its usual bounce. "Constable let Danny Ianello go this morning too. A really talented junior writer, and he didn't even work on Tellco. It just isn't fair. The good people always get it."

"Speaking of good people," Robin said. "Constable let Sandi go too."

"No!" Jill gasped. "I don't believe it."

"It gets worse," Petra told her mournfully. "Sandi's out, but the boss-from-hell is in like Flynn. Now he's the head of production...no "Co-". King of the Hill, Master of his Domain."

"But that doesn't make sense," Jill said. "I heard that Constable's been waiting for a chance to get rid of Nick and put Sandi in charge of the entire production department. Wasn't losing Tellco the perfect opportunity?"

"Well," Robin said. "according to my sources, because of Constable's little performance right before the pitch—remember, Nick was the one who found him at the Waldorf, or so I've heard —he got the mother of all 'get out of jail free' cards. So it wasn't exactly a level playing field. Oh my God –" he whispered. "Another sports metaphor! What on earth is happening to me?"

Petra ignored Robin's outburst. "As they say, it's not what you know, it's who you know," she said, her mouth twisting into a bitter smile. "Or who you blow."

To which Robin added, "Actually, from what I've seen around here I think it is what you know—about Constable."

They all lapsed into brief but uncomfortable laughter, and again eyed the door nervously.

"So, sweet pea," Petra said finally, taking a seat beside Jill on the couch. "You okay?"

Jill nodded. "I saw the writing on the wall last week when we found out that Tellco was gone. Updated my résumé, the whole bit. I just didn't think it would happen so soon—that's the only real surprise."

"Do you know what you're going to do now? I know a ton of people in the business if you need contacts. There are ex-HF-ers at nearly every decent agency in the city."

"That's really sweet Petra, but for the time being I'll pass." Jill folded her arms in front of her. "I need to figure out my next step. I've been on auto-pilot since I started here. This just might be the time to try something else."

After a boozy goodbye lunch with Robin and Petra, Jill spent an hour cleaning out her desk and stripping her work area of all the pictures and mementoes, things she'd brought to Hambleton French or had collected during her four months there. She was removing push-pins from a series of ads that were tacked up on the wall next to her computer, glossy reprints of a campaign Robin had done at his previous agency. An almond-eyed model, gorgeous even with her hair lathered into a foamy beehive, looked quizzically above her head, where a small sampling of NatureShine's all-natural ingredients floated like UFOs. A perfectly-formed lemon, a chalk-white egg, a spray of mint leaves and a miniature honey pot seemed magically suspended in mid-air, though Robin had explained to her in fascinating detail that each element had been photographed separately, and then the entire ad was composed with computer retouching. The magic of advertising had been demystified for Jill when Robin told her how the NatureShine ad was assembled just like something in a factory. And the same thing had happened today.

She rolled Robin's ads into a tube and was securing it with an elastic band when Graham appeared in front of her desk.

"Jill, I just heard," he said, looking crestfallen. "I'm so sorry. It's a terrible thing that's happening here today."

"You're OK, though?" she asked.

"For the time being," Graham said with a shrug. "I'm on clean-up until the account is officially out the door. What a

**Her Latest Supporting Role**

horrible job that's going to be. Then I'm going to be on new business for a while, working with good old Sally again."

"I'm glad you're safe, Graham," Jill told him, and she meant it. "You earned it, you really did." She looked right into his eyes and for a moment there was a heavy silence between them.

"Hey there." Graham finally spoke, and instead of the slick, upbeat account service tone he was in the habit of using at work, there again was the sensitive, almost nervous voice she'd heard in her apartment Friday night. "At least let me buy you a goodbye drink."

They ended up drinking vodka martinis at the Algonquin Hotel. Jill had always wanted to go there, and yet somehow never had. (How had Graham known? Or was it just a lucky coincidence?) She was happy she'd worn something respectable to work that morning—a short black skirt and green ballerina flats—or she would have been embarrassed to be seen in such an elegant, storied room. Hirshfeld drawings of so many famous Broadway shows lined the walls, and because it was early they had the place nearly to themselves. They'd dropped a box of Jill's personal stuff with the mail room—the clerk promised he'd messenger it to her apartment the next day—and then departed the office a little after three. Graham strode to the elevator without giving the hour a second thought. As he told Jill, with an endearingly silly grin, what were they going to do—fire him?

Taking turns, they listed all the people they knew who had been let go, clinking their glasses together after each name in a little tribute. When they had finally gone through everyone they could think of, Graham exhaled noisily.

"I should count my blessings, I guess," he told Jill. "I'm practically the only Tellco account person left. Anyway, I still want to go overseas, and I think this might just make it happen a little faster. Shake the tree."

"Well, I'm happy for you Graham, I really am. I hope you get what you want."

Over the past few days Jill had reconsidered their situation. It had been a week and a half since their big night out (and her humiliating performance); her mortification over the evening's events had slowly ebbed, and gradually been replaced by the suspicion that Graham was the man she should have paid attention to over the summer. And now there was no office (at least for her) and so no worries about an office romance. Only he was lobbying to go overseas and she was going, she suspected, nowhere. She knew he liked her, he'd made that abundantly clear all summer long, but now he was leaving New York and she was jobless, prospect-less, and feeling highly un-dateable.

"Thanks," he said, looking somewhat embarrassed. "So what are you going to do now? Or is it too soon to ask?" Graham reproached himself. "I'm sorry."

"Don't be." Jill waved away his discomfort. "It's not too soon to ask, but the answer is, I don't know. Petra offered me some contacts, but I'm not sure that I want to do the same job at another agency, you know? I spent the long weekend thinking it over. Maybe it's time to try something new."

"Well I hope we'll keep in touch, regardless," he said. He averted his gaze from hers for just a moment, seeming to find something fascinating in the wall of Hirshfeld caricatures to his left. When Graham looked at her again he offered Jill a warm smile, one that she felt from head to tingling toes and that made her momentarily swoon. "I'm glad to hear that you have such a positive attitude about the whole thing."

"Do I?" Jill wondered aloud.

**Her Latest Supporting Role**

# Chapter 18

Jill fought her way off the cross-town bus: on that sunny September weekend it was jammed with sweating and cranky shoppers. She managed to grab the last table at Café Dante, and settled gratefully into the air-conditioned chill with a copy of the *Post* and an iced cappuccino. She was scanning for her waiter, ready to order another when Monika barreled through the door, dressed in the most prized of her many Parisian acquisitions—a black leather biker jacket from Colette—despite the fact that it was nearly eighty degrees outside.

Since Labor Day Monika's workload had cranked back into overdrive. They hadn't seen each other for days, had hardly even talked on the phone or e-mailed, as Monika was very busy with her duties as Associate orientation co-ordinator, guiding her flock of newly-minted young lawyers through a week-long hazing that chiefly involved closing out a different bar every night. Jill was amazed that the week's activities hadn't left a scratch on her chronically overachieving friend; her skin was its usual healthy shade of pink, the whites of her eyes as bleach-bright as ever, sparkling behind their fringe of black mascara.

"Hello, Jill-*ini*," Monika said, in deference to their surroundings. "And Happy Birthday," she added, blowing a noisy kiss and dropping a small Barney's bag on the table between them.

"Thanks." Jill looked into the bag with interest. "You know, I didn't even realize it was my birthday today, not 'til my parents called at the crack of dawn to wish me Happy Happy."

"Twenty-eight's no big deal," Monika assured her. "On my birthday Anya and I went to see a bad action movie on the Champs-Elysée. I wish you'd been there—we could have gotten wild—but now that she's a Parisian *hausfrau* her idea of a happenin' time was an early dinner at Brasserie Lipp."

"At least you got the hell out of Dodge for a while," Jill reminded Monika. She took in the familiar surroundings and grimaced. "I really need a change of scenery. Same places, same faces. No offence," she added quickly.

"None taken."

"I feel like my life has totally stalled." The waiter deposited another drink in front of Jill, and she dumped in three sugars and gave it a too-vigorous stir. "The only thing I accomplished this summer was finishing my degree, and frankly I was supposed to have done that in May. Everything else was either a step backward–"

"Backward how?" Monika looked uncharacteristically thoughtful, ready to listen rather than just launch straight into advice-giving mode.

"The job was a total bust, I lost it in four months." Jill made a sour face. "I've had zits that lasted longer. The Jonathan Wunder thing—disaster! The only thing worse than fucking a gay man is knowing that people are going to talk about it. I'm sure people already are, actually. I love Robin but I can't trust him to keep his big mouth shut. Not to mention Justine DeVries."

"I bet Jonathan Wunder will keep his mouth shut!"

Jill gave Monika the dirtiest of dirty looks. "I guess you and your sister got to gloat over that one. You guys were right—so right—about Jonathan. No one ever accused me of being a good judge of character, especially where men are concerned. I guess my record there remains intact."

Monika gave Jill a goofy smile and rolled here eyes in a way that had always made Jill laugh, ever since prep school. The tension between them lifted. "OK, I know you don't feel like any advice right now Jill, but fuck it," Monika began. "You need to stop torturing yourself over Jonathan. I'm feeling like a broken

**Her Latest Supporting Role**

record here…this is just like the Czerny thing all over again. Let it go."

"I know, I know." Jill stuck a fork into the tiramisu that had appeared between them, and shoveled in a big gooey mouthful.

"So what are you doing to move on? Monika demanded. "Have you started looking for a new job yet or are you still watching MTV all day in your pajamas?"

It had been a week and a half since the big Hambleton French layoff. Over the course of that day fifty-two employees had lost their jobs: no one was certain at the time but just before five an agency-wide e-mail was finally sent, the body count confirmed. Of course she hadn't been there but both Robin and Petra had forwarded it to her Hotmail account. It had been a crazy, emotional day: virtually all work at the agency had ground to a halt as employees waited to learn their fate. The morning had been devoted to the terminations, swiftly followed by the obligatory booze-soaked goodbye lunches (those who had been spared were only too happy to treat their less-fortunate co-workers) and finally there was the sad exodus of cardboard box-toting ex-employees lugging their most personal of personal effects home. A byproduct of the layoff drama was the volley of verbal one-upsmanship it set off in the H-F creative department, as its remaining staffers threw all their nervous energy into developing witty new synonyms for what was happening all over the agency: "Fired" quickly gave way to "Canned", "Pink Slipped", "Booted", "Axed", "Toasted", "Deep Six-ed", "Eighty-Six-ed", "Given the old heave-ho" (that one of course from a Brit), "Shown the door", "Got it" and Jill's personal favorite (from a *Sopranos* fan, naturally): "Whacked."

After a couple of days in her pajamas seeking inspiration from MTV and Häagen-Dazs—sadly, neither had much to offer in the way of career advice—Jill received a strange message, a voicemail from her past. Roddy Cowan was the Musical Director of a dreadful little actors' showcase Jill had appeared in just a few short months before she finally, happily gave up on acting and enrolled at NYU. They'd become great buddies while working together (he was a lot like Robin Devlin, in both good ways and bad) but they hadn't had much contact after their professional collaboration ended. Apparently he didn't know that she'd quit performing, for the message contained an intriguing offer: more of a plea for help, really. Roddy had traded in his off- off-Broadway work for a stint leading a lounge act that performed kitschy pop classics on a cruise ship. One of his female singers ("two girls and two gays" was how he's described the group, at first Jill thought that was the band's name, learning only much later that they were actually known as "The Big Apple Transfer") had gotten pregnant and for various reasons (insurance, cruise line policy, doctor's orders) had to leave the group immediately. He needed someone to step in, someone almost exactly the same dress size and vocal range as the sidelined singer, and that was when he had thought of Jill. She'd laughed her ass off when he e-mailed her a picture of the group—and their set list—but after her initial (and intense) hell no response, became more and more beguiled by the thought of escaping the city, and her mess of a so-called life. It would be like hitting the pause button, getting a do-over. Roddy only needed her for three months and she could probably, from among her network of actors, grad students and advertising friends, find a subletter for her tiny (but geographically desirable) apartment. She needed space, away from everything and everyone that had witnessed her spectacularly awful summer; and time, to get her act together and plot her next move. And a little scenery and sea breeze couldn't hurt either.

**Her Latest Supporting Role**

# AUTUMN

# Chapter 19

From: Jill Barber<barberella72@hotmail.com>
Sent: Wednesday October 4, 2000 4:06 AM
To: Monika Roth <m.roth@psb-law.com>
Subject I was a teenage lounge singer…

Monika,

Got ALL your e-mails, sorry sorry sorry! I am a bad friend. Access to crew computers is VERY competitive and of course I had about a million messages (or fifty) when I finally got online. Life on the "fun ships" is, well, fun. OK not really but it is so great to be out of New York and the weather is nice too, ship is staying out of hurricane region until later in the month (note: weather is nice when I actually get up to the deck, which is not that often, due to my vampire schedule)…I am working until the wee hours every night and after that there is compulsory bonding/drinking time with the rest of Roddy's band. Freak show! OK not really but let's just say that I am SO glad I got out of "show biz" (yes, the other guy in the group really DOES call it that, and no, he's not a total fossil…probably forty, tops) before I ended up as a permanent fixture on the stage of the Lido Lounge or some other godforsaken place. The piano player drinks about a half-bottle of Dewar's a night (but manages never to screw up a song—impressive!) The other girl singer, Janice, keeps calling me "Johnny Bravo" which is apparently some *Brady Bunch* reference to when Greg was hired for a singing gig only because he fit into this super-expensive costume. The first time she said "there's a lot of bread in those threads" it was kind of funny, but after like the FORTIETH TIME IN SIX DAYS I am so over her. This is actually not such a bad temporary job (if waitressing was a 4 this is definitely a 6 or 7, higher marks on everything but pay and the seasickness) but if this were my career I would have offed myself with a kitchen knife after the first performance. Good thing I now have that highly employable MFA in Film Studies to fall back on, hahaha. I have not figured out what to do yet, work-wise, when I get back...weirdly now I kind of miss Hambleton French (more the people than the work, I think?) Trying to figure out what else I could do in that area so I do not end up back to square one yet again.

I miss you lots but I am sure you are working your ass off as always. Don't forget to:

1. eat

2. have fun

3. see lots of movies for me!

And send me some gossip (if there is any?) Staff entertainment options onboard are pretty limited, so I am catching up on my reading and sleep. Also working on a short film idea—creative juices are flowing again, woohoo.

XOXOXO Jill

P.S. NO hot men on board...what was I thinking? Chicks and fags only...I feel like I'm back in film school (or the Hambleton French creative department)!

From: Robin Devlin
<robin.devlin@newyork.hambletonfrench.com>
Sent: Thursday October 11, 2000 9:43 AM
To: Jill Barber<barberella72@hotmail.com>
Subject How are you?

Dearest Julie McCoy:

I hope you are enjoying life on the Pacific Princess or whatever the hell your new place of employment is called. Did I tell you I actually took a cruise once? So sad, it was one of those Pride Travel Gay Singles things...thoroughly depressing; we just sailed up and down the East Coast for a weekend of girly cocktails, drag

**Her Latest Supporting Role**

shows and ABBA. I'm sure your set-up is much more glam. Whenever work is getting me down I just think of you in your sequined mini-dress singing your little heart out to "Waterloo" or "Winner Takes It All" and it makes me feel all warm and happy inside!

Not much to report from the crimson hallways of America's fourth-largest advertising agency. Clean-up on Tellco is almost done and Petra and I have been tragically reassigned: we are now working pretty much full-time on the Big Tony's account. Pizza—aargh! I thought working on toys was bad (shooting all those screaming brats made me want to shoot all those screaming brats, know what I'm saying?) but I had forgotten what a pain in the ass it is to shoot food. The things the stylists do to make that shitty pizza look tasty (let's just say I can think of much better uses for hairspray and nail polish) are positively nauseating. Have sworn off my Saturday night post-drinking slice for the foreseeable future. Petra is her usual crazy self, has started taking kick-boxing and cannot shut up about it (and because she kick-boxes we are all afraid to tell her to shut up about it.) Unlike me she has developed an unhealthily obsession with pizza, she eats it for lunch or dinner or just because she feels like it almost every day. Hence the kick-boxing.

Have been to Boy Bar a couple of times since I saw the Boy Wunder there, also G and Splash and the Boiler Room (I know, I know) but no sign of the bastard. So maybe the sighting was just a weird cosmic coincidence and he has since dived headlong back into the closet? Hope you are over all that now and shagging up a storm with some cruise ship hotty (or hotties!)

Love you miss you kiss you bye,

Robin xx

PS Petra says hello with a big wet kiss but is in a deep food coma from too much pizza and thus cannot type her own missive.

From Monika Roth <m.roth@psb-law.com>
Sent Monday November 27, 2000 8:06 AM
To: Jill Barber<barberella72@hotmail.com>
Subject: GOSSIP!

J,
Thanks for calling from Miami, happy to hear your voice, so sad I missed you!!! This has to be a quick one (sorry, am beyond slammed at work.) But I know you are starved for gossip and news. Not sure which this qualifies as but was with my parents last weekend and Mom told me that Jonathan Wunder's father dropped dead over the Labor Day weekend. I had told her a while back that we had all connected randomly over the summer. Nothing else I swear. He had something called a berry (sp?) aneurism, was apparently dead by the time he hit the floor. Anyway, I don't know how you are feeling about Jonathan at this point but I thought you'd want to know.
Twenty days until your return, right? You are not missing much in New York—last two movies I saw were shit, and the news is so full of post-election hysteria that I cannot bear to look at (or discuss) it any more.
Love,
Monika


From: Monika Roth <m.roth@psb-law.com>
Sent: Tuesday December 12, 8:06 AM
To: Jill Barber<barberella72@hotmail.com>
Subject: Troll alert!!!

Jill,
Weird and random one…I got a call yesterday from Justine DeVries, who was looking for your contact info. She already knew you were working on the cruise ship—don't blame me,

**Her Latest Supporting Role**

your subletter blabbed. I have NO idea what she wants but I thought you would like a heads up. I told her your cell doesn't work unless you are in a U.S. port so e-mail was best.
Prepare! (And then share...)
Love,
Monika


From: Graham Ferguson <graham.ferguson@saatchi-nyc.com>
Sent: Wednesday December 13, 2000 10:06 AM
To: Jill Barber<barberella72@hotmail.com>
Subject: New contact info

Hi Jill,
I hope this finds you well. I wanted to drop you a quick line to a) say hello and b) let you know that I have a new job. After the agency lost Tellco I was put on Big Tony's (perhaps you heard from Robin?) and I just couldn't get excited about another churn-and-burn TV account, or about working with Sally Leyton and Constable any more. So I took a job with Saatchi, and I'm back in the booze business. They're the lead global agency for all of the House of Benedict spirits brands. Now that I'm the new guy I'm not going to be eligible for an international transfer for a while but happily there is lots of European travel on this account. London and Paris especially, which should keep my Travel Jones in check for a while.
I don't know if you heard this or not but Sandi Cusimano has landed on her feet (and I would expect nothing less!) She got a great job, production-company side—there was a big item on her in *Shoot* about six weeks ago. She's now the Executive Producer at GGP Films, which has some of the hottest directors in advertising right now. Good for her. I ran into her recently at a pre-pro meeting and she told me she'd hire you in a second, so if you're not completely down on the ad business you should give

her a call when you get back to town. Let me know if you need her number.

I heard through the grapevine that you will be back in NY before Christmas. I'm sure you'll be really busy after being away for so long, and with the holidays etc. (Are you going to see your folks this year?) Anyhow, it would be great to catch up and say hello if you can squeeze me in. My numbers are 212-662-4703 (home) 212-545-3411 (work) 917-439-9375 (cell). Or e-mail me.

All the very best (and Season's Greetings too)
Graham

From: Monika Roth <m.roth@psb-law.com>
Sent: Friday December 15, 2000 9:44 AM
To: Jill Barber<barberella72@hotmail.com>
Subject: Keys

Can't wait to see you on Sunday. I have to work during the day (shocker!) but we are on for dinner. I made a reservation for 8pm at Isabella's, wear something fabulous to show off your tan (if you still have it...) The keys will be with my doorman, please make yourself at home and help yourself to anything. Call me on my cell the minute you land.

Any word from the troll?

M xo

From: Justine DeVries <DeVries@kirshagency.com>
Sent: Friday December 15, 2000 2:19 PM
To: Jill Barber<barberella72@hotmail.com>
Subject: Hello

**Her Latest Supporting Role**

Jill,

I got your e-mail address from Monika Roth. I heard that you are working on a cruise ship, which was surprising. I think the last time we spoke you were working in advertising, but maybe that didn't work out?

Anyway, I don't know if you are still in touch with Jonathan Wunder or what exactly the deal is between you. You may have heard that his father passed away a while ago, quite suddenly. As you know I work for his agent, Annabel Feldman, and we were very, very excited to get the manuscript of his new book last week. He back-burnered the last thing he was working on and delivered a completely new novel: the working title is The *Jean Genet Appreciation Society*.

Well, I got this weird feeling of familiarity when I read it, and I think you will too. I really shouldn't be sending this to you, Jill, but I thought you would appreciate it. It's just a couple of chapters anyway (there's more of the same of course.) I figured that since the book has already been turned in to Knopf it's not a state secret or anything.

Sincerely,

Justine

*Chapter 3*

*Nell Gardner sat on the other side of the lecturer's cluttered desk in an oxford cloth shirt of pale blue, the exact shade of her eyes. Lazovich noted with amusement that the shirt was unbuttoned a little farther than one might expect from a girl like Nell, saw a flash of milky skin and flesh-tone lace as she shifted in her seat and wondered if her agenda might not be merely academic. He'd found himself on the receiving end of students' advances before, other pretty Connecticut princesses working towards that most coveted and politically incorrect of double majors: the BA/Mrs. Usually they preyed on those self-anointed golden boys, fellow students with rich parents and promising futures, but there were a few (daddy issues, perhaps?) whose long-lashed gazes seemed naturally to fall upon older men. While he listened to her hopeless attempt to impress with erudition, Lazovich swiveled in his chair, studied the blue eyes and aquiline profile with mild curiosity. She was exactly the type that his high-school classmates would have spied on the subway and dreamt about for weeks. Jerked-off to, was more like it, Lazovich thought with a prurient grin. Of course, a chilly Princess like Nell Gardner never would have noticed them, her nose lifted skyward or if not then tucked into* Pride and Prejudice *or* Little Dorrit *or some other worthy volume, too busy or haughty or self-involved to notice a plumber's kid or the son of a taxi driver. Still, those pale eyes, that invisible straightjacket of social class, they had their appeal. He wondered if she had any brothers at home, ones like the endless parade of private school boys that had starred in Lazovich's wet teenaged dreams.*

On and on it continued for another ten pages: details of Nell's failed singing career, the wage-slave job and—worst of all—her sad, benighted pursuit of her sexually disinterested professor. When she'd finished reading Jill felt sweaty, dizzy, physically sick.

From Jill Barber <barberella72@hotmail.com>
Sent Saturday December 16 3:27 AM
To Monika Roth <m.roth@psb-law.com>
Subject FWD: Hello
Fuck. Fuckfuckfuckfuck!

BEGIN FORWARDED MESSAGE

**Her Latest Supporting Role**

# WINTER

# Chapter 20

She'd arranged to meet Jonathan Wunder without having spoken to him, at least not voice-to-voice. Whenever Jill tried to reach him his cell went straight to voice-mail, and she continually missed his calls: was either sleeping, or in the no-call depths of the subway or movie theaters. Still, through a series of messages (brief and tense on Jill's part, while the tone of Jonathan's voice seemed breezily unconcerned, as if he couldn't fathom that she might still be upset with him) they finally arranged to rendezvous on Monday.

Jill sat at a tiny table in Starbucks, feeling feverish, consumed in equal parts by curiosity and dread. She thumbed through the latest issue of *Vanity Fair*, but its images barely made an impression on her. She kept glancing up, eyeing the door nervously, or taking quick little sips from her coffee—so many, in fact, that she'd drained a Grande in under fifteen minutes.

Jonathan Wunder was late, so late that Jill suspected he might have forgotten or blown her off. But then she suddenly glimpsed him on the other side of the glass, oblivious to her as he hurried along the crowded 8th Street sidewalk headed for the entrance. She was happy to have seen him first; it gave Jill a moment to compose her thoughts, get a grip on her feelings. Nervousness (of course), anger (still! she'd been doing a good job getting over everything until those damning chapters showed up in her inbox), and finally a sort of sick curiosity, because those paragraphs signaled that either he was now out in public, honest about his sexual orientation, or if not then some sort of revelation was imminent. About that, she was dying to know.

The door opened and Jonathan Wunder slipped inside. He immediately spied Jill at her front-and-center table, and the tracings of a smile curved across his mouth. Jonathan approached her and began energetically shucking his gloves, striped scarf and suede baseball jacket.

"Jill. hey, Jill, it's good to see you," he said genially, flashing the same winning smile she'd first experienced during that debut lecture. He came to a dead stop next to the table, and this sent Jill into a minor panic. She wasn't sure what she was expected to do next: leap to her feet and invite him to take a seat; extend her hand in welcome; even kiss him hello? He must have sensed her dilemma though, because he backed away slightly and busied himself with stuffing the gloves and scarf deep into one sleeve of his jacket, which he then hung neatly over the back of his chair. This gave Jill a few seconds to catch her breath and then he slipped into the waiting chair, gently leaned across the table a placed one of his all-too-familiar Euro air kisses on each of her hot cheeks.

For an eternal moment she was at a loss for words. The sight of him affected her deeply, even more than she had feared, and Jill fought to quell the choking memory of that long-ago August night (apparently, not long enough ago) when his stubbled cheeks had grazed hers and she'd first become acquainted with the Jonathan Wunder Euro air-kiss. Not the type of kiss that she'd expected that Friday night, or wanted, not at all. If only she'd known.

"Hi yourself," Jill said finally.

"You look really well," he said. "Life on the high seas obviously agrees with you in a very big way."

"That's not my life, Jonathan," she reminded him. "It was a way to get the hell out of New York for a few months. I'm sure you of all people can understand how I might have needed a little break."

Jonathan didn't say anything, just excused himself to go get a latte. She declined his offer for a refill, was already feeling jumpy enough. As he moved away she settled back into her seat and looked across at Jonathan, really took him in. She'd had the chance to assess her own appearance the previous evening in

**Her Latest Supporting Role**

Monika's living room, as Jill had flipped through albums filled with snapshots from their high school and college years. That solitary exercise has confirmed what Jill had half-heartedly suspected for some time, at least since she'd left New York. Her face was a little less glowing, the eyes somewhat tired: she looked older now, measurably older. Whether or not its companion trait, wiser, was part of the package—that was anyone's guess.

Jill surveyed his features much the same way as she'd looked other actresses up and down while they waited together to be called in for auditions: with a critical eye, ready to pick up any physical weakness, any flaw, and use it to make her feel better about her own (real or imagined) shortcomings. Oddly enough, Jonathan Wunder appeared to have grown younger since their last meeting on that dreadful, hung-over Saturday. The wavy dark hair was a good deal shorter, that was the first thing she noticed: it was very short in back and cropped closer to the skull. And although it accentuated his already rather high forehead, the new look nonetheless had a curious appeal, a youthful verve. He was thinner too, much thinner than before; Jill could see it in his vaguely concave cheeks and the angle of his jaw—now almost sharp, though not unpleasantly so. Perhaps his father's sudden death had taken its toll there. His skin, which had stayed the same light olive shade all summer long now had a golden gleam that radiated a combination of good health and, quite possibly, expensive maintenance. And his clothes were different too: a Paul Smith shirt, wild colorful stripes, over a purple T-shirt and beautifully aged Levi's. All these small changes in Jonathan Wunder's appearance didn't just conspire to make him look younger than his thirty-four years. Jonathan looked—at least to Jill—very, very gay.

"Well," Jonathan said when he returned to the table with his latte and a giant cookie. He tore a small piece off the cookie and showily placed the rest on a napkin before Jill like some sort of peace offering. "I was surprised to hear from you, Jill. But I'm glad you called me. I feel like things between us left off…kind of badly, I suppose."

"I'd agree with that," Jill said solemnly. She eyed the cookie, unobtrusively she hoped: wanting a bite but not wanting to give Jonathan the satisfaction.

"I've done a lot of soul-searching over the last few months, Jill." His brow wrinkled into a peculiar expression: concentration and maybe remorse. "A million and one things have change in my life—for better and worse--"

Jill interrupted him. "I was so sorry to hear about your father, Jonathan." He made a quick movement that was half thank-you, half shrug. "It must have been terrible. I know how close you were."

"It's okay, thanks. It was weird though, he died so suddenly, no chance for any of us to say goodbye or anything. Totally surreal."

"Awful."

"Yes and no," Jonathan said. He saw the surprised look cross Jill's face and tried to explain himself. "I mean the shock and suddenness was awful—for my mother especially, she was with him when it happened. But the shock really did something to me, it was kind of like a wake-up call, I guess."

Jill wrinkled her brow. "How?"

"Well, I kept thinking about how I'd tried to be honest with my father ten years ago…about my sexuality. And I felt really bad that I had spent the last ten years of our relationship, well, deceiving him, basically. I mean, I was young then, so young— twenty-three. I'm sure he thought that he was helping me. But I had this weird feeling that I should have come clean with him at some point, that he would have been okay with everything, especially when I got older.

"Anyhow, I decided that I shouldn't have kept lying to my dad, and I wasn't going to lie to the rest of my family any more."

"Jesus, really?" Jill sat back in her chair. "What did you say?"

**Her Latest Supporting Role**

"Well, my whole family was at the house on Sunday after the funeral, we all got together for Chinese food." Jonathan let out a big puff of breath, almost a laugh. "And somewhere between the egg rolls and the sweet-and-sour chicken, I just blurted it out…told my whole family I'm gay."

"Wow," Jill said. Her voice was low with shock. "You actually told them. Good for you…I guess. Did they take it very hard?"

Jonathan gave her an ironic smile.

"That's the punch line, Jill. They already knew! Here I was, I'd been giving myself a goddamned ulcer over the whole thing—since the afternoon of the funeral, that's when I decided to "come out" as they oh-so-tritely call it—and when I dropped the bomb at the dinner table there was maybe, oh, five seconds of uncomfortable silence and then my fucking mother turns to me and says, 'oh, sweetheart, I think we've all known that for years, but thank you for actually telling us yourself.'"

"They knew?" Jill's mouth dropped open as she pictured the Wunder clan, smiling over their Chinese food, nodding their heads in gentle assent as Jonathan delivered his news.

Jonathan smiled blithely at her shock, obviously impressed by his own dramatic delivery of this last and most important morsel of information.

"So that straight guy charade you'd been acting out all those years solely for their benefit…"

"It was all a gigantic waste of time," he explained matter-of-factly. "Who knew?"

Jonathan's nonchalance suddenly made Jill bristle with anger. He was rewriting history in his mind, history that she'd been a part of. Now the events of the summer were being played as a joke: the big set-up, the incredible punch line. He seemed to have forgotten how the dilemma had torn him apart, and Jill too.

"So I guess you didn't need to lead me on after all, then," Jill said. Her voice was coming from low in her throat now, steeped in bitterness. She tried to sound more rational, calmer, but it was a losing battle.

"Sorry?" He gave her his I-don't-quite-understand-you look, all wide-eyed innocence, but Jill wasn't buying it.

"The wining, the dining, the constant 'I want to see you's, the dragging me to your family barbeque and parading me in front of the entire Wunder clan. Our little sham affair. I guess you needn't have bothered after all, huh?"

"Jill..." he said, looking stricken. "I thought you'd be happy for me."

She sighed, and examined her pale thumbs with inordinate interest before arranging her hands in her lap. "No, I am," she admitted finally. "I'm just feeling sorry for myself, I guess. Sad about the way everything has turned out. You know."

"I suppose I did lead you on, a little," Jonathan allowed, tipping his head to one side in gentle contemplation.

"A little?" Jill said with a disbelieving laugh. "And the Pope's a little Catholic!"

"If it makes you feel any better," he said, "I really did want to get to know you, Jill. You were smart and funny and interesting—it wasn't because I thought you were some easy target, some babe-in-the-woods. You know," Jonathan said, and he leaned back and placed his right palm against his jaw line, a familiar gesture from class. It signaled that he was preparing to deliver what he considered a profound insight. "It's too bad you're not a man. If you were I think we'd be really good together."

"Boy, Jonathan." Jill's voice was heavy with sarcasm and she sank down in her chair, mortified. "You sure know how to make a girl feel special."

Missing her irony, he batted the thought away with one outstretched hand. "It's immaterial, anyhow, because I'm back with Kurt now."

"Kurt from the party? The sculptor?"

**Her Latest Supporting Role**

His eyebrows flicked suggestively upward. "The very same."

"Well, I'm happy for both of you," Jill said haltingly. Now she'd heard everything—or nearly everything. The one remaining issue between them—the thing that had spurred her phone call in the first place—was still unmentioned and unaddressed.

As if reading her mind, Jonathan leaned toward her excitedly, and confided, "And that's not all. I have some more news that I think will interest you. Really big news."

"Let me guess. You've written another novel," Jill said, sounding less than impressed, probably just enough to take the wind out of Jonathan's sails. He sort of melted back into his chair, his smile fading.

"Oh, you know."

"Yes, I do know. And congratulations, by the way, I hear it's very funny. Witty, and very true to life," Jill added, delivering the last words with a withering stare.

Jonathan looked perplexed. He flicked his right hand through his hair, a nervous habit that she recalled with an unexpected pang of attraction. "It hasn't even been in the trades yet."

Jill finally gave in to the lure of the cookie, took an angry bite before setting it down, hard, on the table between them.

"Remember that party last summer? The one I came to at your apartment?"

"Of course I do, why?"

"Well, one of my old boarding school classmates was there, do you remember? Her name is Justine DeVries. She works for your agent?"

"Oh…yes." Jonathan gave a slow nod, and smiled. "Sure, Justine…the Ex-lax brownies, right? She thinks you tried to kill her?"

"Well, she e-mailed me last week, and she included a few pages from your new book."

"Oh?" The smile quickly flattened into a thin line of uncertainty.

"The bit that she sent me introduced a character called Nell Gardner…"

Jonathan Wunder placed his suntanned hands flat on the table—palms down and pressing almost imperceptibly against it—and then turned his head toward the floor so that for a moment his face was hidden. She heard him exhale noisily and then he tipped his head up again and looked right at Jill, giving her a full-strength dose of those liquid brown eyes that had once turned her spine to jelly and sent her heart free-falling through her chest. But they had lost much of their power over her: now they were more of an irritation than anything else.

"So you think that Nell Gardner is you, and you're pissed. Is that the deal?"

Jill was extremely pissed, had passed through shock and nausea straight into anger only moments after reading the passage in Justine's e-mail. That was certainly not what she meant when she'd told Jonathan Wunder she wanted to inspire him, to be his muse. Her throat clogged briefly with resentment, and she was unable to squeeze any words out at all.

"That is the deal, Jonathan." Her voice was measured and serious. "I mean, am I wrong? The physical description of "Nell", as you call her, is exactly like me. Her background is mine, practically…I mean Greenwich, come on! Her name even sounds like mine—Bar-ber, Gard-ner —Jesus, what else am I supposed to think?"

He stirred the foam into his latte with an inordinate amount of energy while avoiding Jill's gaze. The silence between them grew longer and more uncomfortable, but she stood firm, refused to change the subject, let the issue blow over. He wasn't going to get off that easily.

"Well," she repeated, her voice steady. "Am I Nell, is she me?"

**Her Latest Supporting Role**

Finally Jonathan lifted his gaze from his cup. He did it in a very hesitant, watchful fashion, as though ready to lower it again at the smallest sign of trouble, as if afraid that she was going to hit him.

"How about, inspired by you?" he said tentatively, and crooked one eyebrow as if unsure whether this was a question or a statement. "I mean, there are definitely elements of you in the Nell character—physical elements mostly. But it's a work of fiction, first and foremost." Jonathan sighed pointedly. "I don't suppose the lovely Justine gave you the entire manuscript, did she?"

Jill shook her head. "Just a few pages, the bit where Nell is in the lecturer's office, dressed like she's trying to seduce him."

"Too bad you didn't read more. The physical description may seem a little close for comfort, but the action itself bears little resemblance to life. 'Nell' figures out his secret and tries to blackmail him, she's kind of a nutcase." He flashed his best aren't-I-so-charming smile. "And that's nothing like you."

Jill's hands twitched with frustration. "Jonathan, that is so not the point. People who know me, who know about our..." she struggled for the least embarrassing phrase, "the time we spent together last summer, they're going to put two and two together. People know I was your student, the character looks like me and has a name like mine. A lot of people are going to think it's me."

"And that's a problem for you?"

She looked at him incredulously; he just didn't get it. "It would be nice not to have people whispering behind my back about your book, too. I'm already in line for my fair share of humiliation over throwing myself at a gay man."

Jonathan shook his head slowly, looked perplexed. "I guess I never really thought about it that way," he said. "I'm sorry. But listen the book is still being edited," he perked up, and beat an energetic rhythm on the table with his palms. "That's what I'll do. I can change the character's name, change her appearance, where she's from...it's a pretty easy fix, believe it or not. The book is in the way-early stages of editing. By the time I get through with Nell Gardner—who is a pretty minor character, by the way—she'll be entirely different and totally unlike you." With a slightly twisted smile, he added, "If you like, I could even turn her into a semblance of your old friend Justine."

"That really isn't necessary" Jill said. "I mean, as weird as it may sound I feel like I owe Justine a big 'thank you'. Like if she hadn't tried to spite me with this juicy little piece of information I wouldn't have found out about your book until it was too late."

Jonathan Wunder gave a small head-bob of assent.

"But look, can I ask you something serious?" she said. "This is the second time you've done something like this to me. You know, used me, that's really what it boils down to. I need to know why. Is it something about me, or was I just in the wrong place at the wrong time?" Jill paused and gave him a direct, unflinching look. Was that a flicker of guilty recognition crossing his handsome face, or was it all in her head? And did it even matter now? "A person could get a complex, if you know what I mean," Jill added, a note of caution in her voice.

"I'm not sure I know what you mean, Jill. It was nothing intentional, nothing about you. Really, it wasn't," he insisted, but she doubted his sincerity absolutely. "I mean, I was going out with women for years, though I'll admit it was all pretty half-hearted.

"Now can I ask you something?" he countered. "Did you really not suspect that I was gay? I mean I know we went out all those times, but I though I was doing enough to keep it from getting physical, to keep you from getting hurt." He gave her a look that was hard to interpret, but might even have been regret.

Jill took a deep breath, and then it all came out: the confusion over their aborted kiss and his rapid retreat from her, the plan to have Robin do a "gay-dar" drive-by at the museum, the dilemma of her attraction weighed against her sense that he might fear the repercussions of sleeping with a student, even the tale of her visit

**Her Latest Supporting Role**

to Czerny's office, the horrible incident that had landed Jill in Jonathan's class in the first place.

When the confession was over at last and Jill sat numbly silent before him, Jonathan shook his head sympathetically. "Jesus, you had quite a summer, didn't you?"

And then it was almost as if telling Jonathan finally relieved Jill of the burden of everything that had happened. She began to feel lighter; her hands unclenched and she eased back into her seat. Suddenly weary of it all, Jill let her resentment go: of Czerny, of Jonathan, of Justine DeVries and of everything and everyone else that had—truthfully or in her own imagination—conspired against her happiness.

She sat back up and gave Jonathan a look that, she hoped, communicated relief and no more hard feelings.

"So what's your new book about, anyway?" she asked, trying to sound casual.

"Well, you know it's called *The Jean Genet Appreciation Society*, right? It's the story of three friends, three closeted gay men who teach at a university in Boston, and the troubles they face when their personal and professional lives keep colliding. It's part satire of academia, part serious exploration of the issues surrounding gender and sexuality. But definitely one-hundred-and-eighty degrees away from *Groundswell*."

Jill smiled. "Art follows life this time, I guess."

Their conversation dissolved into quiet, ironic laughter. Despite the volume of music and chatter around them Jill was conscious only of herself and Jonathan Wunder, and the fact that this was probably the last time they would see each other for a very long while.

"You know Jonathan, I'm not saying this to be mean, but you've spoiled other men for me."

She gazed into his dark eyes: for a moment he actually looked guilt-stricken. Their earlier conversation had made Jill almost certain that he'd lost the guilt gene since the summer: apparently she was wrong. Then his expression gradually turned to disbelief.

"You don't mean that, Jill," he said. When she didn't respond immediately, didn't rush in to salve his remorse, he said it again, and more insistently.

"Yes," she said. "Maybe. Well, probably not," she allowed. Jill saw his expression register relief. "But you know, I really felt something for you. In here." She crossed her arms on her chest, as bad-actress-y gesture as she'd ever made: palms flat, like a body laid to rest. Cheesy, yes, but it summed her feelings up so perfectly. "And God knows when I'll feel something like that again."

"You will." But his voice was hollow in her ears. "I promise you will."

A lost memory suddenly surfaced in her brain. "Hey," she said. "I almost forgot to ask. Did your dreams come back? Is that Salvador Dali film festival playing again?"

Jonathan Wunder flashed his best, most glittering smile: a thousand watts of pure, self-impressed charm.

"Baby," he told her, "I'm dreaming in Technicolor now."

**Her Latest Supporting Role**

# Chapter 21

Jill's body clock was still on lounge-singer-slash-vampire time, despite the two…was it really three margaritas she'd downed the previous evening while she and Monika waited for a table at Citrus, and she'd recounted her discussion with Jonathan Wunder? Despite all the drinks Jill had been unable to fall asleep until almost three-thirty, had burrowed into the sofa bed watching VH1 with the sound really low as Monika snored away in her bedroom.

At around eleven Jill began to regain consciousness; Monika's living room was so dark and silent she had to squint at the VCR to figure out whether it was morning or still the middle of the night. She tripped across her bags on her way to the shower—thankfully Wendy the subletter would be out of Jill's apartment at the end of December; for she was so very tired of living out of two large suitcases. Now that it was winter in New York the city was a gray wasteland of slush and gusting wind, and she needed to beg Wendy for access to her locked closet, would almost certainly freeze to death if she had to wait until the thirty-first for her boots and coat. Until then there was Monika's ample and fabulous wardrobe to borrow from, though when she did Jill looked like a little kid who had raided her mother's closet, so large and long and generally wrong for her was Monika's clothing.

Lunch with Petra and Robin was scheduled for twelve-thirty. They'd agreed to meet at a trendy little café on Ninth Avenue, one that they'd all adored and visited often during the summer. Though they had invited her up to the agency Jill had passed. While she had nothing against Hambleton French—Jill believed what she'd been told, that she'd lost her job through bad timing, a wrong-place-wrong-time victim of circumstance and the crazy instability of the advertising business—she had little desire to run into most of the people she'd worked with, the Sallies and the Nicks, to try to explain what she was doing (or rather, wasn't doing) with her life since leaving the agency. From the ship she'd made vague e-mail plans with a couple of agency friends for after Christmas. Those she wasn't in contact with she'd frankly rather not run into if she could help it.

While Jill had no desire to see Nick Wheeler, she had already gotten in touch with her old boss Sandi Cusimano, called her almost as soon as she'd gotten back to New York. And true to Graham's e-mail, Sandi did indeed sound happy to hear from Jill, and told her that yes, she might actually have a job for her, or at least some freelance production assistant work in the New Year. The prospect of a real job again, a non-singing, non-actressing, non-waitressing daytime gig helped Jill breathe easier, and brightened the prospect of spending Christmas with Tina, her married cousin in suburban Westchester. It gave her a get-out-of-jail-free card for when dinnertime discussion turned—as it inevitably would, the question was when, not if—to what she planned to do with the rest of her life now that she was done with grad school and back in New York.

By the time their food arrived Jill's side was already hurting from too much laughter. Robin was in rare form: even a love story, the mock-heroic tale of how he'd wooed and won his new boyfriend, a Creative Director he'd first met at the GLAAD Media Awards gala, then run into again some months later at The Boiler Room, sounded hilarious when he delivered it. He was happy to report that it had been "love at first date" and they were even considering moving in together. Unfortunately Mr. Quasi-Right—which was how Petra referred to all of Robin's serial love interests (his real name was Brett)—was in Florida on a TV shoot, but Robin promised Jill she'd get to inspect him soon.


**Her Latest Supporting Role**

"But I don't need you to tell me whether or not he's gay," Robin added with an arch smile.

"Ouch," said Jill.

"Robin you get two bitch points for that." Petra pursed her lips with displeasure. When Jill looked confused, she elaborated: "Robin and I award 'bitch points' to each other, all day long. You get either one or two, depending on how mean your comment is. At the end of the day we tally the score, and the one who was the bitchiest owes the other a drink. Of course," she added with a beatific smile, "it goes without saying that he owes me a lot of drinks."

"It's part of our bitch self-help program," Robin added. "We're trying to be nicer people. The bar's pretty low, but I think we're making progress."

"Well, I agree about the two points," Jill said. "But the good news is that I have finally moved on from the whole Jonathan Wunder thing. I actually had coffee with him yesterday, and now I am so completely over it. And over him."

"Really." Robin looked surprised.

"And I bet you'll be seeing him more on the gay bar circuit Robin. He's out now," she gave them both a sour little half-smile, "so totally out, it was kind of shocking. Actually, you may not see him on the circuit after all. He's back with an old flame of his. And he's written a new novel with a gay theme, can you believe it? *The Jean Genet Appreciation Society*. Out next summer." Jill's dark brows arched skyward. "So to speak."

"Jesus," Petra said. "Did he tell you what it's about?"

Jill shook her head. "Don't know, don't care," she white-lied. "I've officially moved on."

"Good for you!" Robin reached across the table and gave her hand a quick, encouraging squeeze. "So speaking of moving on, how is your love life? Any uniformed hotties on the ship? In grade school I had a major crush on that Gopher from *The Love Boat*."

"You know he was in the House of Representatives?" interjected Petra, the reigning Trivia Queen of the H-F creative department. "Representative Gopher from the Great State of Iowa. And he's a Republican," she added accusingly.

"Yuck. That is so disappointing. Thanks for spoiling my happy childhood memories, Petra. That's bitch one point for you," Robin added.

"Not!"

"To answer your questions, Robin," Jill said, "there were no hotties—at least no straight ones—on board.

"No monied young passengers to sweep you off your feet?" He sounded disappointed.

"No young passengers at all. The only cute guys were the crew and they were either married or gay."

"Speaking of married or gay—or married and gay," Robin said. "Did you hear that Constable got the shove?"

Jill blinked, hard. "You're joking."

"I can't believe Robin didn't tell you in his e-mails." Petra shot him a smile, all fake sweetness, before turning back to Jill. "He's nice to look at but—" she lowered her voice faux confidentially, "a little slow."

"Bitch point," said Robin.

"Will you guys give it a rest?" Jill was exasperated. "What happened to Constable?"

"Well, two more accounts had walked out the door—without even giving us the courtesy of a review—and tons of people jumped ship to other agencies too. Saw the writing on the wall, I guess." Petra smiled. "Not me, of course—I'm a lifer. But anyway, the boys from Soho Square showed up right before Thanksgiving and Constable was out. Transferred to the Paris office of all places, which has, like, four accounts."

"And they hate the British over there!" Robin added with a big grin. "They're going to torture his skinny English butt there,

**Her Latest Supporting Role**

and it's about time, if you ask me." His eyes practically sparkled with malicious glee.

"They brought over an account guy from London to be the new President," Petra added. "Then, like a week later Sam Brinder was brought back to be Chief Creative Officer. And can I tell you, for all Brinder's posing and insufferable, cooler-than-thou attitude, the creative department is a much better place to work since Constable got the boot."

"Wow," Jill said. "Constable's gone. That's kind of the end of an era, huh?"

"That's the advertising business for you, sweet pea." Robin shrugged his narrow shoulders. "I've seen it all before. It's like, the King is dead; long live the King."

"So speaking of people leaving," said Petra, "did you know Graham Ferguson left the agency a while back?"

"I did," Jill said. For a moment she stared at her Caesar Salad with inordinate interest. "He e-mailed me about his new job."

"Your dream date," Robin said, and smiled pointedly at Jill.

"Ugh…" She sank down a little on the restaurant banquette. "The Friday after the pitch we went out for dinner, and I was beyond awful to him. He was so nice, and I treated him like shit. He even bought me drinks at the Algonquin on my last day, despite the fact that I was a total bitch to him for four months. If I were Graham I would have written me off the minute I barfed up that extremely expensive dinner he bought me."

Since leaving New York Jill had thought several times of Graham, replayed their conference room all-nighter and their two subsequent nights out over and over in her head. With the benefit of distance and time she finally, completely believed that she and Graham had been right for each other after all. Why did Robin have to be so horribly unpredictable: wrong (so wrong!) about Jonathan Wunder, but right about Graham? And she blamed herself even more. She more than anyone should have seen through Jonathan Wunder's bad acting: it took one to know one.

Monika's ski jacket was draped over Jill's arm, but still she was perspiring as she wandered through the Wallace Wing at the Met. She'd convinced Robin to skip out of work early and join her at the museum: not from any masochistic sense of nostalgia— for it was in this very gallery that the whole gay-dar incident had gone down, that she and Jonathan Wunder had "bumped into" Robin, and that Jill, in a performance as bad as any from her acting days, had convinced Jonathan to hang out with her and Robin in the cafeteria until Robin could give her his verdict. It was just that she had missed her favorite New York museum during her twelve weeks at sea. And art was just so much more enjoyable when you had someone to discuss (or revere…or mock) it with: she didn't want to go alone if she could help it.

She glanced at her watch: five-fifteen. Remembering the concept of Robin Standard Time when they'd made their plans over lunch, Jill had arrived at five o'clock, confident that if Robin wasn't already awaiting her in the gallery, tsk-tsking her lateness in his best calling-the-kettle-black mode, then he'd sail in only minutes after her. And yet it was half an hour after the appointed meeting time, and still no sign of him.

She pulled the cell from her purse to try tracking him down and saw that she'd missed two calls. The first message was from Robin, the litany of I'm sorrys, saying he'd been called back to the office unexpectedly, didn't know that he'd be able to get there before closing. At the end of the message he'd turned from apologetic to mysterious, saying that since he knew how much she hated to museum-hop alone he had someone else coming to take his place. "The first runner-up," his message had said in his comically confidential tone, "you know, in case Miss America is unable to fulfill her duties. Enjoy the museum, sweet pea," he added before hanging up.

**Her Latest Supporting Role**

Jill took a seat in the second gallery, between an enormous Jackson Pollock and a large and murky Rothko canvas. She was in the middle of passing a crumpled tissue across her face to mop up the perspiration when she felt something, a small but unmissable tug on the back of her sweater.

"Long time no see, Jill," said a droll, familiar voice. Jill pivoted in the direction of the sweater-tug and her mouth dropped open in noiseless surprise as if it was the ghost of Graham Ferguson standing behind her rather than the living, breathing man himself.

His lips twitched apart, the amused smile betraying perhaps an undercurrent of nerves. Nothing about him had changed: the ink-blue eyes with their long fringe of black, and the striking, boyish face with that faint pink scar on the chin, that second smile. Though dressed more casually than Jill had ever witnessed—well-worn chinos and a blue oxford shirt beneath a brown leather jacket—he had lost little of that Serious Young Man air, the sheen of earnestness that Jill had detected the very moment they first met, and so many times thereafter.

"Surprised to see me?" He grinned, looking very pleased with himself indeed.

"The weirdest thing," Jill said, the power of speech finally restored. She jammed the damp Kleenex (so old-ladyish!) deep into her purse and got to her feet, then stood on her toes to give him a quick cheek-kiss. "I was just this moment thinking about you."

"Mark Rothko. The shades of black, right? When we were discussing your beloved former boss Nick Wheeler." Graham inclined his head toward the painting before her. "Or in this case, shades of purple."

Jill nodded in wary agreement, thinking, the night that I turned into The Date From Hell. "This can't be a coincidence, can it? You must be the first runner-up?"

"Excuse me?" Graham looked confused.

Jill laughed and shook her head. "Robin left me a message. Said he couldn't make it but was sending along the first runner-up. You know...there's always a first runner-up who can step in should Miss America be unable to fulfill her duties."

"I have no idea what you are talking about," Graham said with a laugh, which made Jill smile: this *one really is straight*. "But yes, Robin did send me."

"Well I'm happy you came instead of Robin. It's really nice to see you, Graham." Jill told him. "I was planning to give you a call, you know, I really was. Now that I'm back in town and getting my act together...or trying to, anyway. And by act, I certainly don't mean lounge singing!" she added with an embarrassed laugh.

"What did you say?"

Jill groaned. "I made a lame little joke about getting my act together. Sorry, too much time listening to bad cruise-ship standup. Not funny," she added, shaking her head apologetically.

He shook his head. "Uh-uh. The first bit."

"Oh, I said that I was planning to call you." She shrugged lightly. "I was."

Graham gave her a hard-to-fathom look: bemused and vaguely intrigued. "That's what I thought you said."

They were hunched over vodka martinis at Bemelman's Bar, looking terribly out-of-place among the early-evening drinkers: Jill with Monika's too-big parka stuffed between the bar and her stool, downtown casual in jeans and a black turtleneck, and both of them a decade or three younger than most of the other patrons. They gorged themselves on nuts and potato chips and olives and, with voices low, poked fun at the crowd surrounding them—the older businessmen on the make, glamorous blonde women who might or might not be hookers, the well-heeled hotel guests in town for a double-header of Christmas shopping and a Broadway show.


**Her Latest Supporting Role**

"I think I've earned enough bitch points for today," Jill said, at last changing the subject. "So how's the new job?"

"The new job is fantastic...especially after doing hard time on Hell-co. They're good clients: fairly smart, pretty reasonable, good creative taste. And the nice thing about working in the spirits business is that the seventies are still alive and well. Generous expense accounts, three martini lunches, first class travel, and I can expense almost any bar bill in the name of 'research' or 'competitive analysis'." Graham smiled pointedly as he drained his glass. "Including this one. I thought I would be bummed out about not doing any more TV spots, but after two years on Tellco this account almost feels like a vacation."

Jill felt a sudden weird urge to do something encouraging, something physical: clasp Graham's hand, reach over and give him a quick hug. But she resisted. In some ways it felt like years rather than months since their big night out, their dating disaster. She didn't know where things stood between them and was suddenly paralyzed by the thought of asking. For all Jill knew he might be married by now, though she'd checked his hand for the tell-tale flash of gold only seconds after they'd connected back at the museum. A wife, a lover, a steady squeeze: Graham seemed like the type to fall swiftly and hard, who wouldn't remain single for long. And now that she'd finally warmed to him he was probably out of reach, off the market—she was sure of it. That was the way things went for her, again and again. Jill's felt a sudden stab of self-pity, and she tipped her head down toward her glass so he wouldn't notice.

"Hey, now it's my turn to change the subject," Graham said quietly. His voice, soothingly familiar, pulled her back to the present. She willed her mouth to smile.

"Please do," Jill twirled the skewer of olives in her glass, still avoiding Graham's gaze.

"Well." He shifted on his stool and then was silent for a moment, so quiet that Jill stopped fiddling with her olives and looked at him. His eyes met hers with an awkward stare. "I was wondering how your politics are these days."

"My politics..." Her mouth dipped into a puzzled frown. "You mean like Democrat or Republican? Well, I missed voting in the election. And at this point I'm sick of talking about hanging chads and Katherine Harris and everything that happened in Florida. If you don't mind."

He shook his head. "No, no, no. That's not what I meant. What I mean is," Graham paused and took a big breath of smoky air, "are you still a Groucho Marxist?"

It took a full three seconds for her to understand Graham's question, and then Jill's face split into an embarrassed grin.

"Oh, God no." She felt a hot flush rise to her cheeks. "I was really hoping you'd forgotten that little bit of stupidity," she admitted.

He stared back at her with that oh-so-confounding gaze: navy blue and sincere. "Forgot that evening, or forgot about you?"

"Oh the evening, I mean the evening," she insisted. "I was so horrible to you, and you were so...so good. There I was making myself sick, physically ill over some other guy, acting like a complete idiot. And you tried to help me." Jill gave him a doleful smile. "To be honest, Graham, I'm not sure that I could be quite so forgiving if I found myself on the receiving end of something like that."

"But did you mean what you said that night? About not wanting to belong to any club that would have you as a member? About always wanting what you can't have?"

"Maybe I did...back then. I don't know." She paused for a moment's reflection. "When I look back on it now that whole week was just a sick comedy. But at the time it seemed so earth-shattering, you know? I was knocking myself over something that had just happened: things I shouldn't have done, stuff I should have noticed and didn't. I guess I was just over-reacting, and you were unlucky enough to catch the full force of my unhappiness."

**Her Latest Supporting Role**

Jill inclined her body toward him slightly, and lowered her voice. "I feel awful about the way I treated you, Graham. I'm so, so sorry."

"Hey. Don't give it another second's thought," Graham said, and he reached over for one of her hands, gave it a comforting squeeze. "You know my policy on regrets, right?"

"Know it?" Jill countered with a nervous laugh. "It's practically my mantra now."

Graham almost beamed at her, and held her left hand tightly. For a moment neither one said anything at all. It was Jill who finally broke the silence. With her free hand she reached for her drink, ditched the olives and drained the glass in one long gulp. Then she leaned slowly toward him, until her lips were only inches from his right ear and her words were transported on a warm stream of martini breath.

"Speaking of moving on," she whispered, "is your apartment near here?"

Jill was the first one awake. It was still evening, that much was certain; outside Graham's half-shaded bedroom window the sky was garlanded with lights from the many high-rise buildings that stretched up Broadway. Far to the north she could see a sliver of the George Washington Bridge, strung with white bulbs like a horizontal Christmas tree. His bedroom was dimly lit, with a single shaft of light pouring through the half-open bathroom door. She craned her neck from the pillow, trying hard not to wake him; his dark head lolled beside her shoulder, and she could feel the in-out breathing of his shallow sleep against her skin. If his room contained a clock radio she couldn't locate it, so Jill settled back into the pillow. Eyes wide open in the half-light, she studied the constellation of moles on his pale shoulder, flattened an inquiring palm atop the silky dark hair on his stomach. Finally she moved down, leveling her ear against his chest and letting the steady heartbeat pass through her like a human stethoscope.

With the tips of her fingers she softly beat out the rhythm against her own bare skin. Jill let her eyes slide closed again and tried hard to memorize the sensations of that moment.

She awakened again, later still. He was studying her face, his expression hard to read. She resisted the urge to squirm away from his gaze and let him study her bed-mussed features while she considered the unexpected path her day had taken and suppressed a smile.

"Hi there," Graham said, halting his study. He drew himself over her and their mouths met in a lingering kiss.

"I didn't want to wake you." He flopped onto his back, making the bed shake, again. "You looked so...I don't know," he faltered. Jill turned her head to catch a very pleased-with-himself expression spreading across Graham's smooth face. "So peaceful, I guess."

'That's a good word," Jill allowed, her voice dulled by sleep. "I feel peaceful." And it was true. After everything that had happened with Jonathan Wunder (and a considerable dry spell before that) Jill had practically forgotten what it was to feel happy—as opposed to horrified—after sex. She decided not to push her luck.

"I should take off," she told him, moving to her side of the bed and swinging her legs out. She sat on the edge, naked back to Graham, and scanned the floor for her clothing.

"Why so soon?" She heard his voice behind her. "Jill, why don't you stay? This has got to be better than sleeping on your friend's couch." He added, with a little less certainty: "Right?"

She located her sweater—Monika's actually—in a twisted ball near her feet and slid it over her head. Because it belonged to her much-taller best friend it was easy to tug the sweater to the tops of her thighs, so Jill didn't have to do the below-the-belt flash as she stood and padded across the carpet to Graham's bathroom.

"Just a second," she told him. "I have to pee."

**Her Latest Supporting Role**

Jill closed the door and gave herself a moment to take in the surroundings. His bathroom was white and modern with little stainless steel accents here and there: sleek toothbrush holder, gleaming trash can, a very Euro-looking scale. And spotlessly, almost surgically clean. Jill remembered Monika's long-standing assertion that men who were too neat and clean, "too hygienic" as she put it, were bad in bed. So clearly not true, Jill reflected, at least not of Graham. She settled herself on the toilet and surveyed the bright white room, suddenly remembering the one time Graham had visited her apartment, and—as if she'd been the audience, not the participant—saw herself kneeling in her own not-so-spotless bathroom, gripping the sides of her toilet as if for dear life while the bitter contents of her stomach streamed out of her. She felt one last stab of embarrassment, then let it go.

When she returned Graham was still stretched out on the bed, though he'd rolled onto one side and propped himself up on an elbow to watch her enter. Jill moved around the room, gingerly picking her clothing off the floor with one hand while attempting to keep the bottom of Monika's sweater pulled low with the other.

"Please tell me you're not leaving," he said. "It's early, not even eleven. Aren't you hungry? I'm starving."

Jill listened hard, trying to read his tone: not desperate for sure, but a little more than matter-of-fact. And of course she was hungry; it had been a full eight hours since the merry lunch with Robin and Petra had ended. But she was suddenly nervous, too; she didn't want to mess up a good evening with a bad ending, overstay her welcome and then come to that sudden and uncomfortable realization that he wished her gone, couldn't wait to see her leave. She paused, placing her discarded clothes on the edge of the bed.

"I am a little hungry," she offered. "But I could always get a slice on the way back to Monika's."

Graham shushed her with a wave of his arm. He stood up from the bed and began his own clothes-hunting. He picked his boxers up from the floor and put them on. Even in the dim half-light Jill could see the bright pattern across them, something that had escaped her notice earlier: smiling cartoon Santas, red and white on a field of Christmas-y green. She let out a little sputter of laughter.

"What?"

Jill pointed to the smiling Santas and made a funny face.

"Hey, I love these!" he protested. "And it is almost Christmas. These are my second-favorite ones, though...the best ones have a Christmas tree pattern."

"Yeah, right. What planet are you from, Graham?" she laughed.

"I can't believe a prep school girl from Connecticut is giving me a hard time about this." Graham gave Jill a chastising smile as he grabbed his T-shirt from the floor and tugged it over his head. "But if you don't believe me then you'll just have to stay over. Because I'm saving the Christmas tree boxers for tomorrow."

They sat in Graham's bed drinking red wine and eating Chinese food straight from the containers as they watched Letterman. Jill's chopstick skills were as spastic as ever: twice already she had slipped up, sent a sticky snow pea sailing into the clean folds of Graham's blue sheets. The first time it happened she'd been mortified—he was so tidy, after all—but instead of looking distressed he'd merely laughed at her. Not meanly, but in a way that made her giggle too.

During a commercial, Graham poked her arm gently with the end of his chopstick.

"Hey, you're a film chick," he said to Jill.

"I suppose I've been called worse."

**Her Latest Supporting Role**

"Well, I was just thinking what a Woody Allen kind of moment this is. You know, a couple eating Chinese food in bed, isn't that in one of his movies?"

Jill tapped her chopsticks against the edge of a container of rice as though it would help her remember. "I think so, but I honestly don't remember which one."

"Me neither," he said. "It might have been *Manhattan*, but maybe it was Annie *Hall*?"

"So you stumped the film chick. I guess I owe you a beer or something, like when the ski instructor falls, right?" Jill paused. "Well, you want to know what I was just thinking?"

Graham nodded his head, chewing intently.

"I was thinking how this kind of Chinese meal is so much more my kind of thing then the last one we had."

"Oh my God, I was just thinking that not five minutes ago. Get out of my brain!" Graham sat up excitedly and imitated the *Twilight Zone* theme music: *doo doo doo doo, doo doo doo doo.* "That restaurant was a little too fabulous for me."

"Though it was beautiful," Jill pointed out.

"Oh yeah," Graham sighed. "I guess I was trying to impress you. Could you tell?"

"Of course I could tell. And I guess I really impressed you that night too, huh?" Jill rolled her eyes at the memory.

"Hey," Graham said. He rested his chopsticks on the tray of food and pulled Jill's from her hand. He slipped one arm around her back and pulled her toward him. For a moment Graham buried his face in Jill's warm neck and hair. "Enough of that," he said finally, lifting his head.

Jill let out a slightly embarrassed laugh. "Feel free to tell me to shut up at any time."

"Like now, for example?"

She turned her head to one side and felt a kiss graze the soft place below her ear.

"Yes," Jill said. "Now would be a very good time."

**295**

# Chapter 22

By the end of January Jill was already perma-lancing at GGP Films. Her old boss Sandi had been as good as her word: better in fact. She'd met with Jill the morning of January 3rd, and called her with a job offer the very next day.

Unlike Hambleton French, this company was tiny, with only sixteen full-time staffers on the top floor of a cast-iron loft building on Mercer Street. Jill sat on one side of "the pit", the largest room in the space, where ten employees—production co-coordinators like Jill, producers, and administrative and accounting staff—sat at a sort of U-shaped mega-cubicle that ran along three of the four walls. In the middle of this giant U was a hybrid conference room/lounge with a meeting table and chairs, two low leather sofas, stereo and video equipment, bookshelves and magazine racks. It looked sort of like a commune for film students, albeit ones with lots and lots of money and who shopped from the pages of Wallpaper* magazine. Jill was in heaven.

There was no consistent rhythm to her workdays, at least not yet. Some were crazy and started way before dawn with a walkie-talkie clipped to her belt and a sheet full of tasks that reminded her of Sally Leyton's much-maligned checklist. But others were unbelievably slow. On the slow days Jill allowed herself only one coffee run in the morning and another after lunch, more afraid of latte-induced poverty than of any ill effects of caffeine or sugar. While she was making a little more money than she had at the agency—no benefits, though—Jill was slowly becoming aware that at twenty-eight she probably needed to stop spending absolutely every cent she made. While she was cruising the Caribbean in a silver sequined mini-dress Monika had put twenty per cent down on a pre-war co-op in the West 80's; and only a couple of weeks after that Jill's college roommate announced that she was getting married and (gasp) moving back to the suburbs after five-plus years in Manhattan. Even Justine DeVries was a property owner, though Jill suspected that her wealthy and indulgent parents, rather than fiscal prudence, were responsible for that.

A slow Thursday morning: Jill was checking out her bank balance online and feeling mildly depressed when she saw her Hotmail account flash:

From: Jonathan Wunder
Subject: News

She had neither seen nor heard from Jonathan since their meeting before Christmas, and frankly that was fine with her. In the spirit of moving on she'd all but put him out of her mind, indeed had spoken of him only twice since then: once to Monika the night after their final meeting, and then (more confessionally) to Graham on New Year's Day. Graham had returned the favor that same evening—if telling someone something so painful and perhaps even disturbing about oneself could even be seen as a favor—by spilling the beans himself. He'd told Jill not only the tale of his erstwhile fiancée, Helena, and the devastating broken engagement that everyone else seemed to think was so comic (she'd run off with a straight florist? Ha ha ha indeed). Even more revealing, he'd shared the details of what had happened afterwards: the binge drinking, the repeated drunk-dialing to Helena and her new man, the letter from her attorney with a veiled threat of police involvement, and finally the twice-weekly psychotherapy session and daily doses of Zoloft that had put him back on track.

Their secrets finally out, they'd fallen asleep together on Graham's couch: fully-clothed, each one so drained that moving to the bedroom had seemed physically impossible. The next morning, her clothes uncomfortable and hot, her mouth dry and tasting even worse than usual, Jill nonetheless felt relieved, relaxed, strangely light. And Graham, still asleep, looked so quiet and at peace that it nearly stopped her heart.

Now she stared at the message in her inbox, half-wanting to delete it, but self-aware enough to know that she'd probably die of curiosity if she did. Knowing Jonathan Wunder it was probably something exciting and self-congratulatory about his new book— perhaps it had been optioned for the movies? Jill couldn't wait…who would play her on the big screen, Katie Holmes perhaps? Then she remembered that the character wasn't her any more—at least not if he'd made good on his promise. Or maybe he and Kurt were having a commitment ceremony? They were all the rage lately. She put her hand back on her mouse and opened the message.

From: Jonathan Wunder <jwunder@rrnyc.com>
Sent: Thursday, February 1, 2001 11:42AM
To: Jill Barber <barberella72@hotmail.com>
Subject: News

Jill,
Happy happy New Year. I hope you are well and generally enjoying life.
I don't know if you saw this in the *Washington Square News* or not (am guessing you have now graduated from the NYU media to bigger and better) but thought you would find it of interest.
Take care and be happy.
Peace,
JW
P.S. Book comes out in June…they are working on marketing etc. now but hopefully I will be appearing at a Barnes & Noble near you in the not-too-distant future ;-)


**Her Latest Supporting Role**

*On Wednesday January 17* The New York Times *reported that Gabor Czerny, an Associate Professor of Cinema Studies at New York University, is allegedly guilty of plagiarism.*

*According to the* Times *at least seven passages in Czerny's new book,* Allegories of Fascism: The Cinema of Eastern Europe *(Oxford University Press, 2000) are "identical or nearly identical" to those found in two other books written by German film scholar Helmut Widener. Widener's U.S. publishers, Schoenman Editions, noted that "in none of the examples (of similarities to Widener's works) is there a footnote to our books. Not one."*

*These allegations come just weeks after another plagiarism charge was leveled against Czerny's book. Anna Kapfer claimed that there are "remarkable similarities" between passages in Allegories of Fascism and parts of her late husband's unpublished volume of film criticism,* Popcorn Politics. *Although Stefan Kapfer died late last year, his wife claims to have proof that the essays which Professor Czerny is alleged to have plagiarized were written more than four years before his death...*

And on it went for another three paragraphs, complete with a quote from Czerny—protesting his innocence, cockily anticipating his exoneration—and closing with a little speculation from the News's reporter, who suggested that if plagiarism was proven, the faculty would almost certainly call for his dismissal.

Jill sat back at her desk, swallowed hard, and then felt the words holy shit form on her lips. She leaned over her keyboard once more, forwarded the message, and then dialed Monika's office. Monika answered on the third ring.

"Hey, it's Jill. Check your e-mail right now."

"I actually have someone in my office," Monika said, in an unusually professional tone of voice. "Can I call you back?"

"Yes, but read your e-mail first."

By the time Jill returned from the ladies room her phone was ringing.

"Un-fucking-believable," Monika exulted, sounding considerably less the buttoned-up big firm lawyer than she had just minutes before. "I told you that karmic payback would kick in at some point. That bastard is finally going down."

"It actually sounds like he might," Jill said quietly.

"You don't sound that happy." There was a note of surprise, even reproach, in Monika's voice.

"I am happy...I guess. I feel kind of stunned, though. I mean I worked so hard to forget about what happened with him, you know? To just put it behind me and get on with everything. You were the one who told me to, remember? The first one, anyway." The truth was that Jill would rather have oblivion—the whole awful incident erased from her memory—than vengeance. But she knew that oblivion was never really an option: the past was sometimes forgotten, but never gone.

"Well, if you're in the mood for a little gossip, I heard something a while back that might make your day. Or maybe make you sick, who knows. But it's juicy..."

"I can take it. Go wild."

"Well, I didn't want to upset you by bringing up the dreaded Czerny, so I've been sitting on this one for a while. But—since you mentioned him..." Monika paused dramatically.

"What?!"

"Well," she continued, "I heard through the Walden grapevine that Justine and the lecherous lecturer have been sort of an item for a while now."

"The troll and Czerny?" Jill's reaction was immediate and physical. "Eeew! Gross!"

After a moment of surprise and disgust, Jill reflected on it: Justine and Czerny, an item? "You know," she told Monika," I saw them together at Jonathan Wunder's party and Justine was on him like white on rice. I can't believe Jonathan didn't tell me when I saw him in December. I told him my dirty little secret, about the Czerny thing. You'd think he would have spilled."

"Maybe he didn't know...I mean, are he and Justine that close? Or he and Czerny, for that matter?"

**Her Latest Supporting Role**

'Do you think the troll has some connection with the whole plagiarism thing?" Jill asked.

"What do you mean?"

"Well, she's in publishing...any chance she got her hands on this unpublished manuscript and gave it to Czerny? I mean, even if it didn't get submitted to her agency, she must know tons of people in publishing, people who could help her get her tiny little claws on some old guy's unpublished manuscript." Jill paused, and considered the likelihood of the scenario. "Do you really think she'd do it?" she marveled. "Do you think she'd steal...for love. For Czerny?"

"Why not? She did it for hate, right? Or not that she hated you, exactly," Monika revised her tone. "But she had a score to settle, and so she sent you those paragraphs from Jonathan's new book to do it, right?"

"I guess."

"The New York publishing world is incredibly small," Monika said with conviction if not actual credibility. "If that is what happened people will find out, and she'll be toast. And if Czerny did plagiarize from either of those authors the faculty will fire him so fast it'll make his head spin."

"Czerny fired," Jill echoed with a small, guilty smile. "The weird thing is, though, I actually feel kind of sorry for Justine."

"You can't be serious!" Monika chided. "After everything she's done to you? Or tried to, anyway."

"But I bet he used her," Jill said, a little more vehemently then she'd planned. "She probably had it really bad for him—I vaguely remember them together at the party, her body language; I think she was into him. God help her. And I bet he did use her, actually," Jill reflected. "I bet Justine and I have more in common than either of us would care to admit to."

Graham had been in Paris since Sunday. When he was in New York they spoke on the phone every day, and exchanged at least a couple of e-mails from their desks, but Jill had barely heard a peep out of him since he'd left. Strange.

Since her return to New York things had seemed blissfully easy. Too easy, in fact: she'd gotten a job that seemed interesting and fun and she adored her boss to boot; she'd moved back into her apartment, which, despite her fears, had not been trashed by Wendy the subletter, but was returned to her not only intact, but a whole lot cleaner than Jill had left it. And perhaps most shocking of all, she and Graham Ferguson had gotten (and stayed) together. The week between Christmas and New Years was especially surprising, had flown right by: their bodies fueled by the feverish energy of the seriously infatuated, their brains scrambled by what seemed, at the time, like near-constant sex. She recalled that first night together in Graham's apartment, the two of them alone; that night, and every time thereafter she'd offered him an escape clause, a graceful exit. Jill knew too well that he'd been deeply wounded, scarred by a romance gone wrong, and she sensed his unwillingness to treat anyone as horribly as he himself had been treated. Despite the way her life seemed to be slowly coming together, all the various little troubles and issues gradually getting resolved, she still felt like a bit of a mess, emotionally anyhow: on edge, a little sensitive (and not the good kind of sensitive either: not the Graham kind) and fairly un-dateable.

And yet things between them seemed so good. The relative lack of discord troubled her; she was just waiting for the other shoe to drop. Every night they were together she made her solemn inquiry, something along the lines of, *Tell me if you want me to go, it's OK, I can take it.* And every time he declined. Mostly he treated it as a joke: *This is where I'm supposed to tell you to shut up, right?* he'd say, again, and flash the smile that for a moment melted the icy fist of trepidation pounding her stomach. In the last week or so, though, Jill sensed that the joke had begun to wear a little thin, and she'd heard a single note of exasperation creep into his voice the last time she asked, right before he left

**Her Latest Supporting Role**

town. Still, when he'd departed for the airport the next morning Graham had given her a movie-worthy goodbye kiss; and Jill's chest filled with helium as she watched him leave his apartment.

That feeling of lightness didn't last though: not long enough. Once in Paris he'd gone virtually radio-silent, just a couple of e-mails (uncharacteristically brief) and one short phone message. It was the first time they'd been separated—so much distance, so many time zones—and she didn't know how to react. As the days passed, and she composed her daily e-mail to him—just checking in, she'd write, or, once, miss you madly (there, I said it!)—she grew more disturbed. By Thursday afternoon, the shock of Jonathan Wunder's e-mail about Czerny already passing—and so leaving her more time to obsess about Graham—she was fully prepared to have love's little A-bomb dropped on her heart. She had it coming, didn't she, after the way she'd treated him? Jill suspected that falling for Graham had been a monumental act of hubris, and she might never, ever recover from it.

Graham was on an early flight back to New York and they were meeting for dinner at eight. She'd finally spoken to him live, right after he landed, and he sounded fine: happy, not tense. But he'd been at the curb looking for his driver, so the call had been very brief.

Jill flew through the door of The Paris Commune at five past. It was a fitting place for his welcome home dinner: he claimed not to be sick of French food, but in fact missed it already—or so he'd told her during their short phone conversation. She caught sight of him immediately. It was a cute bistro in the West Village: warm, crowded and pulsing with music and chatter. Graham sat against the restaurant's far wall, idly sipping his wine; their eyes met and one hand fluttered up in greeting. The buttons on his navy blazer winked at her from across the room, urging her on, and his green and white striped shirt was appealingly open at the neck. She dodged the hostess with her questioning stare and, sucking in a fortifying gulp of air, made her way toward him.

Graham was on his feet long before she reached him, the trace of an ambiguous smile across his lips. Jill stole a glance around her. Except for its attractive clientele, the place could not have been less like Shanghainese: its glossy walls covered with vintage French poster art, the slightly past-their-prime bistro chairs. But somehow the charming surroundings receded from Jill, her peripheral vision faded as she approached him. She became conscious of a weird sensation in her belly, not the surge of nausea she'd felt months earlier when she'd walked through the chilly foyer of Shanghainese, her stomach bloated with self-pity, her well of confidence gone dry. This was more like the flutter of hope and despair she'd experienced in Jonathan Wunder's apartment on that pivotal Sunday night. Again she felt an impending moment of truth, and it weighed heavily on her.

"Hi." Graham kissed her lightly, a public kiss, the merest brush of his lips accompanied by an arm squeeze. He drew back, waiting for her to take a seat.

"Hi," she said. Jill willed it to be strong, but her voice came out a thin echo. "Welcome home. How was Paris?"

"It was great, I love the French. Even when they are being totally exasperating it's kind of endearing. *But I do not understand ze concept, Gray-ham.* This one guy, Philippe, had to have said that about ten times yesterday."

"You must have been busy," Jill offered. She reached across the table for his wine and sipped.

"Pretty busy, not insane. Why?"

"I don't know, I kind of barely heard from you. After a month of non-stop contact it felt weird. I just assumed you were busy." She dipped her gaze down to his glass, and then looked straight at him.

"I know," he said. "I went a little incommunicado while I was there. I was just taking some time to chill, and think. I do that

**Her Latest Supporting Role**

once in a while...you know?" He returned Jill's gaze with a slightly ambiguous look, and it unnerved her.

"Graham." She exhaled more deeply then she'd planned. "Are you breaking it off?"

She seemed to have caught him off guard. Graham peered at her, those blue eyes she'd always found so unnerving suddenly narrowed. He took a huge gulp of his wine.

"Is that what you want?"

"Did I say that's what I want?" Jill sounded defensive.

"Well," he countered helplessly, "did I say that's what I want?"

"No," she admitted with a downcast smile. "But I thought maybe you were afraid to. When you went radio-silent in Paris...I don't know. I thought maybe you were trying to tell me something."

"Jesus, Jill!" Graham rubbed his palms over his face.

"Ever since we got together," she continued, "I keep expecting my wake-up call. You're such a nice guy, and I've been such a mess, and I know you've been hurt...I know that whatever you might be feeling, whatever second thoughts you might be having, that you wouldn't want to hurt me. Even if you are going to hurt me," she added, and looked at him solemnly.

Graham shook his head. "We went through this already, Jill. Like, a hundred times. I mean, didn't we? Didn't you believe me then? Don't you trust me?"

She stared into her lap for a few seconds. "It's more a case of me not trusting myself."

"Sorry? I don't understand," he said.

Jill could feel a single hot tear welling in each eye, but this time she held them back.

"I think I have a blind spot," she explained. Her words came out slowly: calm, measured, rational. "I'm just such a bad judge of character when it comes to men."

Graham looked puzzled, as though he was straining to wrap his mind around the whole concept. "And you think…" he said slowly. "You think that if you feel something for me you are going to get burned?"

"Something like that," she admitted. "I mean, it's happened before. More than once," she added, thinking of Jonathan Wunder and three-timing Phillip and, too, of all her other past liaisons gone wrong, horribly wrong.

"Then…then you do feel something for me," he said haltingly, as if both dying to know and yet afraid of the answer.

Jill nodded, her eyes wide, expression heartbreakingly serious.

"At last!" he practically cried out. Jill watched two women seated a couple of tables down turn their heads, pointedly curious. Their waiter—who had been hovering conspicuously, trying to take their order almost from the moment she had arrived—fled at once, as though threatened with physical injury. "I can't believe you admitted it. Jill Barber," he exclaimed, his voice a mixture of teasing and bliss. "This is a big day for you."

"Can't believe I admitted what?"

"That you feel something for me! I was beginning to think you were going to blow me off again," he told her.

"Why?"

"Oh, I don't know. No, no." He batted his hand through the air, canceling his last statement, suddenly his energetic old self again. "Yes I do. Think back: the restaurant, the wine. You were up and happy and bubbly one moment and then suddenly so ill-at-ease. So ill, period," he added with a sly smile.

"Shanghainese." Jill gave a gentle groan. "Or as I so fondly remember it, the night I turned into The Date From Hell."

Graham gave her a meaningful look, and the intensity of his gaze sent an unexpected shudder of longing right through her.

"When I sat at that table at Shanghainese waiting for you to arrive, I had a knot in my stomach the size of a basketball. I'd been trying to get to know you better all summer long, but you

**Her Latest Supporting Role**

seemed—oh, I don't know." He shrugged and laughed self-consciously. "A little distant, I suppose. Like your mind was somewhere else. Or with someone else."

"Oh," Jill said.

"Then, I don't know what happened, but on the night before the Tellco pitch it seemed like we suddenly connected—finally. And you agreed to have dinner with me. My big chance!" he added, with a nervous exhale. "My last chance, I thought. I felt just awful when the evening turned out so badly. That it was all my fault, like when I kissed you I ruined everything. After you left the agency—left New York—still I was kicking myself over what I'd done. I broke my own cardinal rule," he added dolefully. "You know." Graham mouthed the words in silence: regrets.

She'd told Graham about Jonathan Wunder, but not everything—certainly not about how she'd bolted an entire cheesecake in a fit of self-pity a few short hours before their big night out. Jill took a moment to consider what he'd just said, and then replayed their previous exchanges in her mind. She'd been mistaken about him, though in a different way than with Jonathan Wunder.

"I never knew, Graham," she said quietly. "Really. I mean, I'd kind of figured out that you liked me, that you were interested in me. But I thought it was just this casual thing, like a crush. I thought you probably had one on half-a-dozen other girls at the office too."

"Ha." Graham gave an abashed laugh, his secret finally out. "Actually, the only one who knew the whole story was Robin Devlin. After I saw the two of you in that bar, I was relentless. I pumped him for information all summer long." He grinned, and added, "You would never guess this about Robin, but he's actually very discreet. He was very, very careful with what he told me about you."

Jill gave him a surprised look. "I guess I could say the exact same thing," she said, thinking about all the times Robin had tried to propel her toward Graham, pretending it was all spurred by Robin's matchmaking impulses, never letting her in on his true motivations. And the few times he had come close to telling her the truth Jill had kept herself blissfully ignorant, too wrapped up in her thoughts of Jonathan Wunder.

"So now you know."

"Now I know."

Graham said nothing in reply, but he gave her a smile, wide and genuine, that roused her cautious heart.

Finally she picked up her menu. Jill studied it for a minute or so, then tilted it down and gave Graham a look of comic suspicion. "The size of a basketball? Really?"

He lifted his gaze to meet Jill's, then smiled awkwardly. "And again, tonight."

Those three words sent a wave of happy relief flooding through Jill's overloaded nervous system. She felt suddenly unburdened, alarmingly light. Jill made a noise, the sound of happy acceptance; she vowed to stop obsessing, to stop offering him a graceful exit—at least until one of them actually did something to warrant it. She peered over the top of her menu, stealing short glimpses of Graham as he scanned the restaurant's long list of offerings. She noted with a smile that his face seemed much more at ease—infinitely more peaceful than when they'd first laid eyes on each other that evening.

"Are you hungry, or too jet-lagged?" Jill ventured. She was too hyped-up to choose, had carefully considered every item on the restaurant's lengthy menu but was still drawing a blank. "Everything sounds great, but I just can't decide what to order."

Graham lifted his eyes from the page and offered Jill a guilty look.

"Well...I'm tempted to order—" he paused, actually seemed afraid to say the dish's name. "The duck," he said finally. "I love duck, but I feel like it would be flirting with disaster."

Jill fingered her menu thoughtfully.

**Her Latest Supporting Role**

"*Au contraire, mon cher*," she told him, just the barest hint of irony in her voice. A feeling that had been building for some time finally got the better of her, and she reached across the table to give Graham's hand a squeeze. "I think you should have the duck. No," she gave a pause of consideration. "I take that back. You must have the duck. I insist." Every word made her more giddy. "Tonight we are going to erase the curse of our first date...or die trying. So have the duck. I'm having it too." She set her menu down with an extravagant gesture.

"Okay." Graham smiled, playing along. He set his menu down on the table.

"And then cheesecake," Jill added.

Graham looked puzzled, and mildly intrigued. "Why cheesecake?"

Jill flashed him an enigmatic smile, and decided that they'd made enough confessions for the time being. That one at least could wait until dessert.

# Acknowledgments

Without the wit and wisdom (and editorial assistance) of so many friends and colleagues, this story would be so much duller. Helpful, patient and insightful readers of the many drafts and versions of this story include: Stephen Amidon, Debby Beece, Karen Bronzo, Don Carroll, Atoosa Dorudi Cross, Hugh Duthie, Sarah Fay, Gail Heaney, Josh Kilmer-Purcell, Jennifer Landers, Robert Rodi, Jeffrey Smith and Ellen Stone. Thanks a million.

Thanks also to my friends and colleagues in the advertising business, for constant inspiration and workplace hilarity. And to my wonderful family and to Malcolm: thank you for always cheering me on. I notice and appreciate it.

# About the Author

Cynthia Ashworth is a former television executive and advertising industry veteran who has helped push everything from donuts to credit cards to reality shows. A graduate of the University of Toronto and the University of Virginia's Darden School, she lives in New York City. This is her first novel.

Read more at www.CynthiaAshworth.com

Made in the USA
Lexington, KY
16 August 2011